5

SO-AII-633

Praise for Lynda La Plante's first crime thriller

COLD SHOULDER

"Riveting." —*Los Angeles Times*

"This gripping crime story . . . strong-arms its readers—all the way to the double whammy climax." —*People*

"Ms. La Plante, who wrote *Prime Suspect*, the Emmy Award-winning British television series that stars Helen Mirren as an obsessive police detective, brings the same emotional intensity to this harrowing story about a California police lieutenant who bottoms out when her partner is killed . . . the scenes keep moving as if their wheels were greased, and there is terrific energy in the simple, driving, cinematic plot." —*The New York Times Book Review*

"A female homicide detective in Pasadena hits the skids, then tracks a serial killer in [the] new thriller by the author of *Prime Suspect* . . . Rarely has a British novelist penetrated the cultural undertow of American crime and law enforcement as shrewdly and incisively as Lynda La Plante in *Cold Shoulder*." —*San Francisco Chronicle*

"Tense plotting, well-rounded characterizations, and a realistic story set *Cold Shoulder* up for a warm reception from readers." —*The Cleveland Plain Dealer*

"A winner." —*San Francisco Examiner*

"A compelling story that's both a complex character study and a riveting mystery . . . fascinating . . . intense and suspenseful." —*Booklist*

Further Praise for
COLD SHOULDER

"Admirers of La Plante's Edgar Award-winning TV mini-series, *Prime Suspect* . . . will want to give this novel anything but the cold shoulder . . . finely tuned characters, a well-wrought plot and plenty of suspense made this novel a success across England; its appeal should cross the Atlantic with ease."
—*Publishers Weekly*

"A thriller . . . a police story . . . a good-hearted, fun read."
—*The Miami Herald*

"Accomplished . . . exciting . . . intriguing . . . impossible to put down."
—*The Wichita Eagle*

"*Cold Shoulder* cries out to be a movie. And Lorraine Page is interesting enough for mystery readers to make her a star."
—*The Virginian-Pilot*

Praise for Prime Suspect
the Emmy Award-Winning TV Miniseries Created and Written by Lynda La Plante

"Nothing about *Prime Suspect* is much less than extraordinary. One of the most absorbing, well-acted and mercilessly nerve-racking dramas of the season. 'Sensational' should not be too strong a word."
—*The Washington Post*

"Gritty and graphic . . . keeps you suspended in an edgy state of perpetual doubt. La Plante's script is a beauty."
—*USA Today*

"*Prime Suspect* is a mystery that builds to a powerful climax . . . although there's not a single explosion, a gunshot, or a car chase, the suspense never flags."
—*The Wall Street Journal*

Also by Lynda La Plante

COLD BLOOD

Lynda La Plante

JOVE BOOKS, NEW YORK

If you purchased this book without a cover, you should be aware that this book is stolen property. It was reported as "unsold and destroyed" to the publisher, and neither the author nor the publisher has received any payment for this "stripped book."

This is a work of fiction. Characters, events, institutions, and places either are products of the author's imagination or are used fictitiously. Any resemblance to actual persons, living or dead, is purely coincidental.

COLD BLOOD

A Jove Book / published by arrangement with
Random House, Inc.

PRINTING HISTORY
This work was originally published in Great Britain by Macmillan,
an imprint of Macmillan Publishers Ltd., in different form in 1996.
Random House edition / November 1997
Jove edition / April 1999

All rights reserved.
Copyright © 1996, 1997 by Lynda La Plante.
Author photo by Brian Aris.
This book may not be reproduced in whole or in part,
by mimeograph or any other means, without permission.
For information address:
The Berkley Publishing Group, a division of Penguin Putnam Inc.,
375 Hudson Street, New York, New York 10014.

The Penguin Putnam Inc. World Wide Web site address is
http://www.penguinputnam.com

ISBN: 0-515-12479-6

A JOVE BOOK®
Jove Books are published by
The Berkley Publishing Group, a division of Penguin Putnam Inc.,
375 Hudson Street, New York, New York 10014.
JOVE and the "J" design
are trademarks belonging to Penguin Putnam Inc.

PRINTED IN THE UNITED STATES OF AMERICA

10 9 8 7 6 5 4 3 2 1

To Liz Thorburn

ACKNOWLEDGMENTS

I sincerely thank Suzanne Baboneau, Arabella Stein, Philippa McEwan, the real Lorraine Page whose name I borrowed, Susanna Porter and Harold Evans of Random House, Gill Coleridge, Esther Newberg, Peter Benedek, Hazel Orme. With special thanks to Alice Asquith, researcher at La Plante Productions, and Vaughan Kinghan, editor at La Plante Productions. To everyone at the Pasadena Police Station and Sheriff's Office, thank you for your time and expertise.

With thanks for their contribution to: Eliot Hoffman, Arthur Q. Davis, Clara Earthly, Geoffrey Smith, Paul Lovell, Priestess Miriam Chawani, Brandi Kelly, the Voodoo Museum, Yosha Goldstein, Center for New American Media, Sergeant Barry Fletcher and Lieutenant Sam Fredella of the New Orleans Police Department, John Gagliano, New Orleans Coroner's Office, Dr. Munroe Samuels, Tyler Bridges, Arthur Hardy, Mardi Gras Guide, Luke Delpip, Zulu Social Aid and Pleasure Club, Warren Green, NOMTOC krewe, Ed Renwick, Institute of Politics, New Orleans, John Maloney, Lakefront Airport, Dr. Ragas, University of New Orleans, Kim Brown, Housing Authority of New Orleans, Kara Kebodeaux, New Orleans Chamber of Commerce, Wayne Everard, New Orleans Public Library, Jerry Romig, University City Hospital, Rodney and Frances Smith, Soniat House

Hotel, Norman and Sandra King, Betty Baggert, Longue Vue House, Wade Henderson, 6 WDSU Television, Courtney Marsiglia, WVUE TV Channel 8, Alcoholics Anonymous, L.A. County Coroner's Office and *The Times-Picayune*.

But above all my thanks to a very admirable lady who brought me the story of her life.

COLD
BLOOD

PROLOGUE

Mojo is an African word denoting a fetish or sacred object, which can be used either for good or for evil. *Gris-gris*, meaning "gray gray" in French, is the name given in New Orleans to the combination of "black" and "white" mojos made by a voodoo practitioner to achieve his or her ends— to safeguard the life of a person to whom the charm is given, protect against disease and ward off the evil wishes of enemies in order to avoid bad luck in love and life. A personal gris-gris must be kept secret, and will lose its power if seen or touched by anyone other than the owner. For that reason, gris-gris are usually worn close to the body, on the right side by men, on the left by women.

CHAPTER

1

Anna Louise Caley remained under the shower for a full half hour, scrubbing herself clean, making sure every inch of her perfect body was cleansed. She could blank out from her mind what she had done—that was easy—but it was the abuse she inflicted on her body that worried her, and she examined herself with care, pleased to see that there was no bruise or other marks to show what she had done the night before.

With just a soft white towel swathed around her, she re-examined herself, checking and patting her flesh until she was satisfied, then oiled and powdered her body and got dressed. White tennis socks, white cotton panties, white tennis dress and, lastly, pristine white tennis shoes. She laced them up, then chose one of a row of professional-standard rackets and unzipped the cover, tapping the taut strings with the flat of her hand before she slipped the cover back on. She checked her hair, putting on a white stretch headband to keep her long blond hair back from her face.

Anna Louise left nothing out of place in her room, placing in the laundry basket the towel she had used along with the previous night's soiled clothes. She liked the fact that she was not like a normal teenager, prided herself on being meticulously neat, and she slowly appraised her immaculate room before she headed for the tennis court. She passed through the kitchen, still empty at six-thirty in the morning, before any of the domestic staff had begun to prepare breakfast, and went outside, where a gardener was already turning on the sprinklers and sweeping up any dead leaves that might have fallen during the night. He did not look up, however, as Anna Louise headed for the changing room, where the tennis balls were kept, and picked up a large basket of them, then made her way to the court. First she examined the net, making sure it was precisely the correct height, then fed the balls into an automatic delivery machine and set the dial for speed and direction. She carefully removed her racket from its cover and switched on the ball machine, ready to begin to play against it—against herself. She stood on the service line, her weight thrown onto the balls of her feet, poised and ready for the first ball to shoot out, then began to practice her double-handed backhand. She was a precise player, fast, meticulous and very powerful, and she slammed ball after ball up the court until she was sweating with exertion, each stroke accompanied by a low grunt of satisfaction.

Her concentration lapsed for a moment and she missed the next ball, which struck her hard in the chest. Someone was laughing, and she recognized both the laugh and the accompanying soft, low giggle.

The balls continued to pop out of the machine, but Anna Louise ignored them now and walked off the court toward the summerhouse through the shrubbery, where she knew her approach could be neither seen nor heard.

Sometime later, the machine fired out its last few balls, but now Anna Louise was slashing furiously at them, sending them crashing around the court as Tilda Brown, her closest friend, opened the court gate. Tilda was as blond and as pretty as Anna Louise and was dressed in a similar white tennis dress, but Anna Louise didn't stop playing even for a moment to acknowledge her.

"Hi, Anna!" Tilda called. "Sorry I'm late, I've got a terrible headache. Maybe I won't play this morning, I feel real bad," she continued, pulling a face.

Anna Louise made no reply, but switched off the machine and picked up the basket to begin collecting the stray balls. Tilda, still complaining of a headache, balanced some balls on her racket and carried them across the basket to tip them inside.

"Did you hear what I said? I don't feel like playing."

Anna Louise smiled. "Oh, but I've been waiting for you. I want to show you my backhand, it's really progressed."

"It was always good," Tilda replied.

"Yes, but now it's better," Anna Louise said nonchalantly.

"Maybe later!" Tilda carried the basket over and tipped the balls into the machine. "I'll refill it for you."

Anna Louise stood on the service line, bouncing a ball up and down on her racket, then suddenly took aim. The ball slammed into Tilda's back, making her turn around, gasping. The blow hurt so much she could hardly speak, and the next ball hit her so hard in the stomach that she staggered backward, winded.

"Stop it, Anna, *stop it, that hurt . . . you hurt me.*"

Anna Louise moved closer. "Get Polar to kiss it better. . . ."

Tilda was scared and tearful; her belly ached, while her back felt as if it were burning, and Anna Louise was bouncing another ball, ready to aim at her again. Tilda ducked for cover as the third ball came toward her.

"What are you doing? *Stop it!*" she screamed.

Anna Louise grinned as she picked up a fourth ball.

"You can't get away from me, Tilda Brown." She was now throwing the ball up in the air as if to serve. Tilda moved farther back and bumped into the ball machine, hitting the switch with her arm. The machine began to pump the balls more rapidly toward Anna Louise, who laughed as she swung her racket, forehand and backhand, every ball viciously directed at the cowering Tilda, who screamed, running this way and that to avoid the swift hail of tennis balls, until she squatted, sobbing behind the net.

Even behind the safety of the net, balls slammed into her arms and legs through the mesh, Anna Louise first taking aim at Tilda's body, and then at her face.

"Stop it, please stop it," sobbed Tilda, looking up to see Anna Louise standing over her.

"You stay away from him, Tilda, he's mine. I see you with him again and I'll make you sorry. I'll hurt you more than any tennis ball, I'll hurt you so bad, Tilda Brown, you're gonna wish you were dead.' ''

Tilda was crying like a baby, terrified as much by Anna Louise's verbal threats as by her violence, and she sobbed with relief when she recognized the figure coming toward them. Anna Louise saw him too, and gave Tilda a final quick, hard blow on the side of the head, then lowered the racket, smiling sweetly, her whole manner altered.

"Hi, honey." Robert Caley smiled to his daughter, then looked toward her weeping friend. "What's happened, Tilda?"

Anna Louise linked her arm through her father's. "It was my fault. You know that serve o' mine, Papa, poor little Tilda here got right in the way of it . . . and you got to take some of the blame for coachin' me to serve so hard, but I didn't mean to hit her, I guess she just isn't up to my standard."

Robert Caley had one arm around his daughter as he reached out to Tilda with concern. "You all right, sweetheart?"

Tilda wouldn't look into his eyes, but held her hand to her head, feeling the lump where Anna Louise had hit her. "I want to go home, Mr. Caley, today," she said in a low but firm voice.

"She is just bein' silly 'cause she lost the game," Anna Louise said petulantly. She tried to hang on to her father's arm to stop him from following Tilda, but he pulled free of her, and she was infuriated to see him help Tilda to the gates and walk her back to the house. She smashed the racket against the Har-Tru court, then examined it, afraid she had damaged one of her favorites. Long strands of Tilda's hair were caught between the strings.

Tilda had packed, and refused to say anything else to Anna Louise through her locked bedroom door other than that she was going home at once. Anna Louise tried to cajole her, saying she was sorry, that she hadn't meant to be nasty, but Tilda refused to unlock the door. Now Anna Louise was worried about what Tilda might say to her mother, and was beginning to think that perhaps the sooner she left the better.

"Fine—you leave, Tilda Brown, I don't care," she said

angrily, but she was worried enough to decide to go and sit
with her mother. Tilda would certainly want to say good-
bye to her, and more than likely would tattle. Anna Louise
tapped on the door of her mother's suite and waited; it was
often locked in the mornings, as Elizabeth Caley hated being
seen without her war paint, even by her own daughter. Anna
Louise knocked again, then walked in: all the curtains were
drawn and the room was in darkness. She called out to her
mother, but receiving no reply she wondered if Elizabeth
was still sleeping or, worse, had gone downstairs and would
see Tilda. She hurried through her mother's sitting room
toward her bedroom.

"Mama," she whispered, then pressed her ear to the door,
listening. "Are you awake, Mama? It's me, it's Anna Louise."

She eased the bedroom door open and peeked inside, ad-
justing her eyes to the darkness of the room, then called out
softly again, but saw that the bedcovers had been drawn
back. Her mother was known to fly into an even worse rage
if she was woken from sleep than if she was surprised without makeup. She suffered from severe insomnia and her
sleep was precious, if rarely natural.

Anna Louise looked across to the bathroom door and
heard the soft sounds of bathwater running. She was about
to leave when she noticed the low, flickering light of a candle on her mother's bedside table. The candle was sputter-
ing, and she crossed the room in order to snuff it out.

The gris-gris had been consecrated, because it was posi-
tioned on top of a worn black Bible, a small white cotton
sack of salt to the left and a tiny green bottle of water to
the right. Above the Bible a blue candle, representing the
element of fire, guttered in its candlestick; below the book
was a square of sweet-smelling incense, the symbol for air.
Anna Louise felt the hairs on the back of her neck prickle
when she opened the gris-gris bag and looked at the contents, unaware of their meaning and of what it meant to have
seen and touched a consecrated gris-gris. Fascinated, she
picked up the old Bible and opened the flyleaf: in old-
fashioned scrolled handwriting whose ink had faded from
black to brown there was an inscription to Elizabeth Seal—
her mother's maiden name. Anna Louise carefully replaced

the book, flicking through the tissue-thin pages to try to make sure it was in the same position she had discovered it in.

Back in her own room, she sniffed her fingers and decided they smelled musty, so she filled her washstand basin with hot water and soaped her hands clean. She was just drying them when she heard her mother calling for her and returned to the suite.

"Tilda wants to go home today," Elizabeth said, toying with a silver spoon on her breakfast tray. "But that's silly because we're all leaving tomorrow."

Anna Louise sat on the edge of her mother's bed, noticing that the bedside table had been cleared. "Oh, we had an argument, we'll make it up." She was anxious to change the subject, so asked with concern, "How you feeling today?"

"I'm just fine, honey. Now you go and talk to your friend—it's stupid for her to go if we're all going to New Orleans tomorrow."

"Okay, I'll make up with her. Do you want me to take your tray?"

"Mmmm, I'll sleep awhile maybe, I had a bad night. Kiss kiss?"

Anna Louise leaned over to plant a kiss on her mother's cheek and then carried the breakfast tray out of the room and closed the door behind her.

Tilda had already left by the time Anna Louise returned her mother's tray to the kitchen. Anna Louise was unconcerned: she'd make it up to her, buy her something expensive. She wandered into the kitchen, where Berenice, the housekeeper, had just baked a tray of fresh blueberry muffins, and began picking at one with her fingers, remembering the strange, musty smell from the Bible she had seen upstairs.

"Tilda told me something weird, something she'd seen. . . ." She began casually, still picking at the muffin's crispy top.

Berenice was emptying the dishwasher, not paying too much attention to her employers' daughter, only half listening as she went back and forth stacking the clean dishes in the cupboards. She poured a glass of milk for Anna Louise and set it beside her.

"Miss Tilda sure was upset about somethin', crying her eyes out. We thought maybe she'd had bad news." She continued putting the clean dishes away.

"What does it mean if you've got a Bible, a blue candle and funny little bags of salt and incense, you know, like those gris-gris bags they sell back home?"

The cupboard door banged shut. "You don't wanna know, Miss Anna Louise, an' you stop pickin' at each muffin. You want one, then you take one."

"What does it mean?"

The housekeeper was replacing the cutlery in its drawer now, buffing each knife and fork quickly with a clean cloth before she put it away.

"Well, it depends on which way the cross is placed on the Bible."

"Ah, so you do know what it means?"

"All I know is, if you and Miss Tilda are playing around, then you stop and don't be foolish. That's voodoo, and nobody ought to play games with things they don't understand because evil has a way of getting inside you, like a big black snake. It sits in your belly and you never know when it's gonna uncoil and spit . . . and if you touch another person's gris-gris, then you got bad trouble."

Anna Louise broke off a large piece of muffin and stuffed it into her mouth. "You don't believe in all that mumbo jumbo, do you?"

She took a gulp of milk, swallowing it the wrong way, and started coughing and spluttering as the muffin lodged in the back of her throat. She gasped, her eyes watering and her cheeks turning bright red. She couldn't breathe—it felt as if she was being choked, and Berenice had to hit her hard in the middle of her back as she retched and clung to the edge of the table before at last she coughed up the mouthful of food, heaving for breath.

The housekeeper fetched some paper kitchen towel to wipe up the mess.

"You see, what did I say about that snake? It just come and hissed an' spat right now, almost chokin' you, so you hear me right and don't go meddlin'." But when she turned back Anna Louise was gone, so she went out into the hall, catching sight of the girl as she ran helter-skelter up the stairs.

"Are you all right, Miss Anna Louise?"

Anna Louise looked down and then leaned over the banister, whispering, "It was in my mama's room. It wasn't Tilda that saw it but me!"

She laughed suddenly and continued running up the stairs, not seeing the fear on Berenice's face as the housekeeper slipped her hand inside her uniform dress to feel for her own gris-gris. It was safely tucked into her slip, on her left-hand side, beneath her heart.

Berenice returned to the kitchen: that silly spoiled child had no notion of what went on in the house, and she hoped to God she never would. She cleaned up the mess from the table, and finished putting the dishes away, then tipped all the freshly made blueberry muffins into the trash. She would make a fresh batch, just in case a drop of the snake's venom that had hissed from Anna Louise Caley had touched them: there were some chances that just weren't worth taking.

The following afternoon, accompanied by her parents, Anna Louise flew from Los Angeles to New Orleans. It was February 15 and the next day, Anna Louise was officially reported as missing. Police in both Los Angeles and New Orleans attempted to trace her, and when they failed to do so, her parents brought in private investigators.

The weeks became months—no body and no ransom note were discovered, and even with top investigation agencies on the case, no clue as to the whereabouts of the missing girl, or her body, ever came to light. After nine months the disappearance of Anna Louise Caley was no longer news, and she had to all intents and purposes become just another statistic, another photograph on the missing persons files.

Eleven months passed, and with no new information, Anna Louise's distraught parents faced the possibility that she might have been murdered. By this time, more than fifteen investigation agencies had been involved with the case; the Mississippi had been dragged and helicopters had searched the swamplands of Louisiana. Agnew Investigations, along with three other less well-known agencies, were still retained on the inquiry: the Caleys had paid out millions of dollars, but the expenditure had yielded no motive, no suspect, no results. All the grieving parents were left with was an aching period of waiting, while they longed for a sign that their beautiful Anna Louise was still alive.

All the PI agencies involved had made a lot of money, and some had even traded information with one another, but finally the Anna Louise Caley bonanza was coming to an end. Pickings were getting slim for private investigators—it was a tough business in which contacts and recommendations by word of mouth were a necessity, as Page Investigations, a small PI company, had found out the hard way. Even getting a foothold on the lowest rung of such a competitive ladder had proved impossible, and the attempt had been financially crippling for Lorraine Page: now, her agency was virtually bankrupt.

Even though she was a former police lieutenant, her own case history as an alcoholic and an officer who had shot dead an unarmed boy while drunk on duty meant that instead of being welcomed into the PI fraternity, she was being frozen out, just as she had been kicked out of the LAPD. The hardest part was explaining to Rosie, the assistant whom Lorraine jokingly called her partner, and who was also a recovering alcoholic, that they were going under. Dear Rosie, who still hoped, Rosie who still maintained that business would pick up—but there had never been any business. There was nothing to pick up from; it had all been a gamble, a dream even, but now it was over.

Lorraine had the phone cupped in her hand, half listening to the call, half wondering whether tonight would be the night she would tell Rosie—she knew she would have to do it soon. She listened, interjecting twice how sorry she was as the man's deep rumbling voice made incoherent references to his wife's passing.

Rosie Hurst, a plump forty-five-year-old woman with a kind, open face, was reading her horoscope, a cup of coffee and two orange-chocolate cupcakes beside her. She had flicked a glance at Lorraine when the phone had jangled through the silent office and sighed when she had heard Lorraine's overcheerful "Hi, Bill, how ya doing?"

Rosie had been trying a new diet: proteins one meal, carbohydrates the next, with fruit forty minutes either before or after each meal, and no fats or fried food. She had stuck to it for a month and felt better for having lost a few pounds, but today she was indulging in a binge of chocolate cupcakes, hating herself with each bite. Still, it was just one of those days—she couldn't face another chicken breast without crisp golden skin or French fries or another salad without dressing, and a whole month with no fresh crusty bread spread thickly with peanut butter had been excruciating.

At last Lorraine was able to replace the receiver. "That was Bill Rooney," she murmured, lighting a cigarette. "His wife died."

"I didn't know he had a wife," Rosie said, lowering her magazine.

"I don't think he did," Lorraine said as she counted the butt ends in her ashtray. She sighed and leaned back in her chair. By turning her head a fraction she could just make out the cheap sign printed in fake gold leaf on the outer office door—PAGE INVESTIGATIONS AGENCY. There was a stack of business cards on her desk with the same inscription. It was a farce.

"Well, the end of yet another overactive sleuthing day." Rosie chomped on her cupcake, staring at the free digital alarm clock she got from ordering some nonstick pans. It was almost six. Unaware of the smear of chocolate over her right cheek, she looked over at Lorraine, watching her as she inhaled deeply on her thirtieth or so cigarette of the day. Her eyes were staring vacantly across the small white painted office. Rosie hated it when she did those vacant stares. Sometimes her silences could last over an hour, and Rosie could never tell what her partner was thinking. She hoped this was not going to turn into one of Lorraine's moods. "You should cut down," she said with her mouth full.

"So should you," Lorraine retorted, looking at the trash can filled with empty silver-foil cupcake molds.

"I don't smoke, so it's expected I should crave sugar. That's half of what alcoholism is about too, you know— sugar craving."

Lorraine pushed her secondhand typist chair back from her empty desk. "Is it? Well, well, isn't that interesting. And just what are hamburgers and fries, are they a craving too?''

"For Chrissakes, don't start hassling me! You and your
brown rice and your vitamins make me wanna throw up."

"Might do you some good!"

Rosie now pushed her ample rear back in her catalog-
sale-of-the-month office chair. "Right, that is it."

"Yep, I guess it is, Rosie."

It was hard for Lorraine to explain how each day she felt
more isolated, because in physical terms she wasn't: Rosie
and big Bill Rooney were always there. It wasn't that she
didn't have anyone to talk to, interact with—it just felt that
way. Her mind seemed to be atrophying and she felt drained,
lethargic; sometimes she wanted to weep, out of a deepening
feeling of utter loneliness, or was it lovelessness? Whatever
it was, it was having a more and more destructive effect on
her, and she felt its undertow sucking her down.

Lorraine flicked the old venetian blind that didn't quite
fit the windows. She gave a sly look at her plump roommate
as she stubbed out her cigarette. She didn't even live in a
place of her own, but was sharing Rosie's small apartment
in a run-down district off Orange Grove. She was thirty-
seven years old; almost six of those years had been lost in
a sea of drugs and alcohol addiction, and sometimes, especially at times like this afternoon, she felt it was all a waste
of time; the reality was that she was never going to get back
into the only business she knew or had known when she
had been a cop.

The two women had met when Lorraine was recuperating
from a near-fatal hit-and-run accident. It wasn't the vehicle
that had almost killed her but her drinking and self-abuse.
Now she had been sober and attempting to get her life or-
ganized for nearly two years. As an ex-lieutenant attached
to the Pasadena Homicide Squad, she had experience not
only in the field but as a detective, and she had been a very
good one. "Had" being the operative word: after drinking
took over her life it had cost her the husband she had loved
and the two daughters she had adored.

"What you thinking about?" Rosie asked, pretending to
be immersed in her magazine.

"Nothing," Lorraine answered, but this quite obviously

wasn't true. She wondered if she should attempt another reconciliation with her kids. Yet as always whenever she thought about them, she decided they were better off without her intruding on their new life, a life she had not been a part of for too many years. Added to that, her ex-husband had remarried and her daughters called his new wife Mother. They didn't even want to see her.

Rosie pored over her magazine again. Lorraine's long sighs made her aware that something was coming, but she said nothing, flicking over the pages to a new diet that guaranteed you could lose weight with ease if you sent off for their specially priced "slimming drinks." But since she'd attempted most diets, including slimming drinks, and none had worked, she flicked over to a knitting pattern.

"This is a farce—you know it and I know it. I mean, I dunno what else we can do. How many more ads can we afford to run, if we don't drum up any customer by the end of the week?"

Here it comes, thought Rosie, scowling. "You've said that every week." She hated it when Lorraine started on this tactic, partly because she knew everything she said was true but also because it made her afraid. Afraid Lorraine would leave, afraid that without Lorraine she would go back on the booze, afraid Lorraine would too.

"Got to face reality." Lorraine prodded her empty cigarette pack, hoping she'd overlooked a stray one. But it wasn't to be, so she looked over the stubs in her ashtray again.

"Yes, I know, I know, and I hear what you are sayin', but at the same time we got to stick to it. Everyone knows any new business takes time to take off—even Bill Rooney told us that."

Lorraine appeared not to be listening as she rummaged in her purse and started to check her loose change.

"I mean, we could get a case in tomorrow that'd make everything you just said obsolete," Rosie said a little too cheerfully.

"What?" Lorraine asked challengingly.

"Obsolete," Rosie repeated flatly.

"Really? Well, you've been saying that for the past month and we haven't had so much as a telephone call. And if you want to check the logbook out, we are hardly likely to get some case off the street that'd pay for your cupcakes and my cigarettes, never mind the rent on this place and your apartment. So get it straight, Rosie. Shit, I need a cigarette.''

Lorraine crossed to the hooks by the toilet closet. She yanked down her raincoat.

"Maybe the rain'll stop soon."

Lorraine pulled on her raincoat. "Oh yeah, so it's all gonna be okay if the sun shines?"

"Maybe."

"You're a dumb optimist."

"What?"

"Optimist, Rosie. Even if the sun cracked the pavement, that's not gonna help us. Two stray dogs, a missing senile grandfather, a two-week stint in a department store to cover for their in-house detective's vacation, five car traces, four warrants and a woman suspecting her husband of having an affair with his secretary, and since the wife was your size and his secretary looked like Julia Roberts, it didn't take us long to investigate, and that . . . that is it, Rosie, that's all there's been for the past nine months."

"You always gotta get personal. If you look on the good side, you've been sober nine months more, and so have I, come to think of it, so my guess is we'll make it. This is just a bad patch."

Lorraine clenched her teeth. "No, it isn't, Rosie, it's just a fact. We are flat broke and searching my ashtray for butts is not exactly what I had planned for the future. We might as well admit it, face it, before we get any deeper in debt."

"But we are facing it," Rosie said stubbornly.

Lorraine closed her eyes as if talking to a child, her voice sounding annoyingly overpatient. "No, we are not. Fact is this whole idea was shit, and to be honest I don't feel like patting myself on the back 'cause I remained sober. Truth is, right now I feel like tying one hell of a load on and the only thing stoppin' me is that I have no money."

"Never stopped you before," snapped back Rosie.

Lorraine's eyes were like cold chips of ice. "What's that supposed to mean? What are you suggesting, Rosie? Come on, spit it out, are you saying I go out and screw a few guys to keep this place open? That what you think I should do?''

Rosie blushed and turned away. She loathed Lorraine when she was like this, she could get so cold, so unapproachable, so downright nasty. But unlike the times they'd bickered about the agency before, there wasn't another sarcastic retort forthcoming, just an ominous silence.

Lorraine was staring at herself in the small mirror glued to the back of the door. Her hair needed a cut and new highlights. She leaned closer, frowning, as she checked the scar running from her left eye down to the middle of her cheekbone; that needed to be fixed but plastic surgery cost. She stepped back, giving herself a critical appraisal. Considering the punishment her body and insides had taken from all the abuse, her skin looked remarkably clear, but there were fine lines at the sides of her eyes and they were getting deeper. Either way, she didn't like what she saw, and kicked the door closed.

Lorraine picked up her gym bag and flicked off the main overhead light switch. Her shadow etched across the main office wall as she reached for her purse. Caught in the half-light from the lit-up screen on Rosie's word processor, Lorraine's chiseled features never ceased to make Rosie's heart lurch. She obviously didn't see herself as Rosie did, because she was still a very attractive woman. Perhaps not as stunning as Rosie thought, but for her age, and considering what she had been through, Lorraine Page was still a looker. The stronger she became physically over the past twenty-one months, the more her natural beauty shone through. Lorraine's strict diet, her almost obsessive workouts at the gym, had proved that a woman who lost six years drinking herself into oblivion, who had become a hopeless, scrawny, sickly alcoholic when she and the overweight Rosie had first met, could now pass for an athlete. The only thing ex-lieutenant Lorraine Page could not recapture was her career, and her husband and two daughters. She never spoke of them, either to Rosie or at AA meetings, whereas Rosie spilled many tears about wanting to be reunited with her son.

Rosie now let out a long deep sigh; maybe, as she herself had half suggested, the failure of their business would send Lorraine back to the bottle, back to a life in the gutter. Rosie was therefore totally unprepared for what Lorraine had to say as she hovered by the main office door, about to leave.

Lorraine swung the door slightly with her foot. "I meant to tell you, the department store offered me a full-time job as their store detective. Remember the job I took over for two weeks? Well, apparently she had one hell of a holiday and came back pregnant."

"What?"

"So, we close up at the end of the week and at least I'll have enough for the rent on the apartment."

"What about Page Investigations?" Rosie asked as the tears started.

"Like I said, it's over—end of the week we close up shop."

"What about me?"

Lorraine, still tap-tapping the door with the toe of her shoe, wouldn't look at her friend. "Well, I guess you got to go out into the big world, Rosie, and get a job. Shouldn't be too tough, you can use a word processor and—"

Rosie turned away, her eyes brimming, and Lorraine felt awful. She went over and slipped her arm around her friend's shoulders.

"I'm sorry, sometimes I say things and they come out all the wrong way. What I am trying to say is—you got a life, Rosie, and maybe I have too, not just doing what we're doing, okay?"

Rosie nodded and felt in her pocket for a tissue. Lorraine hesitated, knowing that to stay with Rosie would only involve going over old ground, but was saved by the ringing of the phone. Rosie snatched up the receiver, hoping against all hope that the call would mean a job, but didn't even get to say "Page Investigations." It didn't matter anyway—it was only her sponsor, Jake, wondering if she'd be at AA that evening. By the time Rosie had replied that she would, Lorraine had gone.

"You okay, Rosie?" Jake's friendly rasping voice inquired.

"Nope, we're shutting up shop. Can I see you tonight before the meeting?"

Jake agreed and Rosie replaced the phone, feeling the tears welling up again. Was it ever going to end? Did she have a life of her own, as Lorraine had said? Hell, without

Lorraine, Rosie knew she was hopeless—sure, she could use a word processor, but she didn't have enough confidence to go out alone into the big wide world. That was the difference between them—Rosie needed Lorraine, and without her the world scared the shit out of her. Or maybe it wasn't the world, just her own weakness and low self-esteem. Just seeing the empty cupcake carton made her want to weep—she couldn't even stick to a diet! How could she cope without Lorraine? By having a drink, that would be how, and that realization made her want to weep even more. She badly needed to go to that meeting.

Lorraine went to her weight-lifting class. She pushed herself to breaking point, wanting to exhaust herself so she'd crash out and sleep when she got home. She blanked out Rosie's doleful face. In truth, she was just as sad at the failure of the business, but unlike Rosie she knew she could not let it swamp her. If she had to move on, then she would do what had to be done. She knew she could not take responsibility for Rosie, it was tough enough taking it for herself, and if she was to survive she had to put herself first, otherwise she'd go down. She had not been kidding when she had said she wanted a drink. She did. But she was not going to take one, well, not tonight. She knew by now that it never ended, the "thirst" was never over. It was, and would continue to be, a constant battle for the rest of her life. Part of her wanted to fight it, but sometimes, just sometimes, it seemed so pointless.

Rosie was in floods of tears, sitting beside her dear friend Jake Valsack, who was patting her hand.

"Well, maybe she's right, Rosie. If it's not working out on any front, more specifically financially, why flog a dead horse?"

Rosie blew her nose. "She just came out with it, like she must have known awhile back about this offer of a job. You see, she's pregnant."

"What, Lorraine?"

"*No!* The goddamned store detective, the bitch!"

Jake raised his thick, matted eyebrows. He was having a tough time following what Rosie was going on about, but surmised that Lorraine had a job and Rosie didn't, and their so-called investigation business was kaput.

"I mean, how could she do it, Jake? I decorated and painted the place, we got all that office furniture. . . . I know it's not much, but we got phone extensions put in, I got a word processor to pay off, a fax machine and a . . . It was me that got the desks, you know, and the furniture. It took us months to set up, how could she do this to me?"

"She did it, Rosie, because you had no work coming in, right? Am I right?"

"That is not the point," she said stubbornly.

Jake sneaked a look at his watch; the meeting was about to start. Rosie could carry on like this for a long time, as he knew from past experience, and no matter what he said she paid no attention; she just went round and round in circles.

"What about that ex-captain, Rooney? I thought you said he was gonna drum up work?"

Rosie blew her nose. "Oh, him! He's boozed out, his wife's just died."

"Oh, I'm sorry. I don't know him, but how is he coping?" Jake asked, trying to change the subject.

Rosie continued as if there had been no interruption. "I mean, if you don't stay with something, you know, really see it through. . . . We got the office furniture and I schlepped all over yard sales for that."

Jake gripped her hand tighter. "Rosie, sweetheart, maybe Lorraine did just that, saw it through and came to the conclusion it wasn't gonna work. It hasn't worked."

"She never gave it a chance," Rosie snapped back.

Jake sighed in frustration. He was chairing this evening and he could see that the crowd of people arriving for the meeting was thinning out as they entered the hall. "Rosie, I got to go in now. Maybe talk this through afterwards?"

"I need to talk it through now, Jake."

He was trying to hold on to his temper. "Rosie, I have been talking it through with you for over an hour, but you won't face facts."

"Facts are, Jake, she just dumped me. We might have gotten overflow work from the other agencies."

"No, honey, facts are Lorraine's talking sense. I mean, you think about this, you know her history, she was a drunk cop on duty, she got kicked out of her station, she shot a young kid, for Chrissakes. You ever think that maybe, just maybe, none of the other agencies can take the risk of an ex-junkie, ex-alcoholic orderin' their toilet paper, never mind taking on any overflow of cases? They know about her, so even if it's tracin' stolen vehicles—''

''But we did a trace, we got three.''

Jake rumpled his thinning hair; she was refusing to listen to him. ''I got to go in, Rosie, like now, so come on, wipe your nose and let's go in. You need a bit of stabilizing.''

''I need a drink, Jake.''

He closed his eyes. It was going to be a long, long night.

They were just about to go back to square one when there was a tap on the window of his beat-up Pontiac. ''Jake, it's me, only I've welcomed everyone because I don't think we're going to get any more here tonight. Coffee is served and everyone's waiting for you to take the chair.''

The thin-faced middle-aged woman in a rather expensive tailored suit stepped back from the car. Phyllis Collins didn't even glance at Rosie, who was blowing her nose loudly.

''Okay, Phyllis, I'm comin' now.'' Jake stepped from the car and bent down to Rosie. ''Let's go, Rosie.''

''No, I'm not coming in.''

Jake gestured to Phyllis. ''Do me a favor, Phyllis, she needs a bit of encouragement tonight. You've met, haven't you?''

Phyllis nodded and peered toward the passenger seat. ''Good evening.''

Rosie didn't even acknowledge her as she delved into her bulging purse for a clean tissue. Jake raised his eyes to heaven and Phyllis gave him a reassuring smile.

''You go in, I'll stay with her. Go on, you can't keep everyone waiting.'' Phyllis bent down to the car. ''We've met a few times. I'm Phyllis Collins.''

Rosie glared. She had no recollection of ever meeting the woman before and she had no intention of getting out of the car.

''Jake can't not go in, he's chairing tonight. You mind if I sit with you?''

Rosie shrugged, looking away, but she didn't stop Phyllis from getting into the car. If nothing else, she was someone she could repeat the entire scenario to; she'd have spilled it all out to anyone, she was feeling so wretched.

"My partner just dumped me."

"Oh, I am sorry, were you married long?"

"My business partner. I've worked my butt off and to-night she just told me she had another job, just like that."

Phyllis nodded, her thin, plain face concerned. "Oh dear, no wonder you're not feeling good."

Lorraine eased the wet iced cloth further over her sweating face. The heat in the sauna was so intense she could take only another few minutes. She was lying naked on the high-est bench, two other women were flat out on the benches beneath her. No one spoke.

Lorraine was wondering if Rosie was okay, but she fig-ured if Jake was with her she wouldn't do anything stupid. She decided to clear out the change in her purse and get a bottle of alcohol-free cider to cheer Rosie up. It looked like champagne and tasted like gnat's piss, but Rosie loved it.

"Excuse me," Lorraine murmured as she swung her legs down to the lower bench and then eased her body past one of the prone women, who leaned up on her elbow to allow Lorraine to pass. She remained half upright, staring at the tall woman as she left the sauna. She envied the beautiful, straight, muscular body and then became curious when she saw the patched scars across Lorraine's arms, the small jag-ged razor lines and round burn marks.

The same woman caught sight of Lorraine again in the changing room. Using a brush, she was blow-drying her fine silky blond hair rather expertly.

"I wish I could do that."

Lorraine turned, slightly puzzled, wondering if the woman was talking to her.

"Save a fortune at the hairdresser's. I can never do the back of my head."

Lorraine switched off the hair dryer. "Oh, it just takes practice," she said politely, and concentrated on finishing her hair. When she walked out from the changing cubicle the nosy woman was talking confidentially to someone else, both their overweight bodies cushioned together in their white club-issue towels.

"She used to be a police lieutenant, drunk on duty, that was what I was told. She knows the gym instructor and he told me that—"

Lorraine let her cubicle door bang hard and they whipped around like startled hamsters. She would have liked to tell them where she would like to ram the hair dryer but she didn't. She said nothing. And all the tension her exercise and sauna had relaxed from her body was back. By the time she passed through reception she was wired and angry.

Arthur, the gym instructor, gave her a friendly grin and called out, "Good night."

Lorraine kept on walking.

Some friend he'd turned out to be. She decided she would not come back. She just knew she had better head directly for home instead of getting Rosie's cider because that feeling of wanting a real drink was getting out of her control.

Three bottles of Evian water downed between them, Phyllis and Rosie were sitting in a small café. Only it wasn't Rosie spilling out her tales of woe, it was Phyllis, and she had Rosie's rapt attention.

"I suppose in some ways I stayed on because it was all so dreadful and I keep on saying to myself, When it's all over, I'll leave. But it's not over, maybe it never will be. Sometimes it gets so bad with her I just don't think I can take any more of it. She is so demanding, expecting me to be ready to drop whatever I am doing anytime of day or night. If she wakes up at four in the morning, she can't be bothered to use the intercom, she just screams my name. Sometimes I wake up in a cold sweat because I think I've heard her shrieking for me, and other times, when she's very sick because she's taken so many pills to sleep, I just get rigid with fear and all I do is feel her pulse to see if she's still breathing. It's a wretched, terrible time for all concerned, a tragedy really. . . ."

Rosie took a big breath. "I used to see all her movies."

Phyllis poured the rest of the Evian into her glass. " 'Used to' being the operative words. She hasn't made a movie for maybe fifteen years."

Rosie leaned closer to Phyllis. "Why, why do you take

it? Is it the salary? Oh, I'm sorry, that was rude, you don't
have to answer that, I'm sorry.''

Phyllis pursed her lips, becoming defensive. "No, no, it's
not the salary, believe me, and lately we've not traveled the
way we used to—she's hardly left the house.''

Rosie nodded. "Yeah, I guess it must be awful.''

"It is, every time the phone rings. Not that she answers,
just screams for me to do it, and so I get all tensed up, over
and over again, hoping for news and afraid it will be bad,
the worst. . . . She was such a pretty girl.'' Phyllis started to
sniffle, opening her purse to take out a small lace handkerchief. Rosie noticed it was a very expensive suede-lined
purse, with a gold chain threaded with leather for a strap.
"I'm so sorry to get like this, but I don't have many friends,
no one to really talk to. That's why since I joined AA, it's
meant so much to me, you know. And Jake, he's such a
dear man, he's been wonderful.''

"Oh yeah, I know, he's a godsend to me too. Would you
like another glass of water, Phyllis? Or we could go on to
something stronger, like apple juice?''

Lorraine was waiting to apologize to Rosie when she heard
heavy footsteps on the stairs leading up to the apartment.

"Rosie?''

Jake opened the screen door and then peered in. "Nope,
it's me. She's not here, then?''

"Nope.''

"I'll drive around, see if I can find her. She took it hard
about the business folding.''

Lorraine lit a cigarette. "Yeah, well, I'm not out celebra-
tin' myself, Jake, but one of us has got to earn the rent.''

"You're right, you're right. So stay put, I'll drive
around.''

"Was she at the meeting?'' Lorraine asked with just a
tinge of concern.

"Outside it, I left her with Phyllis whatever her name is.
I just hope the two of them aren't out someplace tying on
a load. See ya.''

Her heart sank when not long after Jake had left she heard
a bellow from the street and then Rosie's footfalls. The

small apartment, which had only one bedroom, a tiny bathroom and a living room with a kitchen crammed into a corner, was on the second floor of an old house on Marengo Avenue. The apartment below was occupied by an ever-growing family of Latinos. Luckily, they created much more noise themselves, their radio and TV sometimes turned up so loud you could hardly hear yourself speak; anyone else having to live beneath the thunder of Rosie's footsteps would have had a nervous breakdown.

"Hey! You won't believe what I got to tell you." Rosie's cheeks were flushed pink with the exertion of hurrying home. She gasped for breath.

"Rosie, how much have you had?"

"I've got more bottled water swilling around inside me than the main water tank." Rosie kicked off her shoes and chucked her coat aside, hurling her purse onto the sofa, and then, with her hands on her wide hips, she beamed from ear to ear. "I think we just got lucky."

"You want some coffee?"

"No, sit down and listen, right now. Go on, siddown. Okay, now, you ever heard of a very famous movie star called Elizabeth Seal?"

"Nope."

Rosie threw her hands up in the air. "Of course you have. *The Maple Tree*, you remember that one. And you gotta remember *The Swamp* and *Mask of Vanessa*, yes?"

"Nope."

"For Chrissakes, we saw it on cable. The movie star Elizabeth Seal is famous, you gotta know who I'm talking about, late fifties, sixties, she was—*huge*!"

"Have you been drinking with her?"

Rosie flopped down on the sofa bed, which creaked ominously. "Don't be dumb, as if Elizabeth Seal would be out drinkin' water with me in Joe's Diner. She's a *big movie star*! Maybe you heard of the name Caley? Elizabeth Caley? That's her married name."

"Nope."

"Holy shit, I don't believe you. Elizabeth and Robert Caley have been headlines, well, almost a year ago they were. Every paper ran their story, even the TV, it was headlines because of her bein' so famous. Their daughter disappeared, you listening? Their eighteen-year-old daughter, Anna Louise Caley, disappeared.''

Lorraine was trying to recall their names, but she still drew a blank. Nothing new in that—there were big gaps of months, even years, when she hadn't even recalled her own name, never mind anyone else's.

Rosie sipped the coffee. She was so excited she was sweating, her eyes bright like a child's. ''She disappeared without a trace. They had the police involved, they had mystics, psychics, 'cause they had a big reward on offer. But they got no ransom note, no phone calls, no notes, nothin'. Like she just disappeared into thin air. Cops reckoned she might have been kidnapped and it went wrong and they killed her. They think she's been bumped off and . . .''

Half an hour later, Lorraine was sitting with her head in her hands, still unsure what Rosie was so excited about. ''I mean, Rosie, if according to this Phyllis woman the Caleys have hired the top private investigation agencies, why come to us?''

''Because nobody has found her yet and they're still spending thousands. They're megarich, Lorraine, and they keep on shellin' dough out.''

Lorraine held up her hand. ''Wait, wait, Rosie, please, just listen to me. If the . . . Caleys, yes? have already over the past . . . how long did you say?''

''Eleven months or so, happened during Mardi Gras in New Orleans,'' Rosie said eagerly.

''What? In New Orleans? Are you serious?''

''Yeah, what you think, I'm makin' all this up?''

Lorraine sighed. ''Rosie, if it happened in New Orleans they're not likely to hire private dicks located in LA, are they?''

''Yes, they already have, Phyllis told me. Cops were working on it here also. After all, they live here, right?''

Lorraine raised her eyes to the ceiling. ''If they have paid out all this money and still got no result, what makes you think they would be willing to shell out some more—say, to us, which I presume is what all this hysteria is about?''

''I'm not hysterical, for Chrissakes.''

''Okay, but facts are facts, Rosie. Why do you think they'd be interested in taking on Page Investigations

Agency, i.e. you and me? Just because you're in AA with
the family's secretary is not what I would call a great intro-
duction.''

Rosie yelled, "I never fuckin' mentioned *you* were a
soak. I built you up, said you were one of the best. I even
gave a good line about havin' Rooney as part of our team,
you know, him bein' ex-captain, that kind of thing. She was
impressed, she was real impressed.''

"She was?''

The sarcasm was lost on Rosie. "Yeah, she was. I gave
her our card and she said she was gonna talk to Mrs. Caley.''

"Oh, and when she's talked, then what?''

"Look, she's trusted by them, worked for them for years,
right? And she knows that Elizabeth Caley is desperate, like
going nuts, because she just wants to know what happened
to her daughter, and she'll pay anythin' to find out.''

"And you gave them our card?''

"*Yes!* An' I'm not stupid, you know,'cause first I was all
upset, right? Like tellin' her about my partner quitting, but
soon as I smelled a big fish on the line I sort of made out
the new job you got offered was some big murder investigation, not just actin' as a store detective. I'm not dumb, I
know how to spin a good yarn when I need to. I said you
was in demand.''

"So how long do we wait for her to get back?''

The phone rang. Lorraine stubbed out her cigarette, nodding to it. "That'll be Jake, you got him all wired up. He's
been looking for you, so you answer it.''

Rosie snatched up the phone. But it wasn't Jake, it was
Phyllis, and she wanted details of Page Investigations' com-
pany background sent around as soon as possible for Mrs.
Caley. Rosie replaced the receiver with a smirk.

"See? She did talk to her, just like I said.''

The following morning, after a hurried session on the word
processor, they had what they felt looked like a reasonable
folder, Lorraine giving full details of all her recommendations as a police lieutenant, listing the cases she had been
involved with. They also included as part of Page Investigations' team the experienced and dedicated ex-captain William Rooney, recently retired from the Pasadena precinct.

Rosie went off to deliver the freshly printed folder to the Caleys' home in Beverly Hills. Lorraine sat in the empty office brooding over the new events. She had a couple of days before she had to give the store job a yes or a no, so she didn't see any reason why she shouldn't hang in there. Rosie *may* be right, they might be able to earn a few bucks, but she somehow doubted it.

The buzzer on the office front door sounded as Bill Rooney wove in with an overbright "Hi, you called, didn't you? So as I was just passin' . . ."

"Oh yeah? Via which bar, Bill?"

Rooney gave her the finger as he squashed himself into Rosie's swivel chair. He looked unshaven and well hungover, his big, florid face and bulbous nose a shade of mulberry. One side of his shirt collar stuck up at an angle, and his tie was food-stained and pulled to one side; the seat of his pants was shiny, and the whole suit had a crumpled, worn-too-often look.

"You look in good shape," Lorraine said, smiling.

"I feel it, I feel real good. Lost half my pension on the PI agency I never got off the ground—in fact, I think the paint's still wet on the door. Never was a businessman, never any good with figures, an' the bastard that sold me the place must have seen me coming—he fuckin' saw 'sucker' written right across my forehead. I got a computer compatible with no one, least of all myself, a cockeyed telephone system, and I had my cell phone no more than half an hour before I lost it. I hadn't gotten the insurance arranged, so I got no cover, an' now I can't sell the equipment for what I paid for it. So, I don't know about passing any overflow cases to you. I'm looking around for myself, business pretty thin on the ground. You got much going?"

He looked over the office and smiled. "I see business is flourishing, can hardly hear myself talk for the sound of telephones ringing!"

"Very witty, considering your own fiasco." Lorraine fetched some clean mugs and prepared coffee. Rooney had glossed over the fact that he had been in no shape to run an agency—with Ellen dying, and making arrangements for her funeral, he had been in a deep depression for weeks. Lorraine felt sorry for him, since for all his bluff manner he was probably lonely, and she watched out of the corner of her eye as he leaned on Rosie's desk and looked at the new Page Investigations Agency folder.

"Makes interesting reading. I like the way you skim over the missing years, sweetheart. Readin' this it's as if you left the force with glowing recommendations instead of out the back door on your ass."

"Yeah, your section reads pretty good too." She banged down the mugs.

Rooney laughed as he read about himself and then he let the folder drop. "I tell you Ellen passed on?"

"Yes, I'm sorry."

"Yep, went to collect her urn. I said to the guy, 'How can I be sure these are my wife's ashes? I mean, I know it's the urn I ordered but you could've filled it with any crap.' " Rooney shook his head as he continued. " 'It's your wife, Mr. Rooney sir, you see her name is on it!' Fucking crazy, whole life and it's packed into one tiny brass jar this size." He indicated with his hands and then rubbed his face. "She was in the kitchen, cooking. Her radio was on, always had her radio playing, used to drive me nuts. And she fell, I heard her sort of thump to the floor."

Lorraine poured water into the percolator. He didn't seem to be talking to her or to care particularly if she was listening.

"She was lying on the floor, still with a wooden spoon in her hand, and she had this sort of look of surprise on her face. She was dead."

"I'm sorry, Bill." Lorraine leaned on the lavatory door.

"Yeah, I guess I am. I mean, I know I haven't been easy to live with. I haven't even cleared her clothes out yet, hadda move into the spare bedroom. It's like any minute she's gonna call me, tell me food's on the table. I dunno what to do with myself, Lorraine, I'm goin' nuts. The house is quiet, I even miss her goddamned radio."

"Don't you still see all the guys down the station?"

"No. I did for a while but you know the way it is, once you're outside it, you're an outsider. Old drinking bars don't feel right anymore, they all talkin' about this or that case and I gotta be honest, it's all high-tech nowadays, you know, everything's computerized, breeds a different kind of cop."

Lorraine went to his side and patted his big, wide shoulder. He gripped her hand for a moment.

"I'm not in the way, am I?"

She felt sorry for him, so she punched him lightly. "Like you said, we're not exactly rushed off our feet. I'm sorry it hasn't worked out for all of us."

Rosie stormed in.

"What a place, it's like a palace, I've never seen nothin' like it . . . gardeners and servants, and the grounds are like some showpiece, ferns and flowers and swimming pools, two pools, and pool houses, and tennis courts and . . . Hi, Bill, how ya doin'? I was real sorry to hear about your wife."

Rooney rose to his feet. "Thank you."

"You ever heard of a movie star called Elizabeth Seal?"

Rooney nodded. "Sure, used to have the hots for her."

Rosie turned, pointing to Lorraine. "See? I told you she was famous. Well, that's where I just come from, Elizabeth Seal's home, like some kinda palace."

Lorraine passed coffee to Rooney and indicated a mug to Rosie.

"I'll have some," Rosie said as she took off her light coat. "They even got an English butler, I'm not kiddin', and a maid. They left me in the hallway awhile until Phyllis came down. It's enormous, the hall, like you could roller-skate around it. They got some cash, tons of it, got paintings worth millions, I'd say. These old movie stars sure know how to live in style."

Lorraine poured Rosie a coffee. "Did Phyllis say anything about us working for them?"

"Nah, she just took the envelope, thanked me for coming around and said she'd see me at the meeting day after tomorrow. Never even offered me so much as a glass of water. To be honest she seemed edgy, know what I mean? Kept looking over her shoulder. . . . Maybe we should have sent it by messenger."

"Elizabeth Seal, I remember her," Rooney said, closing his eyes. "She's originally from New Orleans, starred in a movie called *Swamp* somethin' or other, while back. She was real sexy. . . ."

Rosie nodded and began to list Elizabeth Seal's later

films. Lorraine sat at her own desk with her coffee. Rooney frowned as he listened to Rosie, then nodded his head.

"Yeah, yeah, I remember now, she was all over the papers a while back, somethin' about a girl—kidnapped, wasn't she?" Rooney was pinching his nose, trying to recall what he'd read about the case.

"I said it made all the papers, didn't I?" Rosie was nodding and beaming.

"Her daughter, her body was never found?" Rooney pondered. "Right, and they are still trying to find her. But it wasn't here in Hollywood, it was in New Orleans. She disappeared there, didn't she?"

Rosie pointed. "Yes, disappeared into thin air. She went there with her parents during Mardi Gras. She goes out and is never seen again."

Rooney chewed his lip and then looked at Lorraine. "I think a friend of mine, Jim Sharkey, handled the case here . . . all comin' back to me."

"Lorraine didn't even know who Elizabeth Seal is," Rosie interjected.

The phone rang, making Rooney jump as he was sitting on the edge of the desk closest to it. Rosie answered, feeling very superior by now.

"Page Investigations." She then commenced a waving pantomime to Lorraine, gesturing toward her desk and her phone. "Would you hold one moment and I will see if Mrs. Page is free to take your call." Rosie covered the phone with her hand and took a deep breath. "Elizabeth Caley, line one!"

CHAPTER

2

Lorraine checked her appearance. Her tan shoes looked scuffed, so she kicked them off and Rosie was ready with polish and a brush. Rooney would drive her to the Caley house, not only saving money on a cab but, as an ex-captain of the Pasadena Homicide Squad, his presence might add extra weight to Page Investigations Agency.

Rooney had jumped at the opportunity of filling up his empty days and had tracked down a few back issues of the papers that had run the story about the missing Caley girl. He had also used his police contacts to try to get further details from the officers who had been overseeing the case. Jim Sharkey, the officer heading the LA side of the investigation, had not been very helpful; Rooney reckoned he'd have to take him out and give him a night on the town to gain any decent information. But Rooney did have something regarding the private investigators who had already been hired—and it was an impressive list. Lorraine adamantly refused to allow him to begin digging up anything from the agencies because she felt it might all be a waste of time. They didn't have finances to fritter away; they didn't have finances, period.

She gave herself one final checkup. Rosie finished polishing her shoes, and then they heard the blast of a car horn from the street as Rooney arrived to collect Lorraine.

He had made an effort: his shirt looked as if it had come straight out of the wrapping paper, with two large creases

adorning the front, and his tie had flakes of cigarette ash but
not the usual breakfast stains, Lorraine was relieved to note.

"Rosie not coming with us?" he asked as he pushed open
the passenger door of his Hyundai.

"Nope, no need to overplay it. Just you and me."

"Fine. I drove by their place last night, impressive. It's
a mile past the Bel Air Hotel. In fact, it's so impressive I
almost hadda double-check it wasn't a hotel."

"So, how you reckon we play it?" Lorraine asked.

Rooney drove carefully, wearing his shades, since the
mid-January sun was so strong it already felt like summer.
"Let 'em do most of the talking, we sit and listen. We don't
have to do a hard sell—well, not to begin with. Don't look
good. We don't want to look desperate."

Lorraine nodded, staring out the window.

"What you make of it?" he asked nonchalantly.

Lorraine leaned back against the seat, eyes closed. "Well,
from what I've read in those newspapers you got it sounds
to me as if it was maybe a kidnap case that went wrong—
no note, no ransom . . . she's probably dead a long while.
What do you make of it?"

Rooney headed off the San Diego Freeway, the 405, then
on to the Sunset Boulevard turnoff heading toward Beverly
Hills.

"Well, as far as I can make out, the kid didn't seem the
type to go off with any kind of rough trade. She knew the
area, been there many times, parents have homes there.
Maybe she went freely, but it was Mardi Gras, so who
knows. . . . If we get the case we'll get to know more details
from New Orleans. Can't do much this end, guys in LA just
covered statements, you know, from family and associates,
to see if there was a possible link to the case back here."

"Was there?"

"Not as far as I know, they got diddly-squat here."

"No ransom note," Lorraine repeated to herself. She remained deep in thought for another ten minutes or so as
they drove on, then she opened her eyes. "Remember that
case, 1986, young girl disappeared, turned up eighteen
months later in Las Vegas as a showgirl? The family really
thought she'd be found dead; instead she was found wearing

a G-string and her new silicone tits decorated with a few sequins.''

Rooney shook his head. "Nope, don't remember it." He stopped at traffic lights, then turned into Beverly Hills. Lorraine lit a cigarette, puffing it alight from the car's dashboard lighter.

"Reason I remember it is because of the time it took tracing her, eighteen months. If they want us on this, we gotta think about how long it takes tracing anyone, alive or dead," Lorraine said thoughtfully.

Rooney reached over to the glove compartment and, flicking it open, handed Lorraine an envelope. "They're a sort of guideline of expenses. Pal gimme them a while back, you know, when I first thought about bein' a private dick, useful information. If we get the job, we got to know how much to ask for. Check 'em out."

Lorraine skimmed over the notes and tucked the sheets back into the envelope; she already had a good idea how much to ask for, but nowhere near what some of the agencies were charging for their high-tech equipment, from bugging and tracking devices to computerized files and camcorders.

"We'll undercut those other agencies but give the same crap about our high-tech gear. We don't wanna come on cheap." She replaced the envelope and snapped the glove compartment closed on seeing the stashed bottle of bourbon.

"Right," Rooney grunted as they drove past the high hedgerows and the ornate houses patrolled by security guards with dogs at electronically barred gates. "Some of these places remind you of a prison?" he asked, and Lorraine laughed softly. "No way, man. If you'd been behind bars, no way you'd describe these millionaires' mansions as prisons."

They reached a small rotary with an arrow sign pointing to the Bel Air Hotel. They turned left, passing the Bel Air, and continued up the quiet road.

Rooney slowed down. "Next house on the left." He noticed that she straightened up in her seat, pulling her jacket down. She looked great, and, in contrast to his bulky, unhealthy self, she looked fit. Amazing, considering the punishment she'd heaped on herself. Her resilience constantly amazed him, and he admired her for it. Not too far back in the past she had been arrested for drunkenness and vagrancy, but she'd come a long way since then.

He swung the car in front of the gates, opening his window to a blast of hot air. "Shit, it's hot. Weather's crazy, one second it's pissing down, the next they're saying it's going to be way up in the eighties today." He reached out to press the intercom and announced their arrival.

The gates remained closed for a couple of minutes, then eased smoothly open. From the entrance the house could not be seen, but the lush gardens were even more exotic than Rosie had described. They were like a hothouse jungle of ferns and carefully planted screens of evergreens, with palms of every shape and size covering each side of the pale gravel drive. They drove slowly past tennis courts, manicured lawns and flowerbeds blazing with color where water-sprinklers ensured they flourished in all the seasons. The water-spraying jets spinning in a wide arc gave the garden a hazy, surreal quality. Not until they turned a bend in the drive did the house itself come into view. The white pillars of the three-story Southern-style house were reminiscent of something out of *Gone With the Wind*—any moment one expected Scarlet O'Hara to come running down the white stone steps saying, "Why, I do declare." But instead of Scarlett, a butler in a black suit and white waistcoat stood poised at the ornately carved front doors.

"Rosie said it was some place." Lorraine was in awe.

"Money," muttered Rooney.

A manservant appeared as if from nowhere to open the passenger door for Lorraine. She hesitated a moment before she stepped out and noticed that Rooney had broken out in a sweat by the time they began walking up the steps.

"Good morning, would you please follow me, Mrs. Page, Mr. Rooney?" said the butler stiffly. He was English, his frozen face devoid of any expression as he gestured for them to go ahead of him into the hall. The white marble floor was so polished it glittered, light sparkling on the surface as they followed the butler toward closed ceiling-high white and gold-embossed double doors leading off to the right of the hall.

"Mrs. Caley will join you directly," the butler said as he

gestured for them to head into the room. White sofas with white frilled scatter pillows in satin and silks were everywhere, and everything was white on white with a gold embroidery finish. The white silk Japanese wallpaper had faint outlines of shimmering birds, and hanging between the impressive gilt mirrors on every wall were large oil paintings of Elizabeth Caley in all her many movie roles.

"Ah, I remember her in that one," murmured Rooney as he stared at a painting. "*The Swamp*, it was called, and she danced with a big snake."

"May I offer you any refreshments?" the butler asked as if he'd just smelled something bad.

Lorraine asked for a glass of water. Rooney would have liked a beer but he shrugged. "Fine for me too, just water."

The austere butler departed, and they were able to have a good look around the white palace, almost afraid to sit and disturb the carefully arrayed pillows. Rooney chose a white Louis XV chair, not that he had any notion it was the real McCoy. Only after he'd eased himself down into it did he worry that he might be too heavy for its spindly legs.

Lorraine looked around the room, noting the many beautifully framed photographs of a young girl. She gestured to one. "This must be the daughter." She looked toward the doorway and then moved closer to inspect a photograph. The girl was exceptionally pretty, with waist-length natural blond hair, a small, uptilted nose and wide pale eyes.

Lorraine sat down in the center of the vast white sofa, sinking so low into it that she felt self-conscious: her weight had disturbed the carefully arranged scatter pillows, which tumbled inward.

"I don't suppose I could light a cigarette," she said almost to herself, looking over the white marble-top coffee table with its carefully placed objects, all either bronze or gold. None resembled an ashtray. She stared down at her shoes, almost hidden by the dense white pile of the carpet, and worried that Rosie's quick brush might have left a smear of brown boot polish. She looked up as she heard the clink of ice cubes.

A maid in a black dress with a white pinafore entered with a tray of iced water, fizzy and still, with lemon, all in tall crystal glasses in silver and gold containers. Lorraine could barely hide a smile as Rooney murmured his thanks and his chair creaked ominously. The maid passed each of them the water of their choice and then put the tray down. As she returned to the door, Phyllis appeared.

"Don't get up, please. I'm Phyllis Collins, Rosie's friend. You must be Lorraine? If I may call you, er . . . Lorraine?" She scurried across the room and shook Lorraine's hand, and then acknowledged Rooney. "And you are William Rooney, Rosie told me all about you. Please don't get up, Mrs. Caley knows you are here and will be with you shortly."

Lorraine nodded her thanks. Rooney felt even more awkward in his chair but at least no longer felt the heat because the room was icy cold.

"This has been a very distressing time," Phyllis said, hovering by the matching Louis XV chair opposite Rooney's.

"Will you be staying for—" Lorraine couldn't think how to describe the meeting.

"No, no, Mrs. Caley has asked me not to. I am really just her companion. She should be down any moment."

The moment stretched to three quarters of an hour. They discussed Elizabeth Caley's films and paintings, and Phyllis's English background, but whenever Lorraine tried to steer the conversation toward the reason why they were there, Phyllis changed the subject. Lorraine had drunk two tall glasses of water and refused any more because she knew she would need the bathroom. Rooney had gulped his down and wished he hadn't asked for carbonated water—he could feel the gas roaming around in his belly. A clock chimed and all three looked at the large gold-embossed and glass-domed ormolu clock on the white mantel.

"I presume these are photographs of Miss Caley?" Lorraine asked, quietly indicating one of the ornate silver frames.

Phyllis nodded, and was about to say something when they heard footsteps in the marble hall, the *click-click* of high heels, and then the doors were opened by the butler.

"Mrs. Elizabeth Caley."

Phyllis made the introductions and Lorraine rose to her feet, the pillows scattering around her. Rooney creaked out of his chair, but Mrs. Caley fluttered her hand in his direction and he eased himself back down.

Elizabeth Caley gently brushed Lorraine's outstretched hand, just giving it a light feather touch, then smiled warmly at Rooney, who blushed bright pink. She was, as one would picture a movie star of the late fifties or early sixties, perfectly made up—neatly clasped in a tortoiseshell comb, her black hair was glossy and worn swept up from her beautiful, strong face. At a distance she could still be taken for a woman in her thirties, yet she was very much the wrong side of fifty, her many face-lifts giving her skin a tight, fragile falseness. Her creamy, low-cut blouse showed just enough cleavage of probably equally fake breasts. She wore a straight, tight black skirt and pale stockings, which showed that her wondrous legs were still like a young woman's, and her high-heeled sandals accentuated her slender ankles.

Rooney was almost overcome. He could feel his heart thudding as her perfume seemed to wrap itself around him, a heavy magnolia that made one even more aware of her soft white skin. Elizabeth Caley was still a very stunning and sexy woman. She had full red lips, matching long red fingernails, and on her wedding finger a diamond and emerald ring with stones the size of a small bird's eggs. She was also charming in her manner, almost deferential as she sat poised as if for flight on the edge of a small, hard-backed gilt chair. She gave only the slightest incline of her head to indicate that Phyllis should leave them alone. Phyllis silently closed the doors behind her.

"My daughter." Mrs. Caley gestured slowly toward a large color photograph on a glass-topped corner table. Rooney and Lorraine both turned in the direction of the fluttering hand.

Anna Louise Caley was as fair as her mother was dark. Similar wide eyes stared from the photograph, but Elizabeth's were a dark tawny brown while her daughter's, judging from the photo, were light blue, and she had a faint smile on her sweet, childish lips, a secretive, shy smile.

"She is very beautiful," Lorraine said softly.

"Yes, she is." But Rooney couldn't take his eyes off Mrs. Caley, recalling all her films, one after another, and almost had to pinch himself to realize that he was sitting within a few feet of her.

"I know you have already hired a number of private investigation agents," Lorraine began, as Mrs. Caley stared vacantly ahead. "If we are to reopen the case—"

"It is not closed," Mrs. Caley said quietly.

"I'm sorry, of course it isn't. But if Page Investigations is also to begin making inquiries into your daughter's whereabouts, then we will have to ask you a lot of questions. It may be very upsetting for you, but perhaps we will be able to uncover—"

Mrs. Caley bowed her head. "A clue?"

"Yes. Often an individual or a company like my own, coming into a case fresh, can uncover something that might have appeared inconsequential to others."

Mrs. Caley nodded, her eyes studying the sparkling ring on her finger. "The reason I was interested in meeting you is that Phyllis explained to me that you had been involved in other similar cases."

Rooney frowned, giving Lorraine a questioning look. She ignored it, wondering just what Rosie had embroidered, and covered fast, keeping her voice low and encouraging.

"Tracing missing persons can be a lengthy and costly process and we cannot give any guarantee of success. But that said, I am very confident that with my previous experience as a lieutenant with the Pasadena police, and with the assistance of my partner, Mr. Rooney, ex-captain, we will promise you—"

"No stone will be left unturned?" Elizabeth Caley's wide eyes looked from Lorraine to Rooney and then returned to her ring. She laughed softly. "They have all promised me that, dear, and quite honestly I am not interested in the cost or how long it will take. I want my daughter found because every day is like a nightmare, every phone call a hope, and every night . . ." She caught her breath and swallowed, taking a moment to gather her composure. If this was any indication of her acting prowess, her films must have been good. "I have never given up hope, even though it has been implied that after so long . . ." Another intake of breath and her delicate hand stroked her milky-white neck. "Do you have any children, Mrs. Page?"

"Yes, I do, two daughters," Lorraine said softly.

"Well, then, you must be able to understand what it means to a mother. Every night I mark in my diary, another day passed, another night ahead without my darling, and I pray, I have prayed so much. And I have wept so much that I don't think I have any more tears to shed."

Again came another slow, flowing hand gesture in the direction of her daughter's photograph. "I stare at her face, saying over and over, Where are you? Oh, my darling, dearest child, where are you?"

Rooney was almost in tears. Lorraine looked suitably moved but was still of the mind that Mrs. Caley was talking, or acting, as if she were in one of her movies. She thought this all the more when Elizabeth Caley sprang to her feet and began pacing up and down, her emotion spilling out as she moved soundlessly back and forth on the whiter-than-white carpet, her voice lifting slightly.

"It was February fifteenth. We went to New Orleans, we always go for Mardi Gras. She didn't come down for dinner, but we had arrived only a few hours earlier and we just thought she wasn't hungry."

Elizabeth Caley began to move toward one of the gilt-and-glass-topped tables displaying one photograph after another of her pretty daughter—as a debutante at one of the Mardi Gras balls, at a special surprise birthday, at a film premiere. Elizabeth seemed almost to be dancing in front of them, then she traced one small gilt frame with her finger, tears brimming and then spilling down her perfectly made-up cheeks. "I will not give up, I cannot give up."

Rooney could have fallen to his knees, a fan for life. Lorraine simply wished that Mrs. Caley would stop the dramatics and talk straight so that they could discuss how long they would be given to work on the case. Throughout Mrs. Caley's monologue, she had been calculating how much she could charge to keep three of them on the case, including traveling expenses and meals, and as they would obviously have to go to New Orleans, they would have hotel expenses, car rental, etc.

Lorraine coughed to draw Mrs. Caley's attention. "Mrs. Caley, if you wish Page Investigations to begin work, can we discuss finances for a moment?"

Mrs. Caley spun around on her high heels to face Lorraine. "Of course I want you to begin, why do you think I've asked you to my home? I want to hire you, I want you to find my daughter, haven't I made that abundantly clear?"

Lorraine licked her lips. "Good, but we must discuss what contracts you have with other private investigation agencies, because they are a little territorial and—"

"They've done nothing! It's been eleven months, *eleven months, and I don't care who we've hired.* Not one of them has found a single clue as to where she is." She was giving an Oscar-winning performance, her voice rising as she became more and more emotional. She picked up one of her daughter's photographs and clasped it to her chest. "She is a sweet, innocent girl, she could not just disappear, she must be somewhere. Someone is doing this to me, it's breaking my heart."

Lorraine looked at the bedazzled Rooney, wishing he'd help her. She could tell that Mrs. Caley was building to a climax and could well collapse on them. Then they'd have to return, maybe even go through this a number of times before they had an agreement on paper. Then, to her consternation, the doors banged open.

"Elizabeth, *Elizabeth*!"

Mrs. Caley turned toward the door, holding out the photograph of her daughter in a theatrically helpless gesture.

"She is alive, Robert, I know it, she is alive. I won't give up, *I won't give up.*"

Robert Caley didn't even glance at Lorraine as he gestured to Phyllis, hovering behind him in the doorway. "Phyllis, help Elizabeth to her room, please, right away."

"No, Robert, I won't go. I need to talk to these people, they will trace Anna Louise."

Robert Caley was like a movie star himself. His face was etched with deep lines, made more prominent by his suntan, and his thick black hair, with two wings of gray at the temples, gave him an austere quality that matched the steel of his controlled voice and piercing dark blue eyes.

"Please, Elizabeth, go to your room. It is pointless to upset yourself like this, to put yourself through this over and over again."

Elizabeth placed the photograph back in its position like

a naughty schoolgirl. She pouted petulantly. "They are highly qualified, darling. At least give them a chance ... give Anna Louise a chance."

Robert Caley studied the carpet for a moment, and Lorraine detected that he seemed to be desperately trying to control his anger. Then he looked up and stared coldly at her.

"My wife, as you can see, Mrs. Page, is distraught. I think it would be better if you leave. At the moment we have more than enough investigation agencies, along with the police, attempting to trace my daughter without needing to hire anyone else. This is a waste of your time."

Elizabeth Caley confronted her husband, her hands clenched tightly. "I want them to begin as of this afternoon, Robert, I insist. Mrs. Page has daughters of her own, she knows what it is like for a mother, and she has come very highly recommended—"

"Really? I think all Mrs. Page is interested in is ripping you off, Elizabeth. This has got to stop. I will not have you bringing these people into the house."

Lorraine stepped forward. "Excuse me, Mr. Caley."

He turned that cold, arrogant stare on Lorraine again. "No, you excuse me, Mrs. Page, because I don't know what cock-and-bull story you have fed my wife, but I do not think you are in any way qualified to assist us in tracing my daughter. We have had enough of journalists, enough of bloodsucking people calling themselves private investigators, people who care only for what they can milk out of us, people who are no better equipped to find Anna Louise than—"

"Excuse me," Lorraine blurted out again.

"I will not allow my wife to be subjected to yet another—"

Lorraine interrupted him. "Yet another what, Mr. Caley?"

He took a deep breath, looked away for a moment and then turned back to Lorraine. "Sham, Mrs. Page, and I think you are perhaps the lowest we have sunk to date. You see, I know all about your agency, if you can call it that, just as I am aware of your record for drunkenness. You were thrown out of the police for shooting a young and, I believe, innocent boy. You are an alcoholic with no experience whatsoever in private investigation work. And as for being a mother! You have had no contact with your daughters since you were divorced. Perhaps the agencies hired to trace my daughter have been incapable of gaining results, but they were very swift and very informative regarding you. I would therefore be grateful if you would leave my house and not come back."

Lorraine felt the thick-pile carpet rising up and choking her. She turned and picked up her purse. Rooney, who had sat like a silent Buddha, now stepped forward, his face flushed red.

"Mr. Caley, I am Bill Rooney, and before you start in on me, if you have also done some background work on me, then you'll know I recently retired from the police. I have started working with Mrs. Page—"

"Just leave, please."

"Oh, I'll leave, Mr. Caley, but not before I set a few things straight. Mrs. Page may have been an alcoholic but she isn't now. And whatever she did, she's paid hard for it. But what she's doing now is what she was good at, and I should know because I worked alongside her for long enough. She's got more street knowledge, more intuition than any of the officers I've ever worked with, and she's better than any hired dick you could find in or outside LA. If your daughter's alive, she'll find her, and without ripping you or your wife off, because first and foremost Lorraine Page is a professional. Thanks for the ice water."

Rooney's face was even redder as he turned with his hand out for Lorraine. She had never needed it so badly since she quit drinking. They would have both walked out there and then had not Elizabeth Caley caught hold of Lorraine's arm.

"No, please don't leave, please. . . ." She was not acting now, she was for real, and up close her youth had flown, leaving her face etched with pain. "Find my baby for me, please. Dear God, I beg you to help me, please."

Rooney tried to ease Lorraine out of the room as Mrs. Caley turned pleading to her husband.

"Don't send them away, you can't send them away. Don't let me give up hope, don't do this to me, please."

Robert Caley deflated, refusing to look at any one of

them. He had lost all his anger, and now he sounded simply tired out. "You're hired for two weeks, all expenses paid, whatever you need, whatever your charges. If you wish to talk with me, I can be contacted at my office during office hours. Phyllis, please take Elizabeth for a rest and then draw up whatever contract is required." He walked away.

Elizabeth Caley sighed, leaning against the door. "I'm too tired to talk now, you'll have to come back. Tomorrow maybe. Phyllis will organize everything."

"Thank you, Mrs. Caley," Lorraine said.

Elizabeth beckoned to her. Not in any way out of control now, she was almost steely. "I want a private word with you. Will you assist me to my room?"

Rooney watched them leave before he smiled at Phyllis. She closed the doors with an abruptness that made it obvious she was angry that Rosie had misled her. She turned her small, frosty eyes to Rooney.

"Well, what payments do you require, Mr. Rooney?"

"There are three of us who will be working on this. Thousand a week."

Phyllis nodded, moving further into the room. "Three thousand a week and expenses, which I presume will be at the same rate the other agencies have requested?"

Rooney's jaw dropped a fraction; he'd sort of calculated the thousand dollars was for the three of them.

"I will need receipts of all your expenses," Phyllis said curtly as she flipped open a small notebook.

Rooney beamed. "You'll have them, Miss Collins."

He couldn't believe their luck.

Lorraine did not get in to see Elizabeth Caley's bedroom. As they reached the door to her suite she drew Lorraine closer.

"Can you find her?"

"I will most certainly try, Mrs. Caley."

She nodded, chewing her lip, and then leaned closer still. "I will give you an incentive. If you find her, you will get a one-million-dollar bonus."

Lorraine blinked. "One million."

"Yes. I want my daughter traced, Mrs. Page."

Lorraine turned to look down the wide staircase and then

after a moment, keeping her voice as steady as she could, she repeated, "One million?"

Mrs. Caley nodded.

Lorraine eased her weight from one foot to the other. Her voice was soft, as low as Mrs. Caley's, but she didn't hesitate. "Dead or alive, Mrs. Caley?"

"If you trace her, dead or alive, Mrs. Page, you will receive one million dollars."

"Can I have that in writing?"

The soft white hand with the bloodred nails gripped Lorraine's in a firm, fast handshake, and she once again got the impression that Elizabeth Caley was like two people; publicly, she was the showcase movie star, the consummate actress, but beneath the show there was something else, something she had not picked up on earlier—and it wasn't the underlying steely quality she'd expected. Elizabeth Caley was very, very frightened. Up close, the pupils of her slanting brown eyes were overlarge, and Lorraine knew she was using drugs of some kind.

Not until they had driven out of the electronic gates did Rooney let out a whistle. "One grand each for two weeks, all expenses on top. Plane tickets, hotels, we got total carte blanche, no expenses spared. Rosie was fucking right, this is a big cash deal all right."

Lorraine gave him a sidelong look and then stared ahead. "There's a bonus," she said quietly. He looked puzzled. "If we find Anna Louise we get one million dollars."

He braked, and she had to press her hands on the dashboard to stop herself from sliding down the seat.

"What? Are you kiddin'?"

"No, not kidding. She's going to put it in writing." She slipped on the safety belt.

"Fuck me, one million. Holy shit."

Lorraine gave a tiny smile. "Dead or alive."

"Fucking hell." He shook his head in disbelief.

"Just one thing, Bill, two actually. Thanks for backing me up in there with that bastard Caley."

Rooney accelerated again. "Think nothin' of it, only said what I meant, he got to me. So what's the other thing you wanna talk about, the split?"

Lorraine smiled. "No, that goes three ways. It's just I run this investigation, Bill, not you, me. I give the orders, understood?"

He nodded. "Yeah, I hear you, it's your show."

"Yes, it is," she said softly and then let out a yell, thumping his big wide shoulder. "One million!"

CHAPTER

3

That same afternoon, Lorraine, Rooney and Rosie discussed how they would begin the investigation into the disappearance of Anna Louise Caley. First they would invoice the Caleys for an advance of salary. Rooney would approach the officers he knew had been or were still involved on the case in LA. This would cut down a lot of questions they would have to ask Mr. and Mrs. Caley, and before Lorraine talked to either of them she wanted as much background information as possible. All back issues of newspapers that had featured the girl's disappearance had to be checked over at the library and xeroxed copies filed at the office.

They felt they were on a roll. One million dollars was one hell of an incentive.

That evening, Rooney met with the Dean Martin look-alike Detective Jim Sharkey for a liquid dinner. To begin with, Sharkey was noncommittal; as far as he was concerned, the police had done about all they could do at their end.

"Consensus is, or was, she was kidnapped by persons unknown, though no ransom note was delivered. Other cases with similar characteristics would not have been kept open as long as this one."

Rooney sniffed. "You sayin' you had a lot of girls just disappearing?"

"Yeah, a lot, Bill, and you gotta know it. We got a file as long as my arm on missing kids, and we try checkin' out most of them. Believe me, we spent more time on this one because of the high profile of the Caleys. She disappeared in New Orleans anyway, so there was not a lot we could do here. We even sent a few guys there to dig around but they came up with nothing, and the guys there aren't the friendliest bunch of bastards, kinda suggested we back off.''

"So you did?''

"Yeah, we got nothin' from LA, and we interviewed every kid she knew.''

"Was the Caley girl into drugs?''

"Nope, squeaky clean. You know, with no body discovered after eleven months, some of the guys reckoned the girl maybe just took off.''

Bill sighed, leaning back in his chair. ''Anythin' come up against the parents?''

Sharkey looked askance. "What? Give me that again? They've fuckin' hired the best in the business, if they'd had anythin', anythin' to do with their own kid's disappearance, believe me, we'd have sniffed it. And the broad, she was weepin' her heart out.''

"Mrs. Caley?''

Sharkey nodded. "She must have been one hell of a woman, still is. Geez, what a figure, and I'm tellin' you, Bill, I never been one for older women, know what I mean? But fuck me, well, I'd like to give her a roll in the hay, no kiddin'.''

Rooney nodded. They sank a few more beers, then switched to vodka. The dinner had been a long one. At midnight they called a cab, and made their way back to Sharkey's precinct in uptown LA. Sharkey held his liquor well, and even though he was off duty he refused to let Rooney come into the station with him. To have ex-captain Bill Rooney in tow breathing beer fumes over everyone could cause problems, even more so considering what he had agreed to do.

Rooney waited in the cab. It was almost an hour before Sharkey rejoined him and slipped him a thick xeroxed file of information. It had been an expensive evening, Rooney thought, as Sharkey accepted the folded bills with a wink. He'd asked for five hundred dollars and a guarantee that if any questions were ever asked the files never came from

him. Rooney never even mentioned the thirty-five-buck cab
fare, he was too eager to get the statements back to Lorraine.

Lorraine worked on Sharkey's information till daybreak.
As far as she could make out, Anna Louise Caley was a
well-liked, friendly and very pampered young lady. The students in her year who had been questioned didn't have a
bad word to say about her. All the students and teachers
alike made references to her being very pretty or even beautiful; none referred to her academic prowess but she was
said to have been an excellent tennis player, swimmer,
horseback rider and all-around athlete. She had no steady
boyfriend, but Lorraine ringed the names of the boys who
had admitted to dating her up until the time of her disappearance. She decided she would target them first. She had
the names of numerous female students who all claimed to
have been Anna Louise's best friend, so they were lined up
second. Then came the coaches and the college teachers. It
was going to be a race against time: with only two weeks
on the case, she had set aside only two days to complete the
LA research.

Next morning, Page Investigations Agency was busy for
the first time since it opened. The phone in the office rang
constantly, and Rosie was flushed bright pink and sweating
as the calls came in.

Lorraine pointed to a large corkboard on which she had
pinned lists of names for interview, and those for her to
cross-reference and delete when necessary.

"Okay, Rosie, you list every name, all the students I got
to see in alphabetical order. We cross them out as we go
along." Rosie nodded. There was a buzz in the office and
it felt good.

Rooney had been assigned to make very discreet inquiries
into the private investigation agencies hired by the Caleys,
to see if there was an ex-colleague working anywhere he
could palm money to, like Sharkey, and if they had any
information worth digging into. He listed the companies on
Lorraine's big board.

"My God, are they all on the same case?" Rosie asked.

"Yep. Caley's sure been shelling out a lot of cash." Lorraine chewed her pencil and then stuck it in her hair.

"Okay, this is how we work it, I do the college kids.

You, Bill, start seeing what you can come up with about Caley, tap your old associates, whatever you need to do. Rosie, you'll be the anchorwoman, you hold the fort here, we call in if we get anything. Most important is that we get moving and come up with what we can as fast as possible—agreed?''

Rooney nodded as Rosie made a note of Lorraine's cell phone number and passed it to him. "We can all keep in constant touch.'' She beamed.

Lorraine flicked a look at Rooney and winked. "That's what it's all about, Rosie!''

Lorraine began the tedious and laborious interview sessions and rented a car, an '88 Buick that had seen better days, with a cellular telephone to keep in touch with the office while driving herself from one meeting to another. Armed with two photographs of Anna Louise, she talked to fifteen students at UCLA. To be confronted with fresh young girls, eager to talk and full of youthful exuberance, made her feel tired and jaded beyond belief, but the mental picture she was gradually forming was basically the same one that had already emerged from the old police files. Making the kids feel relaxed with her was painstaking work and her fixed smile was wearing thin, but she persisted. By twelve in the afternoon she had only two names left on her list and went to the tennis courts to meet Angie Wellbeck, listed on Sharkey's statements as a "best friend.'' After Angie, she was meeting one of the kids listed as dating Anna Louise, Tom Heller.

Angie was wearing tennis shorts, a white T-shirt and Reeboks. She carried her tennis rackets in a very professional-looking white shoulder sports bag. She constantly plucked at it as she answered very politely the routine questions Lorraine had asked all the students. Did she get on with Anna Louise? Did she know of anyone who did not like her? Anyone who might have a grudge against her? Who did she socialize with? Did she take drugs, drink too much? In essence, what was the missing girl like?

Angie sat on a bench, staring at her tennis shoes, and Lorraine could see faint freckles on her lightly tanned skin.

"Well, she was real pretty, and always wore the most up-to-date clothes, you know, if something was in, AL always was the first to have it.''

"AL?" asked Lorraine, knowing full well that it was a nickname because it had been repeated to her so many times.

"Yeah, we all called her AL. You know, Anna Louise is boring. I don't mean she was boring, just her name.''

Angie said nothing untoward, or even gave the slightest hint that her friend wasn't anything other than perfect. She just reiterated that although Anna Louise was not exceptional academically, she was great at sports and very competitive.

"Like how competitive?" Lorraine asked.

"Well, she liked to win—at tennis anyway. We played a lot together, sometimes we played doubles. Her dad is a great player. He used to play with her, I think, that's why she was so good. Great backhand, very strong, although her serve wasn't so hot, but she was a good player. Got enough practice in, I guess.''

"Did she get angry if she lost?"

"Sure.''

"Aggressive?''

"Sometimes.''

"Did she argue or get angry with anyone specific?"

"No, she was kind of more angry at herself.''

"How do you mean?"

"Well, if she missed a volley she'd shout and yell at herself, you know.''

"Ah! So you never saw her fighting or shouting with anyone?''

"No, but maybe you should ask some of the others. I mean, I played a lot with her but I wasn't the only person she played with. Tilda Brown played with her mostly. She was closest to AL, but she hasn't come back to school, not after AL disappeared, but I guess you know that.''

Lorraine nodded, underlining Tilda's name in her notebook.

"Did you all have the same coach?"

"Geez, no way. AL was rich, you know, and her coach was ex-Olympic standard, a real professional. We'd all have liked to be coached by him.'' She giggled.

"Did this create jealousy?" Lorraine was boring even herself.

"Yeah, but nothin' to do with tennis."

Lorraine looked at Angie, who had removed her headband and was plucking at it with her fingers, picking off strands of fluff. "How do you mean?"

"Jeff Nathan, the coach, is like a movie star, I think he coaches a lot of famous people. Sometimes when I went over to their place he'd play with us, you know, make up a four with her dad. That was the only time I got to meet him."

"The coach?"

"Yeah, and her dad; he was real nice."

Angie's tennis partners were hovering, so she asked if she could go. Lorraine could think of nothing else to ask. Like everyone else she'd spoken to, Angie hadn't given any real insight into Anna Louise but, like three other girls, she had mentioned the handsome tennis coach.

"Were you her best friend?" Lorraine asked as Angie sprang to her feet, eager to leave.

She turned and smiled. "I dunno about her best. I think Tilda was, but everyone liked her—she was a real nice girl." Angie's face puckered for a moment and she hesitated, chewing her lips. "You think something terrible has happened to her?" Lorraine looked away as Angie moved closer. "Some of them say she's maybe been murdered, is it true?"

"I really don't know, but thanks for your time."

"That's okay. 'Bye now."

Lorraine watched Angie join three other girls, all in similar white tennis outfits. They looked over and smiled. She sat for a few moments, watching the girls warming up, slicing the ball over the net. Judging by the hard thudding crack of the ball she could tell, even though she was no tennis player, that the girls could play well. So if AL, as she was known, was better, she must have been very good.

"I'd say she could have turned professional, if she'd had the inclination."

Lorraine was outside the squash courts, talking to a gangly boy with a white sweatshirt slung around his shoulders.

Tom Heller was at least six feet two and good-looking in an ordinary, neat-featured way.

When Lorraine asked if he had played regularly with Anna Louise, he shrugged.

"Yeah, sometimes on weekends at her house. Her dad is a great player."

Lorraine nodded. "What about the coach, er . . ."

"Jeff Nathan? Yeah, I played with him at her place. He gives private lessons."

"Did you like him?"

He frowned. "I didn't really know him."

"Did Anna Louise like him?"

"I don't know."

"You used to date her, didn't you?"

"Few times—nothing serious, beach parties, we were just buddies really."

"Did you have sex with her?"

He blushed. "No."

"Do you know if she was sexually permissive in any way?"

"No—well, no more than anyone else."

"How many boys do you know had a sexual relationship with Anna Louise?"

He blushed again. "I don't know—like I said, we dated a few times but no more than that."

"What about the coach? This guy Nathan, did he have something going with her?"

He looked with distaste at Lorraine. "I have no idea."

She was suddenly pissed off by his supercilious attitude.

"Look, it's Tom, isn't it? Well, I am trying to trace Anna Louise, she's been missing for eleven months and she could be lying in a shallow grave or she could be dancing in Las Vegas. I am just trying to do my job, okay? So if she was screwing this tennis coach, and you maybe knew about it as her buddy, then I'd be grateful if you'd tell me—"

"I have no idea."

"Do you know where I can find the tennis coach, Nathan?"

"Maybe in the Bel Air. He plays there."

"Thank you, Mr. Heller. Sorry to interrupt your game!"

It was almost lunchtime when Lorraine called the office on her cell phone.

"How's it going?"

"Fine, waiting for Bill to call in with any developments," Rosie said.

"I'm on my way to see the tennis coach—what are you doing?"

Rosie pursed her lips. "A lot, I've got to arrange hotels, flights and—" The second phone rang on Rosie's desk. "Hang on, Lorraine, it might be Bill on line two."

Bill it was, to say that he wasn't getting much of a result from any of the other investigation agencies attached to the Caley case, but he was still plugging away. Rosie passed this on to Lorraine, who suggested that perhaps he should interview the psychic the Caleys had hired in LA. Rosie repeated this to Rooney and listened to his reply with both receivers pressed to her ear before coming back to Lorraine. "He says they're all a fucking waste of time."

Lorraine snapped back to Rosie, "You tell him that so are a bunch of racket-swinging rich kids, but before we hit New Orleans we gotta cover ourselves here, *you tell him that.*"

Rooney could hear her and laughed, and, still laughing, told Rosie to tell Lorraine she was the boss, but when she tried to do so the line was dead. Rosie put both phones down and began to check out the telephone manual for a way to connect calls on two lines.

Jeff Nathan had the kind of muscular body that most women fantasize about. His tight white T-shirt and his brief white tennis shorts showed strong tanned limbs that were very desirable, but within minutes Lorraine had figured out that all his masculine muscles would more than likely be wrapped around another equally tanned male's body.

"You gay, Mr. Nathan?"

"My, my, you are very aggressive."

"No, I don't think I'd say that was an aggressive question but one I need to ask and know the answer to. You see, Mr. Nathan, I am trying to find a young girl who's been missing for eleven months, and if you had sexual relations with her, then—"

He smiled, and relaxed his macho tennis pro image. "Yes, Mrs. Page, I am," he said, looking at the card she had passed him.

"Thank you. So, tell me what you know about Anna Louise Caley."

"Well, I was her personal coach, so I've lost a nice income. Anna Louise could have played professional standard—she was very coordinated, strong, but she had a major fault; if she made a mistake she couldn't forget it. She became very angry at herself and it usually fouled up the rest of her game. The more anger she felt, the worse she played." He cocked his handsome head to one side. "You see, I really did know her only as her coach. I can tell you about her game but nothing about her personal life."

"What about her father?" Lorraine asked.

Nathan shrugged. "Good player, hard hitter, but no speed. He'd wait for the ball to come to him, never used the court. She was never interested in being a serious player. All she ever wanted was to beat her father, but whenever they played she lost it. And she could have beaten him."

"Did she come on to you?" Lorraine asked as they walked toward the court. She found his fake capped-tooth smile unattractive but realized that for a young kid it could be devastating.

"Come on to me? My dear, that is, sadly, the main part of why people—well, women, girls or whatever—keep hiring me. I have to look and act the stud."

"Were you?" She tried one more time.

"Was I what? A stud? Oh, please . . ." Nathan's tanned neck stretched, his perfect features wreathed in smiles.

"So she was, say, infatuated?"

He smiled, showing his perfect white teeth. "Maybe, but I assure you it was not in my interest to encourage her in any way. Like I said, the Caleys paid me well to coach their daughter and I would have been foolish to foul up a good weekly income."

"Weekly?"

"Yep, although sometimes I'd get to their place and she didn't feel like playing, but I was always paid." Nathan turned as a petite blond woman with a frilled white tennis skirt waved to him from across a court. "I gotta go, but if you need to speak to me again, anytime. Do you play?"

Lorraine looked at the blonde attempting to knock a ball over the net. "About as good a game as maybe she has!" He laughed—she rather liked him. "Thanks for your time, I appreciate your seeing me."

She hadn't got much from Nathan, again nothing that had not already been recorded by the police files. She watched him in action with his "student" and realized on closer inspection she was well into her late forties. Poor woman, she thought, she must have the same infatuation with Jeff as his students, staring at his rippling muscles as he began to drag his ball basket to the center of the court opposite the blonde.

"Let's just warm up with a few easy ones, shall we, Mrs. Fairley? See how you've progressed."

Lorraine made her way back to the parking lot and she heard Mrs. Fairley squeal a lot of "Ooops" and "Oh, I'm so sorry . . ." as the balls she attempted to swipe expertly dribbled into the tennis net.

Lorraine felt totally drained by the time she drove out of the university complex, and she was also irritated. Maybe it was the students' youth, their nonchalance, but no one had given her any real insight into the missing girl. Just as nobody seemed to have a bad word to say about her except that she got pissed when she missed a fucking volley.

Lorraine called Rosie at the office from her cell phone. "Any developments?"

"No, not yet," Rosie replied.

"Rooney gone to see that psychic?" asked Lorraine.

"I think so, but he sort of thought it was a waste of time."

"Yeah, okay, I'm on my way to the Caleys'. I haven't come up with anything positive yet, so I'll interview them and then call in when I'm through."

"Oh, I think Rooney wanted to be in on your meeting with the Caleys, didn't he?"

"Rosie, I am running this case, not Bill Rooney."

No sooner had Rosie replaced the phone than Rooney barged into the office.

Rosie smiled. "Lorraine just called in, she's on her way to the Caleys'."

"Shit, I wanted in on that meet."

"I know, I told her, and she said she was running the case, so . . ."

Rooney tossed his hat at the stand and missed, then took off his jacket, showing his sweat-stained shirt. "Well, I got a contact. Old buddy of mine used to be on the force 'bout ten years ago, now works with the top investigation agency hired by the Caleys, Agnew. To be honest, I didn't think he'd still be working, got a good pension when he was invalided out. Poor bastard got a leg full of lead. . . . I've arranged to see him tonight."

"What's his name?"

"Nick Bartello." Rooney frowned.

"Italian, is he?"

"At one time. She won't like him. Dunno if they met, they were attached to different departments. He was drugs, she was with me on homicide."

"Why won't she like him?"

"He's a dead ringer for her old partner, Lubrinski, same kind of guy. Nick and he were partners, short-lived 'cause Lubrinski moved over to my team."

"Who's he?"

Rooney frowned. "She never mention him to you?"

"No." Rosie crossed to the coffeemaker and began to brew up a pot.

"They were partners at the old station."

"So why won't she like him? If he's a pal of yours maybe he can give us some inside information."

"Maybe. So she's never mentioned Lubrinski to you?"

Rosie returned to her cluttered desk. "No . . ."

"He's dead."

"Well, maybe that's why." She sat down.

"He was one hell of a guy, Lubrinski, great cop. In fact, I gotta tell you, Rosie, during my time I saw a lot go down. Not all died, some just folded, you know, mentally, but Lubrinski, when I was told he'd bought it, he was the only officer I cried for. Not because he was one hell of an officer, he was that, but he was also a great guy, could drink any man under the table. Loner, crazy son of a bitch. When I partnered him with Lorraine I reckoned on fireworks . . ."

"And?" Rosie asked, only half listening. But because

Rooney remained silent she looked up. He was staring into space.

"They were one fucking good team, best I ever had. He was injured in cross fire, took three bullets. He bled to death in the ambulance. She'd made a sort of tourniquet to try and stop the bleeding, used her panty hose . . . but it didn't work. He was dead on arrival at the hospital, and she wouldn't let go of his hand. Orderly told me they'd had to force her to let go, that she kept on saying he was gonna be okay."

Rosie raised her eyebrows. "Well, she's never mentioned any of this to me. What happened afterward?"

Rooney sighed, shifting his bulk. "She requested to be returned to duty immediately. About six weeks later she killed that kid . . ."

Rosie knew about the boy Lorraine had shot by mistake, a young kid caught up in a drug bust. "Maybe this Bartello isn't such a good idea. Maybe she won't want to be reminded of the past."

"It was a long time ago," Rooney said, trying to change the subject. "And the guy's good." Then the phone rang, so Rosie's attention was diverted. As she answered she didn't hear Rooney say softly, "I think she was in love with Lubrinski."

Rosie held one hand over the phone, waving the other to Rooney. "It's Nick Bartello."

"Hey, Nick, how you doing? You got my message, then? So can we meet, have a few drinks? Sure, where are you?" Rooney jotted down a note on Lorraine's note pad. "Okay, I'll be there, gimme half an hour. . . ." He slowly replaced the receiver. "Okay, I'm out of here. If she calls in, tell her I've gone to Joe's Diner, lemme check the guy out." He picked up his jacket. "Rosie, maybe you shouldn't say anything about Lubrinski. Like you said, it was a long time ago and I don't want her to think we've been gossiping, okay?"

Rosie nodded, distracted yet again by the telephone. By the time she answered Rooney had departed. The call was from Robert Caley, asking to speak to Lorraine to say his wife was indisposed and he would be at home rather than at the office as arranged. His manner was abrupt, cold. A man, Rosie determined, very used to handing out orders.

Rosie called Lorraine on her cell phone and passed on

the message. She got a blast of foul language, as Lorraine had actually been on her way to Caley's plush office complex, the Water Garden, in Santa Monica. She did not mention Nick Bartello or Lubrinski because Lorraine cut off her call as abruptly as Robert Caley had, but she wondered about what Rooney had said about Lubrinski. The dawning realization of just how little she knew of Lorraine's past life made her feel uneasy, perhaps because it also meant, if she was truthful, that she didn't really know ex-lieutenant Lorraine Page, the woman she shared her home with.

The same austere butler ushered Lorraine into the Caleys' lounge and asked her to wait. She did not sit down, choosing instead to study the other photographs of Anna Louise in their ornate frames. One particular picture caught her eye: Anna Louise was standing between Nathan, her tennis coach, and her father; Robert Caley's arm was around her shoulders, as if he was showing her off to the camera, a look of paternal pride on his face.

Ten minutes ticked by. Lorraine now studied the large oil paintings of Elizabeth Caley's film roles. She really was an astonishingly beautiful woman. She crossed over to one that Rooney had pointed out, which depicted one of Elizabeth's earliest starring roles in which she looked no more than twenty years old. She was wearing heavy golden hooped earrings and a pale blue silk turban like the headcloths black women sometimes wore, arranged in an odd way Lorraine had never seen before, with the material knotted into points to give the impression of a crown over the young woman's head. Her shoulders were bare, the skin of her whole body tinted a tawny brown, and she was covered only by the brief draperies of a brightly colored scarf. A small plaque was set into the embossed gold frame, inscribed with the words *Marie Laveau, Queen of New Orleans*. Looking from paintings of Elizabeth Caley to the photographs of Anna Louise and her father, Lorraine could see little family resemblance.

Twenty minutes passed and Lorraine checked her watch, then the ormolu mantel clock. It was almost 5 P.M. She was about to walk out of the room when the butler returned, and, remaining at the open door, gestured for Lorraine to follow him, giving no apology for the fact that she had been kept waiting.

Lorraine followed the silent black-uniformed figure past the wide sweeping staircase and into a corridor, turning left into a wonderfully light, glass-enclosed sunroom. The vast conservatory was, she thought, some kind of extension to the main house. Tropical plants were in such profusion that it resembled a florist's, with the heady perfume of magnolia and jasmine lingering in the air and condensation misting the lower glass panes. They continued through the jungle, out into a courtyard shaded with plants growing from white painted tubs. Crazy-paved paths and a gazebo with white trailing curtains dominated the end of the courtyard, and primrose-yellow cushions adorned the white garden furniture. A table with chilled orange juice, an ice bucket with two bottles of Chablis and an array of glasses stood in the center of the gazebo.

"Mr. Caley will join you shortly." The butler wafted his hand for Lorraine to sit, and hovered over the table. "May I offer you wine, juice, or . . ."

"Still water," Lorraine said curtly, irritated that Caley was still keeping her waiting. She sat on a white wicker chair, shifting the yellow cushion to one side, glad of the shade given by the trailing muslin curtains. The butler poured her some still water into an ice-filled glass, and with a pair of silver tongs expertly picked up a slice of lemon to rest on the edge of her glass.

"Thank you." She accepted the glass, watching as he uncorked the wine, first feeling the bottle with his hand, then wrapping a napkin around the neck before placing it in the ice bucket.

"Excuse me, Mrs. Page." He actually backed up two steps before he turned and walked back into the house. Lorraine looked at her watch; she had been there well over an hour, and with only two weeks on the case, it was an hour lost. She sipped the ice water, and, seeing a large glass ashtray, leaned forward to draw it closer. She hesitated for a moment, then lit up a cigarette. She looked around the yard, and turning in her chair, she could just see the edge of the tennis courts. She got up and walked to the narrow pathway. To her right she could see the entire double tennis courts, to her left was a vast swimming pool with rows of lounge chairs, each with pale lemon towels, with small tables between, as on a hotel patio. Beyond the pool was a large pagoda-style building, which she assumed held the changing rooms and showers. Water fountains at either side flanked a path that led into a Japanese garden or what she supposed was one because of the bonsai shrubs and trees. There was no one visible, not one gardener, swimmer or tennis player. Apart from the chirping of the birds, it was all strangely silent: so silent it was unnerving. Again she checked her watch and physically jumped when Caley appeared as if from nowhere.

"I'm sorry for keeping you waiting. Did your secretary explain that my wife is indisposed, which is the reason I am here and not at my office?"

He did not seem to require a reply to his apology. He was standing by the table, pouring himself a glass of wine. There was a moment of hesitation and she saw him flick a glance at her glass of ice water. He did not offer her wine but filled his glass and sat on one of the yellow-cushioned wicker chairs. Half turning, he picked up the cushion and tossed it onto the chair nearest him. He was dressed casually in light brown slacks and loafers. His arms were bare, his pale blue silk shirtsleeves rolled back casually. Robert Caley lifted his glass to her and sipped the wine, but she could not see the expression in his eyes behind his gold-rimmed shades. Everything about Robert Caley had that LA gloss, that mark of high fashion, from the thin gold wristwatch on his left wrist to the single fine loose gold band on his right. He wore no wedding ring.

"You have a very beautiful garden."

"Mm, too manicured for my taste, and this flimsy thing reminds me of something off a movie set, but it has a purpose."

Lorraine sat down and drew her glass closer, feeling very self-conscious.

"My wife never sits in the sun, she is too pale-skinned." He obviously did; he was one of those men Lorraine presumed had a year-round suntan. Caley was also a very confident man and apparently in no hurry to ask why she wished to see him.

Lorraine stubbed out her cigarette and felt his eyes giving her a swift appraisal from behind the shades. She coughed lightly and crossed her legs, reaching down by the side of the chair to retrieve her purse.

"Do you play tennis, Mrs. Page?"

"No, I don't."

He smiled, and sipped his wine. "I didn't think you did, but you work out, correct?"

She hated the fact that she was blushing, and busied herself with opening her purse to take out a notebook. "Yes, but since you checked up on me I am sure you must be aware I was not, until recently, in what one could describe as the best of health."

He lifted his glass to her. "Well, you certainly look well today. Is your hair naturally blond?"

"Yes, but I have streaks." She suddenly laughed, finding their conversation ridiculous. No man had ever asked her whether or not she was naturally blond.

"My daughter's hair is as blond, ash-blond, but then you must know, you have photographs."

"Yes, I have, thank you. And thank you for sending the retainer fee so promptly."

"Ah, that will be Phyllis's doing." Caley reached for the bottle again and refilled his glass. "Would you like more water?"

Lorraine shook her head. "I don't think I can deal with your butler—he reminds me of a character from one of those British television series on PBS."

Caley laughed, a lovely deep warm laugh, and he crossed one leg over the other, leaning back in his chair. "Close to the truth, actually. He used to be an actor, a lot of Brits come out here for the pilot season hoping for work. When they don't get it, I suppose they take what work they can, but Peters has been with us for many years. I think he's refined his role rather well. The other servants are from home, or Elizabeth's old home in New Orleans—Berenice is our housekeeper, and we have two maids, Sylvana and Maria, plus Mario the chauffeur. I think we also have about four gardeners who maintain the grounds and the pool."

Lorraine made a note of the servants. "Can I ask you some questions?"

"Of course, that is the reason you are here, go ahead."

"I gathered from talking to her friends that your daughter was very well liked. In fact, it's a rare occurrence when—"

"She is very well liked," he corrected, as if resenting the use of the past tense.

"I met her coach, Jeff Nathan."

He nodded. "Yes, he's a good coach and Anna Louise is an excellent player. I'd hoped she would think about turning professional; she is a natural athlete."

"Are you?"

He leaned forward. "Sorry?"

"Are you a natural athlete?"

"Good God, no, but you're not here to talk about me. Did anyone you have spoken to come up with anything new?"

"No, they did not, so it will obviously be necessary for myself and my team to go to New Orleans when I've completed my interviews here."

He nodded, sipping his wine.

"I know you have gone over this over and over, Mr. Caley, but would you tell me in your own words exactly what occurred the day your daughter disappeared?"

He drained his glass and stood up. "We had breakfast. My wife was checking her packing, so she did not join us; it was just Anna and myself. She was in good spirits, looking forward to the trip. We usually go for the last weeks of Carnival—we've done it for many years. The date of Mardi Gras itself is worked out backward from Easter, so it can fall on any Tuesday from early February onward, from February third through to March ninth."

Lorraine smiled and consulted her notes. "Thank you. So last year you left on February fifteenth?"

"Yes. At about nine-thirty I spoke to my wife and said she and Anna should be ready to leave at noon. I had some business to take care of at the office, and when I returned a little before twelve the cases were already in the limousine. I showered and changed and we left for the airport just after twelve-thirty." His voice was expressionless, having repeated this many times before. He stuffed his hands into his pockets and walked to the side of the gazebo, leaning against

one of the pillars. "I have a private jet. I did not fly it myself
because I had some papers to sort through on the flight, so
we used my pilot, Edward Hardy. Anna sat with her mother,
looking through the magazines on the central table, and
asked Elizabeth if she could arrange for Phyllis to pick up
one of the dresses she liked on the fashion pages. Elizabeth
called Phyllis and arranged it there and then, shortly before
we landed. My car was waiting at the tarmac and we went
directly to the hotel. Anna Louise was as excited as she
always was. She was planning to see a friend."

Lorraine flicked through her notes. "Friend would be
Tilda Brown, yes?"

He nodded, so Lorraine continued, "And you all went
straight to the hotel?"

"Yes, we always have two adjoining suites booked for
the entire Mardi Gras month."

"That is the Hotel Cavagnal?"

"Yes, Rue Chartres. It's an old hotel in the heart of the
French Quarter. The balconies overlook the courtyard on
one side and the streets on the other."

"Why do you choose to stay at a hotel when you have
houses in the city?"

"Well, during Carnival it's good to be central to all the
action."

Lorraine looked at Caley, unconvinced, and he continued
evenly, still meeting her eyes, "And sometimes I prefer to
conduct my business away from a domestic setting."

Lorraine looked back to her note pad. "So you arrived at
the Cavagnal—"

"Yes. The maid—she's called Alphonsine—unpacked
my wife's clothes first, then mine, and then she went to
Anna Louise's suite. We have various functions and parties
we always go to, so she checks that everything is pressed
or that nothing requires laundering."

Lorraine nodded, and waited. "Alphonsine lives in New
Orleans?"

"Yes, we have staff at one of our homes there. They help
us at the hotel, see if we want anything taken to the house
and get everything ready there, because we generally go to
one or the other residence when Carnival ends."

Lorraine flipped through her notes. She had the addresses

of the Caley households and lists of their staff. "So what time—"

He interrupted her. "As soon as we arrived, Elizabeth arranged for a massage; I remained in the suite making some business calls. Anna Louise joined us for tea, and we decided we would dine at the Cavagnal, early, as we had a number of invitations and er . . . She has a wicked sense of humor, and began to mimic some of the more elderly ladies who had asked us for cocktails. At one point Elizabeth got angry, said that after that evening she would be free to see her friends, but for now she had to behave. Elizabeth is quite a celebrity and enjoys being the center of attention on these occasions. Probably reminds her of the old days when she really was a star."

"Did Anna Louise argue with your wife?"

"No, in fact they began to discuss what they would wear—girls' talk. I went for a swim, came back around seven. I showered and changed, Elizabeth was already dressing, her hair had been done. She always used the same hairdresser, again someone she has known for many years."

"Oscar Cloutier?"

"Yes. He left at about seven-fifteen. We both went down to the dining room at seven-thirty. We had some champagne ordered. At seven-forty-five Elizabeth asked me to call Anna Louise's room, so I did. There was no reply, so I returned to the table, assuming she was on her way down."

Lorraine looked over her notes. Robert Caley had repeated his original statement almost word for word, even down to the dates of the Mardi Gras. He went on to say that he and his wife began to order, and he even ordered barbecued shrimp, his daughter's favorite New Orleans dish, for Anna Louise.

"When it got to about eight and Anna Louise had still not come down, I asked the waiter to call her room again. He said there was no reply, so I went up to her room, and as it was locked, I used the connecting door between our suite and Anna Louise's. Nothing that I could see was out of place and the gown she was going to wear was laid out for her on the bed. I went into the bathroom and the sitting room and saw her purse, or at least the one she had been carrying on the flight, so I simply thought she had gone out to visit someone and had been delayed. I returned to the dining room."

"But you had asked her to join you for dinner. Did she usually disobey?"

"Well, sometimes she would say she would do something, but like any teenager she could not always be relied on."

"But your wife had specifically asked her to join you both on this particular evening."

"Yes, yes."

"Did she seem to not want to? You said your wife reprimanded her for mimicking some of the people who had invited you for cocktails later in the evening, correct?"

He sighed, irritated. "I wouldn't call it reprimanding—I said she was ticked off, but it was not a very serious exchange."

"At any other time when you were in New Orleans had Anna Louise agreed to dine with you and not turned up?"

"I suppose so, but I can't recall any single time it was of importance. She knew the city and was very aware of the obvious dangers of being out alone in certain neighborhoods. We had both been very firm about her not wandering out alone at night. And she never did, or not to my knowledge."

"She knows the city well, knows the old French Quarter?"

"Yes, of course. Elizabeth is from New Orleans, so Anna Louise had been there off and on since she was a child. She even made her debut at one of the Carnival balls."

"So Anna Louise also has many friends there?"

"Yes—well, not that many because she was educated here, but one, Tilda Brown, is a close, if not her closest friend. She was also studying at UCLA but came from New Orleans, so they have much in common."

"So you assumed that she might have gone to see Tilda?"

"Yes, I did."

"Did Mrs. Caley also think she had gone to see Tilda Brown? But I believe Tilda had been staying here in LA with you shortly before you left."

He nodded, then shrugged. "They'd had some tiff and

Tilda left the day before we did. Stupid, really, because we were going to give her a ride with us, but—''

"Did you know what the girls argued about?''

"No, I did not.'' He seemed irritated, his foot tapping. These were obviously questions he had been asked before.

"According to previous statements you did not call Miss Brown's home until very much later that evening.''

"Yes, that is correct.''

"Why did you not call Tilda Brown immediately?''

"Because we finished dinner and, as I said, we had engagements—commitments, if you like.''

"So even though you saw your daughter's purse left in her room—''

Caley turned to face Lorraine. "I did not call Miss Brown's family or anyone else because I did not think anything untoward had happened and neither did my wife.''

"How did your wife react to your daughter not coming down to join you for dinner?''

He sighed. "Elizabeth is a little more volatile than myself. She was very angry with Anna. We left the hotel at about ten to go to our first engagement. When we returned to the hotel at about fifteen minutes after midnight, we became concerned. We called Miss Brown's family. Tilda was in bed, so we spoke to her parents and they told us that Anna had not been by or phoned. They had not seen her.''

"May I ask if you are wearing prescription lenses?''

"What?''

Lorraine stared at him and he slowly removed his sunglasses. "Thank you.''

He moved closer so she could see his eyes. He leaned on the table. "You think I'm hiding something?''

"No, but I like to see—''

"What, the whites of my eyes? Or do you and your type get a kick out of the pain? Because, Mrs. Page, every time I have gone through this, every statement I give, you don't think I feel somehow to blame? That if I had acted faster my daughter might have been traced? Well, I do blame myself, every minute of every day. My daughter has been missing for eleven months, Mrs. Page, and every phone call, every letter is a hope, and every hope makes my heart thud in my chest. What did you expect from me, tears?''

"I'm sorry, but I have to ask."

"You ask whatever you want and I will try to answer, just as I have with every single agency we have hired. I know the police here have given up, but I also know the case is still open in New Orleans. How do you expect me to behave? I want my daughter back, I pray she is alive. Whether she has run off with some unsavory character or whatever she has done, I will forgive her because this is hell. All I want is to see her again. I love her, I was proud of her, and I miss her."

He was bitterly angry and yet his eyes brimmed with tears. It was unexpected and it threw Lorraine. His open emotion and obvious declaration of love for his daughter were distressing. This sophisticated, handsome man was suddenly more vulnerable than any man she had ever met because he was unable to control himself. Half turning from her, he started to cry, awful low sobs.

"I miss my lovely daughter, Mrs. Page. If I pass the tennis courts I hear her laughing, shouting out to me. Just sitting here in this stupid fucking gazebo hurts because I hear her laughing about it, sending it up, like the ridiculous Japanese garden we both hated. And then I have to listen to my wife crying every night, watch her face when the telephone rings. This house is dead without our little girl."

"I'm so sorry."

"I don't need your sympathy, Mrs. Page, I need my daughter found. Or worse, I need to know she is never coming home, then I can get on with my life." The tears spilled down his face and he wiped them away with the back of his hand before replacing his glasses. "Excuse me, if you need to ask any more questions go ahead."

Lorraine closed her notebook. Everything he had told her was on record, he had given no further insight into what had actually happened to Anna Louise. She picked up her purse and replaced her notebook, then hesitated.

"There is just one more thing, Mr. Caley. You said you made calls from the hotel, to business associates, I presume, and I have no record of who you actually called."

"You'll have a list delivered by morning."

"Your business is real estate. Could I ask you to give me

a more precise account of your business transactions in New Orleans and here in Los Angeles?''

He turned away. ''What in God's name has my business got to do with my daughter's disappearance?''

''Maybe nothing, but then again it might, so I really would like to have as much background on you—''

''You'll have it. Now if you would excuse me.''

''Yes, of course. Er, just one more thing, I know your wife is indisposed, but would I be able to speak for a moment with Phyllis?''

He nodded and walked to an intercom phone she had not noticed at the side of the gazebo. He picked it up. ''Phyllis, would you come into the yard, please? Mrs. Page would like to speak to you.''

Robert Caley collected the open bottle of wine and walked out toward the tennis courts as Lorraine remained seated, looking after him.

Rosie was trying to decipher Bill Rooney's appalling handwritten scrawl. ''I can't make this out, what is this?'' she asked.

Rooney yawned. ''The psychic the Caleys used. She wasn't at home and I been back twice. I left two messages.''

''Juda?'' Rosie enquired.

''Yeah, that's her name. I reckon she's a waste of time, all flakes if you ask me. I'm gonna go for a few more drinks with Nick Bartello, he's on to something, so if her ladyship calls in, tell her she can catch me at home later. A lot later, if I know Nick.''

Rosie nodded and jotted down Juda's name, phone number and address. ''I gotta go to a meeting tonight but I'll leave a message for her here and at home.''

''Good, you do that. See ya!'' Rooney thudded out as the phone began to ring.

''Mr. Rooney there?'' said a thick, drawling voice with a real downhome Louisiana accent.

''No, I am so sorry, he's not available. Who's calling? Can I take a message?''

''I'm just returnin' the man's calls. It's Juda Salina. You know what it's about?''

Rosie perked up, becoming the partner in the investigation

agency. "Yes, we are investigating the case of Anna Louise Caley and—"

The phone went dead. Rosie looked at the receiver, wondering if it was something she had done at her end. She wrote a memo for Rooney and Lorraine, saying the psychic had made contact. Rosie also noted the time and date the call had come in. She was being very professional.

Phyllis toyed with her glass of mineral water. "She needs pills to make her sleep and sometimes she can't get up. Today is one of them. We had the doctor come but he prescribed a different sedative. It's all very sad, poor woman, but I'll make sure she can see you tomorrow."

"Thank you."

Lorraine sipped the melting ice, the deftly placed slice of lemon now floating on top of the residue of tepid water. "So you didn't see or hear anything untoward the day the family departed for New Orleans?"

"No, I did not."

"And Anna Louise was happy and carefree, excited by the forthcoming trip?"

"Yes, they were often more like friends than mother and daughter. I mean, they had the odd little argument, only natural—she was quite willful but she never sulked."

"The day they left, February fifteenth, you received a call from the Caleys' private jet?"

"Yes, I did. Anna Louise had seen something in *Vogue* she wanted me to purchase for her."

"Did you?"

"Yes."

"Did she often just call you to get what she wanted? According to the files a thirty-five-hundred-dollar black chiffon Valentino dress. I would say that stinks of a spoiled kid."

Phyllis pursed her lips. "The Caleys happen to be extremely wealthy, Mrs. Page, and I assure you that was not unusual. You may say she was spoiled, but at the same time she was also one of the sweetest, most natural young girls I've ever known."

"But she was spoiled."

"No more than any other child of rich parents."

Lorraine hesitated, and then said quietly, "Or parent . . ."

"I'm sorry, I don't quite follow?"

"Yes, you do. Surely it is obvious that the main money in the Caley family is Elizabeth Caley's."

Phyllis pursed her lips. "Mr. Caley is also a very successful businessman."

"But he was not that successful when they first married. An old press cutting hinted that he was not a wealthy man and they met when he was showing Mrs. Caley a property."

Phyllis froze. "I am afraid this is not something I can answer. I have worked for the Caleys for only ten years, so I have no knowledge of whatever happened previously. All I do know is Mr. Caley works exceptionally hard."

"What work is he involved in specifically in New Orleans?"

"Mrs. Page, I am not privy to Mr. Caley's business. I am Elizabeth Caley's companion and secretary."

"But you settle the bills. You did, I believe, pay my fees and will continue to pay them, is that correct?"

"Yes, Mrs. Caley instructed me to pay your retainer."

"You didn't discuss it with Mr. Caley?"

"I made a note for him to be aware of exactly what I had done, as I always do."

Lorraine made no mention of the million-dollar bonus Mrs. Caley had promised to pay. She was beginning to feel tired; it had been a long day and she had to drive back to Pasadena.

"Thank you. Oh, just one more thing—Tilda Brown, Anna Louise's girlfriend, was staying here and she was supposed to return to New Orleans with the Caleys but instead left the day before. Do you know why?"

Phyllis rose to her feet. "No, but probably over a tennis match—they were always playing tennis. I think Tilda used to make up her own rules and it infuriated Anna Louise."

"Did you hear them arguing at all?"

"No. Tilda just asked me to arrange a ticket for her, and she was driven to the airport by Mario."

"Thank you, Miss Collins. I'll walk out via the gardens."

Phyllis nodded and said she would tell the security guard to open the gate.

"Is there a full-time guard on duty?"

"Yes, since Anna Louise's disappearance we've had a lot of press hanging around outside, and Mr. Caley didn't want his wife disturbed, so we now have full-time security guards patrolling the estate. To begin with, it was feared that perhaps Anna Louise had been kidnapped, so the guards were employed for everyone's peace of mind."

Lorraine prepared to leave. Just as she was walking away from Phyllis she stopped. "Is this house Mrs. Caley's?"

"Yes, I believe so."

"And the property in New Orleans?"

"Yes, I think a lot of it belonged to her family."

Lorraine hesitated, wondering whether or not she should ask Phyllis the next question, or leave it until she spoke to Elizabeth Caley personally.

"Was there something else?"

"Er, yes, it may be nothing, but who is the main beneficiary of Elizabeth Caley's will?"

Phyllis glared, and Lorraine knew she had made a mistake.

"It's probably irrelevant to the investigation but at the same time you must understand that I—"

"I really can't help you, I'm sorry."

"That's okay. What time shall I call in the morning?"

"About eleven."

"Thank you, I'll see you tomorrow, no doubt."

"Yes, you will." Her sharp features were even more pinched as she stared at Lorraine. "You certainly do a lot of research." She did not say it as a compliment, but Lorraine smiled as if it had been one.

"I believe that is the point, is it not? And you must understand; Phyllis—I hope I can call you Phyllis—that everything you say to me is in total confidence. If there is anything that you feel would help my investigation, anything at all, I hope you will feel free to call me at any time."

She caught it, just a flicker of hesitancy, but then Phyllis covered with a tight, brittle smile. "You keep to the left walkway and it will lead you around to the front of the house. Good afternoon, Mrs. Page."

Lorraine walked from the courtyard along the immaculate paved path. She passed the tennis courts and stopped. Robert Caley was sitting on a white painted bench, the bottle of wine held loosely in his hand, seemingly staring at the empty tennis court. She continued on past the vast swimming pool with its carefully laid out lounge chairs, and could see a maid folding up the unused towels.

Lorraine would have gone on, but Robert Caley called her and she turned to face him. He still wore the dark glasses but removed them slowly as he looked at her.

"I'll be going to New Orleans. If you need to go there within the week, please call me. You can . . ." He gave a boyish smile. "I'm offering you a ride."

She returned his smile. "Thank you, I'll call you."

He nodded and stood watching her as she walked around to the front of the house.

Lorraine had found Robert Caley very attractive—she'd known it when he had leaned toward her across the table in the gazebo—but any sexual desires had to be dismissed because if she discovered that he could benefit from his daughter's disappearance or death, he would be under suspicion. And by now Lorraine intuitively felt that Anna Louise Caley was dead.

CHAPTER

4

"Rooney said he reminded him of someone called Lubrinski."

Lorraine reacted, giving Rosie that funny half-squint look, her hair covering part of the scar on her cheek. "Did he now?"

"Yeah, said he was injured in some shoot-out. He's got a nickname, Nick the Limp."

"Really?" Lorraine said noncommittally.

"So who was this Lubrinski guy? And what was that about you using a pair of panty hose as a tourniquet, is that true?"

"You should know Rooney by now, Rosie, he's full of crap. He should have been doing what I told him to do, like contact the psychic. We got two weeks, Rosie, just two weeks."

"But you told Bill to check out all the agencies, and I'm not exactly sittin' on my butt doin' nothing all day, thank you very much!"

"Oh, shut up. And if you don't wanna use the shower I will. Maybe see if I can see her tonight."

Under the shower, face uptilted, eyes closed, the memories came back. The way Jack Lubrinski had looked up at her in such agony and gripped her hand.

"You're gonna be okay," she had lied. "Ambulance's gonna be here any second, you old bastard, but in the meantime . . ."

"Hell, if it takes being shot to see you whip off your panties I'd have done it before."

"Shut up, you perverted shit."

He'd died in her arms fifteen minutes later as the ambulance, siren screaming, cut its way through the traffic to the hospital. He was still holding on to her hand like a child when she saw the light go out of his eyes. They'd had to pry his hand away from hers. She hadn't wanted to let go, sure that maybe there was hope, but there had been none. The black-haired, dark-eyed Lubrinski had left a deep empty place inside her. Was that why she wanted Robert Caley? Was that going to be the game plan for the rest of her life, the look-alike Lubrinskis? Was that why she was attracted to Robert Caley, because he was dark-haired, with fierce, scared eyes? That was what she had seen when he'd taken the shades off, fear and pain. Lubrinski had always hidden behind the smart remarks, the tough exterior, until he was dying; then she had seen something in his eyes that had squeezed her heart. What was it? Why did it attract her? What she felt was in no way a mothering feeling. She didn't want to mother Robert Caley: she wanted him to screw her, just as she had wanted Lubrinski. But at that time she had been married with two kids. She wished she had just once told him before he died that she loved him. She shut her eyes tightly, clenched her teeth together; she wasn't going to cry now, it was all too long ago. But she couldn't stop the tears, because for the first time she was admitting to herself that she had been in love with Jack Lubrinski. She had fought and denied it, even after his death, but now all these years later she wept for him and whispered to herself, "I loved you, Jack, and I still miss you."

Rosie opened the shower curtain. "I called the psychic. She says she won't see nobody."

Lorraine reached for a towel. "Wanna bet?"

"You going there now?"

"Yep. We've got two weeks, Rosie, just two weeks."

"Oh, can I come with you?"

Lorraine was about to refuse, but Rosie's childlike eagerness changed her mind.

"Sure, why not?"

The address was good, but the apartment was in the lower

ground floor and at the end of a corridor. The apartment
block was an expensive one with intercom buzzers, top-level
security and an underground garage for residents. Lorraine
had been lucky; she had simply followed a car into the parking area, waving at the woman in front, who had smiled
back, unaware that Lorraine had no right to be there.

"Bingo, we're in. We can surprise Mrs. Salina unless she
saw us coming in her crystal ball," said Lorraine as she
followed the woman into the garage.

"Learn something every day," Rosie said, impressed, but
Lorraine was already hurrying out of the car.

"Good evening." Lorraine smiled as the woman parked
her Saab convertible.

"Good evening," she replied, switching on her blinking
alarm and heading toward a private entrance door.

Lorraine moved quickly to join the woman as she
punched in the security code to access the elevator into the
building. "Weather's strange, nearly eighty already today."
She glanced behind her, irritated to see that Rosie was still
getting out of the car. The woman nodded, more intent on
getting her house keys out from her purse than concentrating
on Lorraine. The elevator door was still open, and Lorraine
rammed her foot against it in case it began to close.

"Are you having problems with your air-conditioning?"
Lorraine asked, keeping up the conversation and giving Rosie a glare.

"No, but I noticed it was a lot warmer today."

"Yep, could be heading up in the eighties according to
the weather report."

Rosie stepped in and the elevator door shut.

The elevator from the garage opened onto the main corridor by the apartment elevators. The woman turned toward
them as Lorraine hurried down the corridor with Rosie tag-
ging behind, neither of them realizing that they were in fact
heading in the right direction for Mrs. Salina's place.

"Yes, who is it?"

Lorraine leaned close to the door. "My name is Lorraine
Page."

"What do you want?"

"Mrs. Salina, I really need to talk to you. I am a private
investigator looking into the—"

"I don't know how you got into the building, but you'd better leave immediately or I'll call security."

"You go right ahead and do that, Mrs. Salina, but I'm sure Mrs. Caley won't like it."

There were a few moments of silence. Rosie stood to one side, still more impressed by Lorraine. Then came the sound of a chain being removed, a bolt pulled back, and a higher lock opened before the door inched open.

"I'm goin' out in five minutes."

"Fine, this won't take long. Can I come in?"

"You with the police?"

"No, this is my card, my name is Lorraine Page of Page Investigations, and this is my assistant, Rosie."

Mrs. Salina snatched the card, and then the door inched further open. "Five minutes."

Rosie pursed her lips—she didn't like the assistant line, since she was a partner in the agency, but she said nothing as they were led along a dark, narrow hall. The main room of the apartment was at the end of a narrow corridor, the walls lined with framed photographs of well-known and not so well-known stars, alongside certificates for psychic readings, palm readings, crystals, tarot cards and more. It seemed Mrs. Salina dabbled in every form of psychic phenomenon and had a certificate to prove it. Rosie glanced at everything, wishing she had brought a note pad. This was really interesting, she thought—no wonder Lorraine liked her job, you got to meet all kinds.

It was not until they followed Juda into the small sitting room that they got a good look at her. She was exotic-looking, olive-skinned, with thick, black crinkly hair tied in a knot at the nape of her neck. She weighed at least 280 pounds, yet, like a lot of very heavy women, she moved lightly and had tiny, delicate hands. Lorraine estimated her age to be about fifty, and her shawls, bangles and thick beaded necklaces were reminiscent of the Flower Power days. In contrast, her perfectly made-up face was very much a nineties work of art, with well-placed false eyelashes, lipstick similar in color to the one Mrs. Caley had worn, and even the lips outlined in the same way.

"Sit down," she said as she eased her bulk into a hard-backed armchair. "Like I said, I got five minutes. Why do you want to see me?'' She had a New Orleans accent, not heavy but easy to detect by the way her voice drawled and lifted in a musical manner.

She stared hard at Rosie, who tried to blend into the wallpaper, uncomfortably balanced on a stool. She had let Lorraine take the better chair, or rather, Lorraine had taken it automatically: she behaved as though Rosie weren't there.

''Tell me about Elizabeth Caley.''

''I'm sorry, but unless I have Mrs. Caley's permission I cannot discuss her. My business is just like a priest's or a doctor's; my clients' private consultations with me are exactly that, private.''

''But, like me, you have been hired to help trace their daughter.''

''Yes, that is correct.''

''How much contact have you therefore had with Mrs. Caley?''

''I am afraid I cannot divulge that.''

''Did you travel to New Orleans?''

''I did.'' She levered herself up from the chair and crossed to the dresser. She opened a drawer and took out a photograph. ''She is a very strong presence.''

''Anna Louise?''

''Why, yes. This was given to me by Mrs. Caley.'' She thrust it in front of Lorraine, and there was the sweet face, the long blond tresses.

''She is very beautiful.''

Juda nodded, then passed the photograph to Rosie, who leaned forward to look at it.

''Yes, she is very pretty.'' Rosie nodded. Juda returned the photograph to the drawer.

''She most surely is, and I would say she is still in New Orleans.''

''Alive?'' Lorraine asked sharply.

Juda shut the drawer and remained with her back to Lorraine. Then she turned slowly and, with her eyes closed, pressed herself against the dresser. Rosie studied the big woman: if she had been worried about her own weight, Juda had even more of a problem.

''I sincerely believe Anna Louise is alive.''

''Why?''

The false eyelashes fluttered. "Why? Like I said, she has a presence. The little girl is alive, I am sure of it."

"Why?" Lorraine persisted.

The eyes opened. "I have just told you, I feel her presence."

"Well, that may be so, but I am not quite as fortunate as you, Mrs. Salina. My job is to find her. I can't feel any presence, I am not in touch with the . . . forces, so to speak."

"They are forces, Mrs. Page, strong ones, and I am telling you that little girl is alive. I take my work very seriously, and when I feel her, become her, she is not saying to me she is cold." She turned her dark eyes to Rosie again, and Rosie felt a frisson of fear. She looked away, biting her lip: there was something unpleasant about the woman, about the whole apartment.

"So, what is she saying to you?"

Juda pointedly looked at her watch, and then at Lorraine. "Mrs. Page, you ain't paying, Mrs. Caley is, and I have told her all that I have been able to receive—that is, Anna Louise is alive."

"Well, I'll pay you, is that what you want?"

Juda stared hard at Lorraine. "I have to go out now. If Mrs. Caley personally tells me that I can give you what I have received, then you may call again. But right now all I can tell you is that I feel her presence, an aura of light, every time I look at her sweet angel face."

"Well, if this presence should indicate where Anna Louise is, then I'll talk to Mrs. Caley and I'll come back and make you tell me where she is. You see, I deal in facts, not fantasy, and she has been missing nearly a year. Now, that is a very long time to have no word, no letter, no contact. I'm hired to find her."

"But I presume you are being paid."

"Yeah, but then so are you."

"No. The husband has refused to allow me to see my poor dear Elizabeth."

"Did you tell him his daughter was alive?"

Juda crossed to the door and stood there. "I have had no dealings with Mr. Caley, but I have known Elizabeth for many years."

"She's a drug addict, isn't she?"

Juda gave Lorraine a surly look. "I said five minutes, now I ask you to leave. I only agreed to see you because you implied Elizabeth had asked you to see me, but I think you are lying, just like all the others who have tried to talk to me. My clients have my total loyalty."

"What other people have talked to you?"

Juda again gave that direct, rather eerie stare. "Private investigators, and the police. They treat me with no respect, Mrs. Page, I can feel it, see it in their faces. They don't have to say a word, I know what they think of people like me." She moved back to the dresser and opened a drawer. "Here, take this, but now you gotta go."

She handed Lorraine a cheap computer-printed document, clipped together. Juda didn't wait for her even to glance at it before moving impatiently into the hallway. Lorraine handed it to Rosie and indicated by a nod that Rosie should follow her to where Juda stood by the open front door, waiting.

"Good afternoon, Mrs. Page. Er, just one thing, will you come real close to me for a moment?"

Lorraine stepped closer and Juda stared up into her face. She lifted her delicate hand and touched the scar running down Lorraine's cheek. "Honey, you should get that fixed, you'd be real lovely. What was your first name?"

"Lorraine."

"Nice to talk with you, Lorraine."

Rosie was squeezing past her when the woman leaned forward again.

"Rosie. Your name is Rosie, and your spirit is kind. You take care now, honey."

The chain was replaced, the bolts banged across. For someone who was about to go out, it was weird that she should lock herself in. Was she expecting someone or simply lying? Lorraine suspected the latter; Juda Salina was not about to go out.

Lorraine and Rosie had to wait fifteen minutes in the garage before a resident came down and used the special code to open the security gates. They sat discussing Juda and, as Bill Rooney had done before them, came to the conclusion she was one big fake, able to make a lot of money from people as desperate as Elizabeth Caley. Her computer-printed advertisement was crude and unprofessional, stating how many people had been saved by Juda Salina predictions, and how many times. She also listed a number of police cases she had assisted in. It was all rubbish; saying she felt a presence and that Anna Louise Caley was alive only meant she could keep asking for more money from Mrs. Caley.

Rosie read the printout, and frowned as she turned the pages. "I hope she's right."

"About what? Your sweet soul?"

"No, that the little girl is alive. I hope she is."

Lorraine was now more convinced the girl was dead, but she decided that Rooney should at least check out the so-called police investigations listed in the printout and Salina's part in them. She had gained only one thing of interest: Robert Caley did not like Juda Salina. She respected him for that.

Juda sat wondering whether or not she should call Mrs. Caley. She didn't like the fact that yet another private investigator was questioning her, and supposedly with Mrs. Caley's permission. In fact, it annoyed her that she had been told by some faceless employee of Robert Caley's that she was no longer allowed to visit his wife and that there would be no further payments. She had made a lot of money out of their misery, even a trip back home. But this time she was worried.

She went over in her mind everything Lorraine had said. The woman hadn't asked anything new, so what was it? The scar? She had a feeling that it had been inflicted by a man, but the message had been very hazy. She sighed, feeling tired, unsure whether or not to put herself through it, and without being paid. But even as she fought against doing it, she got up, drew the dark crimson curtains and turned off the overhead lights so the small room was in virtual darkness. She sat down again. An onlooker would have thought she was nodding off to sleep, her eyes drooping like those of someone heavy with exhaustion, unable to keep awake. She moaned softly, as though with sexual gratification, and sank deeper into the chair. Her big bosom rose and fell as she took slow, deep breaths.

"Yes, oh yes, yes," she whispered, and her tiny, delicate hands clung to the carved arm of her uncomfortable chair. She continued to take deep labored breaths, her bosom heaving, her head beginning to feel light as she began to go slowly into a trance. The darkness seeped into Juda's consciousness. Nothing for a while, then it started to happen, just as it had when she had been with Elizabeth Caley. First came the distorted sounds of music, then of a street. She couldn't grasp the area, it was happening too quickly and she couldn't control it, but she felt the place was familiar. Exactly as it had played out before, something began to terrify her, and this time she felt it even more strongly. She began to gasp, her hands clawing at the chair; there was a pain in the center of her chest, as if a weight were pressing down, squeezing the air from her lungs. She began to flap her hands; someone or something was astride her, a man, it was a man and he was taking out a knife. She couldn't see his face, just knew he was going to slice her throat.

Her own scream cut through the dark void of panic, and she lurched forward, coming to fast, fazed for only a few moments before she realized she was safe in her own apartment. The sweat trickled down her cheeks and she involuntarily patted her neck and chest, frightened by the still-awful feeling of choking, of someone squeezing the life out of her. But it wasn't her, she knew that, it wasn't Juda Salina being murdered, it was someone with a name beginning with the letter L.

The initial L: did it stand for Lorraine Page? She was tensing up, remembering what she had just put herself through, and for a second time. Juda had had a similarly jumbled message when she'd gone into the trance at Mrs. Caley's, someone's name beginning with the letter L. She knew she had frightened Elizabeth Caley, but she didn't know what it had meant. Often she didn't, the messages for one client could get confused with another's, but this one had been particularly strong. She'd presumed then that the letter L was for Louise, Anna Louise, because she had had an overpowering feeling of imminent danger, and of death. She had lied to Mrs. Caley, said the powers had been strong and that her daughter was alive, but she had felt death very close.

Juda tried to recall the exact day she visited Mrs. Caley. She found the entry in her diary and turned over the page to the next day. She read the scrawled message from Robert Caley's secretary that she was not to see his wife again. They were the only notes in the diary for that day. Juda drummed the blank pages with her painted fingernails, made a decision and dialed the Caley residence. Phyllis answered.

"Phyllis, this is Juda—"

"You must not call here again—I thought Mr. Caley had made that clear to you. He will not allow you to speak to Elizabeth again."

"I know. It was you I wanted to talk to."

Phyllis was almost whispering. "If it's about any further payments, I have been instructed by Mr. Caley that—"

"It isn't, I just need to know something. I've had a visit from a woman working for a private investigation agency."

"You mean Mrs. Page."

"Yeah, Lorraine Page, isn't it?"

"Yes, she's been brought in."

"What day did you hire her?"

"The same day you last came to see Mrs. Caley. You know she was very distressed after you left and . . . hello?"

Juda was silent.

Phyllis sounded worried. "Hello? Are you still there? Is something wrong, has Mrs. Page said something?"

"No, no, I just needed to clear up my diary entries. Thank you, Phyllis, and please tell Elizabeth I am thinking of her and keeping Anna Louise's presence in my mind, and I'll wait for her to contact me. 'Bye now."

Juda replaced the phone before Phyllis could ask anything else. She could tell herself it was coincidence, but she knew it wasn't. She sensed much more strongly than she would ever admit that Anna Louise Caley had been dead a long time—she knew that. What she hadn't been able to make sense of until now was that on Tuesday night the message she'd received was so strong it had made her physically sick. A connection to the letter L had come up and burned in her brain, surrounded by fire and imminent danger. Now she was sure the L was for Lorraine Page, and there was a lot more than imminent danger . . . she was sure the woman was going to die, and in the same way as she had seen so clearly

in her second trance state—Lorraine was going to get her
throat cut.

Lorraine had borrowed Rosie's heated rollers to style her
hair. She wore a cream silk blouse, a tight, straight skirt
with a slit down one side and high-heeled shoes. She eased
a dark blue linen jacket around her shoulders and stepped
back to admire the effect.

Rosie stood in the kitchen, spooning up a vast bowl of
cereal. "I dunno how you manage to get bargain of the
month at every yard sale—nothin' ever fits me. Very
smart."

"Thank you, I need to feel good to take on Elizabeth
Caley."

"Mm," Rosie muttered, milk dribbling down her chin.
"You gonna take up his offer? Be nice to travel in style,
private jet."

Lorraine checked her purse and slim briefcase. "I'm not
ready to leave LA yet, so we'll see. In the meantime, there's
a list of things for you to be doing: arrange tickets, hotels
and start packing. Call me if you need me on the cell phone,
maybe early afternoon, and see what Rooney and this hop-
along guy come up with."

"Okay." Rosie looked down the neatly written list.

Shortly after Lorraine drove off down the road, Rooney
screeched to a halt outside the apartment. He tooted the car
horn; he'd started giving Rosie a ride into the office if he
was passing. She thudded down the wooden steps and
crossed over to his car as he opened the passenger door.

"You just missed Veronica Lake, she's gone to the Caleys'. But we have a list of orders and she wanted to know
how you got on with Nick Bartello."

Rooney pushed his shades up his shiny nose. "I got one
bitch of a hangover, but I'd bet any money he's got an even
worse one."

Rosie looked at him more closely. "Jesus, where in hell
did you get those shades?"

"Found 'em in a drawer—I think they were my wife's,
why?"

Rosie grinned. "Well, I just didn't reckon you'd be the

kind of guy to wear pink-framed shades, but they suit you, match your coloring, sorta flushed.''

Rooney drove on, his gut pressed against the steering wheel. ''Well, when I'm through with 'em you can have them. They'll match whatever color you describe your hair.''

''Aw, shut up, you, it's the perm. I'm a natural redhead and if you want I can prove it.''

''God forbid, I couldn't take that even without a hang-over!''

Lorraine and the butler had another formal bowing session before he led her toward the drawing room.

''I won't be kept waiting again, will I?'' she asked.

He actually half smiled. ''Mrs. Caley is expecting you, Mrs. Page.''

At that moment Phyllis appeared and gestured for Lorraine to follow her up the wide staircase.

''Please bring Mrs. Caley's breakfast, and for you, Mrs. Page?''

''Oh, I'd like a coffee, black with honey if you have it, thank you.''

He gave a curt nod and departed toward the kitchen corridor as Lorraine continued up the stairs.

''What's his name again?''

''Peters, Reginald Peters.'' Phyllis tapped on the double doors on the first landing.

''Come in.''

Phyllis stepped back and ushered Lorraine into Elizabeth Caley's drawing room, almost bumping into her as she stopped dead in her tracks. The drawing room was a profusion of perfumed flowers in vast displays on almost every available surface, and even though the shutters were drawn over the open windows, the pale lemon walls, drapes and carpet seemed to blend into each other as if the room were ablaze with sunlight. White muslin curtains billowed from brass curtain rods in contrast to the stillness of the designer-draped silk curtains with their golden fringes and tiebacks.

Elizabeth Caley was reclining on a white shot-silk chaise longue, wearing a flowing kimono of dark green and yellow printed flowers. Her thick pitch-black hair was braided in a long plait down her back and a tight white bandanna was wrapped around her head. She was creaming her delicate hands and smiled warmly at Lorraine.

"Come in, darling. Please excuse me for not shaking hands, but I have just had a manicure and the girl never uses enough moisturizer. Sit down."

Lorraine looked around. There were scatter pillows in profusion on every lemon shot-silk chair, and before she could decide which one to sit on, Phyllis made the choice for her, drawing forward a spindle-legged armchair.

"Thank you, Phyllis dear. Is Peters bringing refreshments?"

"Yes."

"Good, then you may leave us."

Phyllis crept out, and Lorraine sat down, unzipping her briefcase and taking out her notebook.

"Have you done something different to your hair?"

Lorraine smiled. "No, just washed it."

"You do it yourself?"

"Yes. Thank you for seeing me."

Peters entered, wheeling in a gilt trolley, which held coffee, croissants, tea and ice water. He eased the trolley over to Mrs. Caley, passed her a white, stiffly laundered napkin and poured a greenish-looking tea. The china was fine porcelain. He poured black coffee and indicated a silver dish with honey for Lorraine.

Mrs. Caley eased herself to a sitting position and wafted her hand. "Thank you, thank you, I'll ring if we need anything else."

"Very good, Mrs. Caley." He performed his backward half-bow out of the room and closed the doors silently behind him.

"Would you care for a croissant?"

"No, thank you."

Lorraine spooned in the honey, careful not to let any drops fall on the white tray cloth. Elizabeth Caley picked up silver tongs and placed a warmed croissant on a plate, then some jam from a silver pot. Lorraine noticed that her smooth hands with their long, talonlike red nails were shaking, and she had to use both hands to sip from her delicate teacup.

"I'm sorry I couldn't see you yesterday, but I am sure Phyllis made my apologies."

"She did."

"I don't know what I would do without Phyllis. That is a very pretty blouse."

"Thank you." Lorraine balanced her cup and saucer on the arm of her chair as she eased her notebook onto her lap. "I am sorry if I ask you questions that must have been put to you many times, but it is important. I will try not to take up too much of your time, as it must be distressing to . . ."

Elizabeth Caley nodded. She resembled Merle Oberon, with the same high forehead, enhanced now by the bandanna, and flawless skin. Her makeup, like everything else about her, was immaculate, her lips lightly outlined in a dark fuchsia. Whether or not her beauty had by now been assisted by surgery was immaterial; even at this close proximity her face appeared unlined. In comparison, Lorraine felt jaded, as any woman would. Elizabeth Caley had a fragility and femininity that in this day and age were ridiculed by feminists because, perfect creature as she was, she belonged to a different era. She would not dream of opening a door for herself—this was a woman used to having men break their necks to get to the door first.

"Could you just tell me about February fifteenth, the day you left for New Orleans?"

"How do you mean?"

"Well, I know you and Anna Louise were together before your husband returned from his office and—"

"Oh, I see, yes, well, I had to oversee all the packing, we had some engagements, cocktail parties, dinners. . . . Peters usually packs for Robert, but I am very particular, I always have special tissue paper; it avoids creases, you know, if you lay tissue sheets between each garment."

"Did you pack for your daughter?"

"Good heavens, no. Anna Louise is dreadful, and you know how young girls dress these days, jeans and T-shirts, and more jeans and T-shirts, sneakers. I think whoever invented those awful things should be shot. She just hurls things into cases—in fact, we had a little tiff about it because I asked Phyllis to make sure she had some of her nice things because we had a few formal engagements. Anyway,

Phyllis oversaw her packing, I think, and then we had brunch on the terrace and waited for Robert. We then went to the airport and . . .'' She frowned. ''Oh, yes, on the plane she saw something in *Vogue* or *Elle* magazine, a little black cocktail dress, and I was surprised because she really liked it. So we called home to ask Phyllis to pick it up and arrange to have it delivered for when she returned.''

She frowned again, one long fingernail tapping the center of her forehead. ''Anna Louise was in high spirits, really looking forward to the trip and seeing her friends, especially Tilda Brown, an adorable girl. She often stayed here; we are all very fond of Tilda.''

''Tilda Brown was scheduled to travel with you to New Orleans but—''

''Oh, yes, yes, yes. She said she wanted to go earlier, so Phyllis arranged it. I've no idea why, but you know young girls, silly waste of money, I suppose. Anyway, we left, drove to the airport and . . .''

Lorraine listened as Elizabeth Caley repeated, as her husband had done, almost word for word her original statement given to the police, from the moment that they arrived at the hotel until the dinner.

''Can you think of anything, no matter how trivial it may seem, that you have not mentioned to anyone else?''

''My dear, I have gone over and over those hours, as if seeing them on a screen, trying to find some clue, but there is nothing, nothing at all that I can recall. And that is what makes it so horrible, because I cannot think of a single thing that would be of help. She was happy, cheerful and looking forward to Carnival. . . .''

''Had she ever gone off alone before?''

''Of course, but never without letting us know where she was going to, or who she was seeing. She is an intelligent girl, aware of the dangers of being out alone in the evenings, especially in the old French Quarter. I had even discussed with her the importance of always making sure we knew where she was. Obviously any young girl from Los Angeles is made very aware of the dangers of going off with strange men or accepting a ride, or drugs—''

''Did she ever use drugs?''

''I'm sorry?''

"Did Anna Louise to your knowledge ever use drugs— smoke marijuana, for example?"

"No, most definitely not, she doesn't even smoke cigarettes. And very rarely drinks—perhaps a glass of champagne, nothing more. She is, you see, very health-conscious, very athletic really. She loves sports and obviously any overindulgence in drugs or alcohol would be damaging to her. I am not making her out to be a Goody Two-shoes, she is not perfect. She can throw tantrums and get angry, just like any other girl of her age."

"Tantrums?"

"Well, I don't know if that is the correct description. She is very spoiled, I know, more by Robert than myself, and she can twist him around her little finger, always has since she was a baby. He dotes on her, but he can also be very firm."

"Is your daughter the main beneficiary of your will?"

"Why do you ask?"

Lorraine chose her words carefully. "Well, there is no evidence that your daughter has been kidnapped, no ransom note, no contact. I am simply trying to find if there is a motive. . . ."

For a fleeting moment Lorraine saw Mrs. Caley hesitate.

"Yes, she does benefit from my will."

"Your daughter is the main beneficiary?"

"Yes, but she is also the main beneficiary of my husband's will. Did you ask him the same question?"

Lorraine kept her eyes down as if concentrating on her notes. "Yes."

"Ah, I see. Yes, well, if anything happened Anna Louise would automatically be the sole beneficiary. And if, God forbid, anything did happen to Anna, then Robert is obviously the next of kin, and vice versa."

Lorraine looked up, concerned, because Elizabeth Caley was shaking, and now it was not just her hands, her whole body visibly trembled.

"Are you all right?"

"What has happened to my daughter?"

"I don't know, Mrs. Caley, but I will do everything I can to find out."

"Do you think she is dead?"

"Until I have more details I really can't answer that question."

Elizabeth slowly rose to her feet, holding on to the edge of the chaise longue. Lorraine watched as she used the furniture to cross the room, grasping the back of a chair for a moment, then the edge of a cabinet. "Excuse me, just a . . . Please help yourself to more coffee."

Lorraine stood up, ready to assist her, but Elizabeth supported herself against the door leading into her bedroom and, before Lorraine could help her, had walked out, the door banging shut behind her.

Lorraine poured herself a cup of fresh coffee and then noticed a dark wet stain on the chaise longue where Elizabeth Caley had been reclining. Was she incontinent? She tried to recall the moment when she had noticed Mrs. Caley shaking or trembling—was it when she asked about who was to be the main beneficiary?

Phyllis entered, nodded curtly at Lorraine and uttered a quiet "Excuse me" before she slipped into the bedroom.

Lorraine waited about ten minutes. Phyllis came out of the bedroom and gave a brittle smile. "I'll just get some fresh tea. Would you care for more coffee?"

"No, thank you, I'm fine. Is Mrs. Caley all right?"

"Yes, she just gets tired very easily, so I hope you won't keep her much longer."

Phyllis quickly slipped one of the scatter pillows over the stained chaise longue and then began wheeling out the trolley. As she got to the door a shrill, high-pitched voice from the bedroom called out her name. *"Phyllis . . . Phyllis!"*

Lorraine watched as the woman scuttled back to the bedroom and disappeared from view. She could hear her whispered voice but was unable to make out what she was saying. Then Peters walked in, and before Lorraine could say a word he had wheeled the trolley out. She saw the intercom on the telephone flashing and again heard Phyllis's low voice. This time she crept closer to the bedroom door.

"I think you should. I can ask her to leave. Fine, yes, I'll tell her."

Lorraine only just made it back to her chair when Phyllis walked in from the bedroom. "Peters took out the trolley."

"I think, Mrs. Page, you had better leave because—"

"Get out, Phyllis." Elizabeth Caley now wore a different kimono and was tying the silk sash tightly around her waist. "I'll tell Mrs. Page when she can go, not you. Go on, get out. And I want some fresh tea and she wants whatever she was having."

"No, I'm fine, thank you. And if it is inconvenient for me to stay—"

"It isn't. Go on, Phyllis, go away."

Phyllis sighed and walked out.

"She can be so damn interfering." Elizabeth crossed to a glass-topped table crammed with photographs and ornaments. She opened a cigarette box and took out a long, thin cigarette. She flicked an onyx lighter, shaking it.

Lorraine took out her own and was just about to light Mrs. Caley's cigarette when the onyx lighter caught. She sucked in the smoke and tossed the lighter down onto a chair.

The beauty had gone, her perfectly made-up face like some kind of mask. *"I don't want you interfering!"* Her voice was shrill, and her hands, with the clawlike nails, tightened the kimono sash. Like a cheap whore, she let the cigarette dangle from her fuchsia-colored lips. "Mrs. Page, you do what I paid you for. And I will withdraw my offer of a bonus if you see Mrs. Juda Salina again. She knows nothing about my daughter." Elizabeth held up a sheet of her private notepaper. Scrawled in her own handwriting was her agreement to pay the bonus. "As I said, one million if you find my daughter. But if you talk with Juda Salina, I will not pay you a cent. Do you understand what I am saying? You won't get one more payment."

Elizabeth Caley's voice had changed. The elongated vowels were creeping in, as if she was reverting to her Louisiana accent. It fascinated Lorraine, and she knew that whatever Elizabeth Caley had taken in her bedroom was either cocaine, speed or some kind of stimulant because she was hyper—smoking, pacing, clutching continually at the belt of her kimono. "I need to trust you."

Lorraine folded the note. "You can, Mrs. Caley, you can trust me."

"Okay, okay, that's fine, that's good. Yes, that's good, I

need to trust, I need to, understand me? You understand me?''

''Yes, I understand.'' She didn't, she still didn't know what was going on, but just as she might have found out, the doors opened and Robert Caley walked in. He ignored Lorraine and went straight to his wife, seeming to wrap her in his arms.

''Come on, come and lie down now, sweetheart. Say good-bye to Mrs. Page.'' He kept his arms around her, steering her toward the bedroom. ''I think you had better leave, Mrs. Page.''

Lorraine was getting into her car when Robert Caley hurried out of the house. ''Mrs. Page.'' He had a vivid scratch mark down his right cheek.

''Yes,'' she said innocently.

''A moment, please, er, perhaps I was not as, er . . . honest as I should have been when we spoke yesterday.''

''I'm sorry?''

''I told you my wife could not speak to you, that she was indisposed, as a good PR agent would say. Well, you just saw what my wife's indisposition is. . . .''

Lorraine didn't let him off the hook but looked at him with as much innocence as she could muster. ''I'm sorry?''

He turned away, rubbing his head. ''My daughter's disappearance has obviously affected my wife deeply. I don't know what she has said to you but I think you should be aware that she can be very irrational and . . . Elizabeth has had, over the past few years, a drug-related problem mainly due to an old injury. . . . During the filming of *Santa Maria* a gallery collapsed on her and she suffered extensive injuries. The studio doctors made sure she would be on the set the following day by prescribing heavy painkillers and . . . er . . . well, she still suffers a great deal of pain, and over the years . . .''

Lorraine waited, watching him trying in every way to explain or excuse his wife's behavior.

''She is, I suppose, a sick woman, and with Anna Louise's disappearance . . . what I am trying to explain to you is that my wife has a dependency on these so-called painkillers. It is controlled, obviously, but now she is not using these drugs for any physical pain, just mental—"

"I understand."

"Good, because I would hate to have you misconstrue anything or, God forbid, report this to the press."

"I wouldn't do that."

"Good, thank you. It's just that I have been able to control her dependency with the help of her doctors, but sometimes if I am not here she . . ."

If he was lying he was good, because he seemed genuinely disturbed and caring.

"I do understand, Mr. Caley. This must be a very distressing time, not just for your wife, and obviously anything that is said to me, or anything I see, will remain strictly between us."

He turned away. "Just try and find out, Mrs. Page, if my daughter is dead or alive, because not knowing is destroying me, and killing my wife."

CHAPTER
5

Rooney lolled in Lorraine's chair behind her desk. The door buzzer went off, and both he and Rosie looked toward the door. Nick Bartello lounged in the doorway, gazing down at the doormat. He wore his thick black and unruly curly hair almost to his collar and he needed a shave.

He limped into the office. His crumpled denim shirt and torn jeans didn't detract from his immediate attraction. He was one of those guys you knew just by looking at him had a big case history. His limp wasn't bad; it just made his walk a bit lopsided.

"Hey, Nick, how you doin'?" bellowed Rooney.

"I'm fucked, I feel it an' look it. You got some coffee brewing?"

"Sure. Nick, this is Rosie, by the way."

"Hi, Rosie." Bartello slumped into her vacated chair. "Hey, man, did we tie one on last night or didn't we?"

"We did, Nick, we did."

Rosie started to brew some coffee as Nick pulled a crumpled note pad and bits of paper out of his pocket. "Okay, this is how the land lies. I know I only got handed the case when our top dicks gave it the thumbs down, maybe because they'd like to stick one up my ass. Like I said last night, I get fired if I don't get a result an' to date I got diddly-squat. And today, like ten minutes ago, Robert Caley is threatening the agency to get screwed unless we get some results."

Rosie returned to her desk. "Coffee is on." She hovered, and he gave her a marvelous smile.

"Thanks, sweetheart, make it strong and black." He turned back to Rooney, who grinned.

"Nick's being paid a grand a week plus expenses, Agnew is getting about five grand. They probably put out to Caley they got three of you workin', right, Nick?"

"Yeah, but in reality the main guys are on a new gig finding some bitch's ex-husband. They'll drag it out as long as possible, so basically I got the Caley case solo. Company don't wanna lose their five g's per week, I don't wanna lose my job."

Rooney cocked his head at Nick. "You tell 'em about us?"

Nick shrugged. "I didn't say nothin'. They know you're on the Caley payroll and, hey, Rosie, what about that coffee? This is a desperate man you're looking at."

Rooney snorted as Rosie checked the coffeemaker; it was just bubbling. She liked Nick Bartello, crude maybe but there was a lovable quality to him. That smile he had was a killer.

"Bill, I am prepared to split my fee, you gimme what you got and vice versa."

"But you got squat."

"Correct." Nick laughed. It was as good as his smile, a lovely chortling sound.

"So why should we pool with you? We're doing okay ourselves."

"Yeah, well, maybe I got a bit extra that bein' drunk didn't loosen out of me. You think I didn't know what you were up to?"

Again Rooney snorted; for all his easygoing manner Nick was nobody's fool. "It'd have to be somethin' if you want in with us."

Nick Bartello rubbed the stubble on his chin. "Well, maybe I just got somethin' that'd be worth wantin' to split that one million Mrs. Caley promised as a bonus."

Rosie looked at Rooney; he'd obviously been drunk enough to tell Bartello, and for a moment he looked abashed.

She banged down the mug of coffee. "Don't you think we should discuss this with Lorraine?"

Bartello laughed. "Look, I know her type, if Jack Lubrinski rated her, she's cool, she'd go for this. She's a drinker, right?"

"Not anymore," said Rosie angrily.

"Okay, maybe she isn't, but all I am suggesting is we pool info and you cut me in on the one million. I dump my job and everyone is happy and able to pay the mortgage with a few extras on the side."

Rooney gave Rosie a frown and then turned to Bartello. "Okay, I agree. Lorraine will, what you got?"

"We should wait for her to be in on this," Rosie interjected as she poured more coffee.

"Come on, you only got two weeks," Nick said.

Rosie glared at Rooney, knowing he must have told Nick everything about their case.

"You're already one day down and I been on this for a few weeks, so I got information that'll save valuable time."

"You got nothing," Rooney said flatly.

"Okay, I'll come clean, I got something I didn't tell you last night, but no way am I gonna spill the beans unless we shake hands."

Rooney looked at Rosie and she shrugged. "Okay, we got a deal."

The two men shook hands. Then Bartello sipped his coffee. "Right, try this for starters, I got from a very reliable source that Elizabeth Caley is into drugs in a big way. So maybe, just maybe, the disappearance of her precious daughter is connected."

"Fuckin' hell, is that true?" Rooney asked.

Nick sipped his coffee. "Yep, it's true, like she's got a habit of over three thousand dollars a week. I'm checkin' into dealers, I mean, she might owe some shit that got nasty with her daughter. I got the name of her doctor as well. He's like top drawer for the stars, but he's also known on the street for passing on risky prescriptions."

"Is it cocaine?"

"Apparently the lady will take whatever she can lay her pretty hands on. She's been in two drug rehab centers, the type with a lot of glamour." Nick passed over some crum-

pled xeroxed medical sheets, stuck together with a safety
pin. "Got those from a sweet-faced nurse for a hundred
bucks. By the look of the doc I'd say this angel could make
a few thousand bucks on the side passin' this kind of stuff
to the tabloids."

Rooney looked over Elizabeth Caley's medical sheet.
"Says the woman is called Maureen Sweeney."

"Yeah, well, she's not likely to put her real name on their
register, is she? But it's substance-abuse routine—"

Rooney finished reading and then passed it to Rosie.
"That it?"

Nick rocked back in his chair. "Well, for starters. What
you got?"

"Lorraine went to see this psychic," Rosie said, and got
a kick from Rooney.

Nick stared at Rosie. "Juda Salina?"

Rosie frowned. "Er, I'm not sure."

Rooney turned back to Nick. "She give you anythin'?"

Nick shook his head. "Nah, she's a fake."

Rooney nodded. "Yeah, I agree, that's why I never bothered seein' her. Dunno why Lorraine's so interested."

"So, what else you got?" Nick waited, saw Rooney
glance at Rosie, and then threw his arms up into the air.
"Holy shit, you lyin' bastard, you got diddly-squat."

"Rooney did *what*?" Lorraine yelled into the receiver of
her cell phone.

"Now calm down," Rosie said, quivering.

"*Calm down?* Are you crazy? You tell me that stupid fat
bastard has brought on some half-assed guy, not only *told*
him everything we got, but even offered him a share of the
million-dollar bonus and you tell me to *calm down*?"

"They were trading information," Rosie stammered.

"I don't give a shit what they were trading."

"But Nick's information was good—"

"It stinks. You think I didn't already know Elizabeth
Caley was stoned out of her mind? Jesus Christ, Rosie, I
knew it the first time we met her."

"Well, I didn't."

"You've never met her," Lorraine snapped.

"Well, maybe we can sort it out," Rosie said nervously.

"Oh, yeah, the bastard works for Agnew, doesn't he? Yes? Yes? *And don't you think he's gonna go straight back there and tell them?*"

"I don't think he will," Rosie said nervously.

"You don't think, period, and neither does that stupid son of a bitch Rooney. How could he do this?" Lorraine thumped the dashboard in frustration. "Where are they now, Rooney and this Bartello character?"

"I think they're at our place."

"I'll see you there."

It took Rosie about twenty minutes to walk from the office to the main Orange Grove intersection, then she headed down Marengo Drive. She saw the rented car parked at a bad angle, right under the NO PARKING sign. She also saw Rooney's car across the road from the apartment.

Rosie could hear them arguing from the street.

"I told you, Bill, that *I* was running this case, not you. *Me.*"

"Okay, okay, I'm sorry, but no way is Nick gonna report back to his agency."

"Oh yeah? You know that for sure, do you?" Lorraine was shouting.

"I fucking know Nick Bartello, an' I'm telling you he's on the level."

"Oh, you're telling me, are you?"

"*Yes!* An' if you'd just get off your box for a second and calm down—"

"Don't tell me to calm down, Bill, because I am steaming!"

Rosie banged in, but neither Rooney nor Lorraine even glanced at her. Rooney was red-faced and looked guilty.

"Nick'll be here any minute and we can talk this through."

"No way am I splitting this four ways!"

"Shouldn't we put this to the vote?" Rosie interjected, and then wished she hadn't.

Lorraine glared at her as she unbuttoned her blouse, heading for the bedroom. "When are you two gonna get it? This is my case, *mine*, no fucking votes, I make the decisions!"

Rosie was on a carb meal of pasta and salad and had actually lost four pounds since they started on the Caley case. She was surprised at how much better she felt, and decided that she really would cut out cupcakes and pastries between meals.

"What is this?" Lorraine asked, jabbing a spiral piece of pasta with her fork.

"It's just fusilli with garlic and tomato sauce. You don't like it, there's more for me and Bill."

Lorraine took a mouthful and grimaced. "My God, you went heavy on the garlic."

"You wanna cook, then the kitchen is all yours," Rosie said.

"So what time is this Nick guy arriving?"

"Anytime now," Rooney said.

Lorraine got up and fetched her notebook. "Okay, Juda Salina told me nothin' apart from the fact she was hired not by Robert Caley but by his wife. She wouldn't say much because of her so-called client confidentiality shit, and Mrs. Caley is prepared to withdraw the bonus if we make contact with her again. I'm gonna have to have another talk with Mrs. Movie Star, who is hooked on so-called painkillers. Robert Caley admitted his wife is hooked on drugs, and to my mind she seemed scared of her husband, or if not of him, maybe of me finding out she's a druggie. Anyway, he was pretty straight, but as a possible suspect his motive could be that if his daughter is out of the way, he stands to inherit the fortune because he's the main beneficiary. That's just supposition because Mrs. Caley said that they *both* named their daughter in their wills, so whoever should go first, bingo, the other's a hell of a sight richer." She looked up as Rosie lifted her plate, about to fork her leftovers onto her own. "Shit, Rosie, I haven't finished."

"Sorry, but I thought maybe the garlic—"

"No, it's great." Lorraine drew her plate closer and took a mouthful.

"He a suspect, then?" Rosie asked.

"Right now maybe, I need to know the financial—"

They turned as Nick Bartello opened the screen door and peered in, having overheard the last few lines of their conversation.

"I'd say it's a motive, the will. Elizabeth ex-movie star Caley is worth about fifty-five million dollars."

Rooney pulled his napkin out of his shirt collar and rose to his feet. "Hi, Nick, lemme introduce you, this is—"

"Lorraine Page of Page Investigations," Nick said, smiling, his hand outstretched. Lorraine did not take it, but lifted her glass of water.

"So you're Nick Bartello?"

"Yep, that's me."

"Have we met before?" Lorraine continued to eat.

"Nope, but you got one hell of a reputation."

"Have I?" Lorraine said.

Nick looked at Rooney, puzzled by her coldness. He drew up a chair and Rosie poured him a glass of water.

"What's your reputation, Nick?" Lorraine said sarcastically. "Or is 'the Limp' sufficient?"

"I'm a real lovable motherfucker, how's that for starters?" The smile that had smitten Rosie cut no ice with Lorraine. She'd come across a lot of Nick Bartellos, invalided out of the force or not, and he didn't even have that much of a limp.

"What division were you in?"

"Mine—well, at one time, when I was with the drug squad," Rooney said flatly.

"Really? So you an' Bill are old friends?"

"Yep, insomuch as I got a leg full of lead courtesy of this fat fucker sending me out on a domestic, but not informing me that the cokehead had a personal armory that'd make the U.S. artillery think twice before they sent in tanks."

Lorraine nodded. "So you reckon Bill here owes you?"

Suddenly Nick Bartello quit the jokes. "I got nobody but myself to blame, Mrs. Page, nobody owes me nothin'. What I did was my business and I got a pension to prove it. Bill and me are just old buddies."

Rooney, feeling very uneasy, thought he'd better get it in before Nick blurted it out. "Nick partnered Jack Lubrinski for a few weeks. When I moved I took Jack with me."

"Yeah, thank Christ, he was a mad fucker."

"My, my, you must have been some double act."

Nick hesitated. "Yeah, we were, Mrs. Page, for ten minutes."

She turned away. "And now you work for Agnew Investigation Agency? Lubrinski would be real proud of your progress.''

''Yes, ma'am, I most sincerely do work for them and maybe I know what Jack would think a whole lot better than you. Way I heard it, you were quite a lush.'' He lifted the glass to his lips, trying to figure her out. She was cool, he'd give her that, because she didn't rise to the cutting remark.

''So, have you informed Agnew about us?''

''No.''

''You haven't? Really? Not even tipped them off we've been offered a big bonus?''

''No, I'll tell them squat, especially not if I get a cut.''

''Does that mean you will tell them or you won't, Mr. Bartello?''

''Nick.''

''Okay, Nick, why should I believe a word you say?''

He put his glass down carefully. ''Because I'm just a hired hand and a cut of the bonus would mean the finger to Agnew and all who sail in her. What is it with you? You want a fucking résumé? Hasn't Bill told you we worked together?''

''Yes, but limping around is not what I'd call a really good recommendation, Mr. Bartello.''

''Fuck off! Hey, Billy, what is this? What's with this broad?'' He was angry, and his eyes glinted at Rooney as he tried to control his temper.

''She's the boss, Nick.''

He turned and stared at Lorraine. ''My, my, my, haven't you cleaned up your act. Lady Boss now, huh?''

''*My, my, my*, Mr. Bartello, haven't I just, so why don't we cut the bullshit and you tell me why we should cut you in if we find Anna Louise Caley? Because what Bill here got from you about Mrs. Caley I already knew, and it's not worth enough to give you a slice of our possible bonus.''

He leaned closer to her. ''Maybe, bright eyes, I got something else.''

''I'm all ears, Mr. Bartello. Can you match what we got?''

He smiled that killer smile again. ''Oh yeah, what you want me to do, give you a round of applause? So far you got shit—''

"You haven't come up with much better," she said, and she was warming to that smile. As Rooney and Rosie watched their interaction they could almost see the sparks between them.

Nick rocked back in his chair and took out a crumpled pack of Kool cigarettes. He flicked one out and flipped open his lighter, then gave Lorraine a hooded look. "You got Robert Caley earmarked as a suspect? Well, you might be close. Way I see it is, with his daughter dead, he's the main beneficiary, isn't he?"

"Yep, but he'd have to kill the old movie star to get his hands on her cash."

"Maybe he's planning it."

"Maybe he is."

"You think a guy who has bumped off his own daughter wouldn't go to those lengths? The top agencies were hired not by Mrs. Caley but by her husband, so the same reasoning could apply to her. She might want his dough." Nick waited for the comeback.

"Has he got any? Old newspaper articles say he was just selling real estate when they married."

"That was more'n twenty years ago. Now he's got a lot of real estate. I checked up on that too, so he's not short of cash. Anythin' else?"

Rosie and Rooney were out of it, watching Lorraine and Nick as they concentrated on each other across the table like chess players.

"If you only have Robert Caley as a possible suspect, then you are in a very small canoe, Mrs. Page, and you got no paddle."

"Why?"

"Because if I had done my own daughter in, I wouldn't hire half of LA's top private dicks, myself included. . . . But your problem is, if Caley is our guy, he *would* hire the world an' its mother but only if he was goddamned sure there was not a shred of evidence to prove his guilt. With me?"

"Not really."

He smiled. "Oh, I think you are, Mrs. Page, I think by now you have me figured out."

He was knocked sideways by her husky laugh. He was beginning to like everything he saw about Lorraine Page.

At the same time he would not give her any indication that he did. He reckoned this lady ate Nick Bartellos for lunch.

Rooney lit a cigarette, "So, we together on this or not?"

Nick looked at Lorraine and cocked his head to one side. "Up to the lady."

"What you got, Nick?" Lorraine asked bluntly.

He dug into his pocket and brought out a quarter. "Toss you for who goes first."

She took the coin. "Okay, heads or tails."

"Your call."

"Heads." She tossed it onto the table and prodded it. "I guess it's me first."

Nick watched her get up. He was aware of every line of her body as she seemed to uncoil from the chair. She lit a cigarette and inhaled deeply. He liked the way her mouth pursed up, how it hung half open as she let the smoke trail out.

"I think the girl is dead; trail is too quiet, no sightings, et cetera. Then again, people have been found after a much longer time on a few cases, but my gut feeling is Anna Louise is long dead."

Nick nodded. "But Bill said the million dollars still stands, dead or alive, right?"

Lorraine hesitated. "That mean you agree with me?"

"Yeah, I do, and Bill's of the same opinion."

Rooney looked at Lorraine. "Yeah, I think she's a goner."

Nick lifted his hand. "Chick's dead, we all agreed?"

"No," said Rosie. "I'm not sure she is dead—well, not until we've got more information. She could have just taken off. Kids of her age do. I mean, I know kids that have taken off and years later resurfaced. Maybe Anna Louise is one of them."

Lorraine met Nick Bartello's bright blue eyes and there was mutual understanding; they both believed Anna Louise was dead.

"Yeah, I guess you may be right, Rosie." Lorraine kept looking at Nick. "You talk to this Juda woman?"

Nick nodded. "There're a lot like her, all she needs is a fuckin' crystal ball and a tent. She's full of bullshit and the money rolls in 'cause we got a town full of desperate people.

I'd say she's been cleaning up with Elizabeth Caley, you know how these movie stars get into this kind of psycho stuff. Her rap about client confidentiality sucks, and it's bullshit about her being used by the cops for their inquiries, I checked it out. She more'n likely read it in the *National Enquirer*. From police records she never came up with anything they could use, she just got in the way and got publicity for herself.''

Rooney felt he should put in his two cents worth. "You want to see her again? Mrs. Caley doesn't want you to see her." He looked at Nick. "She told Lorraine she would withdraw the bonus—"

Lorraine interrupted. "We've gotta get to New Orleans. Robert Caley offered me a trip in his private jet. I'll accept. It'll give me more time to talk to him."

Nick smiled. "Oh yeah, gonna join the mile-high club, are you?"

"What's that supposed to mean?"

Nick ran his hands through his unruly mop of hair. "No offense, but he's a looker and . . . Come on, just a joke. Is this all you got so far?"

"If you and Bill here have talked it over, you know we got squat."

"Yeah, I hear that, but what are *you* holding out on?"

Lorraine laughed at him. "Who says I'm holding out, Nick?"

"Call it intuition, sweetheart. You got a gut feeling the girl is dead—what else is your gut saying?"

Lorraine sat down, drawing her chair close to him. "There is something going on in that palace the Caleys call home. Elizabeth Caley is scared, maybe of Robert Caley, I dunno."

"But you intend flying out on his private jet?"

"I intend to try."

Nick smiled at her again; it was too intimate and she turned away. He rested his hand on her arm. "Don't get uptight, he's a great-lookin' guy. If I was in your shoes, I'd try and get in his pants."

"For Chrissakes, get off my back."

"No, you do what you have to."

"What's that supposed to mean?" she snapped.

"If you can get information, fuck him. Like I said, if I was in your position, and a woman, I'd maybe do the same thing because the three of you haven't got much, and not a lot of time either. An' screwing the guy is just a way of cuttin' corners. However, that said, maybe I have—"

"Have what?" Rooney asked, leaning forward toward him.

Nick lit a cigarette from the butt of his last and rocked back in his chair. "Okay, is that it? All you got so far? So I guess it's my turn, right?"

"Right," said Lorraine, annoyed and yet slightly embarrassed by his innuendoes, because it was as if Nick Bartello had read her mind. Robert Caley *was* attractive to her. But he'd also hit the nail on the head on another matter—she, or Page Investigations, had little to go on so far. Maybe a few hunches, but she never mentioned those. "Well, we're waiting, Mr. Bartello," she said, cocking her head to one side mockingly. "I'm sure you must have so much more. You've been on the case awhile, so stop fucking around."

He took a drag on his cigarette and then slowly removed a crumpled mess of paper from the back pocket of his jeans. He carefully straightened out a couple of pages, taking his time. The edges were ragged, they looked like pages torn from a small notebook.

"I'll check my files, see if there's anything I can cross-reference." Nick grinned, indicating his scruffy bits of paper.

"Why not start with the drugs?" Rooney prompted. He felt tired and in need of a drink.

"Okay. I picked up a guy called Gerry Fisher 'bout ten years back. Anyway, he turned out to be married to one of the officers on the drug squad—not my team—but I kind of got a hint to go easy, you know the game. I let Fisher off the hook, so he owed me, right? And then I pick the bastard up again eighteen months later, still running drugs, and I say, 'I'm gonna bust you, an' I don't care if you're married to the president.' Fisher was a kind of middle man. He scored from his main dealer and then did backdoor deals with a society-type doctor called Hayleden with a lotta high-profile patients who didn't want straight prescribed drugs. He didn't know who he was dealing for, he'd just take the orders, then deliver to the office. In fact, he said he rarely even saw Hayleden. I was gonna do somethin' about it, but then I got a leg full of lead an' was invalided out. So Fisher—''

''What's this got to do with the case? Get to the point, Nick!'' Rooney banged the table.

''Okay, okay, right. Now, before I was even working on this Caley thing, I was doin' a search for another movie star's kid. His family reckoned he was dealin' because he was loaded all the time, and they hired the company to tail him and sort him out, you know, before the law did, put a bit of a squeeze on him. And bingo, I meet up with Fisher who still owes me, right? So he tips me off that this kid is scoring from him an' dealin' to college kids.''

''Anna Louise Caley?'' Lorraine asked, suddenly interested.

''No, wait a second. I do the business, put the hand on the kid's collar, et cetera, and we cop a nice fee for the agency. Next thing Fisher's scared shitless, thinks it's gonna be an arrest, but the family don't want that, just a rap over their asshole kid's knuckles. So Fisher bargains with me, telling me that he'll give more info on a lotta high-profile people if I don't hand him over to the law. I tell Fisher to fuck off, and to cut a long story short . . .''

They all moaned but Nick held up his hand. ''Hey, hey, wait, I'm getting there. I get pulled on the Caley investigation, so I use Fisher, ask him if the kid was dealin' to Anna Louise. He said he'd never heard of her and didn't recognize the photo, so I say she is Elizabeth Caley's daughter, used to be Elizabeth Seal, the movie star.''

Nick squinted at his bits of paper. ''Now it starts gettin' good. Fisher ain't dealin' to Anna Louise Caley but her mama! Goes like this, one night Fisher gets an emergency call from Doc Hayleden, who's skiing in Aspen or someplace, and asks Fisher to deliver some quality goods to his office ASAP, says a nurse will pay him.'' He listed on his fingers. ''Items required: cocaine, amphetamines, some crack and a load of downers—sleeping tabs, Temazepam— like it's obvious somebody is havin' a party. So he takes the goods to the office, gets paid the usual way, then he goes back to his car. He thinks to himself, Why not cut out the middle man? Fisher waits, and about half an hour later, a thin woman drives up. He sees her go into the office, then come out fast and get back into her car. He follows, 'cause he knows the office is closed, so this chick hadda be the buyer, right? And she leads him straight to the Caley residence. She parks by the security gates and he takes his chance. He goes up to the car, and she freaks and says she doesn't know what he's talking about, she was simply collecting a prescription, and if he doesn't get away from her car she'll call the police. She drives in. . . . He thinks maybe he got it wrong, but he gets a few more emergency calls and sees the same woman collecting, so he figures he was right to start with. He stops her again, and this time she is more than freaked, but he calms her down and tells her he's not the law, just—"

"You talking about Phyllis Collins?" asked Rosie.

"Yep, only now she's scared that he's gonna squeal on her, squeal on her movie star, so she agrees from then on they will deal direct. Phyllis would call him, place the order, meet up in cafés or wherever. So the Doc loses his cut, Fisher is raking it in because he starts doin' the same thing to a few more of the Doc's customers. Then Phyllis tells him no more deals, Mrs. Caley's gone into rehab, nice earner down the drain. But somebody in that house still has a real bad habit—according to Fisher, several thousand dollars a week habit."

"My God, Elizabeth Caley?" Rooney murmured.

Nick shrugged. "Next, an' this may or may not be connected, my friend Fisher—"

"Can I see him?" Lorraine asked.

"Be tough. He was found dead three weeks ago. He's still on the slab, they've got a backlog. Probably back on heroin, had a needle in his hand."

"Shit," Lorraine said as she poured herself more coffee.

Nick turned to the next crumpled page. "So, we know the secretary scored for her ladyship. I'd say that's a good area we can work on, or work on Phyllis because she must know a lot more than she's admitting to. You said you figured Mrs. Caley's still using drugs, so maybe she got another dealer or is dealing with the Doc again. At the same time, we don't want to rock the boat because Mrs. Caley is the one offering the one-million bonus.''

"Did this guy Fisher ever mention meeting or dealing with Robert Caley?'' Rooney asked.

"Nope.'' Nick stubbed out his cigarette.

"Is that it?'' Lorraine asked.

Nick shrugged. "Phyllis should be pushed a bit—we could have a possible drug connection. Maybe Fisher's dealers got pissed, or the Doc, so that's all got to be checked out. Next, and this *is* good . . .''

Nick studied his notes, chewing his lower lip as he flicked a glance at Lorraine. "Right, Robert Caley. He may be cute-looking, sweetheart, but to me he's our suspect number one, and if not him, his associates.''

"Because of the will?'' Rooney asked.

"That's a good opener. We don't know if he's intending to bump off his drug-addled wife in a few months' time, but with no daughter, and *if* Elizabeth Caley dies, he gets the lot. And believe you me, it's a fucking fortune. Like I said before, we're talkin' in the region of fifty million. That mansion they live in is worth twelve million alone, and they've got big property in New Orleans.''

"But this is just supposition, right?'' said Lorraine.

"Yeah, but so is everything until we get results, and when I said earlier that our Mr. Caley is not short of cash, it's not exactly true. You know what business Robert Caley is into?''

"Real estate,'' said Rooney impatiently.

"Yeah, right, businesses both here and in Louisiana, and he's making a lotta dough.'' Nick paused for effect. "Well, he was.''

Rooney and Lorraine glanced at each other. This area they had not yet checked into, so they waited as Nick prodded his crumpled notes.

"Robert Caley and his partners are trying to open a casino in New Orleans, right? Gambling is big business, it brings in the dough, and they've also sold it to the city on the basis that it will jack up the economy and give everybody out of work a job. But somehow, they're being fucked over—suddenly, there's zoning objections, architecture objections, bad-for-family-life objections, and Robert Caley still hasn't got a casino license, while another local consortium has had time to crawl out from under a rock and say it ought to go to them. The reason I put my money on Mr. Caley as numero uno suspect is that he's losing credibility, and every delay makes it more likely that his partners will pull out. If he doesn't get the green light for this casino soon, he's gonna go down millions, because he bought the proposed site.''

Nick beamed at them; he knew he'd opened up one hell of a can of worms. He continued, ''So we got quite a few possible motives: one is the missing daughter could have been kidnapped and connected to a drug dealer; two, she was snatched as a threat to Caley to pull out of the casino deal, maybe just removed as a warning. Caley is mixing with very heavy hitters, and as far as I can make out, it's the wife bringing in all the private dicks not Caley—''

''He didn't want us hired, but he sort of implied it was because he figured we were hopeless,'' said Rooney, draining his coffee cup.

''Lemme wind down, Bill. My number three theory is Caley needs money for the casino, and bad. You know what the politics is like down there—if Caley had a big enough sweetener to slip into the right civic-minded vest pocket, his problems would all just melt out of his way. So he knocks off his daughter, next comes the wife, and we got one very rich and happy guy with a license to print money for the rest of his life.'' Nick folded his scruffy notes and stuck them back into his pocket. ''Well, that's what I got. May I make a suggestion? I think Lorraine or even Rosie should see what we can pump out of Phyllis Collins, I'll do the Doc's drugs scene and, Bill, you see if you can dig up more on the Caley casino property deal.''

''Sounds okay to me,'' Rooney said, easing his sweaty tie up to the equally sweaty collar of his shirt.

Nick lit another cigarette and crossed to the front door. ''Thanks for the coffee, Rosie, and so, partners, I'll be seeing you. . . .'' He hesitated and looked at Lorraine. ''Seeing that Mr. Smoothie has offered you a ride in his private jet, take it, because I don't know about you but I figure he's our prime target.''

Rooney pushed back his chair. ''Yeah, I'm outta here too.

I'll see what I can get from my old department. We all call in, right?''

"I'm looking forward to it," Rosie said, smiling.

"To what?" Lorraine asked irritably.

"New Orleans, I've never been there. And with expenses we can book into a real nice hotel. And I can interview Phyllis Collins, she'll be at the meeting tomorrow."

"See you," Rooney said, already at the door.

" 'Bye, y'all," Nick called.

Lorraine looked up. "Just one thing, Mr. Bartello. This is my case, I run the show, so after today you don't tell me what to do."

"Hey, that's cool."

Lorraine caught the glance between Nick and Rooney as they left. It really infuriated her, and she was angry at herself for coming out with such a crass statement. She should have played her hand far better. She carried the dirty dishes across to the sink.

"Maybe I'll talk to Phyllis, Rosie."

Rosie ran water in the sink and couldn't hide her disappointment.

Lorraine put her arm around her shoulders. "You can see her too at the meeting—two heads are better than one, Rosie, okay?"

CHAPTER
6

Lorraine got on the freeway. Rosie had already contacted Phyllis Collins and she had agreed to see Lorraine, but not at the house. Phyllis eventually suggested they have coffee in the plaza on Rodeo Drive, as she had to be there to collect something for Mrs. Caley from the Georgette Klinger shop.

"What's that?" Lorraine asked.

"I dunno, maybe a boutique, I didn't ask."

"Okay, if you need me, I'll have the cell phone with me."

"Right, over and out."

Lorraine checked her watch, parking the car at a meter on Rodeo Drive. She had over an hour to kill, so she decided she'd have her hair trimmed and chose a salon at random, asking if her hair could be done right away.

"Okay, Lorraine, gonna make you a new woman."

Lorraine watched as Noël, the flamboyant African-American hairdresser, cut and snipped, looked at her with critical eyes, cut and snipped some more. She noticed on the shelf below the mirror some white tubes, the name Georgette Klinger printed down the side.

"What is that stuff?"

He looked up. "Oh, those are the real expensive treatments, they have a shop farther up the Drive. Some of our customers"—he made a sweeping gesture with his scissors—"swear by it."

• • •

At two-forty-five, armed with Noël's card, she walked out.
She still had fifteen minutes before she was to meet Phyllis,
so she walked down Rodeo until she got to the Georgette
Klinger shop, peeked in, and then stepped back to admire
herself in the window. The cut was good, tapered to the
nape of her neck and long at the front. He'd made one side
much longer, the scar side, and she liked the way it hid half
her face when she leaned forward. In fact, she liked her new
image. She was so busy admiring herself that she didn't see
Phyllis parking on the opposite side of the road, didn't see
her continue on to another parked car, a metallic green
stretch Lincoln with black tinted windows, and get into the
backseat.

"Hi, I'm supposed to meet a friend, collecting something
for Mrs. Elizabeth Caley."

Lorraine's confidence in her new look faltered slightly as
the elegant Frenchwoman behind the counter swished back
her waist-length blond hair.

"I am zo zorry, who?"

"Mrs. Elizabeth Caley."

"No, I am zo zorry but I am not expecteeng anyone,
unless . . . one moment, pleeze." She checked a leather-
bound book. Lorraine busied herself looking over the various Georgette Klinger serums and lotions. "No, Mrs. Caley
is waiting for some of our sunscreen creams, but they have
not arrived yet, not until next week. I am zo zorry."

Lorraine asked for shampoo and conditioner and had a
near-heart attack when the bill was rung up. A second assistant walked in from the back of the shop, eager to help
sell more products.

"Theeze lady is a friend of Mrs. Caley's, she said she
was expecting a delivery—"

The second woman smiled at Lorraine. "I called two days
ago to apologize for the delay. The sun creams won't be
here until the end of the month."

Lorraine collected her goods in their neat white plastic
bag and left the shop. She checked her watch, worried she
was going to be late for Phyllis.

Juda's heavy breathing and sweet perfume made Phyllis feel
sick; she disliked the woman intensely. "I am afraid Mrs.

Caley's husband has put his foot down, there is nothing I can do. Please do not call the house again. Mrs. Caley said she would contact you at a later date."

"I see—well, it's up to her. But you know she can't make appointments and just keep canceling like this. I make the time for her and I have a lot of clients."

Phyllis handed Juda an envelope. "I think this will suffice . . ."

Juda took the envelope. "Please tell my dear Elizabeth not to give up hope. I still feel a strong presence of Anna Louise, tell her not to give up hope."

"I will."

Juda nodded, passing Phyllis a small square package, wrapped in brown paper. As Phyllis reached for the door, she said, "Perhaps Mr. Caley is going away and Elizabeth can see me?"

"I am sure Mrs. Caley will call you. I must go . . ."

Phyllis got out of the car. The driver half turned toward the backseat; he was only about twenty, with deep olive skin, and he wore a white shirt open at the neck. He watched as Juda opened the envelope and began to count hundred-dollar bills, a lot of them.

"Where to now, Aunt Juda?"

Juda glanced up, quickly stuffing the money into a soft leather purse. "Get me back home, Raoul, then go do some grocery shopping. And keep your eyes to the front or you'll be on the next bus."

He chuckled. "Nobody messes with you, huh?"

She leaned back, staring out of the dark window. "You said it, sugar, an' when they do, they get real sorry. Wait, stop a second, I just seen someone."

Lorraine hurried along Rodeo toward the plaza. She saw Phyllis get out of the Lincoln, saw her waiting at the roadside, but by the time she had actually crossed the road, she was already ahead of Lorraine.

Lorraine presumed the Lincoln was Mrs. Caley's, the chauffeur dropping Phyllis off for their meeting, so she didn't give it a second glance. But Juda leaned forward in her seat as the nose of the Lincoln eased out from the parking bay. She was sure the blonde was the woman who had called on her, and by the look of it she was tailing Phyllis.

"Lorraine," Juda said softly.

"What? We stopping or moving on?"

"Drive," Juda snapped.

"A client?" Raoul asked.

"No, she's no client that one, she's a private investigator." She repeated the name Lorraine to herself and then clasped her fat sweating ringed hands together. Her chest heaved as her breath caught in her throat in loud rasps.

"You got trouble?" Raoul asked.

"No, I not got trouble, but that lady is gonna have it, bad trouble."

He didn't joke anymore. When she said stuff like that, when her big, false-eyelashed eyes stared sightlessly as if she was seeing through and beyond him, his aunt scared him like his mama could—but then they were sisters. His hands clenched the wheel as he took another furtive look at Juda, then at the side-view mirror, wondering if he would catch a glimpse of the woman his aunt had referred to. But Lorraine had disappeared.

Lorraine caught her breath, joining Phyllis just as she sat down at one of the small white tables outside the coffee shop.

"Sorry I'm a bit late, but I wasn't sure exactly which shop." Lorraine smiled. "Would you like coffee?"

"Yes, please, a cappuccino. No need to go to the counter—a waiter'll bring it, it's not self-service." Phyllis spoke fast, nervously. She couldn't fail to see Lorraine's plastic bag from Georgette Klinger.

"I don't think you've been very truthful, Phyllis."

Two pink spots appeared on Phyllis's cheeks and her mouth tightened. "I'm sorry, but I can't imagine why you think that. You've had your hair cut."

"Yes, I had time to spare, and I also went to this store." She held up the bag and smiled.

"Ah, yes, I was going to collect something for Mrs. Caley."

"But it's not in until the end of the month. I know."

"Yes, very irritating, waste of a journey. Still, I am free

to see you, and you did want to see me, Rosie said, rather urgently.''

A waiter hovered and Lorraine ordered the cappuccinos. Phyllis's right foot tapped nervously against the chair.

"But you knew they wouldn't have Mrs. Caley's sunscreen, they called you. Well, so the assistant told me.''

"Good heavens, did you ask them? Well, really, I think that was all rather unnecessary.''

"Maybe, but since I was there—''

"If that is what you term being dishonest, then I am sorry. I was going to call in just to make sure it hadn't arrived. I also have other things to collect, so I wasn't lying, and I rather resent your implying that I have been. Mrs. Caley suffers so much from the sun, she cannot sit out in it at all. . . .''

Tap-tap went her foot, the table rocking a fraction, but Phyllis seemed unaware of it, constantly looking around, fiddling with her blouse collar. Lorraine let her stew for a while. The two pink spots on Phyllis's cheeks faded before she spoke again. "Your hair is very nice, good cut, it's all in the cut really, isn't it?''

"Yes, I just got lucky, I went to the salon further up the drive.''

"St. Julian's?'' Phyllis asked. Her face reminded Lorraine of a bird's pecking, her thin nose sharp as she twisted her head and kept up the nervous kicking of the table. "My, you are taking your work to rather silly lengths.''

"I'm sorry?''

"That's Mrs. Caley's salon. Well, it was—they come to her now. But Anna Louise used it, she was always very particular about her hair.''

"Really? Then it was just a coincidence, I walked in off the street. As I said, I got here early.''

The coffee arrived, with tiny flaky pastries. Lorraine smiled her thanks to the waiter.

"How long has Mrs. Caley been a drug addict?''

Phyllis's pink spots returned with a vengeance. She stirred her coffee, her foot still tapping, and now her head twitched. "I have no idea what you are talking about.''

"Yes, you do, and that's why I wanted to see you.''

"I really do not see that whatever medication Mrs. Caley

requires is any business of yours or Rosie's.''

"Medication? Come on, Phyllis, I know she's on uppers, downers, cocaine, speed, you name it. Even her husband admitted—''

"Mr. Caley told you?'' Phyllis said, astonished.

"Yes, but he implied they were simply painkillers for an old injury and that Mrs. Caley had, well, become dependent on them. But speed, cocaine, et cetera, are not what I would call painkillers, and when I last saw her she seemed very hyper. She was also very disturbed.''

Phyllis's jaw was working overtime now. "I think in the terrible circumstances, Mrs. Page, anyone would be disturbed. Her daughter is missing, she could obviously be dead—''

"Yes, I know, Phyllis. That's why I have to investigate every possible motive.''

"You mean you suspect Mrs. Caley?''

"No, but I need to know who she was getting her drugs from because there may be a connection.''

"There isn't, I assure you.''

"Your assuring me, Phyllis, is not good enough, I'm afraid. And if you care about finding out the truth, then you'll stop this silly game. You could be arrested for procuring drugs, you know that, don't you? You see, I know how it used to work, Phyllis. The friendly, sympathetic doctor—he could be arrested for dealing. I know you collected from his office, just as I know you later dealt directly with a man called Gerry Fisher.''

"Oh, God,'' Phyllis was shaking now. "Does Mr. Caley know you are talking to me?''

"No, this is a private discussion between you and me, it won't go any further. But I need to know if anyone got nasty or made threats to Mrs. Caley. A three-thousand-dollar-a-week habit is big money for some, it gets to be competitive, understand me? And I know you cut out the doctor at one point, so he lost his share.''

"It's not three—''

"Come on, Phyllis, we're not here to worry about a few hundred dollars this way or that.''

"It's five—''

"What?''

"Sometimes a bit less, and obviously I would say a lot of that is for . . . confidentiality. I mean, if it was ever to get out—she is very famous, sits on a lot of charitable boards—and then of course there is Mr. Caley to consider. If it was ever to be made public, it would be dreadful for him."

"He doesn't use drugs of any kind?"

"No, no, not at all, he's very much against them. He has tried every means possible to persuade Elizabeth to stop. She's been in so many clinics, but no sooner is she released . . . it starts again, and with this tragedy it's made things a lot worse. She's in a stupor for most of the day, and then when Mr. Caley comes home she starts taking anything that'll wake her up, so then of course she can't sleep and the spiral begins. It's a wonder she hasn't killed herself yet. She must have the constitution of a horse, the abuse her poor body takes, but she still manages to put on a good show when it is needed. Nobody would know, and that's part of the problem. She's very sly, very devious, and will swear on a Bible that she was clean if you asked. . . ."

Lorraine drained her cappuccino. Phyllis had hardly touched hers, but she was not so agitated now, her hands folded in her lap.

"How we've managed to keep it secret for so long I don't know, I really don't, but at least I haven't got to meet that dreadful man."

"So who do you deal from now, Phyllis?"

"Please, I don't deal, Mrs. Page. When Mrs. Caley went to a rehabilitation center, I told Mr. Fisher his services were no longer required. Then it started again, I picked up her prescriptions from the doctor's office again, just something to help her sleep and relieve the anxiety. She's not using the other things, that is the truth. His license should be revoked, but if he didn't get what she wanted she would go elsewhere."

Lorraine nodded, really needing a cigarette. "So you never contacted any other street dealer, just the doctor?"

"Yes."

"So no one else knows, nobody is putting any pressure on her to use their goods?"

"If they are, I don't know about it."

"Mr. Caley knows you are getting the stuff for her, does he?"

Phyllis chewed her lips. "He knows about the painkillers."

"Do they sleep together?"

Phyllis looked shocked. "I cannot discuss that, really."

"Do they share the same bedroom?"

"They have different suites. What they do in their own time I really have no notion of. He is, to my mind, very caring and patient with her, and she can be extremely difficult, you know."

"What about Anna Louise?"

"I'm sorry?"

Lorraine sighed. "Phyllis, did Anna Louise know about her mother's addiction to drugs?"

Phyllis looked away. "Perhaps, well, it is hard not to if you live in the same house. Mrs. Caley has extreme mood swings and sometimes she is quite irrational."

"Did they argue a lot?"

Phyllis nodded.

"Did Anna Louise use drugs?"

"No, no, she hated them, she wouldn't even smoke a cigarette, hardly ever drank. In fact, sometimes she seemed more like the mother than the child, which is why this is so awful for Mrs. Caley."

Lorraine picked at her tiny pastry. "The day they left for New Orleans, what state was Mrs. Caley in?"

"She . . . she had taken something. She was very tense, always made the excuse she hated flying, that she needed something to calm down her nerves, but she was . . . I think the expression is 'wired.' She kept on changing her mind about whether or not to go, but we got her packed and ready, and by the time Mr. Caley returned, she was quite calm."

"How was Anna Louise?"

"Well, she hated it when Mrs. Caley got anxious, and I think at one point she said she didn't want to go. But when Mr. Caley came home they talked for a while, and then they all left."

"So the last time you spoke to Anna Louise was from the plane?"

"Yes, that was the last time. She asked me to pick up a dress, but you know this."

"And she sounded okay, not stressed out?"

"She sounded relaxed and happy, as did Mrs. Caley."

"So you also spoke to Mrs. Caley?"

"Yes, she was making sure I'd get the dress sent to the house, and then I was to give it to the pilot who would return for it and take it on to New Orleans." Phyllis suddenly bowed her head. "It was a lovely dress, and . . . she never got to wear it. You think she's dead, don't you?"

Lorraine signaled to the waiter. "I am not in any position to say that, not until I know more. Do you?"

"Pardon?"

"Do you think she's dead, Phyllis?"

She nodded, twisting her hands. "Yes, she would not do this to her mother, and especially not to her father—she was a very thoughtful girl. You know, if she was going to be late she'd call home, and when she went away she would call her father two or three times a day."

Lorraine settled the bill for the cappuccinos; she could have bought a full meal in an Orange Grove coffee shop for what she paid. She was rising to her feet, preparing to leave, when Phyllis spoke again.

"It was very hard when she had friends to stay." She had sipped her cold cappuccino now and had a froth stain on her upper lip. "She was protective about Mrs. Caley, afraid anyone would find out. You know, in this day and age it's so difficult to trust people not to sell to the tabloids. Poor Anna Louise was worried about how it would affect her mother; it seems so incongruous that she should be the one to make such headlines, in every paper too. And you know something extraordinary, sick really . . . after fifteen years, during which she could not get a phone call returned—well, not for serious work, maybe television, but she would never do television parts—she's suddenly been offered numerous scripts from some of the big studios. And one, it's hard to believe, even hinted that they may make a film about Anna's disappearance and they wanted to discuss Elizabeth playing herself. Disgusting, just disgusting. So it is understandable why she is so dependent, isn't it? Even if it is very hard on me."

"Thank you for agreeing to see me and for being so honest, Phyllis. Obviously everything we have said was in confidence. And if there is anything, anything at all that you think may help me, will you call me? Or Rosie."

"Yes, yes, I will and . . . well, thank you for coffee."

Lorraine hurried out of the plaza onto Rodeo, leaving Phyllis still sipping her cappuccino. She was relieved that Lorraine had wanted to discuss only the drug situation. She had been afraid she knew more, and she could not, would not have talked about Juda Salina—she daren't. She dabbed her lips with her napkin and looked around. Not until she saw Lorraine actually disappear from view did she get up and go into the café to use the public telephone. She gave a quick, furtive look around as she punched in the number, and waited.

"The Caley residence."

"Peters, will you check on Mrs. Caley? And will you say to her that everything is all right and she has no need to worry. I will be home in half an hour or so."

Lorraine sat in her car. It was sweltering, the seat burning her backside, so she opened her windows all around. The cell phone buzzed and hissed.

"Rosie, can you call Robert Caley? He'll probably be at his office, so try there and ask if he'll see me."

"Sorry, hang on a second." Rosie was munching a carrot, her cheeks bulging. She swallowed quickly. "Sorry, let me put Bill on, he wants a word. While you're talking to him I'll call Caley, okay?"

Rooney picked up the phone. "I've been trying to check out this casino deal."

"Yeah, what you got?"

"Not a lot but I got what I could. Caley heads a consortium made up of him, a couple of local moneymen and a casino outfit from out of state. They're ready to back the deal to the tune of around two hundred and fifty million."

"What?"

"Yep, lot of dough, but Caley will take the major slice of ownership because he laid out the initial payment for the land, massive site near the riverfront. The complex will have a hotel and a lot of high-class shops as well as the casino."

"So what's Caley's problem?" Lorraine interjected.

"Well, there's a number of little hitches. One, he's been wanting to set this deal up for five years, but unfortunately the state of Louisiana hasn't been too quick about getting legalized gambling on the statute book, while their good neighbors next door have been straight off the blocks—a lot of the gambling revenue for the whole of the southeast already has a happy home up the coast in Mississippi, and maybe it ain't gonna move. Second, there's some old-money elements in the city that are dragging out some case about rezoning the area, saying it's prohibited by federal law—load of fucking horseshit—but they could hold things up quite a while. And third, get this, there's some very fucking weird provisions in this gambling statute—the city gets to choose the guy who develops the site, but the state gets to say who runs the casino. Everybody has been thinking it would be Caley and his friends, as soon as they can get this legal mess straightened out about the site, but lately people are getting to wondering what's holding things up. Some other rich guys down there seem to have gotten the message that maybe somebody else might just get the license to run the show, so now Caley's got a rival consortium to worry about, call themselves Doubloons. One of his backers has dropped out until he has the operating license in his pocket, and the other may walk too."

"You got the backers' names?"

"Yep, two guys named Bodenhamer and Dulay. They're big-time owners of major corporations, Bodenhamer construction, Dulay liquor. They both stand to make a bundle out of the casino, not only out of the gambling but by selling the stuff they got to sell, and as yet they don't stand to lose a cent. Caley's in a lot deeper, though."

"What do you mean?" Lorraine asked, trying to assimilate all the information.

"Caley paid for the land leases on the site. If he doesn't get the license he's stuck with them. This is all common knowledge in New Orleans, but I'd get a lot more from being there."

"It might be common knowledge, Bill, but how come this isn't detailed in any of the reports your pal Sharkey xeroxed for us?"

"Maybe he was looking out for his own ass, I dunno, or maybe they didn't think it was important."

"No? Well, I think it is. You're sayin', in so many words, Robert Caley's got to get the casino deal?"

"Sure. He's been cash-poor for years—he liquidated a lot of his assets, sold off properties in LA and Louisiana. If the deal is greenlighted he stands to make megabucks. So maybe Nick was right about Caley. He's up against very tough opposition, mainly from this other consortium, but the door's wide open now for anyone else to walk in."

"We got to get as much as we can and fast. I'll see if Caley will give me further details. Rosie contacted him yet?"

Rosie took the phone. "Yes, be there about four-thirty. He's warned security to expect you."

Lorraine tucked the phone under her chin and started up the engine. "Okay, I'm on my way."

Rosie replaced the receiver and bent down to start removing tinfoil dishes from a plastic bag of takeout, spreading a newspaper as tablecloth on Lorraine's desk.

"It's Japanese, Bill, nothing fattening—that's prawn, that's salmon and that's fish, raw fish. It doesn't taste so good first time, but give it a good chew and a dip in the sauce. Then we got grated radish and broccoli."

"No thanks, I'll get a hamburger."

"This is better for you—at least just try it."

"No thanks, I'll wait."

Rosie laid out all the dishes, then speared a piece of fish on a fork and carried it to Rooney.

"Just have a taste—it's good, healthy, and if you don't mind me saying so, that suit'd fit better if you lost a few pounds."

Rooney made a face, but opened his mouth and chewed, while Rosie leaned over him, waiting. He swallowed, nodding his head.

"Not bad, bit like Chinese, isn't it?" Rosie prepared two platefuls as Bill hovered over the dishes, picking up a prawn and nibbling it.

"No rice? Didn't you get any rice?"

"No, you can't eat rice with protein because it's a carbohydrate and you can't mix them. Next meal we can have a huge plate of pasta, as much pasta as you can eat, but no protein.''

"That's interesting. Where you getting all this from?''

"Lorraine, she put me onto it.''

Bill sat down in front of his plate, tucking a paper napkin in his collar. "She knows a thing or two, does Lorraine.''

Rosie nodded, pouring some spring water into two cups. "She always impresses me, sort of takes me by surprise. She's a funny woman, though, and I don't mean to bitch about her behind her back, but sometimes she can have a sharp tongue, and then other times she's as soft as a baby.''

Rooney had his mouth full, or he would have contradicted her vehemently, because in all the years he had known Lorraine Page he had never seen a side of her character that could be described as soft as a baby, but he said nothing, chewing in unison with Rosie. Even if what he was eating did taste like rubber and he would have preferred a huge hamburger special with sausage and bacon on the side, he liked the fact that he was not sitting at home alone. French fries he could get on his way home, sweet company he could not.

A young man with slicked-back hair, wearing a gray designer suit and floral tie, led Lorraine into Robert Caley's office. He tapped at an immense floor-to-ceiling door, a green light blinked on an intercom by the side and the floral tie opened the door. He peered in, Lorraine just behind him.

"It's Mrs. Page, Mr. Caley.''

He turned with a whiter-than-white capped-tooth smile. "Please . . .''

The office was a vast windowed room, with blinds cutting out the afternoon sunlight. An enormous black desk with black glass top dominated the room. The carpet was gray thick-pile, and soft leather bucket chairs formed a semicircle in front of the black monster. Expensive prints lined the walls, but there were no filing cabinets, no stray tables. Only a bronze sculpture of what looked like an elongated man on a plinth pointing to heaven was placed discreetly in a corner.

Robert Caley was speaking on one of the eight telephones lining his desk. The high back of his chair was facing Lorraine, so she couldn't see him, but his assistant indicated one of the bucket seats.

"Fine, Bel Air, see you there." Caley eased around to face Lorraine as he replaced the phone. "Excuse me one moment, Mrs. Page."

He looked at his assistant. "Call my five o'clock appointment and move him to six—I have to go out to the Bel Air for a while. And grovel some more to Dulay's office, Mark, he's really pissed off."

"Yes, sir. Do you want any refreshments?"

"No, unless . . ." Caley turned his attention to Lorraine.

"Nothing for me, thank you."

Caley gave a curt nod and the doors were closed silently. "You wanted to see me, Mrs. Page?"

He swiveled from side to side, and, not waiting for her to answer, tapped the phone he had used with his forefinger. "That was trouble."

"I'm sorry, if it is inconvenient . . ."

Caley smiled glumly and leaned on his elbows, cupping his chin in his hands. "It is, but maybe I need something to take my mind off the fact I might go belly up. You want to see something?" He sprang out of his chair and pressed a button at the side of the desk. Lorraine turned as part of the gray wall to her right slid back to display a large architect's drawing. "This is what might do me in. Come here, let me show you." He showed her the proposed casino site, hotels and shopping precinct, and told her about his plans, much as Rooney had outlined. "Looks good, huh? As I owned the entire site, I would of course be the main shareholder. But I didn't count on the state dawdling around for fucking years while they commission fifty reports on how gambling corrupts widows and orphans and makes you go blind, before they get around to deciding that actually it's an emerging area of the leisure industry, a worthy new area of economic development, which provides employment, economic stimulation, just what the city needs. They realized all of that first time around up the coast. Five years of my life go into this plan; and my partners, who unlike myself have not laid out so much as a dollar, are getting cold feet, while a gang of other guys around town decide they might like a piece of the pie and get themselves into a little huddle too. So . . .''

Lorraine looked over the model. "So if your partners pull out, what are you left with?''

"A lot of land, and no money. So you see, I need those partners, without them I couldn't build myself a shed. That's how deep in this mess I am." He clicked off the screen, pulled back the wall panel across the model and returned to his desk.

Lorraine sat back in her chair. "Are your partners dumping you?''

"Yep, one gone and one just about ready to. He called in the last hour—asked me what I propose to do to ensure this goes through, when he's the one pushing the governor's fucking golf cart for him every weekend. It's only so long you can string people like Lloyd Dulay—the brewery magnate, if you don't know who he is. When you have his kind of money, there are a lot of people like me dangling deals, and you know these megarich bastards are always intent on anything that's gonna make them even richer, they just don't want to wait.''

"You mind if I smoke?'' she asked.

"No, go ahead.''

He opened a drawer and placed an exquisite onyx-and-gold box on the table. She took a cigarette, and he clicked open the gold Cartier lighter from inside the box for her. As she inhaled she looked up and met his eyes. They stared at each other for a brief moment, then he let the cigarette-box lid close with a snap. He passed across a black glass ashtray. "I need a drink.''

She watched him cross the thick-pile carpet to yet another hidden section in the pale gray walls. Another panel slid aside to reveal a large bar. She could hear the clink of ice against the glass and her heart began to beat rapidly. Was he going to offer her a drink? More important, would she be able to refuse it?

Lorraine was there for a specific reason—to discover if Caley was financially in as much trouble over the casino deal as Rooney had surmised. Yet he had, without any prompting, told her. Either he was a consummate actor and had preempted her reason for being there, or he was being honest. He had confused her and she was at a loss as to how she should continue the meeting.

"This office is a bit crass, isn't it?" he chuckled. "When I first took it over, I used to go down the corridor and down a back flight of stairs to the john. I didn't know which button to press for my own private bathroom. Fucking nightmare of gray on gray, but it's only rented." He placed a long crystal glass of sparkling water with ice and lemon on the desk. He had a small square cut-crystal glass with brandy.

"Thank you," she said softly.

Again he met her eyes, and this time he smiled. "You didn't think I'd offer you alcohol, did you?"

"For a moment I did."

"I wouldn't do that to you, I know you have a problem. I should, I live with a woman who has not one but a number. But then I think we have already discussed my wife's situation."

She nodded, wondering if one of the gray walls also slid back to reveal a bed. If it did and he revealed it, she wouldn't know how she would react. She found him even more attractive today, liking everything about him; his hands were strong and tanned, his suit more casual than the floral-tied assistant's, and he wore simple loafers. Everything about him was casual, apart from his blue eyes: they were as dangerous as his smile.

"As I told you, I have to go to New Orleans—tomorrow maybe. You want to come with me?"

"Yes." She sipped the ice water.

"I guess you want to see what you can dig up there." He laughed.

" 'Dig' being the operative word. I might be digging ditches for the rest of my life if I don't pull this deal off."

"But surely your wife has a considerable amount—"

He interrupted her. "Let me make this very clear, Mrs. Page. My wife's money is hers, I make my own. We have separate bank accounts, always have, and in case you haven't unearthed it yet, I signed a prenuptial agreement. What is my wife's is hers, what is mine is mine, for what it's worth."

"If she dies . . ." Lorraine said quietly.

He glared. "What?"

"You are her main beneficiary, aren't you?"

"No, Mrs. Page, my daughter is—"

"But if Anna Louise is dead?" she said, keeping her voice soft.

"I hadn't thought of that. Dear God, is that the reason you are here? What the fuck do you think I am, huh? We are talking about my daughter, what do you think I have done, killed her so that I can get my wife's money? Do you think I'm making plans to kill my wife, is that it? What do you think I am?" He shook his head. "Jesus Christ, that is so sick."

"I'm not here for that."

"Well, I'm glad to hear it, because if you were I'd throw you out of here myself."

"I'm looking for motives for Anna Louise's disappearance, Mr. Caley. Maybe you've given me one."

He glared again. "You seriously think I would be capable of murdering my own daughter?"

"I don't know you, Mr. Caley, but as an investigator I have to look at all possibilities. You are, as far as I can see and in view of what you have just told me, the only person that, like it or not, would benefit from Anna Louise's death."

"And I'd benefit a whole lot more if my wife also died, yes?"

"Yes."

"So you think I am arranging to kill her? Is that what you came here to discuss? To find out by what means I intend to murder my wife? Well, in your capacity as a so-called investigator, maybe you could give me some tips."

"I am not, Mr. Caley, a so-called investigator."

"You weren't much of a cop."

She stood up and leaned toward him across the desk. "You have no idea what I was and I am not prepared to sit here and be insulted."

"But you can insult me? Anna Louise is my daughter— now you get out of this office and do the job my wife hired you to do, because I did not kill my daughter and I have no intention of murdering my wife."

Lorraine coughed, trying as best as she could to appear

nonchalant. "Perhaps one of your business associates may
have a connection."

He sat back in his chair and stared at her, then swiveled
around so she could not see his face. His voice became
deeper, quieter. "Go on, Mrs. Page. . . ."

"Well, you've just made it perfectly clear; there's a lot
of money to be made, there's you and a rival consortium,
and things would be a lot easier for them if you were just
suddenly to lose interest in this project. Plus their business,
right? So there is a possibility that your daughter may have
been part of some kind of plot."

"Like what?" he snapped.

"Well, someone may have kidnapped her to persuade you
not to go ahead with your project. You own the land, and
your partners haven't put in a cent so far . . ."

He remained silent for a moment and then slowly swiveled around in his chair to face her. "Go on."

"It's just a theory, but someone may have been considering using her to make you back off. Has anyone approached you directly, warned you off personally?"

He stared, then shrugged. "No, no, they have not. You
mean hold her for a ransom?"

She nodded. "Has anyone offered just to buy out your
land?"

He began to toy with his empty glass, moving it slowly
along the desktop. "No, but tell me this: why, if what you
are saying was true, was there no ransom note, no request
for a meeting, no contact whatsoever? The Doubloons consortium has so much muscle that I do not believe for one
moment they would resort to kidnapping Anna Louise as a
means of threatening me."

"But they may have used some unsavory goons to pick
her up, maybe hold her, and it went wrong."

"You mean they killed her?"

There was that awful pain in his eyes, and she had to look
away. "Possibly, which would explain why there was no
note or no contact with you. All the publicity surrounding
your daughter's disappearance must have had an adverse
effect on the deal."

Caley pushed his chair back and stood up. "But they are
successful enough at blocking any advancement of my de-

velopment without my daughter, they didn't need her. And if I continue to lose my partners, then—''

"You've considered this, haven't you?"

He nodded, sighing. "Yes, briefly, but then I dismissed it because I truthfully do not think they would sink so low."

"When millions are at stake you would be surprised how low people are prepared to sink, Mr. Caley. So, if you had even considered the possibility, then you must understand why I must also look into it and why I will need to know who all the other parties are, specifically your competitors. Then by a process of elimination—''

"You won't get anywhere with this so-called elimination."

"Try me," Lorraine challenged.

"Okay, you want to talk to the opposition, yes?"

"Obviously."

"Well, Mrs. Page, I think you will come up against the same brick wall that every other agent has met with, but far be it from me to dissuade you. In fact, I will do everything I can to assist you, as I have done throughout the inquiries. Now if you'll excuse me . . .''

"Did the other agents and the LA police question you about these people?"

He strode toward the huge doors. "Of course, and they also at one time suspected me."

"I see."

"No, Mrs. Page, I don't think you do. I had expected, after we had talked, that you would have believed I could not have harmed a hair on my daughter's head, let alone be the type of man who would put his wife through such torment. You have suggested nothing new, nothing that I have not been subjected to before. Now excuse me, Mark will give you all the details you require."

He walked out, closing the door behind him. A few moments later, the floral-tied assistant appeared with a thick file and crossed the office to Lorraine.

"Mr. Caley has asked me to give you these files, but please understand this is private and confidential information. You may make notes but not remove the file from the office. Mr. Caley's secretary will give you every assistance if you need anything clarified—''

"So I remain in here?" Lorraine took the files.

"Yes, Mr. Caley suggests you use his office so that if you require any assistance, or anything xeroxed that we agree to be released, his secretary or I will be on hand to help you. The file contains plans for the proposed casino development and—" Again he was interrupted as Lorraine moved around Robert Caley's desk.

"Fine, thank you. I'm sorry, I didn't actually catch your name."

"Mark Riley, I am Mr. Caley's personal assistant."

She sat at Caley's desk, opening the file. "Thanks, Mark. If you could just show me what button I press to talk to you or—"

"Margaret is on line five, I am on line two."

She smiled. "Thank you very much, Mark."

He hesitated at the half-open door. "I'll leave you to it."

"Did you know Anna Louise, Mark?"

He looked surprised. "Yes, of course."

"Did she come here a lot?"

"No, just occasionally for lunch with Mr. Caley."

"Did you ever see her socially?"

"No. I met her only when she came to see Mr. Caley."

Lorraine was left alone in the vast, cool office, sitting in Robert Caley's soft leather chair. She opened the file and then reached for her purse to get her notebook. She found it, but no pen, so she looked down the side of the desk to rows of black steel-fronted drawers discreetly built into each side, to try to find one. There were no handles. She tried pushing at them, trying to fathom how they opened, but they all seemed to be locked. She frowned and looked over the vast desktop and saw that it had a built-in square directly in front of the chair. She pushed at it but nothing happened. Then she noticed a small black raised button, so she pressed it and the inlaid section eased back. The opening housed a blotter, a row of pens and pencils, notebooks, memo pads, paper clips, all in neat compartments, and two photograph frames facedown. She turned one over and it was of Anna Louise; the other was of Elizabeth Caley.

Sitting at his desk in his office, Mark Riley watched Lorraine on a small monitor. He turned to a dark-haired woman who was typing on her word processor.

"Mrs. Page is having a good snoop around the office."

Margaret looked at him. "Yes, I noticed, but I've secured all the drawers so she can't poke her nose any further."

Mark looked over the date book. There was no record of the new appointment. "Who's he meeting right now?"

"Who do you think?" Margaret said, half raising an eyebrow.

Saffron Dulay was late—she always was—and Robert Caley checked his watch again, missing her entrance. But no one else did—she was hard to miss. Saffron moved gracefully between the tables, led by a maître d', who bowed and gestured toward Caley's discreet table in one of the alcoves of the Bel Air garden restaurant. Pausing just a moment to smile and acknowledge a number of people she knew, Saffron gave only a slight incline of her beautiful head, behaving as if she were royalty, and the maître d' was treating her as such.

Caley immediately rose to his feet as Saffron joined him, bending her head toward him for a kiss on the cheek.

"Robert," she said huskily, "I'm sorry, I know I am late, please don't get up."

He did, pulling her chair out for her as she sat down with the passing swans at her back. He knew she liked to get a good view of the place and invariably knew anyone who was anyone. Saffron was rich, the only daughter of a brewery magnate, sole heiress to billions. She wore her wealth in that covert, simple way that only the truly rich can. Almost six feet tall, the sheer simplicity of her white negligée-type dress enhanced her height, while her glowing golden tan was set off by slim gold sandals and a million dollars' worth of solitaire diamonds in her ears. As she eased her slender body onto the cushioned seat, she removed her only accessory—her gold-rimmed shades.

"Hi, how you doing?"

Saffron was the wrong side of forty but one would be hard-pressed to estimate her age; her confidence in herself, boosted by her millions and her obvious physical perfection, gave the appearance of youth. Four marriages and endless lovers had not managed to dent her innocent girlish act, one she had perfected better than any hopeful starlet half her age.

"You got any news about that little girl o' yours?" she asked in her Southern drawl.

"No."

She reached over and touched Caley's hand lightly. "It must be s'ah hard."

"Yeah, it is."

Her eyes flicked around the tables, then back to Caley. "You always choose this place."

"Yep, I can smoke, outdoors." He signaled to a waiter. "I've already ordered you your usual—I take it your tastes haven't changed."

She laughed, her eyes still darting around the restaurant, and all he could think about was Lorraine Page. She was as blond, almost as tall, but so flawed, so real a woman in comparison with Saffron. He no longer wanted to fuck Saffron; that had been over a long time ago. He had never disliked her before, but now he did. Perhaps Lorraine attracted him because she was so direct. He would like to screw Lorraine, and just thinking about it made him smile.

"You got one hell of a smile, Robert Caley," Saffron said softly.

"Why, thank you . . ."

She cupped her chin in her hands. "What you want, darlin'? You runnin' short of funds again?"

The waiter brought her an elaborately decorated cocktail and another whiskey sour for him. It irritated him that she knew instinctively why he had asked to see her, that he had to play out the game. She sipped a tiny drop from the glass and then placed it on the table; she wouldn't touch it again, she never did.

"Ah'll never understand why you don't get that movie-star wife of yours to finance you."

"I don't want money from my wife."

"No, but you sure as hell need it, an' you'll take it from elsewhere." She leaned back, only now giving him her undivided attention. Being rich, she knew how to handle anyone about to put the touch on her—she was an old hand at it.

"I don't want a cent from you, darlin', but I do need you

to talk to your daddy. No need to go into details, you know we're into this development deal together, but he's hinted he might pull out and I know you can bring him around, so—''

''Ah already talked to him, darlin', soon as Ah put down the phone from you he called me. In fact, we must have been playin' telephone games—he calls you, you call me, then he calls me. He may be more than seventy years old, but, man, he is a wily old bastard. Said he wants me to go to some function back home, you know, always keepin' tabs on me and it drives me crazy. Since Mama died, he is trying to get me to go live back home, find a nice steady man and produce a grandchild.''

''It's understandable, you're his only daughter. So did he mention my project at all?''

''Why don't we drive around awhile to discuss this?'' She smiled sweetly, not waiting for him to reply, then tossed her napkin aside. Caley half rose from his seat, watched her get up, then finished his drink, knowing she would be table-hopping for a good fifteen minutes. He paid the check, and knew he was now about to pay even more. As he threaded his way through the tables he checked his watch; he had only forty-five minutes before his next meeting.

The driver could not see or be seen through the dark-tinted glass partition. Saffron's limo had a wide couch section, a television and bar, plus a fax machine, telephone and a lap-top. Caley sat opposite her; she was lying across a deep-cushioned seat, unwrapping a peppermint.

''You want a sweet?''

''Nope.''

''No calories.''

He opened the bar, filled a crystal tumbler with ice cubes and topped it up with water. He looked at Saffron, holding up the glass, but she shook her head.

''I have to be back at my office by six.''

''Fine, we'll drive nice and slow . . . just the way Ah like it.''

She eased one shoulder strap down, then the next, and wriggled out of her white dress. She wore no underwear and was totally unself-conscious as she carefully folded her dress and spread her long tanned legs wide. She wore only her thin-strapped gold sandals. Caley watched her as he sipped the water and then drained the glass, leaving just the ice cubes. He jangled the glass for a moment, and she giggled.

"Well, well, it's been awhile since Ah was cubed up, and you know how Ah like it . . ."

He didn't even loosen his tie or remove his jacket; he didn't need to. Saffron didn't want to be held in his arms and wouldn't want to have her discreet makeup disturbed by frantic kisses. She knew exactly what she wanted, and so did he. She began to massage herself, cupping her neat breasts in her tapering fingers until the nipples hardened. He knelt between her legs. With his right hand he stroked her nipples with an ice cube, making her moan softly, as his left hand began slowly to caress her thighs, inching up gradually between her legs until his thumb rubbed her, knowing the exact spot to arouse her, and she spread her legs wider and wider, eyes closed.

"Oh, yes, yes, Ah like that, Ah like that."

Slowly he let the ice cube slither down from her breasts, making her shiver, and her body arched as he adeptly inserted the melting ice cube high up into her vagina. He quickly reached for the rest of the cubes still in his glass and pressed in one after another until he could feel the cold ice with his thumb.

"Oh, God, yesss, yess . . ." She bent forward, drawing his head down as he began to suck and lick her clitoris. She came quickly, letting out a scream, but still held his face between her legs with her hands. "Ah wanna come three times, make me scream three times, baby, do it, do it."

Nick breezed into the office eating a hamburger, and Rosie wrinkled her nose.

"That's full of cholesterol, not good for you, Nick."

"I know, but I like it."

He sat in Lorraine's chair and swiveled around, stuffing the remains of the burger into his mouth as Rooney walked in.

"Caught you, you've had a hamburger, I can smell it," Rooney said accusingly to Rosie.

"I have not," Rosie replied self-righteously, "but he

has." She pointed to Nick, who was wiping his mouth on his shirt cuff.

"What the hell is this place? A health clinic?"

Rooney sat on the edge of the desk, amused, looking at Rosie.

"Just a private joke. What you got—anything or nothing?"

Nick dug in his pockets, bringing out his scraps of notes.

"I got a line into Elizabeth Caley's doctor, pal of mine is sniffing around for me, and . . ." They waited as he thumbed his way through his crumpled papers.

"Fisher's girlfriend is rapping to a pal of mine on the drug squad, and . . ." Nick continued.

"And?" prompted Rooney. Nick ruffled his already untidy curls.

"We got to move fast—word is they're going to arrest Doc Hayleden for dealin', so I'd kind of like to get to him before the bust. Maybe nice if her ladyship came with me, you know, see how a real pro works . . ."

Rosie said she'd call Lorraine on the cell phone, and was about to dial when Nick held up his hand.

"What is it with her? She got a problem with me?"

Rooney shrugged, looking across at Rosie.

"No, why do you ask?"

Nick cocked his head to one side. "Well, I'm working my butt off, but I don't want to get screwed."

"By Lorraine?" Rosie asked.

"Yeah, I know she's edgy about me being on this gig, so . . . I'm asking you straight: I'm in, aren't I?"

"Of course you are," Rosie replied, and Rooney jabbed a finger into Nick's chest.

"Listen, we cut this four ways and that's it."

Nick grinned. "Okay, just needed it confirmed. And hey, is she screwing anyone? Not metaphorically. Just wondered."

Rooney laughed. "You don't stand a chance, Nick. Does he, Rosie?"

She hunched her shoulders. "I dunno, but do you want me to contact her or not? She's over at Caley's office."

Nick grinned again. "Sure, you call her, but don't you say a thing—about anything personal."

• • •

Lorraine remained at Caley's office desk, making notes, monitored by Mark and Margaret, but she called for no assistance from either of them. She sat at the big desk, plowing methodically through the thick file, knowing it had been checked over by all the other investigators, but she could not afford to skim just in case she missed something. By six o'clock she had half filled her notebook, and she sat back in the big leather chair.

Robert Caley's finances were stretched to the limit. It appeared that all his money was tied up in properties, which still made him a rich man but one with no ready cash flow. As he had told her, he had banked everything on the casino deal, and if it did not come off, he would still have to pay off the outstanding monies due on the land. If his partners pulled out, he would lose millions and would be forced to sell properties fast and thus at a loss in order to pay his debts. Lorraine had no access to information about Elizabeth Caley's fortune, and as far as she could ascertain, the Caleys did not have any form of joint finances or joint accounts.

Mark looked at the monitor and saw Lorraine stand up and stretch her arms above her head, yawning. He watched her close the file and begin to pack away her things.

"I think she's through," he said to Margaret. She was talking to Robert Caley's chauffeur, who had just got back to the office.

Margaret pursed her lips. "I hope he's not going to be late. Mario left him at the Bel Air. That bitch Saffron Dulay—dunno why he even sees her."

Mark shrugged as he pointed to the video screen. "It's called being fucking rich, Margaret! Mrs. Page is leaving. Can you blast the air-conditioning on in there? She's been smoking . . ."

Mark hovered as Lorraine walked out of the office carrying the file. "You all finished?"

"Yes, thank you. Is Mr. Caley here?"

"No, I'm sorry, he's at a meeting and then he has another one at six o'clock. Do you need to speak to him?"

"Er, well, not really, just thank him for me, would you?" She passed him the file. "And, oh, just one thing. Mrs.

Caley, she has nothing to do with the business here, am I correct?''

''Yes.''

''I see, and she has not financed any of the real estate companies?''

''Not to my knowledge,'' he said tartly.

''They have no joint interests?''

''None that I am aware of.'' He carried the file to a cabinet. Lorraine followed, standing just behind him.

''She is very wealthy, then, in her own right?''

''Yes, I believe so, but I work for Mr. Caley. I have never been privy to Mrs. Caley's private finances.''

''But you must have some idea of what she's worth. I mean, is it a few million, one million or a sort of clutch of millions?'' she smiled jokingly but he would not give an inch.

''I really have no idea, perhaps you should discuss it with Mrs. Caley herself.'' He turned as Margaret approached with Mario. ''Mario, will you walk Mrs. Page to the elevator? I'll inform security she's leaving. This is Mr. Caley's chauffeur, Mario, Mrs. Page.''

Mario nodded and headed for the door, holding it open for her. They went down in the elevator together.

''I thought Mr. Caley was still out.''

''He is, ma'am.''

''Are you employed by both Mr. and Mrs. Caley?''

''Yes, ma'am, eight years now.''

He gestured for her to go to the security desk and she unpinned her badge, handing it over. He then opened the main doors of the building for her.

She hesitated, ''Did you know Anna Louise?''

''Yes, ma'am, I sometimes drove her and Mrs. Caley.''

''Did you drive her to any specific place? Particularly just before her disappearance, anywhere unusual?''

''No, ma'am, I only used to drive them on shopping trips, sometimes to a social event, but Miss Caley had her own car. She was a really cute girl, always polite, always treated me with respect.''

''And Mrs. Caley?''

''I'm sorry?'' He looked away.

''Did Mrs. Caley treat you with respect?''

"Yes, ma'am." He still held the door open, but she got the feeling he wanted to get rid of her.

"Did you drive Mrs. Caley to and from her doctor's at all?"

"No, ma'am."

"Really? So you only drove Mrs. Caley infrequently? Just shopping trips, a few social events?"

"Yes, ma'am, that is correct."

"Did you ever take Mrs. Caley to a Mrs. Juda Salina's apartment over on Doheny?"

"I did sometimes take them."

"Them?"

"Ah, well, yes, Miss Anna Louise went to see Mrs. Salina a few times. Mrs. Salina used to come by the house, but Mr. Caley didn't like it, so then they used to go to her place."

"Did Anna Louise ever go by herself to Juda Salina?"

"Er, maybe, once or twice."

"Immediately before she disappeared?"

"I don't want any trouble, please. Mr. Caley doesn't know I took them. He didn't like her, and I don't believe in all that stuff."

"So Anna Louise went to Mrs. Salina's just before they left for New Orleans, yes?"

He nodded his head.

"You're from New Orleans, aren't you, Mario?"

He seemed to be very uneasy, and the sweat stood out on his forehead. "Yes, ma'am, a number of the Caleys' employees used to work for her family, and sometimes we go back there with them, when they're gonna stay awhile."

"If I need to talk with you, Mario—"

"You can call me at the house or here, Mrs. Page. I live in, I got an apartment over the garages."

Mario looked at the security section, then back at Lorraine. He took out his card and wrote on the back. "That's my cell phone, you can always get me on that, but you got to know I got nothing to say about Mrs. Caley, or Mr. Caley. They're fine people and I am real upset about Miss Anna Louise, just like everyone that knows them."

Lorraine slipped the card into her pocket and smiled. "I'm sure it must be a very distressing time for everyone. Thank you, Mario."

She walked out of the building and headed toward the parking lot. She saw the white stretch limo parked by the security gate. Robert Caley was bending into the passenger side, with his back to her. Lorraine hurried along the neat pathway and took a shortcut across the grass, ducking under the white barrier. She was within feet of Robert Caley, who seemed angry.

"All I'm asking is for you to see if he'll give me time. Jesus, you play games, you know that?"

"Me? *You* play the games, Caley, you get what you deserve. What you want me to do? Tell my daddy that you'll go down on him?"

"I'll tell your daddy what his fucking bitch of a daughter gets up to—"

"Hi, I was just leaving," Lorraine said from directly behind him. He whipped around, the door of the limo ajar, and she could see the still-naked Saffron lying on the backseat. He slammed the door shut; the car backed away from the barrier and did a U-turn.

"That was some meeting," Lorraine said, smiling.

He covered fast, shrugging his shoulders. "Yeah, but sometimes old partners can push their luck."

She could see a small muscle at the side of his jaw twitching and she continued to smile. "Thank you for letting me use your office."

"Anytime." His hands were clenched at his sides, and although she knew he was trying hard to be civil, his eyes gave him away. "If you'll excuse me, I have an appointment."

"Sure, if I need to speak to you again . . ."

He was walking away. "You know where I am, Mrs. Page."

As Lorraine turned around to go to her car, the security guard tipped his hand to his hat and headed toward her.

"Evening, Mrs. Page." He walked with her to her car. He even took her keys to unlock the car for her, holding the door wide. Everyone in the place seemed overpolite.

"Must have been up in the eighties today," he remarked, making conversation, waiting for his tip. She passed him five bucks.

"That was a nice limo."

"The big white one?"

"Yeah, with the Louisiana plates. Whose is it?"

"Used to come by a lot but not lately—business associate of Mr. Caley's." He shut the car door, tapping the roof with his hand. She wondered if she gave him another five bucks whether he would recall whose limo it was, and she lowered the window, keeping a fixed smile in place.

He lifted the security pole for her to drive through. As she came along-side him, she let the smile drop.

"Who owns the limo, pal? Save me time checking it out at the station. Yeah, that's right, I'm a cop, we come in all shapes and sizes now."

He hesitated. "Miss Saffron Dulay, she's Lloyd Dulay's daughter—he uses her limo when he's here in LA."

"Thank you," Lorraine said crisply, driving out through the barrier. So that was the business meeting. Well, maybe it was; Lloyd Dulay, Robert Caley had told her, was one of the casino partners, the brewery magnate.

Lorraine was heading back toward Hollywood when Nick called her on the cell phone.

"Hi, honey. If we wanna talk to Caley's doc, we got to make it quick. I got tipped off that he's gonna get busted, so meet me there as soon as you can make it."

"Okay, I'll head straight over there, I've just got to make one call on the way." She punched out the office number.

"Hi, Bill, anythin'?"

"Nope," he answered. "How you doin'?"

"I had a couple of hours at Caley's office, I got some names to check out. He gave me access to the casino-deal file, which makes interesting reading. Will you dig up what you can about Lloyd Dulay's daughter? She's in Hollywood, name's Saffron Dulay. I think Robert Caley's got a thing going with her, so can you check her out?"

"Sure, but, Lorraine—"

She knew he was about to hassle her about wasting time in LA. "I got to go now, I'm on my way to meet Nick."

The line went dead. Rosie leaned over Rooney's shoulder, reading his notes. "Who's Saffron . . . what's the name?"

"Dulay, daughter of one of the guys on the casino deal—rich, rich family. Lorraine seems to think Robert Caley's screwing her, so I'll check her out, start ringing around the social columns and gossip sheets.''

Rosie nodded. "I'll do that, if you like.''

"Okay, thanks. You smell nice, you wearin' perfume?''

Rosie beamed. "It's gardenia.''

Nick watched Lorraine drive into the parking lot adjacent to the doctor's office on Santa Monica and Bedford, get out and head toward the building. He liked the way she walked, with long, easy strides. A raunchy woman, he thought to himself, *all* woman. Even with her blond hair all ruffled and her suit crumpled, she looked good to him. He'd always liked leggy, tough blondes, and Lorraine was a natural, kind of coordinated. He couldn't help smiling, intuitively guessing she was also raunchy in bed.

"What's so funny?'' she snapped.

"Nothin', but you look like you want to sock somebody. You in a raw mood, are you?''

"Yeah,'' but she was smiling when she answered. Nick Bartello had that ability to put you at your ease immediately.

He gave her that great smile of his. "Okay, this is what's going down. You wanna sit in my Jeep? I'm in the Doc's parking space. He's inside, by the way, but he's also gonna be *inside* inside sooner than he knows.''

They crossed to a beat-up Jeep Cherokee; even the seats were torn and shredded.

"Holy shit, Nick, where'd you get this?''

"Engine's good an' it was cheap. My dog screwed up the seats.'' He whistled, and a weird long-haired head shot up from the backseat.

"This is Tiger. Tiger, meet Lorraine Page, of Page Investigations.''

The dog, part German shepherd and part sheepdog or maybe wolfhound, was as unkempt-looking as its owner, its freaky pale blue eyes like Nick's.

"Found him in a trash can two years ago, he's a great guard dog but he craps everywhere, so he kinda lives in the Jeep.''

"Yeah, I can see that.'' Lorraine looked over the disgusting Jeep's seats; a food bowl, a water bowl and an old blanket, along with Tiger, occupied the entire backseat. As

Lorraine sat inside and shut the door, Tiger gave a low, rumbling growl.

"Hey, back off, this is my partner."

Tiger settled down, his head resting on his master's shoulder as Nick tapped out a cigarette from a squashed pack of Kools.

"Remember the Fisher guy I told you about? My now deceased informant?"

Lorraine nodded.

"Well, I made some more inquiries. Autopsy report revealed it wasn't a heroin OD but a blood clot, caused by injecting Temazepam, that caused death. Kind of makes sense because he'd said the last time I met him he wasn't using, but I just presumed he'd got back on the smack. His type usually does. This doctor is sellin' prescriptions like it's going out of fashion and he's still supplying Temazepam to Elizabeth Caley. But if we want to go in there, let me do the talking. We won't have long because Fisher's girlfriend has been rapping to the cops—they picked her up a couple of nights ago. Don't ever accuse me of not movin' my ass, I been at this since early morning. Anyway, I know they're gonna bust him any second, so if we need a bit of a lever to make him talk we can use Fisher."

"Okay, let's go talk to the guy."

The office was like a luxurious lounge, deep sofas, drapes and coffee tables, while Dr. Hayleden, with his rimless glasses, pristine suit, coiffured hair and facework, resembled something from a waxworks.

"I cannot discuss any patient. Unless, of course, he or she is privy to the discussion or you have a legal, written consent form."

Lorraine said nothing. Nick remained silent.

"So I think that concludes our interview."

"Not quite," Nick said softly.

"Oh, I think so. You walk in off the street, you say you are a private investigation company, you ask questions about one of my patients, and obviously one that the media know only too well, and expect me—"

"To cut the bullshit," said Nick quietly, "I know you have been prescribing Elizabeth Caley not just painkilling drugs but sleeping tablets, mild tranquilizers, right? And over a long period of time—only she's got enough to tranquilize a fucking elephant."

"I don't like your insinuations, Mr. Bartello."

"Quite honestly, Doc, I don't give a fuck. I know nobody, no matter how much of an insomniac they may be, who requires per week the bulk load of Temazepam you have been prescribing for Elizabeth Caley. Enough to melt down the tabs and inject six or seven times daily. Now, we're not talking the usual prescription-sized orders here, I mean two hundred a time. The reason I know this is a friend of mine was also dealing for you, a Mr. Fisher. He and his pals were breaking into warehouses at chemical plants and delivering to your door. I know and you know, Doc, anybody doing that amount of drugs is heading for thrombosis, like our pal Mr. Fisher. He is dead, you know that?"

Dr. Hayleden stared hard at Nick, trying not to show that he knew exactly what he was talking about. But they'd got to him, they could feel it. The sweat was breaking out on his forehead and his eyes widened in panic. Lorraine kicked Nick's ankle lightly—no way did they want to frighten him too much.

Lorraine leaned forward. "We're not from the drug squad, this is a private investigation. All we need to know is if Robert Caley is aware of what his wife is hooked on."

"I don't know of any patient on my books called Fisher." Dr. Hayleden was sweating profusely, his perfect hairweave now damp around the edges, his lips dried out as he constantly flicked his tongue from corner to corner of his mouth. "You must understand, if a patient insists on misusing prescribed drugs there is little I can do about it."

Nick got up. "If a doc continues to prescribe drugs knowing the dangers, I'd say he was in shit up to his armpits. Why don't you answer the question? Better still, tell us if Robert Caley has ever picked up one of your little sweetie bags for his wife in person."

Fifteen minutes later Nick and Lorraine knew that Elizabeth Caley was sometimes ordering over a thousand tabs a week and that Hayleden, never having met Robert Caley, had no reason to believe he was in any way aware of his wife's drug abuse. Mrs. Caley's personal assistant had on occasion collected the tablets. Anna Louise Caley had never at any time been to his office.

By the time Nick and Lorraine had driven back to Pasadena, the LA drug squad had arrested Hayleden. He was to be charged with the selling of prescriptions and illegal drugs, would probably get off with just a fine, and be struck off the medical board. But his type just moved on and started up again in another state. Elizabeth Caley, using an assumed name, was only one of his many clients. Her real name would probably never even be linked to the case.

Over dinner back at the apartment, Nick remained adamant that Robert Caley was still their main suspect. Rooney listened as Nick and Lorraine filled him and Rosie in on their session with the doctor. The consensus was that they should now begin work in New Orleans. Only Lorraine held back, not satisfied that Robert Caley was their number one suspect. The others felt she was becoming obsessive with the Juda Salina scenario, and she insisted she still needed to talk with Phyllis again and have yet another session with both Elizabeth and Robert Caley.

Nick threw up his hands in agitation. "Why the fuck are you wasting time, sweetheart? It's Caley, he's got the motive."

Rooney nodded in agreement. "Yeah, we got to prove it, though, Nick."

Nick wound some spaghetti around his fork and looked at Lorraine. "You give us reasons why we don't go for him, push him hard."

"I honestly don't have one, just a gut feeling."

"You mean you want to get into his pants," Nick said, laughing.

Lorraine sprang up. "Fuck you, that isn't true. All I'm saying is, if he was involved in his own daughter's disappearance, why give me access to his private files, why give me reasons or a fucking big motive? He's not hiding anything—on the contrary."

Nick poured a beer, which he had brought himself because he knew neither Lorraine nor Rosie drank. "Hey! Let's just hold it there. A guilty man is bound to want you to know before you find out. Rules of the game, Lorraine, you know that. And you caught him with Saffron what's-her-name. We have got to move fast so that Elizabeth Caley doesn't kill herself before we get him or we'll lose out on that million-dollar bonus.''

Lorraine felt tired out. ''You got anything on Saffron Dulay, Rosie?''

Rosie, more official than ever, opened her notebook. ''For starters, she's had more husbands than I've had hot dinners. She's the only daughter and heir to a fortune. I contacted Melissa Dewhurst from the Hollywood grub mag, and she filled me in without much preamble because Saffron sued her magazine for a lotta bucks 'cause Melissa wrote some article implying she was a nympho. By the way, she sued another mag because it hinted that she'd had breast implants. Judging from the pics I got sent over, I'd say she's had a lot more than her tits lifted, she looks fantastic. And take a look at the apartment she lives in.'' Rosie spread out the magazine pictures.

Nick leaned forward and whistled. ''Now, she's a motive. What a body, and rich with it, nice one. Lorraine, have a look at her with clothes on. You saw her in the back of a limo at Robert Caley's place bare-ass naked, right?''

Rooney stared. ''You're kiddin' me!''

Lorraine sat back, pushing her half-finished plate away. She opened her briefcase and passed out her notes from Caley's office files, putting them on the table. ''Don't get food over them, but you two, and you, Rosie, should get clued in.'' She got up from the table.

''What about Robert Caley?'' Nick asked, uptight.

''That is about him, Nick—just read it, all of it.''

Nick yawned, winking at Rooney. ''How about a drink? We can go through these in a bar.''

Rooney snapped the book shut. ''Okay by me. See you tomorrow, Rosie, thanks for the spaghetti.'' He leaned over and kissed her cheek. It took her by surprise, and she blushed.

Nick gave her a wink as he held open the door for Rooney to pass. ''Good night, see ya tomorrow.''

Rosie started clearing the table. It was nice having men around the place, it was a good feeling, and as she passed a mirror carrying the dirty plates to the sink she gave herself a quick glance. Maybe tomorrow she should have her hair trimmed, start wearing a bit of makeup. Rooney's peck on the cheek had meant a lot; she hadn't been kissed by a man for a very long time. Not that Rooney had kissed her properly, but it was a show of affection and she hadn't had much of that either.

Lorraine remained sitting at the table as Rosie began clearing up. She could hear Rooney and Nick laughing in the street below. She got up and stood by the window, looking out, then turned to Rosie.

"Good night, Rosie, go to bed now, it's late, and I'm tired out."

"Good night. Turn off the air conditioner or you won't sleep."

Lorraine turned off the air-conditioning, then the lights, and stood in the semidarkness by the window, arms folded, deep in thought. Nick Bartello had virtually taken over the case. She knew it, and she knew she would have to top him, to prove not only to Rosie but to Rooney that she was still running the show. He was ahead of her and he was good, she knew that. He might be laid back but he had come up with motives, and good ones. Was she losing her touch? Had her physical attraction to Caley made her fail to see through him? She sighed as she lay down on her sofa bed.

Was Robert Caley capable of covering up why his own daughter had been abducted, possibly murdered? Or was it Elizabeth Caley covering up not only her drug addiction but something more sinister? If so, why the hiring of private investigators? Unless it was a role she was acting out from one of her old movies?

Lorraine yawned, feeling her eyes droop with tiredness. Either way, she was convinced that the key to the disappearance of Anna Louise Caley was connected to her parents. The question was, which one? They had only two weeks to get that million, and two days were already gone.

The faces became blurred; one moment Nick Bartello was calling out to her, then Lubrinski. She was trying to drag the body to safety from a hail of bullets. . . . She was screaming, the body was heavy, bleeding and moaning. Lubrinski's face became Nick Bartello's, then Lubrinski's again, and she was weeping, unaware she was crying out loud. It was her own cry that woke her; just before she came to, the man cradled in her arms had become Robert Caley. She sat up shaking, panting for breath, her body drenched in sweat, and it took her a moment to realize where she was. Then she flopped back onto her pillows, closing her eyes, but she couldn't go back to sleep. She didn't want the nightmare to return, didn't want to go back to the memory of Jack Lubrinski dying in her arms. She felt cold, very cold.

Nick Bartello was so like Lubrinski. He too always kept his notes in his back pocket, ripping pages out of her book to scrawl in his thin, unorthodox shorthand.

Rosie had heard the screams. She had sat bolt upright in her bed, listening, then crept to her door. She eased it open and peeked into the living room. She saw Lorraine curled up like a little girl, hands clenched under her chin.

"You all right, partner?" she whispered.

"Yep, just had a bad dream. Did I wake you?"

"Nope, see you in the morning."

"Rosie, you always go for the same kind of guy?"

Rosie leaned over the sofa and gently stroked Lorraine's hair. "Listen, I been without one for so long, I'd go with anything offered, short or tall, fat or skinny, bald, blond or dark. Maybe not a redhead, never fancied red-haired guys."

Lorraine turned over and smiled up at Rosie. She had such a lovely, sweet smile, it was sad she so rarely used it. "I always liked dark-haired guys. You know, maybe that is what I need."

"What?" Rosie looked worried.

"A man."

Rosie laughed. "Thank Christ for that, I thought you were gonna say a drink. Mind you, in my experience they're both as bad for you."

"Yeah, I guess so."

Rosie's gentle hand stroking her head was calming, and Lorraine was asleep before she knew it. She didn't even feel Rosie carefully lay her duvet cover over her, didn't know Rosie waited until she was asleep, watching in fascination as Lorraine's long, slender hands slowly uncurled from fists. It was moments like these that made it all right between them; only to Rosie did Lorraine show her frightening vulnerability. Whatever bad dreams made her scream in such a terrible way were never referred to. But they were now less frequent, like her sweet smiles.

CHAPTER
7

Lorraine arrived at the Caley home at two minutes to eleven, exactly two minutes before the appointment time, which had been agreed upon through Rosie and Phyllis, but Mrs. Caley was with her beautician and asked if Lorraine would be kind enough to wait. Lorraine was furious, and told Peters, the dour butler, that it was impossible for her to wait because she had other pressing business. Eventually Elizabeth agreed to see her despite the inconvenience, and she was led into the sunroom.

Elizabeth had a thick mask on her face, a terry robe belted at the waist and a towel wrapped around her head. Two young women in white uniforms were hovering around her, one giving her a pedicure, the other a manicure. They were in the small massage room off the gym built on to the rear of the house, with a polished pine floor, weights, bicycles and a punching bag, and leather reclining chairs. Classical music drifted from hidden speakers, and all the blinds were drawn on the arched windows, excluding the morning sunlight.

"Mrs. Page, this is Angela at my feet, and Barbara."

The two pretty, immaculately groomed girls smiled and continued working.

"Pull up a chair, darling."

Lorraine drew a wicker basket chair forward and sat down. "Thanks for seeing me, Mrs. Caley."

Elizabeth was sipping her usual mint tea from a china cup

placed on a small side table. "My dear, I am paying you. If you need to ask me about anything, it would be rather stupid not to see you, would it not?" She eased up into a sitting position and sipped her tea again. "You have any news for me?"

"No, not yet, I'm sorry."

Barbara finished the last coat of bloodred polish on Mrs. Caley's left hand and stood up. "I'm all through, Mrs. Caley."

"Thank you, Barbara."

"I won't be a moment, Mrs. Caley, then I'll take your mask off," said Angela, as she carefully massaged oil into the delicate feet.

Lorraine did not want to ask any questions until the face-pack had been peeled, the skin cleaned with tonic lotion, then massaged and moisturized. It took a long time. Elizabeth kept her eyes closed throughout.

Angela gave a series of small discreet smiles to Lorraine and then whispered, "She's asleep."

Lorraine smiled understandingly back, when what she really would have liked to do was get up and shake Elizabeth Caley awake. But she sat there like a fool as Angela crept around, packing up her vanity case. When she finished, she gave a silly little wave and crept out, closing the door silently.

Elizabeth remained motionless, head tilted back on the headrest, seemingly fast asleep. Lorraine stared at her first with irritation, then with a strange fascination: there wasn't a line on the woman's face or neck and, completely devoid of makeup, her skin was still flawless. Her beautiful hands rested on the white robe, and she was absolutely still.

Lorraine was suddenly panic-stricken—was she dead? She eased out of her chair and crept closer, sighing with relief when she could see her breathing, deep, slow, rhythmic breaths. Elizabeth Caley had a perfect face: cheekbones, nose, chin, lips—whether they were man-made or not was immaterial. Lorraine looked over the sleeping woman—could she really be ramming that amount of junk into herself? She could see no needle tracks, none on her slender marble-white arms, and none between her toes. Then she saw a small bruise and needle puncture on the right side of her neck, but only one. If Elizabeth Caley was injecting herself, then she must be very adept, possibly using her groin. But to move aside the robe could wake her, and God knows what the implications of that would be. Lorraine checked her watch and walked out, leaving the sleeping Mrs. Caley to her Beethoven concerto.

Peters was unsure, but Lorraine made it clear that as she had been hired by Mr. and Mrs. Caley to trace their daughter, it would be necessary to see Anna Louise's room.

"Perhaps you should ask Mr. Caley for his permission," she said impatiently.

"I'm afraid Mr. Caley is out at lunch."

"Well, it's up to you, Peters, you are capable of making a decision, aren't you?"

It was no simple room but a vast suite consisting of a bedroom, lounge area and a bathroom bigger than Rosie's entire apartment. It was like a showcase: unreal, unlived in, nothing out of place. The furnishings were soft shell-pinks and whites, and the king-size bed had a row of white stuffed bears so pristine they were obviously for show rather than ever having been used as toys.

Lorraine slowly looked around; no normal, full-blooded young girl could occupy this room and leave no trace of herself. She sat on the bed and let her eyes take in every corner, as if hoping the room itself would talk to her. She asked herself where she would put something if she wanted to hide it. Was there some kind of hidden safe?

She moved through the suite, her feet buried in the soft thick oyster-pink pile of the carpet. She looked under the bed and found nothing, she searched behind the curtains, underneath the scatter pillows and the bears: nothing. She went into the bathroom, looked inside the huge cabinet, the toilet cistern: nothing. She went back into the vast walk-in closet and looked through the shelves: nothing, not even a faint smell of old perfume on any of the clothes. They seemed, like everything else, unused and unworn. She was just about to return to Mrs. Caley when something caught her eye. All the shoe boxes had the contents stamped on cards—sandals, mules, loafers, brown, black, cream, etc.— apart from one; it had the same neat card, but without any description at all; it was blank.

Lorraine eased the box out and discovered it was a designer-made shoe box, the cardboard covered in white silk. She took the lid off and smiled to herself. Inside she found little bundles of letters, birthday cards, mementos, a Valentine card. At last she was finding something interesting, something she could get a fix on. She opened the Valentine card: *My one and only Valentine. Love, Polar*

Most of the other birthday and little gift cards were from Anna Louise's various aunts and uncles, her mother and father, but five cards in all, accompanying floral deliveries, were from the same Polar guy. Lorraine sifted through the box, reading the letters. There were poems and a couple of invitations to college functions.

She found nothing of interest until she had almost emptied the box—then she saw the condoms, held together with an elastic band. Anna Louise sure as hell had a neater-than-neat complex. Next came out several matchbooks, also tied together, not from any elegant restaurants but from the Viper Room, On the Rox and the Snake Pit—all notorious nightclubs. But not until she drew out the pornographic magazines did she sit back, because they were not cheap material bought over the counter but heavy hard-core porn.

She flicked through them and found a folded note Scotchtaped to one of the centerfolds. Written on the note in tiny neat capital letters were the words:

I LOVE YOU, I WANT TO FUCK YOU, I WANT YOU TO WANT ME, I WANT TO TAKE IT UP THE ASS, I WANT YOU TO LICK MY PUSSY UNTIL I COME AND I WANT YOUR DICK IN MY MOUTH. SMACK ME HARD, PLEASE, PLEASE HURT ME AND KISS ME BETTER.

Lorraine slipped it into her pocket; it was the only thing she took out of the room. She had determined that the childish print was Anna Louise's by checking it against one of her poems before slotting the ''shoe box'' back into place.

Peters was standing at the bottom of the stairs as she slowly made her way down.

''It is a very beautiful room.''

''Yes, it is. Mrs. Caley is still sleeping, and I really do not think I should wake her.''

"I'll come back tomorrow morning, say about nine."

"Mrs. Caley does not rise until ten-thirty."

She hesitated. "I'll be here at eleven. Good afternoon."

Lorraine called Nick from the car.

"Hi, how ya doing?"

"You fancy going clubbing?"

"What?"

"You know the club the Viper Room?"

Nick laughed. "You're a bit old, sweetheart, and far be it from me to say, not famous enough. You won't get past the door."

"Wanna bet? Pick me up from Rosie's about eleven-thirty."

Nick hesitated. "Shit, Lorraine, I ain't no dancer, I got one and a half fuckin' legs. What's this about? You come across another chick screwing Robert Caley?"

"Nope, I just got an insight into our sweet angel Anna Louise. Some guy called Polar was givin' it to her up the ass. See you later. And, Nick, have a bath, maybe a shave, huh?"

Lorraine replaced the cell phone, well pleased. She figured she had now come up with something that no one else had even hinted at knowing. She was buzzing, and fully intended driving straight back to her apartment, and then on to an AA meeting before meeting Nick at the Viper Room. She had no intention of going to see Juda Salina again, but she pulled over as she drove along Doheny Drive, checked the time, and sat thinking for a moment. She couldn't understand why she felt so drawn to following up Juda Salina, but she did—maybe because Anna Louise had visited her, maybe because she knew intuitively that the woman knew a lot more about the missing girl than she was admitting. If she had the mystic connection she claimed with Anna Louise, maybe she might have some insight into who the character calling himself Polar was. . . . And as Lorraine was virtually on her doorstep, why not?

Lorraine pressed the intercom from the main apartment entrance. This time she was not about to play games trying to get in or out without permission. A bored voice asked who was calling.

"My name is Lorraine Page, I need to speak with Mrs. Salina."

"She's sleepin' right now."

"Then wake her up, this is important."

"What you say your name was?"

The main door to the apartments opened and she stepped inside, heading directly down to the apartment along the narrow corridor.

Juda slapped Raoul across the face, hard, and he pressed himself against the wall.

"I dunno who she was, and you gotta a lot of freaks comin' in, all jumpy and sayin' it's important. I thought she was a client."

She pushed at him again. "I said you check out my appointment book, you don't let nobody in here unless *I* say so. Now you've gone and let this bitch in—well, I'm not seeing her."

"I said you was sleepin' and she said to wake you."

"Fine, now you tell her I'm sick and not getting up for her or nobody else, you got it?"

The doorbell rang and Juda swayed down to her bedroom, slamming the door shut. Raoul inched open the door, leaving it on the chain.

"Hi, it's Lorraine Page."

"She can't see you, she's sick."

"Who are you?"

"Raoul, Ah'm her . . . Ah is her driver."

"Okay, Raoul, go tell Mrs. Salina that unless she gives me ten minutes, I'm gonna go to the guy who runs these apartments and I'm gonna tell him that your aunt is runnin' a business out of this exclusive apartment block. Now you go and make sure she understands that I am not moving away from this door."

Banished to the kitchen, the door firmly closed, Raoul put the kettle on. He was already wishing he hadn't come to LA, but he couldn't go back home, not for a while, and he had no other place to go. Living with his aunt was hideous; only if he sat in the boxlike kitchen could he escape her bulk, but it was dark and claustrophobic, and Raoul didn't like the dark, didn't like what happened in the darkness.

Juda lit an incense stick and wafted it for a moment. Lorraine sat in the same chair she had before.

"I didn't mean to be so pushy, Mrs. Salina, but I really needed to ask you some questions."

"I'm sick, I got a migraine." She was wearing big dark glasses, another tentlike creation folded around her massive body and a green turban. The long red talons wafted the heady incense perfume across the room, making Lorraine's eyes water.

"You never told me that Anna Louise Caley came to see you."

"I don't recall you askin'."

"Did she come to you the day before she left for New Orleans?"

Juda sighed. "I'll check my book, but you know, I already told you I have to respect my clients' confidence." She eased herself up and swayed slowly to the door, opening it. The apartment was so small she didn't need to shout but she did. "Raoul, get me mah appointment book."

Raoul appeared at the door and passed a red leather book to his aunt. "Go get the car, Raoul, I need to be someplace in fifteen minutes. Park outside, go on now, get your butt moving." She shut the door and flipped open the book.

"Mrs. Salina, I don't want to see your appointment book, I want you to tell me if Anna Louise—"

Juda shoved the book under Lorraine's nose. "You see, Miss Page, you threaten me and tell me you're gonna report me. Now, there it is in black and white, whole weeks before February fifteenth, and there is no Anna Louise listed, okay?"

Lorraine stood up, flicking through the book, and saw that Juda did actually have an appointment that afternoon with a client called Eunice Bourdreaux. She closed the book. "Thank you. Why did Mrs. Caley bring Anna Louise—were you reading her cards too?"

"Sometimes she needed assistance, she used not to feel so good."

"I know why she didn't feel so good, she was out of her head on drugs, so Anna Louise used to . . . what? Help her down the corridor?"

Juda shrugged. Like her nephew, she seemed to enjoy

slipping in and out of her Southern accent, sometimes accentuating it, other times not. Now she drawled, elongating her vowels.

"Ah do not know about any drugs, Ah don't know what you are trying to imply or why you are so interested. The little girl came, sat awhile and when Ah finished the session with her mother they left."

"Did you talk to Anna Louise, I mean, read her palm or tarot cards, for example?"

"I may have, I don't recall . . . mah client was Mrs. Elizabeth Caley."

Lorraine sucked in her breath; with her singsong voice and her huge dark glasses, the woman really annoyed her. She crossed her legs, one foot swinging with irritation.

"You read tarot cards, you read palms, you feel people's auras, and according to all those credentials you got pinned up on your walls, you also call yourself a medium . . . and you're saying you cannot remember? Now, I personally don't believe in all this, but that is just my opinion."

"You are entitled to your opinion, honey."

"I also know that you hand out a leaflet, where you state you assist with police inquiries. But the police told me you never helped solve any case. You just got a lot of publicity from it, and judging from the red appointment book, I'd say you need a whole lot more. It's not exactly bulging with clients now, is it?"

Juda smiled, her hands resting over her belly. "Right now I'm not doing' so much business—in fact, I might just well retire."

"Unless you don't always note down your clients. So let me ask you again, did Anna Louise Caley ever come to see you alone?"

Juda remained smiling, then shrugged her fat shoulders. "No, she did not. Like I said, she just came a few times with Mrs. Caley."

"Who is the young man that let me in?"

"Raoul? He's my nephew, I am taking care of him, Miss Page, that's all. Nothing illegal about that now, is there?"

Lorraine leaned forward. "What did Anna Louise ask you about? Was she worried about something? Was she scared of something?"

Juda sighed but did not answer. Lorraine was becoming angry at her inability to get Juda to talk. She tried a different tactic, almost pleading. "I am trying to find her, Mrs. Salina, so if there is anything she said to you that would give me an insight into a problem she may have had, even a relationship . . . ?"

Juda turned away.

"Was she seeing someone? Mrs. Salina, don't give me any more clients' confidentiality, et cetera. Please, Anna Louise has been missing without a trace for eleven months."

"I have been interviewed over and over again and if there was anything, don't you think I would have already told the police, told the other private dicks? But there is nothing, and what I saw for Mrs. Caley has nothing to do with anything."

"Okay. What did you see *for* Mrs. Caley? Please."

Juda licked her lips. "I saw nothing good, I saw she needed to go to a rehab clinic, I saw she would have marriage problems, I saw that she might have a resurrection of her career, a lot of publicity, but not good . . ."

Lorraine wanted to snatch the dark shades off her fat face, but instead she gave up. "You know, people like you make me sick."

"I think you made that clear the last time, honey, but to be honest I am not struck by you all that much. You think you can push your way into my home, make threats, only because you're being paid a lot of cash to do so. You ain't offerin' any to me, and even if you did I'd throw it back in your smug face. I suggest you start taking lessons in politeness because you are a rude bitch. Like I said before, I got nothing to say or add to what I already told the police and what I told you the last time you came burstin' into my home."

Lorraine walked to the door, opened it. "You still see a big bright aura around Anna Louise Caley? You still telling that poor woman to keep up hope? Well, I may be pushy, I may be getting paid for my job, but it's sure as hell a lot better than being paid for spouting bullshit to poor desperate people who could probably do with a good shrink. Thanks for nothing."

Lorraine didn't wait for Juda to show her out and

slammed the front door hard to let the whale of a woman know she had left.

Juda remained sitting in her chair, her hands clasping the arms. She sure as hell could feel Lorraine Page's presence; one part was obvious, the bitch was a pushy ex-cop. But the other part confused Juda. To begin with, she had been positive she'd felt something bad, really bad; was it because she was different from all the other PIs? After all, she was digging that much deeper. Or was it because she knew that someone with the initial L was going to be in bad trouble, like a clock whose tick-tick-ticking was about to stop, for good?

Juda had felt it the moment she had met Lorraine, that something inside that lady was about to escape from control. What it was she couldn't put her finger on, but it unsettled her and she began to be afraid, as she knew she would have to go deeper and she feared that the consequences would suck her into the darkness herself.

Lorraine stepped out onto the pavement, which was shimmering in the blistering sun. As she headed for her rented Buick parked at a meter, a limo drove out of the parking lot. She could not see the driver because of the dark tinted windows, but she recognized the car. When she had seen Phyllis get out of it yesterday afternoon, she'd assumed it was Elizabeth Caley's. Now as the driver's window glided down, she knew she had been wrong: Raoul, in his mirrored shades, looked toward her, smiling.

"You were on Rodeo Drive yesterday afternoon with Phyllis Collins."

He looked nonplussed.

"Mrs. Caley's companion," Lorraine said, as she walked toward him.

Raoul gave an even wider smile. "Maybe I was, but to tell you the honest truth, ma'am, I am new around town, so I don't know where I am or who's in the back."

Lorraine moved closer until she could see her own face in his mirrored shades.

"How long have you been staying with your aunt?"

"Oh, a while, maybe a few weeks."

"You came here from New Orleans?"

"Yes, ma'am, I did, no work back home."

"Did you know Anna Louise Caley?"

He turned off the engine and removed the keys. "Who?"

"Anna Louise Caley, you know who I'm talking about."

He sucked at the small monkey-like mascot dangling on the end of his key ring. "I know, well, I read about her but I never met her. I seen her photographs, ma aunty show them to me, and I know she was real pretty."

"Didn't you meet her in New Orleans?"

"No, ma'am."

Lorraine stepped back, sure he was lying. "Thanks for letting me into the apartment."

"That's okay, you have a nice day now." As she walked off he shouted out to her, "Hey! Miss! Hey!"

She turned back to him; he was leaning out of the window, his elbows resting along the rim, still sucking the key ring.

"You shouldn't be so mean to my aunt."

"What?"

"She is not the kind of person you want to get on the bad side of. Trust me, you be nice to her."

"Why?"

"Maybe she's seen bad things for you, she's got the . . ." He tapped the center of his forehead. "You cause any trouble for her and she'll make bad things happen, she's got the sight, know what I mean? 'Bye now, ma'am, and lemme tell you, you got real nice legs."

He eased back inside the car and she heard loud music begin to thud out, some kind of screaming reggae, then the window slowly closed. She felt uneasy, because, although it was the middle of the day and hot, she suddenly felt icy cold.

She unlocked her car and got inside. She could still see the limo parked up ahead of her; Mrs. Juda Salina was obviously not that short of money. She started the engine, pulling her safety belt on. She stayed there for another five minutes and jumped when the phone rang.

"Hi, it's me, just checking in." It was Rosie. Lorraine kept her eyes on Juda's limo up ahead.

"Rooney's here and wants a word," Rosie said, sounding loud and perky.

Rooney came on the line. "We got to get over to New

Orleans real soon, I don't wanna talk to my contacts there over the phone, better face-to-face. You got anything?''

"I want anything you can get, from anyone you can get it from, on this Juda Salina bitch, the so-called psychic.''

"I think we got as much as we could. She's a joke, isn't she?''

Lorraine saw Juda exit from the apartments and get into the waiting car. "She's got a young nephew staying, Raoul, from New Orleans, comes on like a young Lothario, à la Robert de Niro. Get him checked out, try the same surname for starters. If you get nowhere, use the license number; fat woman can't drive and the car's got Louisiana plates.''

Rooney jotted down the registration. "Okay, but you know we got to get over there. Time's moving fast, we only got two weeks—three days down already.''

"Yeah, yeah, I know. Ask Rosie if she's gonna go to a meeting this evening and if it's one Phyllis attends . . . shit, hold on.''

Lorraine saw Raoul drive off, honking his car horn as he inched into the traffic. She swerved out, narrowly missing an oncoming car that hooted at her. She waved her hand in apology, the phone tucked under her chin.

"Hi, it's me. It's Rosie,'' came her bellow.

"You meeting tonight?'' asked Lorraine, heading up Dohney about four cars behind Raoul.

"Yep, you want to come?''

"I will if Phyllis will be there.''

"She will be—she usually is.''

"Okay, see you later, 'bye now.''

Rosie replaced the phone. "She's got a thing about this Juda Salina. Dunno why, waste of time, I think. I mean, I was there, I met her, and Nick checked her out.''

"You think she's a flake too?'' Rooney asked.

"Well, I have to be honest—I couldn't tell you. She was sort of strange, gave me a weird feeling like when she looked at me she was seeing through me. She's got strange eyes, very deep and dark, or maybe it was just the false eyelashes.'' She chuckled.

"I've lost four pounds,'' Rooney said.

Rosie clapped her hands. "That's wonderful. I have lost—

well, not as much as I'd like. Do you think I'm looking thinner?''

Rooney gave her a long, studied appraisal, and then nodded. ''There is just one thing, Rosie—when we get to New Orleans, can we forget the diet? I mean, they have the best food in the world, and I'm not going there to eat raw fish. It might mean a few extra pounds going on, but . . .''

She held out her hand. ''It's a deal—we diet now, but we come off it when we get to New Orleans.'' They shook hands, and Rooney felt suddenly embarrassed. He'd never had this kind of intimate conversation with a woman before, even with his poor wife, who had been stick-thin when he married her and stick-thin the day she died.

''Can I tell you something?'' he asked hesitantly, and she looked over at him.

''Sure, tell me what?''

''Don't tell Lorraine,'' he said, like a kid. Rosie waited while Rooney rubbed his head and pulled at his big nose.

''Maybe it's age.''

''What is?''

He coughed, now pulling at his tie. ''Well, don't take this the wrong way, I mean, hell, I'm not backing out of anything, no way, but . . .'' He sighed, unsure of what he was saying and how to say it. ''I just can't get the energy up the way I used to, you know, that adrenaline that pumps through you on a case. I used to feel it down to the soles of my feet, itching all the time to get to the bottom of something. I wouldn't sleep, couldn't even eat sometimes, and I know I was hell to live with. I must have put poor Ellen through it, and I keep thinking about her, thinking what a bad husband I was. She never had much of a life.''

He seemed so vulnerable, trying to express something that he couldn't release, and Rosie went over and put her arms around him, which embarrassed him even more.

''I just feel so bad about her, Rosie, because she was looking forward to us going on this camper trip all over the U.S., and . . .''

Rosie said nothing, but just held him and rubbed his back. Rooney rested his head against her.

''I'm sorry about this, you must think me a big old fool, but she was a nice woman, Rosie, never would hurt a fly.''

"It's always good to let it out, Bill, you'll feel better, and don't you worry about that itch—I think you're a very special person. Too many people hide their real feelings—I know I hid mine in a bottle, but I'm getting better, much better."

There was a moment of embarrassment as Rosie drew away and Bill blew his nose hard.

"Lorraine should be here any minute," Rosie said to cover her own confusion.

"I'd be grateful if you didn't mention this to her, I don't want her to feel that I'm not giving one hundred percent."

"Nothing happened here, you old buzzard." Rosie smiled warmly, but they both knew something had happened. Perhaps they were afraid to admit it at once, but there was now a bond between them and it felt good.

Lorraine tailed the lunatic Raoul as far as she could, but he then cut across traffic and she lost him. Maybe Raoul knew she'd been on their tail, but judging by the way the kid drove, he was more than likely to get a speeding ticket, and Lorraine with him.

They were parked across the road from the AA meeting. It was almost eight.

Lorraine looked in the rearview mirror. "Here she comes now. Okay, I'm out of here, you wait in the car."

"But I want to go to the meeting."

"Fine, can you just give me a few seconds with Phyllis?"

Lorraine crossed to Phyllis, smiled and shook her hand. Then they walked to a bench seat outside the church hall.

Phyllis clenched her hands together. "I really do not see that it is any concern of yours, I was simply passing the car and Mrs. Salina called out to me, so I went over and—"

"Is she still seeing Mrs. Caley?"

"Er, no, well, Mr. Caley has objected to her coming to the house and so, no, she doesn't see her anymore."

"Does Robert Caley know Elizabeth is pumping herself full of Temazepam—that's what she's injecting, right?"

Phyllis had those two red dots in her cheeks again. "You don't understand."

"I am trying to, Phyllis, I really am. Do you have any

idea how dangerous it is? That she could induce a thrombosis and kill herself?''

Phyllis seemed ready to burst into tears.

Lorraine continued. ''The stuff is lethal, Phyllis, and you would be partly responsible if she killed herself. You're procuring the stuff for her, you have admitted to picking it up, so why don't you stop lying to me? Does Robert Caley know what his wife is taking?''

Phyllis shook her head. ''No, he has no idea. You see, when she last came out of the rehab clinic, she was no longer taking cocaine, not even alcohol, but then with all this terrible thing about Anna Louise . . . She couldn't sleep and she became very anxious and . . .''

''The doc prescribed the Temazepam, right?''

Phyllis nodded. ''Just a small amount to begin with and then she needed more, and . . .'' The tears came and she fumbled in her sleeve to take out a tiny lace handkerchief. ''Oh dear, dear me, I can't stop her. And she's threatened to sack me if I mention it to Mr. Caley, she'll also sack me if I don't collect them. . . . It places me in such a terrible position.''

''Well, she won't be able to get any more, Dr. Hayleden's been arrested.''

''Oh God.'' Phyllis pressed the handkerchief to her watery eyes.

''Yeah, oh God, but you should thank God, Phyllis, because without her supply she's not likely to kill herself, is she?''

Phyllis closed her eyes and sniffed, her mouth turned down. ''Oh, she'll find someone else, or something else. I don't know if I can take much more. That's why I started drinking, you know, she wore me out. She just never sleeps, she can't sleep without something, and now she has an excuse. All she thinks about is Anna Louise.''

''She took her to see Juda.''

''Yes, I think so, but I wasn't with them, she would never let me go with her.''

''And Mr. and Mrs. Caley took Mrs. Salina to New Orleans, yes? To try and help trace Anna Louise?''

Phyllis nodded, chewing at her thin lips. ''Yes, Elizabeth insisted. You see, Mrs. Salina was sure that if she was close to where she had been, in the hotel or wherever, she would pick up her aura.''

''And?''

Phyllis shrugged. ''Well, she was sure the poor child was very much alive, and I think she stayed on for a few days after Elizabeth returned because, as I recall, Mr. Caley sent his private plane to bring her back to LA.''

Lorraine nodded. ''Why did he forbid her to see Elizabeth?''

Phyllis sighed. ''Mr. Caley suspected that the woman was a charlatan, building up Elizabeth's hopes; he never approved of her, and he was deeply angry when he discovered that Elizabeth had taken Anna Louise to Mrs. Salina's apartment.''

''Was that when he banned Juda from visiting the house?''

''No, that was after they returned from New Orleans.''

''But she was a calming influence!''

''*Yes*, she was, but not after the disappearance. Elizabeth would become very distraught and call Mrs. Salina in hysterics. She gave her hope, you see. . . . Mr. Caley was only doing it for the best.''

Lorraine nodded, checking the time. ''Why did Anna Louise go to Mrs. Salina's?''

''I don't think she got involved in any of that mumbo jumbo thing, it was just that sometimes Mrs. Caley was not very steady. I think Mr. Caley had words with Anna Louise, and she promised never to go there again. . . .''

''And did she?''

''No, no, she wouldn't go against her father's wishes. She was a very obedient girl. And she had Tilda Brown staying at the time, so she had other things on her mind. The girl used to stay a lot—well, with her family being so far away, most weekends actually. In fact, Anna Louise was looking forward to going to New Orleans because . . .''

Phyllis suddenly hesitated, turning away from Lorraine. It was as if she had thought of something and was deciding whether or not to mention it. She covered by tucking her little handkerchief back up her sleeve.

''Because?'' Lorraine said softly.

''Er, nothing really, it's just that the girls had a bit of a falling-out, nothing serious, and Tilda went home the next morning. She was meant to stay on another day and travel with Mr. and Mrs. Caley, but you know young girls—probably argued about a game of tennis.''

"Must have been quite an argument for her to leave so abruptly, and also as they were planning to travel together the following day.''

"I suppose so, but you know young girls.''

"Have you ever met Saffron Dulay? I think she's a close friend of Mr. Caley's.''

Phyllis looked at her watch and stood up, smoothing down her skirt. ''No, I have not had the pleasure. Is there anything else you wish to ask me? If there isn't, I really should go in.''

"No, I don't think so. Thank you very much for your time.''

Phyllis patted her hair. ''I am sorry if, well, I know you think I am not always honest, but you see, Mrs. Page, part of me has to be so very careful. I signed a confidentiality agreement with Mrs. Caley, all her staff have to. . . .''

"I understand, Phyllis.''

"It's just I am so scared of losing my job. I have a very elderly mother and aunt I take care of back in England. They are dependent on my income, and the Caleys have been so very kind over my own little problem.''

"Yes, I am sure Elizabeth Caley would be, considering her own.''

Phyllis gave an eerie, high-pitched titter. She put out her hand to shake Lorraine's—rather like a little fragile claw, which clasped for a moment and then released.

"Was Juda Salina paid a lot of money?''

"Money, Mrs. Page, is not something that Elizabeth Caley has any worries over.''

"Just one more thing, Phyllis. How close to the time of Anna Louise's disappearance did Mr. Caley forbid her to see Juda Salina?''

"Oh, weeks before. Then after Anna Louise disappeared, Mr. Caley agreed to allow Mrs. Salina to visit but stopped her coming after about three or four months. Now please, I really should go in. Good evening.'' And with that, Phyllis hurried into the church hall.

Lorraine frowned; why did Elizabeth Caley have such a prissy woman caring for her?

Rosie banged the car door shut, shouting, "I got to go in, Lorraine! *Lorraine!*'"

Lorraine was still frowning as she joined Rosie. "You know, I don't think Phyllis even likes Elizabeth Caley."

"You going into the meeting?"

Lorraine shook her head. "No, you go ahead."

Rosie sighed with irritation as she watched Lorraine walk toward the car. "Maybe you should."

Lorraine whipped around. "We got less than two weeks, Rosie."

"I know that, but how am I going to get home?"

Lorraine sighed. "Ask Phyllis to give you a ride."

Rosie was tight-lipped: sometimes she really didn't like the way Lorraine treated her, and she was just about to say so when Lorraine turned back and gave her a hug.

"Sorry, didn't mean to sound so nasty, but we *are* pushed for time, Rosie, and I think I'm on to something. Not sure what it is yet, but if you can't get a ride, take a cab, okay?"

Rosie patted her friend's shoulder. "Don't you worry, I'll get home. You know Nick will look after you, don't you?"

"What?"

Rosie winked. "I never said nothing, but he's kind of got the hots for you, so you treat him nice."

Lorraine laughed. Sometimes Rosie could be so dumb. "No, Rosie, he just wants a cut of the one million, that's what he's got the hots for—and we may just be getting closer to it. See you later."

CHAPTER

8

It was 11:30 P.M., already the third night of the investigation, and Lorraine was not as confident as she had led Rosie to believe. She gave herself the critical eye; she was wearing a short black dress—secondhand, naturally, but its Donna Karan label showed it had once been expensive. She had also acquired, from the daughter of the Latinos living in the apartment below, a pair of red platform high-heeled shoes. The black stockings were her own. She had washed her hair, still unsure about the new cut, and was just wondering if she should put on even more makeup when there was a knock on the door.

Rosie had got a ride home from her meeting and was sitting in front of the television with a bowl of grapes.

"Come in, it's open," she said.

"Hi, is she ready?" Nick said loudly.

Rosie nodded, and used the remote control to switch off the TV. "What's this Viper Club like?"

Nick sauntered in. "Viper Room—you don't call it a club, Rosie. Is she for real, then?"

Rosie shrugged. Lorraine walked in, and Nick tried not to overreact because she looked so different. "My, my, we are pulling out the stops."

Lorraine looked at him. "Wish I could say the same for you. You rolled out of bed to get here?"

"I most surely did. So this is on, is it?"

"You think I got dressed up like this for fun?"

"Turns me on. I think it's the shoes. Man, you gotta be six foot in them."

Lorraine put on a pair of shades and waved at Rosie. "See you. Come on, Nick, let's go." She peered at his denim jacket. "Holy shit, you got dog hairs all over you."

"Well, I would, I got a dog. G'night, Rosie."

Nick glanced over the note found in Anna Louise Caley's bedroom. He said nothing as he passed it back to Lorraine. He was still taken aback by her appearance, and when she leaned close to him, he got an erection. It annoyed him that she could make him react to her so physically.

"I want to find out who this guy Polar is. She had matches from the Viper Room, so we'll start there. And there were other matchbooks from On the Rox and—"

"Look, no need to explain, we'll figure it out, okay?" He seemed irritated, and she didn't have the slightest inkling that it was because he found her so attractive. They turned onto Sunset and drove past the flash parade of yuppie wanna-be Hell's Angels on their shiny chrome bikes, past the neon-lit zone, the hookers and the pimps, past the open-fronted bars and cafés, until he pulled over into a vacant parking space outside a sleazy joint called Alfredo's Live Striptease.

"We're here?" Lorraine asked.

"Nope, but I need to see a friend. Just hang in there, I'll be a couple of seconds."

Nick hopped out of the Jeep and went into the strip joint. Lorraine waited with Tiger's hot, panting breath wafting past her face.

"Sit back a bit, you stink."

He looked duly miffed and squatted back, then the sides of his huge mouth lifted and he gave a low growl.

"Hey, sit on my knee if it makes you happy, just don't bite me."

She heard the thud-thud of his tail as it whacked against his food bowl. There was no growl, but his lip curled up to reveal his teeth and it looked as if he were smiling, which made Lorraine laugh.

"Good boy. I could get to like you, you know that?"

And she really believed she could when two leather-clad,

drunk bikers stumbled against the Jeep and one looked in, sneering, to ask, "How much?" Tiger went for the jugular, fast, and the biker took off, scared shitless.

Lorraine reached out and patted his big head. "Nice one."

"Winning you over, is he?" Nick said as he opened the driver's door. He started up the engine. "Okay, I got our calling card, so maybe we can get in. . . . But if you don't mind me sayin' so, you're the wrong side of thirty and there are not a lot of chicks in there over twenty. Guys can get in any age so long as they're famous an' their wallets're heavy. Still, we'll have a go."

They drove out into the night traffic and Lorraine asked if Nick had some movie-star contact. He laughed, shaking his head. "Nah! Feel in my pocket, I've gone one better."

She slipped her hand into his denim jacket and pulled out a plastic bag. "Nick, what you playin' at?"

"Cocaine—well, some of it, rest is scouring powder. You ain't somebody unless you have something that the some-bodies want, right?"

"You mean you just scored this?"

"Nope, well, in a way. Remember me tellin' you about Fisher?"

"Yes, but—"

"Tony T. Loredo owns that dive. I busted him in '85, but I did him a favor. Since then he's come up in the world, and he supplies young meat, chicks, dope, you name it, to the movie stars. I'm gonna use him as an intro. All right with you?"

They pulled up outside the Viper Room's dark, nondescript entrance; the only indications that it was a club were the heavy-duty bouncers on the door and the stretch limos pull-ing up and moving off as their clients staggered into the venue.

Nick leaned out of the Jeep and called out to one of the bouncers. "Hey, man, gimme an ear, will ya?" He turned back to Lorraine. "Bend your head forward, look like you're out of it, cover your face with your hair. Do it!" The bouncer came up closer. "Keep your distance, I got a mad dog in the back and a real one beside me. . . . I also got some merchandise Tony said he wants me to deliver."

The bouncer stared at Lorraine, then at Nick, who eased out his bag a fraction. The bouncer stepped back, nodding, and pointed for Nick to park a ways down the road.

"Right, we're in. . . ."

"In" blew Lorraine's mind. The main clubroom was so dark she could hardly see and the music was so loud it was deafening. She tried as best she could to see through the darkness. She focused on a young girl wearing a black bra and panties, and fishnet stockings. "You think she maybe had a dress on when she arrived?" she said to Nick, but he was looking around. He then turned back and leaned in close.

"Over to your right, clutch of supermodels." Nick pointed up above them. "That's a room with a two-way mirror onto the dance floor. Some of 'em get a kick out of screwing up there on top of all these assholes. Still, takes all kinds . . ."

"Yeah, and maybe Anna Louise Caley was one of them. How do we go about it?"

Nick shrugged. "I think we're wasting our time. Come on, that note you found in the girl's bedroom is juvenile dementia, a kid writing dirty, so what?"

"It might mean something if we track down this guy Polar."

Nick signaled to a waiter. She could feel he was edgy, his eyes darting around all the time. He searched in his pockets and took out a picture of Anna Louise.

"You got any cash on you? Like fifties—ten bucks no good—I need a few big notes." Lorraine opened her purse and he suddenly leaned in close and whispered to her, "Head down and stoned, sweetheart."

She looked up as a waiter closed in on Nick. "Hi, man, gimme a Mexican and a Diet Coke. Hey, a second."

The waiter leaned forward.

"I need to get shot of this." Nick jerked his thumb at Lorraine, and then winked at the waiter. "My friend Tony, Loredo T., wants to know if this chick's been in. Reason is she owes him, understand? Lot of dough. And if you can tip him off, there's something in it for you. . . ." Nick drew out the plastic bag. "Worth fifteen big ones—all yours. Act real cool about it, man, but I need to know if she used to hang out down here.''

''Sure, a Mexican beer and one Coke.'' The waiter took the photo without looking at it and two fifty-dollar notes with a nice swift move so they were hidden under his tray.

Lorraine hissed. ''A hundred bucks, Nick, are you crazy?''

He kept looking around the dark dance floor, where a girl was stripping; nobody seemed all that interested. ''That's shit, some of these kids drop ten, fifteen thousand bucks a night down here. I'm gonna take a leak, you okay to hang out on your own?''

She turned away. ''I've been in places a lot worse than this.''

He leaned close. ''This is class, sweetheart. Won't be long.''

He was away at least twenty minutes. Lorraine watched the stoned kids, some openly snorting coke. One girl was so high she sat with her legs apart in a stupor. As guys walked past her they groped her, and all she could do was just about hold her head straight.

Lorraine got up and headed for the rest room. She was pushed and jostled, and saw more lines of coke laid out and young teenage girls huddled together, wearing as little as possible. Lorraine felt old; not that anyone bothered even to look in her direction, they were too intent on getting noticed by one or another of the ''stars.''

Nick had still not shown when she made her way back to where she had been sitting, but the seats were now occupied by a couple on the verge of copulating, so she picked up her glass and turned away. She took a gulp, then freaked because it wasn't straight Coke, it had rum in it, and a lot of it, mixed with God knows what else.

The alcohol hit her throat like a fireball. She swallowed. It took a lot of willpower to put the glass down, but she did. She edged away and was pushed against the wall by a group of guys dancing with one another. She pressed her back hard against the suedette wall, could feel the panic starting and wished Nick would show. Her dress clung to her as she broke out in a sweat; the heat was stifling, the thudding music overpowering, but not as hard to ignore as her need to finish the drink.

"Where's your friend?" the waiter hissed, and she turned to be blinded by spinning spotlights. "He in the john? Or upstairs? Don't look at me, act like I'm taking your order."

She closed her eyes, sweat trickling down her body. She swallowed, her mouth felt rancid.

Nick appeared right behind the waiter. "Hey, man, you got a guy fuckin' a chick in the john."

"So? Listen, I can be out the back door in ten, my break's due, okay?"

Nick nodded, and as the waiter took off he grinned at Lorraine. "Quite a show in there."

"Get me out of here, Nick."

He laughed. "What? Can't take it? But you said you . . ." He suddenly knew she was in trouble and gripped her elbow, easing her forward and out into the cool night air.

Lorraine leaned against the side of the Jeep. "Somebody spiked my drink or I picked up somebody else's and . . . sorry, sorry, I got all hyper in there."

She was so vulnerable, her whole body shaking, and he put his arm around her, walking her to the Jeep door.

"Come on, sit inside, you're okay . . . You want some water?"

She stumbled and he held on tightly as he helped her. He reached over to the backseat. Tiger's head appeared and he gave him a quick pat as he unscrewed a bottle of Evian.

"It's Tiger's but I guess he won't mind."

She gulped at the water; it was lukewarm but it was liquid. She was scared to feel so dependent. "Sorry about this, sorry."

He gently stroked her cheek. "Sweetheart, you don't have to be sorry, I shouldn't have stayed in the john, but the floor show was somethin' else and . . ."

She turned away, her hand clutching the dented old plastic. "Oh, shit, Nick, does it never stop? That was the first drink I've had in months, months. . . ."

He opened the glove compartment and took out some peppermints. He unwrapped one and touched her lips. "Open your mouth." He popped in the mint and cuffed her chin lightly. "You stay put, I don't want to miss out on this

guy. Besides, he's got a hundred bucks of our dough and''—
he tapped his pocket—''he's gonna do some nasal damage
in there with this stuff. You okay if I leave you?''

She nodded, her mouth bulging with the mint. ''Yep, and
I got Tiger. Go on, I'm fine.''

Lorraine wasn't. She couldn't stop the tears as they welled
up and spilled down, and she sucked hard on the big peppermint, angry with herself.

''I lost it in there, Tiger,'' she whispered. It frightened
her how quickly her confidence could be swiped from her,
and to realize that everything she was or thought she was
could be so easily ripped apart. All it took was one drink
and the craving was back.

Nick was leaning against a wall where he could see the
cordoned-off backyard. He waited for almost ten minutes.
They had bouncers even out back with the trash cans, because kids tried to get in that way. He was beginning to
think they'd lost a hundred bucks when out came the waiter.
He had a studded leather jacket slung over his shoulder and
was wearing dark shades.

''Gonna check out my wheels, be back in five,'' he called
out to the bouncers.

Nick remained half hidden against the wall until the
waiter was clear. He was very edgy as he joined Nick.

''My bike's parked up a ways, you wanna walk with
me?''

''Sure, you got a name?''

''Frankie. You got to be real careful, any one of us caught
passin' on anythin' so much as a cigarette pack and we're
fucked. This is a big earner, man, I don't wanna lose my
job.''

''I never seen you, it's cool.''

The waiter's Harley had more bolts and alarms than a
security firm. It was a highly polished, chrome-on-chrome
custom shovel-head.

''Nice bike.''

''Yeah, the fuckin' bastards use trucks now to lift them.
I've only had it a few months.''

''Like you said, you got yourself a nice earner and maybe
you gonna earn even more. You got something for me?''

"This is the chick that's missin', right? An' I'm not gonna get involved with any cops, that's got nothin' to do with the action—"

"I'm not a cop, for fuck's sake. I'm gonna hit on her family for Tony, she owed him. I don't give a shit about anythin' else."

"I don't think anyone knows who she is, they got a lotta this kind of material, know what I mean?"

"I'm trying to, I just want to do the deal an' get out of here."

Nick eased out the bag as a taster and Frankie flicked a furtive glance in both directions. He drew his jacket forward and exposed a newspaper with a brown manila envelope tucked inside.

Nick gave Lorraine a wink as he got back into the Jeep, starting it up straightaway.

"Let's put some distance between me and my new pal Frankie."

He swerved into the traffic with a screech of his balding tires and they headed down the strip. He eased the manila envelope out of his denim jacket.

"Oh, my God," Lorraine said, as she took out the photograph.

"You said it, blew me away. Part of a private collection they got up in the office. You were right, I was wrong."

Nick lived in a house similar to Rosie's, but even more dilapidated. His apartment was a chaotic mess, the bed unmade and dirty dishes stacked in the sink. "Guess the place needs a woman's touch. Problem is, although I get a lot of chicks up here, none of them stay long enough to vacuum."

He wasn't apologizing, he obviously didn't care. Out of the corner of her eye Lorraine saw him open the fridge and take out a bottle of iced vodka. He took a small thick glass, filled it once, knocked it back and refilled it twice, each time downing the contents in one go and letting out a satisfied "Ahhhh."

Everything in her wanted to join him in the neat ice-cold vodka. Her body was shaking.

"Nick . . ." she said softly.

"Yep? Coffee's on, won't be long." He came and stood over her as she sat on a chair and gently patted her head. It was a sweet, affectionate gesture, and she had to swallow hard because she felt herself wanting to weep. "How you doing?"

"Okay."

It was hardly audible and he squatted down in front of her, resting on his old beat-up cowboy boots. "You want to talk?"

Her voice was husky. "I want a drink, it's all I can think about."

" 'Sokay, I can go over to the fridge and pour you one right now, but that would be dumb."

She bent her head. "Just gimme a drink, Nick."

He stood up, hands on his hips. "You want one, *you* get it! You get up off your ass and the bottle is there in the freezer compartment, go on."

She got up slowly, licking her lips, and crossed to the fridge. Her hand reached out and she turned to look at him.

"I'm not stopping you, you know the road you're gonna take better than me."

She rested her head against the cold front of the big old-fashioned fridge, and he remained watching her, hands resting above his snake hips, the old Mexican silver-buckled belt askew. He waited. The way she pressed her body against the fridge turned him on; she was virtually kissing it like a lost lover. She pushed herself away and turned to the coffeepot, her hands clenched at her side.

"How well did you know Jack Lubrinski?" Her voice was strained. She turned to him, her face tilted to one side, the scar hidden by a fold of her soft blond hair.

"Good cop, great guy."

She nodded, and as she pushed the hair away from her face he could see the jagged scar down her cheek. She had the bluest eyes he'd ever seen, but she didn't seem to be looking at him, it was more like looking through him.

"I miss him."

"Yeah, I know."

Suddenly she focused on him, studying his face. He blushed under her scrutiny. "You sometimes remind me of him."

He lit two cigarettes and passed one to her. As he held it out she touched his hand lightly with one finger, then took the cigarette and inhaled deeply.

"You see, what happens, Nick, is like corners of my mind open. It comes on unexpectedly, kind of throws me sideways, and I feel this terrible panic. Just when I think I have it all under control, just when I think I've got myself together . . ." She sucked on the cigarette. "One spiked drink, one goddamned mouthful, and . . . nothing else matters."

"Yes it does, you didn't open the fridge."

"No, I didn't, but I would have if I was on my own. That's what scares me, Nick, that and . . ."

"And what?"

She shrugged and sipped her coffee.

"Go on, tell me, and what?"

"Oh, my kids, I think of them and Michael."

"Who's Michael?"

"He was my husband."

"Ah, well, we've all got ghosts, we've all got corners, Lorraine. Maybe you shouldn't hide them away but talk more."

"I can't."

She suddenly bent her head forward, so he couldn't see her face, and let out a soft moan. He wanted to hold her in his arms, cradle her, kiss her, but he got up and moved farther away. He couldn't deal with the emotions she was wrenching out of him; it had been a long time since he had wanted to love a woman, and that's what he knew was happening: he was falling in love with her. He changed the subject fast.

"Right, we should talk over what went down tonight, sugar, because it's late an' we got to get moving on this case and out to New Orleans."

She sniffed. "Yes, you're right, and I'm okay now." She sprang to her feet, pulling her skirt down, kicking off the red high-heeled shoes. "Gimme the picture, let's have another look. And this Frankie didn't know of anyone called Polar?"

"Nope." Nick picked up his jacket off the floor, fished inside the pocket and brought out the envelope. She took it from him and slapped it against her thigh. No shakes now, no vulnerable lady. She was back in shape.

Lorraine leaned on the edge of the Formica-topped kitchen table, studying the photo. He stood next to her, quite close, but couldn't touch her, not like before; he knew her need for him and a drink had gone.

"Well, she's out of her head, that's for sure, look at her eyes."

"Nice body," he said softly.

Anna Louise Caley was naked, lying on a table. There were bottles around one shoulder, one glass fallen on its side. The three boys were all around twenty, and they looked drunk, their clothes half off, their trousers down, and all their faces in the shot. One boy was fucking her, one was kissing her tits and one was jerking off over her, semen glistening over her flat, tanned belly. Anna Louise Caley was smiling, one hand holding a bottle of tequila.

"Miss Goody Two-shoes," Lorraine said softly.

She was peering at the picture closely. "I think one of the little shits was the freckle-faced kid I interviewed at UCLA, I'm sure of it."

Nick lit another cigarette and inhaled deeply. "According to Frankie, and he only started working at the club about the time this was taken, he only saw her once or twice, with a blond girl about the same age. They came together, got smashed and royally screwed. He didn't know any of the kids fucking her but remembered her from the photo we passed him."

"He also know who she was? Newspapers had her picture on the front page, so how come he didn't contact the cops?"

"Hey, kid's scared to lose his job, and you don't think he was the only guy that must have recognized her and kept their mouths shut."

She frowned. "But if this kind of thing is a regular scene, why would he remember somebody who only used the place once or twice? I mean, you said they were screwing in the john."

"Well, firstly, a so-called bag of coke worth fifteen thousand dollars is a pretty good incentive, and this action we got here wasn't done in the john but in a private room, this happened like real late. You know, just the main guys there, the so-called stars that gang-bang, and only a couple of wait-ers on duty, Frankie being one of them. He said he remem-bered her because he reckoned he'd get his dick wet, but she passed out—"

"But this bunch of shits aren't movie stars, one is a col-lege kid."

"Maybe rich enough, who the fuck knows?"

Lorraine frowned. "Frankie have a picture of her girl-friend?"

"No, he said she was taken up to the top room and he wouldn't get up there, they had their own waiter."

"Who took this photograph?"

Nick cocked his head to one side. "Seems they got hidden cameras in the wall of mirrors in the private room. They take a lot of snaps, so many he wasn't even worried they'd miss one."

Lorraine stuffed the photograph back into the envelope. "Well, I got something to discuss with Mr. and Mrs. Caley, but I don't think they're gonna like it." She started to put on her red shoes and then pulled a face. "I'll go barefoot, you wanna give me a ride home?"

"Sure."

In the Jeep she stroked Tiger's head while the dog tried to lick her face. "I think we really bonded, Nick, he's a real character."

"Yep, he is." Nick slammed his door shut.

"You know, this new direction kind of excludes Robert Caley. You think the photo might have been used for black-mail?"

Nick rammed the car into gear. "Like Frankie said, they got a load of snaps and all they're used for, I'd say, are sick kicks. But maybe we don't exclude blackmail."

As they drew up outside Rosie's place, Lorraine laughed. "Hey! We got one big breakthrough tonight, Nick. I'll talk to the Caleys in the morning, maybe see if I can get that Tom Heller to spill something, and then . . ." She punched his arm. "New Orleans, here we come. . . ." She clapped her hands. "Oh, Nick, one million dollars! I am sure we'll crack this, we'll find her, and like Mrs. Caley said, dead or alive we still get the bonus." Lorraine rubbed Tiger's head and then grabbed her high heels. "G'night, talk tomorrow.

Oh, Nick, you won't give this information to Agnew, will you?''

His smile wiped fast. "No, but is it okay if I collect my paycheck?''

She laughed, and he stayed watching her running barefoot up the stairs, two steps at a time to the first floor. She seemed full of energy, her confidence seemingly restored. She also, Nick noticed, made sure she had the photograph. Lorraine Page was back on the case. He rubbed Tiger's head.

"Dangerous lady, that one. Gets to the core, understand?'' Tiger licked his face. "No, I guess you don't.''

Nick finished the bottle of vodka and lay spread-eagled on his crumpled bed. He picked up his guitar, strummed a few bars and began to tune it. He had liked her when she was vulnerable, liked it when she could take charge, sort of care for her. He hadn't felt that way about anyone in a very long time, and he knew he was caring too much, she was touching him deep down.

"Oh, Lorraine, Lorraine, filled up with pain . . . Oh, Lorraine, let me . . .''

He was a much better guitarist than he ever admitted, but his lyrics stank and he knew it, so he just lazily plucked at the strings and kept on saying her name . . . Lorraine.

Lorraine was curled up on her sofa bed, planning exactly how she would deal the ace she held in the manila envelope to the Caleys. Nick was far from her mind; so was the craving. The vulnerable Lorraine had crept back into her secret corner, along with Jack Lubrinski, her daughters and ex-husband. In fact, the person she was thinking about when she drifted to sleep was Robert Caley, wondering how he would react to the photograph. In a way she was relieved that in her mind he was no longer their main suspect. She was still wondering about his possible involvement in his daughter's disappearance and, lastly, what it would be like to lie naked next to him, when she fell asleep.

CHAPTER
9

Lorraine stood in front of the case chart pinned up on the wall in the office, "Day 4" underlined. It was only seven-fifteen in the morning, and she'd been there since six. She hadn't had more than a few hours' sleep but she wasn't feeling tired; on the contrary, she was buzzing.

Marked under her name were the names Robert Caley, Elizabeth Caley, Tom Heller (the freckle-faced student from UCLA), Noël (the Rasta hairdresser): four people she wanted to interview again.

Listed under New Orleans were Caley's business partners in the casino development, Tilda Brown, Anna Louise's girl-friend, and all the Caley staff. Uppermost on Nick and Rooney's list was to make contact with the New Orleans officers involved in the investigation to get an update and any background on Juda Salina.

Lorraine watched as Noël blow-dried her hair.

"You want the same style, right?"

"Yeah, just like before. By the way, did you ever do Anna Louise Caley's hair?"

He cocked his head to one side, holding the dryer aside a moment. "Yep."

"You ever go to the Viper Room?"

He continued working, his attention on her hair. "Nah, I got better things to do with my time."

"Anna Louise Caley used to go."

He looked at her reflection in the mirror, seemingly intent on her hair.

"Really? Didn't think she was the type."

"Why do you say that?"

"Well, she was always kind of cute, bit shy. Obsessed with her hair, though."

"Was she always on her own?"

He turned off the dryer and leaned against the mirror shelf. "What's this? Why all the questions?"

Lorraine leaned forward, looking at her reflection. "Because I have been hired to trace her and all I get told is that she was a real cute, nice little rich girl. But I don't think she was; in fact, I know there was another side to Miss Caley."

"You think I know about it?"

"Maybe. I'm a private investigator, Noël, not a cop, so there's no need to get edgy. I want to show you something." Lorraine drew out the photograph. "Take a look at this."

Noël glanced at the photograph, then whistled between his teeth, holding it closer. He muttered something to himself and then passed it back to Lorraine. She slipped it back into the envelope.

Noël continued to blow-dry her hair. Twice his eyes met hers, but he said nothing.

"You know any of the guys in the photo?"

He nodded. "You see the cat at the end, right at the end of the salon, finishing a tint? He's the one giving it to her. His name is Cal, Cal Thompson, real little prick, if you'll excuse the pun."

Lorraine looked along the row of salon chairs. Cal had his back to her, so she couldn't get a good look at his face.

She walked down the salon to the end chair. She stood behind the young man who was washing out his tint bowl and brushes.

"Excuse me, it's Cal, isn't it?"

Cal Thompson turned. He was good-looking, tanned like everyone in LA, one of those young men full of confidence in his own looks.

"Hi, could I talk to you for a moment?"

He frowned, looked toward the main reception, back to Lorraine.

"In private."

He hesitated. "I'm busy right now, if you want to make an appointment—"

Lorraine took out the photograph. "You want this plastered over the *National Enquirer*? I'd find a few minutes if I were you, Cal."

Cal drew a curtain across the doorway. Lorraine sat down and took out her cigarettes.

"You a reporter?"

"Nope. Sit down a second, Cal."

He sat down, still holding on to his cool, pushing the ashtray toward Lorraine. "What do you want?"

"Information. I'm a private investigator. Look at the picture, Cal. Gang rape is an offense, right? She was just a kid, so just answer a few questions, then I'm out of here."

"Listen, man, she's no fucking minor. Look at her face, she was loving it."

"I'd say she was stoned out of her mind. You do know who she is, don't you?"

He sighed, turning away. "Yeah, yeah, I know who she is."

Lorraine waited; he was losing his cool now. "So you know she's been missing?"

He nodded. "Yeah, but it's got nothing to do with me. I mean, *that* was just the one time, know what I mean? We were high and . . . that's all there is to it."

"All? There's three guys here fucking a young kid stoned out of her mind and you say that's all? Can you name the others?"

"No."

"So what happened after this?"

Cal shrugged. "I put my dick away, had a few more drinks and went home. She'd already left with her friend."

"Who was the friend?"

"I dunno. She was here once at the salon."

"Tilda Brown?"

"I dunno, I get a lot of clients. Some walk in off the street, so it might not be in the appointment book. Look, I obviously know Anna Louise, but then so did everybody else. She had the reputation of being open to offers, she'd been there a few times before, turning the same tricks. She liked it.''

"Was she always stoned?"

"I dunno, I think it was booze rather than drugs, but everybody's taking stuff down there, it's on sale, know what I mean?"

"I'm trying to, Cal. Did you ever see her with anyone specific? Heard the name Polar mentioned at all?"

"No, like I only saw her that time at the club and a few times in the salon. She's not even my client."

"You saw her leave the Viper Room on the night this photo was taken?"

"Yeah, and her friend. We hung out for a while longer."

"We?"

"Couple of friends. It was real late anyway, the place was getting quiet, so it hadda be around four or five in the morning."

Lorraine slipped the photograph into the envelope. "Do you recall when this was taken?"

"Yeah, because it was my girlfriend's birthday. We had a bustup in the Viper, I hung on in there. February thirteenth last year. Look, I'm being dead straight with you. I'm married now and I don't get into that kind of stuff anymore."

Lorraine stubbed out her cigarette. "You recall how she got home? You said you saw her leaving. Did she drive or was she driven, or did she get a taxi?"

"Man, she was too out of it to drive. I think maybe somebody collected her, but I dunno, I honestly don't remember. I did nothin' wrong, I mean, she was loving it."

Lorraine walked to the curtained doorway. "Thanks. And, Cal, I hope you have been straight with me because I don't want to have to come back."

"Hi, you remember me?"

Tom Heller was drenched in sweat after a tennis game, tying a white cotton sweater around his shoulders. He stared at Lorraine a moment, then took out a pristine white towel from his kit bag and wiped the sweat from his face, rubbing his hair. "No, I'm sorry, I don't."

She opened her purse as he stowed his rackets into their cases. "Lorraine Page, Page Investigations."

He zipped up the bag. "Oh, right, yeah."

"Anna Louise Caley, you said you had dated her."

He slung his bag's shoulder strap onto his shoulder.
"Right. Look, I should go get a shower."

"You also said it was a platonic relationship—just pic-
nics, beach parties . . ." He started to move away. "Wait
one second." Her voice made him pull up fast. "You lied,
you knew her very well, didn't you?"

"No more than anyone else."

She slapped the photo into his chest. "No more than anyone else? You mean everybody fucked her like this? Take
a good look, because that is no beach party or teenage bar-
becue, now, is it? It's a gang bang and you, sunshine, are
jerking off over her belly. It is you, isn't it?"

He stared at the photograph and then let out a long sigh.
"Oh, shit."

"Let's sit on a bench and talk. This time you'd better be
honest with me or a copy of that is sent to your parents, to
the dean of students of this place—you understand me?"

Mario was polishing the Caleys' limo. He turned as Lorraine
walked up to him.

She smiled. "Doing a nice job, Mario. Remember me?
Lorraine Page."

Mario nodded and continued polishing.

"Tell me, on the night of February thirteenth last year,
did you collect Anna Louise from the Viper Room?"

"What?"

Lorraine leaned on the side of the car. "The family left
for New Orleans two days later, on the fifteenth, same day
Anna Louise disappeared, so I'd say you've got a pretty
good memory of events close to that date 'cause you were
questioned by the cops, right?"

He nodded again, still polishing.

"So, February thirteenth last year, did you—"

"Yes, ma'am, I picked up Miss Caley and her friend,
drove them back here."

"Stoned out of their heads?"

"I dunno, ma'am, I just picked 'em up. They was waitin'
on the sidewalk."

"Did her parents know?"

"No, ma'am. Anna Louise called me on my cell phone. I had to get up an' get dressed. It was comin' up to around five o'clock."

"How come you've never mentioned this to anyone before?"

He walked around to a bucket and dunked his chamois into the soapy water. "I didn't want no trouble. They were just foolin' around, the way kids do. I brought them home, no more to it."

"You ever picked up Anna Louise from a club before?"

"No, ma'am. She'd call me from a few parties, never wanted to drive when she was not sober. We hadda kind of arrangement, safer that way."

"Who was she with?"

"Most times with her friend Tilda. She didn't go out much, only when Miss Brown was stayin'. Everyone said that Miss Brown was a nice girl, but me, well, I didn't. I think she was a bad influence on Miss Anna Louise, but I never said nothin' to nobody, not my business."

"You know anyone called Polar?"

"No, ma'am, I do not, an' if you'll excuse me, I need to wash over the wheels now."

Lorraine stepped aside. "Did you take Tilda Brown to the airport?"

"I did."

"She say anything?"

"No, she knew I didn't like her, she never spoke to me. Miss Tilda Brown is a high-and-mighty little minx."

Lorraine turned as she heard her name called. Phyllis was standing on the front steps of the house. She looked confused. "Why, Mrs. Page, I've only just sent off your money. I didn't expect to see you, is there a problem?"

"No, I just need to speak to Mrs. Caley before we leave. She is in, isn't she? Only I arranged to see her at eleven, but I've been held up." Lorraine joined Phyllis on the steps.

"I doubt if she will agree to see you. She never mentioned to me that you would be coming over and she is meeting her agent, so . . ." Phyllis walked into the hallway, as if to close the front door, but Lorraine was right behind her.

"I need to talk to her, it's very important."

"I really can't interrupt her, she is dressing."

"Yes, you can, Phyllis, because I am not leaving this house until I see her."

"I am sorry, but Mrs. Caley cannot see anyone."

"Don't you think you should ask me, Phyllis?" Elizabeth Caley stood at the top of the stairs, looking poised and immaculate. "I'll come down, Mrs. Page, but I only have about half an hour." Elizabeth stepped brightly and steadily down the stairs, her perfume reaching Lorraine long before the delicate white outstretched hand tapped her shoulder.

Lorraine followed Elizabeth into the sunroom. All the blinds were drawn and the overpowering smell of lilies mixed with Elizabeth's flowery perfume made her want to gasp for fresh air. They sat at a small white table on two delicate cushioned chairs amid the profusion of plants.

"I'll get straight to the point."

"I hope you will, darling. My agent will be here shortly—it seems I am being offered work. Since Anna Louise disappeared I've had so much press—disgusting really—I think a lot of people in the industry thought I was dead. Of course, I won't do it, but he is most insistent that I at least discuss the offers. There is nothing sadder than resurrecting old has-beens like myself." She laughed.

"You look wonderful," Lorraine said, and meant it. Not a hair of the coal-black braided bun at the nape of Mrs. Caley's neck was out of place, her makeup was perfect, and her simple pale lemon suit with tight-fitting pencil skirt showed off her slim legs and feet in their white high-heeled sandals. She was wearing a tiny gold ankle chain with a diamond drop, diamond earrings and the large diamond and emerald ring on her wedding finger. Beside her, Lorraine felt and looked cheap; this makeover job on Elizabeth Caley had cost a lot of money and it showed.

At that moment, tea and coffee were brought in by the mute butler.

"Thank you, Peters," Mrs. Caley said as she poured her pale greenish tea. She looked at Lorraine. "You've found out something, haven't you?" Her voice was soft, almost frightened.

"Yes, I have."

She closed her eyes. "It's not good, is it?"

"No."

"Well, get straight to the point, Mrs. Page, don't keep me in suspense."

Lorraine reached for her briefcase. "I am sorry, but what I'm going to show you will be very upsetting." She passed over the photograph and waited, watching Mrs. Caley like a hawk. She saw her eyes widen, saw her swallow once, twice, then breathe in deeply as she stared at the photograph of her daughter. She then passed it back to Lorraine.

"Why? Why would she do something like that? Why?" Her lips quivered, then her brow puckered. She seemed to be trying not to weep in order not to spoil her makeup. "Who are those people with her?"

"I know two. One is a hairdresser and the other a fellow student."

She shook her head. "Dear God, they should be arrested. Where was it taken?"

"In a club. It's called the Viper Room."

"Don't show it to Robert, please don't let him see that disgusting display or he'll . . . he'll kill them. He wouldn't believe it, he has no idea."

"Did you have any idea?"

"What? Did I know my daughter was making a public spectacle of herself? Did I know my daughter was being fucked by a group of men like a whore? *No! I did not know!* But I wish to God I had." She clenched her hands. "What kind of a woman do you think I am?"

"You have a drug problem, I know that."

"I beg your pardon?"

"Let's not play games, Mrs. Caley, I know about your doctor. Do you know, really know, what chances you are taking?"

"Who told you this?"

"I found it out, Mrs. Caley, that is my job. But are you fully aware of the enormous risks you are taking with your own life? You are using Temazepam sleeping tablets."

"Wouldn't you, under the circumstances?" she snapped.

"What you are doing is lethal and you must take medical advice and as soon as possible. I believe you are injecting Temazepam—"

Mrs. Caley pushed at the table. "Phyllis, has Phyllis been talking to you?"

"Your doctor has been arrested—"

"Oh, my God. Did he tell you? What has he said to you?"

Lorraine opened her cigarette pack and proffered one to Elizabeth Caley, who swiped the pack out of her hand.

"You are supposed to be investigating the disappearance of my *daughter*, not delving into my private life. You had no right to make any inquiries about my personal—"

Lorraine interrupted, her voice controlled and very firm. "I am trying to ascertain the whereabouts of your daughter. And I would say your drug problems might have some connection. So I am asking you again, did your daughter also use drugs, Mrs. Caley?"

"No, she did not."

"Did she know of your drug addiction?"

Elizabeth Caley sighed impatiently. "Yes, but she would not even contemplate using drugs herself. She saw too much anguish and pain, regret and dependency in her own mother."

"Were you aware that Tilda Brown also frequented these clubs with your daughter?"

"Tilda was with Anna Louise?"

"I believe so. Did you know the two girls had some kind of argument the day before you left for New Orleans?"

"I don't know what they were arguing about, just that Tilda decided to leave—silly, really. I just let them get on with it."

Lorraine wasn't going to let Mrs. Caley off the hook. She tried again.

"Do you have drug dealers in New Orleans?" She knew she had hit a red zone; Elizabeth Caley's face was glistening with sweat and she was becoming more agitated by the second.

"Oh God, Robert will be so angry, this is terrible. You see, he is in the middle of this big business deal and—"

"I only need a name, Mrs. Caley, someone you usually contact there."

"No, no, please, if this was ever to get out, if anyone there was to know . . ." She seemed to fall apart in front of

Lorraine's eyes, slumping into a chair and crying. The makeup smeared, and she held her head in her hands as though it ached, pulling loose her tightly coiled hair. She continued to sweat profusely.

Lorraine leaned forward to touch her. "Please, I will be discreet, I promise you, but I do need to question everyone possible. You want me to find your daughter, don't you?"

"Yes, yes, I do," she murmured, and then her body began to shake uncontrollably and she screamed, "Phyllis, *Phyllis, Phyllis!*"

Phyllis came running as Elizabeth Caley lost control of herself. Urine trickled down her legs, her limbs jerking and her head twitching.

"It's all right, I'm here, *I'm here, Mrs. Caley*, just hold on to me, you're going to be all right, just hold on to me. Oh, my God, help me, for God's sake, help me, she's going into a spasm . . ."

Peters came running, and between them they helped her from the sunroom. Lorraine followed them out into the hall and watched as Peters carried Elizabeth up the stairs.

"Please stay down here," he said angrily to Lorraine.

"Yes, just leave her alone," Phyllis interjected.

Lorraine sighed with irritation, but there was nothing she could do. She knew she would get nothing more out of Mrs. Caley now, so there seemed no point in remaining at the house. She returned to the sunroom to collect her purse and cigarettes. A maid was already clearing up the tea trays.

Lorraine suddenly picked up the teapot, took off the lid and sniffed; it smelled of mint and something else, a herbal smell. She sniffed again.

"Excuse me, Mrs. Page, may I take that from you?" It was the dour Peters.

"What the hell is in it?"

"Just a herbal remedy. Mrs. Caley has it delivered."

"Where from?"

Peters picked up the tray. "The Natural Health Store, I believe it's called. Excuse me, I hope you won't take offense, but why don't you leave her alone? She is very sick and it's tragic to see her this way, just as she was recovering and—"

"Yes, very reminiscent of *Sunset Boulevard*, but I wonder who will end up in the swimming pool?"

He stared hard at Lorraine and did not hide his disdain. "You should perhaps take great care or it could be you."

He walked out. Lorraine was about to follow him when the maid gave a small nervous cough. Lorraine turned toward her. She gave a furtive look at Peters's disappearing ramrod back before she whispered to Lorraine.

"She gets it from home, ma'am. It's no remedy."

"I'm sorry, what did you say?"

The girl chewed her lip and then tried to pass Lorraine, frightened.

"Wait, don't go. Are you talking about the tea?"

Phyllis hurried in. "Get back in the house, Sylvana, go along, quickly now."

Sylvana shot a frightened look at Lorraine before scurrying away.

Lorraine turned to Phyllis with concern. "Is Mrs. Caley going to be all right?"

Phyllis shook her head and shrugged. "She'll sleep it off."

Lorraine took Phyllis's arm as they walked back to the house. "Phyllis, you had better get Mrs. Caley some treatment and fast—otherwise she's going to kill herself."

"Yes, I know," Phyllis whispered, and then stopped in her tracks. "What did you say that made her get so upset?"

"Who's her drug dealer in New Orleans?"

Phyllis closed her eyes. "Oh God, this is dreadful, if Mr. Caley was to know. Please, is it really necessary to—"

"For Chrissakes, Phyllis, I am trying to find her daughter! Now if you know and persist in withholding information from me, in giving me half-truths . . ."

Just as it seemed that Phyllis was about to confide in Lorraine, Robert Caley strode in. "What has been going on out here? Phyllis, you should be with Elizabeth. I want you to sit with her until a doctor comes to see her."

"I'm sorry, Mr. Caley, I'll go straight to her now."

"And stay with her—if she vomits she could . . ." Robert Caley sighed, waited for Phyllis to go and then looked at Lorraine. "What did you say to her? She's hysterical."

"I'm just trying to do my job, Mr. Caley, but it seems

everyone who works around here is so busy protecting your wife—''

''You saw her, don't you think she needs protecting?'' he snapped.

''Yes, I do, but I don't think you know how serious her condition is, Mr. Caley.''

''How dare you! I get her into a rehab center and she's cleaned up only to get back on whatever drugs she can get her hands on. Well, she's going away this time whether she likes it or not—''

''So you know what she's taking?''

''You name it and she'll shove it up her nose, down her throat or inject it. Unless I put her under twenty-four-hour watch I can't stop her. But believe me, I've tried.''

''Right now, Mr. Caley, your wife is using drugs that could very easily kill her. They are very dangerous used in the quantity she is injecting and she could easily induce a thrombosis.''

He closed his eyes. ''Oh, my God, what is it—heroin?''

''No, they are prescribed sleeping tablets.''

He sighed, making a helpless gesture with his hands. ''The last thing I need right now is some asshole to get hold of her condition and the story to be plastered over every shit-filled tabloid there is. My competitors'd love it, with Anna Louise missing you can bet any money they'd link her drug abuse to—''

''What if it is?'' Lorraine interrupted. He frowned and looked at her. She was sure he was unaware of the exact drugs used by Elizabeth Caley. ''Do you know who she used to procure drugs for her in New Orleans? Your wife has a very expensive habit, Mr. Caley, and she'll either take stuff with her or score it there, so maybe there is a link.''

He sat down, head in his hands as he rested his elbows on the table. ''I doubt it, she has a pretty well-organized network of people who I think procure whatever she needs. And she pays highly for it, I have no doubt.''

''You know any of them?''

''I know her main contact is her own doctor. It's madness, like a catch-22 situation—if I report him he will obviously use my wife's name, even more so now.'' He got up and stuffed his hands into his trouser pockets. He seemed tired out. "I banned Juda Salina from the house but it didn't do any good, she just went to her place—"

"Juda Salina procured drugs for your wife? Are you sure?"

He cocked his head to one side. "Sure as I can be, but what can I do? Put the cops on her and then she informs the press who her client is?"

Lorraine leaned forward. "I don't think her doctor will be able to practice for some considerable time—he was arrested two days ago, and as I believe your wife did not use her own name I doubt if there will be any adverse publicity. Well, I hope not for her sake as much as yours."

"Thank you," he said softly, and smiled, then gestured for her to walk beside him. "I need some air, let's go into the garden."

They walked side by side in silence along the narrow pathway past the manicured lawns and flower beds. She felt him begin to relax and he gave her that gentle smile again.

"You mind if I ask you something personal, Mr. Caley?"

"No, Mrs. Page, you go right ahead. And if you don't mind my being personal, I like this new haircut, it suits you."

Lorraine ignored the compliment. "Do you love your wife?"

He wasn't expecting the question and took a moment before he answered, shaking his head, "Of course I do, but maybe 'care' would be a better description. If it wasn't for her I'd still be bumming around selling real estate. That's all I did, you know, when I met her, I was a real estate agent. In fact, I was trying to sell her a property."

"You got lucky," Lorraine said softly, and his pleasant manner changed. He lost that vulnerable quality, his eyes hardened and his voice was cold.

"No, Mrs. Page, I fell in love with a very beautiful, sweet lady. Now, unless you want to ask any further personal questions, I had better see to my wife. . . . Oh, I offered you a ride, I'm flying to New Orleans tonight. If you wish to join me, call Phyllis, I'll send my car around."

"I accept the ride but I'll make my own way to the airport."

"Fine. Phyllis will give you details of which hangar my plane's parked in. About six-thirty?"

"Thank you, I'll be there."

"I bet you will be, Mrs. Page."

He returned to the house, not looking back, and Lorraine remained standing alone, angry at herself. There was no need for her to have asked Caley if he loved his wife; she knew he didn't, but she believed he really did care about her.

She was getting into her car when she saw the private ambulance pull up in the driveway. She took a long time unlocking the door as she watched the two attendants hurry into the house. A third car was parked in the driveway, a dark four-door Mercedes-Benz. After a few moments the two attendants appeared on the steps, holding Elizabeth Caley between them. She was wearing a pair of dark glasses and a scarf swathed around her head and she was sobbing, needing the support of both men, but she made no attempt to resist as they helped her inside the ambulance.

Phyllis and Robert Caley came out behind Mrs. Caley, accompanied by a tall man in a gray suit carrying a doctor's bag. Lorraine could not delay leaving any longer, as all three turned toward her.

"Good-bye, see you later," she called out, and then at once regretted her failure to say something more appropriate—even more so when she drove past the ambulance and caught a glimpse of Elizabeth Caley just before they closed the doors. She was weeping inconsolably, repeating her daughter's name again and again—"Anna Louise, Anna Louise . . ."

CHAPTER

10

Lorraine had expected a small twin-engined plane, but Robert Caley owned a 1993 Citation Jet, which made her Russian cabdriver whistle with open admiration. As she picked up her suitcase a tanned blond man jumped down the steps of the plane.

"Mrs. Page?" His wide smile seemed overbright. "I'm Edward Hardy, Mr. Caley's pilot. Let me take your case. Mr. Caley has been delayed, but he called in to say he would be here shortly. As it turns out, it's not a problem, because we haven't yet got clearance for takeoff."

Lorraine stepped inside, and Edward moved ahead of her to indicate a plush leather easy chair. He stowed her case away in a compartment at the rear of the plane, keeping up a friendly conversation.

"If you need the bathroom it's right here, and the bedroom is just beyond."

She flicked him a glance, but the remark was innocent.

"If you need to wash, or do whatever ladies do. In the meantime, can I offer you a drink? We have champagne, chilled Chardonnay or a nice Merlot, if you prefer. There's gin, whisky, vermouth, or I can make up a cocktail—anything you want."

Lorraine felt intensely self-conscious as she sat stiffly in the leather easy chair. "Just ice water, please."

A diminutive Chinese man appeared, carrying a deep basket and a large foil-covered silver tray.

"Hi there, how you doing? Young Sin, this is Mrs. Page."

She smiled as the little man began to lay out his many different covered dishes. "You like lobster, Mrs. Page?" he asked.

"Yes."

"Flown in from Maine." He opened a table, deftly placing on it a white linen cloth and napkins, flower bowls, cutlery and cut-crystal glasses.

Lorraine drew a *Vogue* magazine toward her and flicked through the glossy pages. Had Anna Louise Caley sat in the same chair and read a similar magazine?

"Did you know Anna Louise?" she asked as Edward refilled her glass. "Yes, of course."

"You were flying the plane on February fifteenth last year?"

"Yes, I was."

Lorraine smiled, sipping her water. "Anna Louise called home?"

"She did. We have a phone, do you need to make a call?"

"No, thanks. How was she on the flight?"

"I was in the cockpit."

"But you must have welcomed her aboard."

"Yeah, she was like usual, you know, cute kid, always real friendly."

"You've worked a long time for the Caleys?"

"About eight years."

"So you knew Anna Louise quite well?"

Edward hesitated and then put his hands on his hips. "She was my employer's daughter, ma'am. She was a nice kid but I never knew her. I never saw her outside business if that is what you mean."

"You are a nice-looking young man, Edward."

"I'm also married, Mrs. Page, with a two-year-old boy. No way would I start up anything that'd jeopardize my job, my marriage, or show disrespect to Mr. Caley."

"How did you get on with Mrs. Caley?"

Edward was beginning to show his irritation at her questions. "Mrs. Caley is one of the nicest women I know, always friendly. I know she has a few problems, but that isn't my business. When she's aboard she's real quiet, she's nervous about flying. You nervous at all, Mrs. Page?''

"No.''

"No, I didn't think you would be.''

He was about to walk away when she slapped the magazine down.

"Edward, a second. Don't get uppity with me. I'm hired by the Caleys to find their daughter, so I have to ask you a few questions, be they personal or not. I don't mean to insult you, but I've had a lot of people tell me what a cute, sweet kid Anna Louise was, when I know she was not quite so cute, not quite so innocent, and liked to be fucked.''

"Excuse me, ma'am.'' Edward walked to the exit door.

Lorraine sighed, surprised by her own brusqueness. She looked out from the window as Caley's limo drew up close to the plane. Edward was waiting to take Caley's suitcase. The two men smiled warmly at each other.

Caley appeared, waved at Lorraine, and slipped his arm around Edward's shoulders. "Sorry about the delay. Will we have problems with takeoff?''

"Nope, just got clearance, we can go anytime.''

"Right, let's get going.''

Caley started for the cockpit, then turned. "Will you put your belt on, Mrs. Page—just a precaution. I'll be right out.''

Takeoff was smooth, hardly disturbing the cutlery neatly laid out on the dining table. It was a few moments more before the plane began to climb, and Caley returned. He fixed himself a whiskey, checking his watch.

"Flight's just over three hours. We'll eat in about an hour—is that all right for you?''

"Fine, thank you.''

"I hope you like lobster?''

"I do.''

"Good.'' He smiled and picked up his briefcase. He sat opposite her and selected some papers from his case. Lorraine continued to flick through the magazines, aware of his presence, aware of his seemingly paying her no attention. It unnerved her.

"You can smoke if you want,'' he said quietly.

"No, I'm fine, thank you.''

"If you'll excuse me, I just need to read through these, sorry."

"Don't apologize, I'm grateful for the ride. Thank you."

He didn't answer, becoming intent on his papers. As he worked he eased off his jacket, tossing it aside. He then unbuttoned his collarless shirt, one, two, three buttons, still intent on reading, and undid first one cuff, then the other, rolling the sleeves midway up his forearm.

Caley fixed himself two more drinks, checked in with Edward, then sat in another area of the plane and used the telephone for almost three quarters of an hour, his back to Lorraine. She listened, even though he kept his voice low. The calls were to business partners, to Phyllis and the hospital to discuss Elizabeth's condition, then to his staff in New Orleans. There was a lengthy conversation with Mark, his assistant, and Margaret. He listened, swore under his breath, sighed a lot, and then got up to refill his glass. He paused at her side.

"Do you want a refill?"

"Nope, I'm fine."

He smiled, but she could see his mind was elsewhere, so she continued to look at another magazine. By now they all seemed to have the same model wearing similar dresses. She didn't look up when he sat opposite her again.

"I like your suit."

She looked up and blushed. "It's new."

"Are you hungry?"

"Only if you are. If you have to continue working, please, go ahead."

He didn't. Instead he offered her his hand and led her to the table, drew out a thick padded leather seat for her and lit the candles.

During the meal, they hardly spoke. When they finished, he prepared coffee as she returned to her seat. She didn't know if it was the air in the cabin or the churning of her stomach, but she was finding it hard to breathe because she wanted him to touch her. It was driving her crazy; it was all she could think about, and it physically hurt, the wanting.

"I need to use the bathroom."

He pointed to the end of the cabin, a cigar clenched in his teeth as he poured their coffee and then opened a bottle of brandy for himself. Lorraine pressed the door closed and gasped. Not until she had run some water and patted her face did she feel calmer. Her hands were shaking and she felt like a sixteen-year-old, afraid of walking out and seeing him, afraid he'd know what she was feeling.

She knew the bedroom was next door, even had a moment of fantasy that she would walk out and he would be waiting for her. What would she do if he was? It was madness. She flushed the toilet, telling herself to get it together. She caught her reflection in the vanity mirror above the small washbasin—her cheeks were flushed from the cold water, and her mascara had smudged. She spat on a tissue and wiped beneath her eyes. "Suit might look good but you look a mess," she told her reflection, forcing herself to open the door and walk out.

Her coffee was on the table, but there was no Robert Caley. She looked toward the closed bedroom door; had he gone in there? Was he, as she had just fantasized, waiting for her?

Edward opened the cockpit door. "Will you put your belt on, Mrs. Page, we'll be landing in ten minutes."

She nodded, pulling up the seat-belt strap as Edward popped his head around the door again. "Just so you won't panic, Mr. Caley is not landing the plane, says he's had too much to drink. He's finishing up some work, be out when we land."

Lorraine noticed the briefcase had gone, and she shut her eyes with relief; just not having him close made her calmer.

Caley was lying on the bed, the cigar in his hand. He'd had too much to drink, he knew, but he couldn't handle the fact that he wanted Lorraine; it was making him feel like an inadequate teenager. He imagined her walking in and, without needing to say a word, lying down beside him. He could feel the slow downward spiral of the plane matching the churning in the pit of his stomach. He had to force himself to straighten out. He checked his watch, got up and shaved, then put on a clean shirt.

Caley rejoined Lorraine as the undercarriage lowered. He snapped on his safety belt, placing the briefcase he hadn't opened at his side. Lorraine stared out of the dark window.

"I put the candles out."

"Oh, thank you."

He straightened a magazine on the table between them as the plane made a good smooth landing. "Good pilot," he said.

"Yes," she said, but neither of them looked at the other.

The stretch limo was waiting outside the private Lakefront Airport, and beyond the tarmac the dark waters of the huge salt lake stretched as far as Lorraine could see. As Caley helped her into the car he asked her where she was staying. She sat as far away from him as possible, opening her purse to check Rosie's notes. The St. Marie Guest House. The chauffeur waited until Caley gave him instructions to drive directly to his hotel.

"It's the hotel we stayed at the night Anna Louise disappeared. I've booked both suites again because I thought perhaps you would want to question the staff."

Lorraine nodded, and Caley turned toward the window, seemingly staring at the bulk of an old, garishly painted paddle steamer, now refitted as a floating gaming palace, brilliantly lit and emblazoned with a huge casino sign. The competition? Lorraine wondered.

"If you want, you can use Anna's suite . . ."

Lorraine told herself she was being insane, one minute afraid to be close to him, the next wanting to accept a suite in the same hotel. He stared out of the window, asking himself what the fuck he thought he was playing at, one moment avoiding her, the next asking her to sleep in the adjoining suite. If Elizabeth knew, she would scream blue murder, always wary about any scandal that might smudge her fame in her hometown.

"Maybe not," he said softly. "Sorry, I don't want you to get the wrong impression, it's just . . ."

"Just what, Mr. Caley?"

He turned and faced her as the chauffeur swung onto the Interstate to cross town; the houses, all with their southern shutters and verandas and many already sporting Carnival decorations, seemed small and huddled together in the darkness, and the city cramped, spaceless after the sprawl of LA.

"It's a connecting suite," he said with embarrassment.

"Yes, you said." Her heart was thudding, and she knew she should refuse the offer. Instead she gave a tiny laugh, trying to make a joke of it. "You afraid I'll sneak up on you in the middle of the night?"

There was a long, strained pause, and he never took his eyes off her. "I am not afraid of what you would do, Mrs. Page—it's what I would do, or might not be able to stop myself from doing."

There was another strained pause. She inched her hand across the seat toward him. She couldn't speak, and when she felt the touch of his hand on hers she felt as if she would explode. They had left the highway now and were approaching the old French Quarter, and Lorraine was glad of the excuse to look away, pretending to be absorbed in observing the historic streets. Only a few blocks away were the high, modern towers of a business district like any in America, but here was an atmosphere unlike anything Lorraine had encountered before—half village, half cosmopolitan Babylonian city.

The buildings at first seemed low and unimpressive, flat-roofed, two-story town houses for the most part, their plaster fronts painted within a narrow range of muted shades that had once been bright—ocher, putty, ashes of rose, mustard. All had long, elegant shuttered windows and door-frames, often picked out in a contrasting deep green, but most distinctive was the ironwork, as fantastically wrought as spun sugar, with which balconies, galleries, walks and window boxes were all lavishly decorated. In its heyday the place must have been something to see, Lorraine thought, but now the fading paint, peeling woodwork and untended hanging baskets and jardinieres were noticeable even at night.

Caley grimaced slightly as the crowds became thicker and the buildings more and more festooned with the purple, gold and green of Carnival flags, masks and streamers, and they slowed almost to walking pace to avoid the pedestrians of every age and nationality who thronged the streets. "Sorry. There's only a couple of blocks of this—it's tourist gulch down here, I'm afraid."

Lorraine knew he too was making small talk to try to conceal the tension between them, and glanced up at the street sign as they took a left: BOURBON. Farther down the block she could see the neon naked girls and triple X signs of the strip clubs, and every storefront they passed seemed to be a jazz bar, a restaurant, or a gift emporium full of tacky T-shirts, mugs, figurines, Carnival masks and Cajun cowboy hats by the score. Music and the smell of spiced food were everywhere, spilling from doorways and sometimes from broad galleries above; everywhere people were eating, drinking, singing, begging, the young guys staring and calling after the girls, tourist ladies in their seventies holding tight to their purses and their companions' arms. But all were out in the night and the Quarter: the raw life of the place hit Lorraine like a shot of liquor, and suddenly it didn't seem quite so faded and unimpressive. On the sidewalk a young black kid of ten or twelve tap-danced effortlessly, expertly, in a pair of sneakers with metaled heels and toes. He had a wide, ingratiating smile pasted to the lower half of his face, but Lorraine caught the age and the knowing in his eyes, and suddenly she felt the power of the past. This place had seen a lot of human foibles, she thought: there was nothing that couldn't happen here.

They picked up speed again as they drove on and the streets became quieter and the goods for sale changed to jewelry, art and antiques, displayed in ritzier shops closed at this hour of the evening.

"We're almost at the hotel, Mr. Caley," the chauffeur said as they turned into a block as perfectly preserved as a museum, and Lorraine moved her hand away. They pulled up outside an exquisite three-story town house with broad galleries and ironwork as delicate and elaborate as the lace of a ballgown: there was nothing to indicate that this was a hotel, but when the chauffeur rang at a pair of high double doors, a smartly suited young man appeared and greeted Caley warmly by name.

He led them through an arched porte cochere into a lantern-lit, paved courtyard, and Lorraine knew she was entering a world apart from the tacky burlesque of the tourist traps, one where every aspect of her surroundings had been carefully designed to leave no sense unsoothed, unrefreshed. The trees exhaled an intense, herb-sweet scent, strange at first, then delicious, revivifying, while in the background the sound of two fountains was just audible, and an array of

ferns, palms, citrus trees and vines grew lushly and seemingly at will around the courtyard's borders and balconies.
Lorraine knew at a glance, however, that this sweet neglect
was an effect achieved at considerable cost in terms of both
time and money; the balance of wildness and cultivation was
as perfect as a chord in music.

The young man ushered them into a small, graciously
appointed office, and an interminable time seemed to pass
while Caley exchanged pleasantries first with him, then with
the still more courteous and urbane general manager before
their bags were taken by the bellboy. Lorraine noted wryly
that the South, though perhaps in slightly reduced circumstances, still moved at her own grand old lady's pace.

"Lieutenant Page will want to ask your staff a few questions," Caley said as the manager at last motioned them
toward the elevator.

"Anything I and my staff can do to assist in any way,
you only have to ask."

The bellboy was waiting at the elevator, a dainty cage of
mirrors and gilding. Despite the confined space, Lorraine
and Robert Caley remained well apart and said nothing to
each other. When they reached the third floor, Caley took
his keys from the boy, walking ahead.

"Show Lieutenant Page to her suite, if you would," he
said without a backward glance.

"Yes, sir. You follow me, ma'am?" Lorraine was shown
to a plain white door; the hotel was clearly too exclusive
for room numbers, or even names. Farther along the corridor
Caley's suite door closed.

"Enjoy your stay, ma'am."

"Thank you."

Alone, Lorraine glanced around the suite: the sitting room
was large and airy, lit by a heavy crystal chandelier, and
again Lorraine knew that the daybed, the magnificent fireplace and mirrors, and the figured rugs, as soft and fine to
the touch as a cat's ear, were genuine antiques, not the ostentatious reproductions favored by anything approaching an
expensive hotel she had encountered in the past.

Beyond was the bedroom; an embroidered half-canopy
hung from a corona above the double bed, and a separate
bathing and dressing area was screened from the balcony by

muslin-draped French doors. Lorraine opened them and stepped out, noting a narrow spiral staircase—presumably the fire escape—trailing vines and plumbago, which gave access to the balcony below and then the ground. She wondered halfheartedly if Anna Louise Caley had left that way. If she had, no one would have seen her leave unless they'd been in the courtyard.

She unpacked and hung up her new clothes, wondering if she should contact Rosie and the others now, but then knew that if she did she might have some explaining to do. She went into the bathroom, set her few cosmetics out on the imposing marble washstand and ran herself a hot, deep bath.

Nick Bartello knocked on Rosie's door as Rooney appeared at the end of the corridor. "I got five beds in my room—how many you got, Nick?"

"Oh, just a double, a single and a cot!"

Rooney shrugged. "Well, we ain't payin' for it."

Rosie opened her door and beamed. "Hi, come on in. I got a huge room and my own bathroom, it's so cute."

"Any word from Lorraine?" Nick asked as he sat down on a boxy foam-filled sofa, upholstered in the same Dralon and fringes as the drapes. An old TV was perched high on a tallboy; the oversized nylon lampshades were full of dust and the room smelled of cigarettes and air freshener.

"Not yet, no, but I called home and the office and got no reply, so maybe she's on her way."

"I'm hungry," Rooney said flatly, and Rosie beamed again.

"Why don't we go eat, see a few sights, maybe wander around the French Quarter? I mean, since it's our first night we can kind of relax, right?"

"Let's go," Rooney said, grasping for a beer.

Nick hesitated, then shrugged. "Okay by me, but you got to get on to the cop shop here, Bill—find someone we can get some inside information from."

"Way I hear it, any one of the cops'll do anythin' for a few extra bucks."

"Hey, we can get on the streetcar, take a ride, have a look at the riverboat casinos."

Nick looked at Rooney as Rosie headed out. "Dumb broad thinks we're on holiday."

Rooney shrugged. "For tonight we can be . . . why the hell not?"

"Okay, man, why the hell not?" Nick strolled after Rooney as Rosie locked her room, clutching tourist guides and leaflets in her hand. "But we're already four days down. That leaves us ten to break this case."

"I've been looking forward to this," Rosie said as they trooped down the stairs, passing four old ladies with crimped perms protruding from their straw sun hats with "Laissez les Bons Temps Rouler" printed on them.

"Hell, Rosie, this is a geriatric location," Nick said.

"Now don't start, Nick Bartello. Like I said, we're lucky to get into someplace as central as this, it's coming up to Carnival."

"Sure is," Nick said as a group of yet more chattering women met their tour guide in the reception area.

"Ladies, are we all set? Tonight we are going to the historic Voodoo Museum, please all have your special party tickets ready," their slick black-haired guide bellowed.

Rosie slipped her hand into Rooney's arm. "I want to go there, to the Voodoo Museum."

"Let's eat first, huh?" Rooney said, that beer calling him.

Lorraine wrapped the hotel courtesy robe around herself as she dried her hair, conscious of the door to the adjoining room that had remained closed. In his suite, Caley, a towel around his waist, made some calls, the first to Saffron Dulay's father to arrange a meeting.

It was almost ten-thirty, but he still continued to call each of his partners to say he was in town and needed a meeting. Normally, he would have waited until first thing in the morning, but he needed to occupy his mind. The door that connected the two suites drew him like a magnet.

Had he said it? she asked herself, or had she misheard? Hadn't he said he was afraid of what he might do?

"Shit," she muttered, knowing it was ridiculous. "Go repack your things and get out before you do something you'll regret." But she did nothing, telling herself that she should go down to the front desk and start asking a few questions. This was the room Anna Louise Caley disappeared from; the dress she was going to wear had been laid out in readiness, and Caley had said he saw her purse in the sitting room. By which door had he entered the suite—the connecting door? Had he said it was unlocked? She couldn't remember. She finished drying her hair and decided she would go to bed and ask questions the following morning.

Lorraine had closed the doors to the balcony and was pulling back the bedspread when there was a tap on the main door. Her heart lurched as she heard the key turning.

The maid peeked around. "Oh, sorry, do you want your bed turned down, ma'am?"

"No, thank you, er . . . one second. Come in."

The maid hovered at the door. She had two foil-wrapped mints in her hand, and she curtsied to Lorraine as she scuttled to the bed.

"Do you mind if I ask you something?" Lorraine smiled sweetly.

"No, ma'am."

"Do you recall Anna Louise Caley at all?"

"Yes, ma'am, she often stayed here."

Lorraine came closer. "Were you on duty the night she disappeared? It was February fifteenth last year."

"Oh yes, I was, ma'am."

Lorraine looked at her watch. It was ten-forty-five. "Did you turn back her bed?"

"I did not. I knocked but received no reply."

"But you just unlocked my door, so you obviously have keys, and as I didn't reply, you walked in."

"But you didn't have a DO NOT DISTURB sign on the door, ma'am."

"Did Anna Louise Caley?"

"Yes, ma'am, but I came by earlier than tonight. We had a lot of new guests check in this evenin', so I am late on my round."

"So what time did you try to turn down Miss Caley's bed on the fifteenth?"

The maid looked at the ceiling. "Be about eight to half past."

"Did you come back to try again?"

"No, ma'am, I did not, because when I finished my round

there was still the sign on the door. That was about ten-thirty.''

"Thank you. Er, what's your name?"

"Ellie, ma'am, Ellie Paton.''

Lorraine slipped her a couple of dollars and sat on the bed. If Anna Louise Caley had stayed here often, then she would know the routine of the night staff, so she obviously intended not to be disturbed or found out.

"Good night, ma'am, enjoy your stay.''

Ellie closed the door silently and Lorraine listened, wondering if she would also turn down Robert Caley's bed. She could hear nothing, so she inched open the door and stepped into the corridor. She could see the DO NOT DISTURB sign on Caley's suite door.

Lorraine eased off the robe and slipped between the cool sheets. The two mints had been left by the telephone at her bedside. It was now almost eleven, and she used the dimmer switch to lower her bedside lamp. Distant voices echoed from the streets outside the courtyard: music, someone singing. She lay there waiting, wondering what he was doing. No way could she sleep.

Nick was tired out. He'd had too much to drink and the hot spicy food had given him one hell of a thirst. He was also feeling the buzz between Rosie and Rooney. Hard to believe, but they were acting like a pair of teenagers, tasting each other's food, ordering more and more ridiculous dishes. The Cajun restaurant had been as big as a barn, but hot and crammed to capacity, full of tourists being sold the atmosphere by overexpansive waiters, all out-of-towners eager to eat their blackened shrimp and jambalaya off greasy checked oilcloth and add their business cards to the thousands stuck on the posts that supported the roof. A band played rapid, lurching zydeco while the singer yelped about his Cajun queen, and middle-aged couples shuffled around the dance floor as though it were the first time they had touched one another in years. The place irritated the hell out of him.

"You two mind if I split? I'm kind of tired out.''

"Ah, no, don't you want a streetcar ride to the river-boats?" Rosie asked.

"Another time. I'll just get some shut-eye." Nick delved into his tight jeans, but Rosie put her hand out. "It's okay, Nick, all on the agency, remember?"

Nick grinned and eased out of his chair. "See y'all in the morning for grits Creole-style. G'night." He sauntered out, ready to hit some of the strip joints in the real city; the tourist section was all show, all done to hit the wallet, and judging by the packed restaurant a lot would end up well and truly creamed, unaware maybe they'd seen nothing of what really went on just a few streets deeper down.

Lorraine tossed her sheet aside and, stark naked, reached for her robe. She knew if she stopped moving she'd back out, but just as she got to the adjoining suite door, it opened. They didn't say a word. He slipped his hands beneath her open robe and drew her close. She rested her head against the nape of his neck, inhaling his clean smell, like fresh scented soap, and she could feel his heart thudding alongside her own as she curled her legs around him. He lifted her higher and closer, carrying her toward his bed, then eased her down so her back lay flat against the sheets, her legs still entwined around his waist. He slowly stroked her legs as he knelt down until they opened wide for him to kiss her thighs, her belly. She felt herself opening to him totally as he licked her, kissed her cunt until she was moaning, feeling the rush of heat flood through her as she tilted her hips upward. Not until she came with another soft purring moan did he begin to strip off his towel. Then he gently moved her so her head lay on the pillow and he lay beside her, stroking her, kissing her body, gentle, sweet kisses. He eased his body over hers and nuzzled her neck until his lips searched out her mouth and his tongue traced hers. Not until she drew his head closer, not until he felt her hungry passion, did he move his hand down to his erect penis as if wanting her permission to fuck her and she murmured, "Yes . . . yes . . ."

Caley was the most experienced lover she had ever known. He never at any time seemed to be just screwing her; he was caring and in turn rough, but she began to feel that he was only wanting to give her pleasure, wanting her to orgasm, asking softly what she liked, what she wanted him to do. Without embarrassment she told him; it made her feel as if she was in control and yet she knew she wasn't. And not until she began to make love to him, caressing him in turn, did she feel him withdraw slightly, and she pulled away from him.

"Let me love you now . . ."

He closed his eyes as she eased on top of him, looking down into his face. She bent her head close. "Look at me, open your eyes . . . I want you to see me, know me."

Slowly he opened his eyes. Gone was the experienced lover; instead she saw a raw innocence, almost a fear, and she stroked his face. "What are you scared of?"

"You," he said softly, because the countless women he had fucked, women like Saffron Dulay, had never touched him so deeply as Lorraine. He was not used to accepting sexual pleasure, only to giving it, and there wasn't a trick he didn't know. But tonight there were no games, just two people with the same physical passion for each other, and the more she aroused him the more at ease he became with allowing himself to be desired, until they were equal. His first orgasm left him gasping for breath. Their bodies glistening with sweat, they remained clinging to each other as they drifted into an exhausted sleep. They woke alternately, arousing and waking the other. The night felt long and the dawn was still to come, and they could not get enough of each other.

"I am loving you, Lorraine Page," Caley whispered.

"And I you, Mr. Robert Caley." She smiled, leaning up on her elbow, looking down into his handsome face. "It's been a long time for me."

He laughed softly. "Much longer for me, my love, I never believed I could feel this way again."

"Again?" she mocked.

Caley drew her close. "It's as if this is the first time I have ever been with a woman who doesn't play games because . . ." He kissed her lips. "We don't need to—more importantly, I don't want to. That said, what was the last position?"

She laughed, tracing his face in the dim light, feeling his rough chin, liking the fact that it had been so smooth when they had first kissed. "Remind me."

• • •

Rooney looked at the big riverboat casino, gaudy as a Christmas tree with its rows of gold lanterns and golden illuminated crown encircling the funnel, the lights dancing on the wide Mississippi.

"Maybe while we're here we'll treat ourselves to a few chips one night," Rosie suggested.

"That'd be nice, I've never been inside a casino."

They walked on, Rosie now totally at ease about their linking arms. "You know, according to the papers two of these riverboat casinos have gone bankrupt. In fact—"

Rooney stopped and looked around. "We can't be far from Caley's site for his proposed casino."

Rosie was about to get out her street maps when he took her hand and tucked it under his arm. "We'll start work tomorrow. Maybe we should think about getting back to the hotel."

"Okay, fine by me."

He grinned. "You're good company, Rosie. I've enjoyed tonight, good choice of restaurant, real authentic atmosphere. I dunno why Nick dived off the way he did, antisocial bastard."

"I'm glad he did," Rosie said as they continued walking.

"Me too," Rooney said gruffly, and his big arm tightened on hers. "So you were married, right?"

"Yes, and I got a son, but that part of my life is best forgotten. Not my boy, but you know, Bill, I was a lousy mother. I had this drinking problem, and now they've moved to Florida. My husband remarried, like Lorraine and her ex, he remarried and her daughters are settled, so is my boy. But one day, well, I hope one day he'll come to me so I have a chance to explain that no matter what I did I never stopped loving him."

"I'd have liked a son," Rooney said gloomily.

"Maybe walk back toward the big hotels, people bound to be getting cabs there," Rosie said as if reading his mind.

They turned back and continued walking at a slow, unhurried pace.

"You ever think about it?" Rooney asked.

"Think about what?" Rosie said.

"Starting up another family?"

Rosie stopped, looking up into his big round face. "I think about it all the time, Bill, but I'm forty-two now—"

An empty cab passed and Rooney interrupted her as he stepped out on the cobbled road to flag it down.

"What's the name of our hotel, Rosie?" Rooney bellowed.

"The Saint Marie," she said as Rooney opened the passenger door.

The cabdriver nodded, about to do a U-turn when Rooney leaned forward. "We far from the old Convention Center?"

"No, sah, two-minute ride."

Rooney looked at Rosie. "Might as well just drive past, huh?"

"Sure, Bill."

"You know anything about a new casino complex near here?" Rooney asked the cabbie.

"I heard they bin thinkin' about it. These rich guys keep on sayin' they're creatin' work for the locals but it's a load of hogwash. They bring in outsiders, don't hire locals, not classy enough, so they say, not intelligent enough to deal a pack o' cards. Good enough to spend their money there, though. They is corrupt, this whole city is corrupt, an' I know it, my cousin is a cop."

"You don't say," said Rooney, leaning forward.

Nick had walked a little farther than he meant: he'd followed Dauphine quite a ways, glad to get away from the bright lights, and then taken a left somewhere. He was bored now with the cheap bar; it must once have been a strip joint, and still had the pink light to make gray-fleshed and jaded girls look younger, and the stage surrounded by sheets of uneven mirror tiles. Old electric cable and piping now hung off the walls, which were covered in tacky seventies posters, and even the red light couldn't conceal the dirt and neglect. Some young guys played the video poker machines, while an elderly jazz four-piece played with surprising verve and expression under the old glitter ball.

The guys were good, but Nick had had enough, so he signaled the waitress to get his check and she sauntered over. Two kids started screaming at an old black dude who had been sitting on a bar stool for almost as long as Nick had been in the bar. The old guy had played a set and he was a real good horn player. When he had been on, the place had been jumping. One of the kids pushed at the old man, who rocked dangerously on his stool. Nick kept one eye on them as he flicked out his wallet, paying the lazy waitress, who seemed more interested in her tip than in the fracas.

The two boys, both black, were really yelling now.

"We paid you, man, we want the goods, man, you owe us."

The barman was easing down to the bar phone, his eyes out on stalks. The kids got louder.

Nick was almost at the door when the gun came out. There was a hushed silence. No one seemed to want to make a move.

"Gonna blow your fuckin' head off." The muzzle of the gun was rammed into the old man's face.

Everything in Nick was telling him to walk away. But there was something about the old dude and his beat-up trombone.

"Hey, take it easy, kid."

The boy turned, waving his Magnum, and close up Nick could see he was well spaced out.

"Who you tellin' to take it easy, motherfucker? Stay out o' this, none o' your business."

Nick came even closer. "You threatening me?"

"You want your head blown off, man?"

Nick eased into position just behind the old man, who was shaking badly.

"Sonny, I suggest you put that big mama away and cool down because you are kind of making this whole place jumpy."

"You a cop?"

"Nope, just a guy enjoyin' an evening out." Nick smiled, then made his move. He was fast, jabbing the kid hard in the groin and at the same time twisting his arm hard up behind his back. "Drop it . . ." The gun clattered to the floor. Nick kicked it away but not one person reached for it.

"Get the fucking gun, man," Nick said to the old man,

who eased off his stool, placed the trombone on the bar and picked up the gun.

"Okay, now everything's cool. You two walk out and chill out."

Nick pushed the stoned kid off him. He fell onto his backside, and as his friend hauled him up onto his feet his mouth was frothing with fury. "I'll get you, motherfucker."

They ran out, still shouting abuse as Nick helped the old man back onto his stool.

"You okay?"

"Sure, brother. You wanna beer?"

Nick didn't, but he nodded his head. The barman removed the weapon and placed a chilled beer on the counter.

The old man turned to the band. "You guys lost your wind?"

The band started up and the bar buzzed as the old man gave the barman orders to serve drinks on the house. He then turned his lined face to Nick, and when he smiled he displayed four gold teeth, two top, two bottom.

"This is my place, my bar, who the fuck are you?"

"Nick, Nick Bartello."

The gnarled hand gripped Nick's. "Name's Fryer Jones. That was a real nice move you just performed, you a cop?"

"Was, long time ago."

"Ah," Fryer said as he slurped his beer.

"What was that about?"

The old man fingered his trombone. "Nothin' much. Happens most nights, they get high. I got to pay a pot of protection and you can see the place ain't a gold mine. We call the cops an' they ask for even more dough. Sometimes we just let' em shoot up the place a bit—don't bother me, why should it, I had my day."

Nick drank his beer, and another bottle was placed down in readiness.

"So you deal on the side, huh?"

The old guy chuckled. "For somebody that ain't no cop y'all sure ask a lot of questions. What the fuck you doin' in this area anyway?"

"I've been hired to trace Anna Louise Caley."

Fryer kissed his teeth. "Ah, little Caley gal, been a lot 'bout her in print."

"So you know who I'm talking about." Nick hadn't really anticipated such a direct reply.

"Know her mama, everyone knows Eeelizabeth Caley, man. And if you want some advice—"

"Take any you've got," Nick said, liking the old man.

"Git your ass outta here or you'll get burned real bad, man."

"Why?"

"Just like I said, lotta people been here before you."

"What, to this bar?"

Fryer chuckled, shaking his head. "Nah, man, the city is jumpin' right now, afloat with millions of bucks, and just a handful gettin' the pickin's . . . it creates a deep murky pond. Dig up some of the slime and like I said, you'll git yo'self in bad trouble, might have even got yourself into some tonight. Those two kids . . ." Fryer fingered his trombone. "They got heavy connections."

"Didn't look too heavy to me." Nick drained his beer.

"Nothin' is how it looks, man. Some got connections to gangsters, some got deep roots, and I'm just givin' you some friendly advice. Now if you'll excuse me, I got my second set comin' up, I like to keep my wheels oiled."

Nick got off his stool as Fryer unwound from his neck what looked like small animal bones bound with a leather strip. "Here, brother, wear this, and go easy now. Help ward off evil, they're the real thing. Go easy now."

Fryer watched Nick walk out, then turned to his barman with a half-raised eyebrow. "Crazy fucker." He signaled to a young guy drinking solo at the far end of the dark bar, who immediately took off after Nick.

The barman stashed Nick's empty beer bottles in a crate beneath the bar. Right by the side of the crate was a double-barreled shotgun: if Nick Bartello hadn't stepped in to help Fryer, the kids were within inches of getting their heads blown off. But he was not to know, Fryer Jones was old and he hadn't survived this long without taking good precautions. There were a number of dudes quietly drinking who were ready to step in, but Fryer usually took care of things his own way, and unless they got a nod from him they left him to it.

"Lookin' for that little Caley girl," Fryer said as he

sucked at his trombone piece, wiping it down on his dirty
shirt front. The barman washed out some glasses, gave a
dead-eyed stare around as the place was filling up. Nothing
really kicked off until after midnight, when a lot of the regulars would come in from their work at other clubs and
restaurants. Some of the musicians, having trotted golden
oldies all night, needed to jam, and played at Fryer Jones's
bar. These sessions were almost a nightly ritual, and a lot
of hookers would drift in at dawn to have a few beers and
a dance before crashing out to sleep the day away.

Fryer made his way to the small raised platform with the
old beat-up plastic chairs, a microphone and sound box circa
1956. He patted a few shoulders, then stopped by a young
black girl with her hair plaited and decorated with metal
beads. She was fanning herself with a folded-up newspaper,
eyes closed, her cheap synthetic version of a satin slip dress
clinging to her young pubescent body, showing off rather
than hiding her small tits with their large brown nipples.

"Hi, Sugar May, your mama know you're out this late?"

"Yeah, she knows. I wanna be a singer, Fryer, she knows
I hang out here, she don't care either way."

"Mmm, you said you were gonna stay with your aunty
in LA, said you needed two hundred bucks, so how come
you're not singing at one of them Hollywood clubs?"

Sugar May shrugged her pretty little shoulders. "Mah
brother took mah money, Fryer—Raoul'd take mah cherry
if I didn't keep my legs crossed. He's been gone a few
weeks now. So you gonna let me sing?"

Fryer looked around, then bent really close to Sugar May,
gripping her braids so he drew her head back. "You tell
that mama of yours if she send any mo' your relatives squee-
zin' me for protection I'll shove my trombone right up her
ass. That was dumb, hear me, girl?"

"I didn't know my brothers was comin', Fryer, they're
just stoned."

"They shoot their mouths off, threaten me with an old
pistol in front of my cli-hon-telle, Sugar May, an' one of
'em was an outsider."

"I'll tell her, Fryer, I will truly, and I wasn't lyin' about
going to stay with Aunt Juda, honest I wasn't."

Fryer released his hold on her braids. "You also tell her

the guy was looking into Anna Louise Caley, and this one
don't look like he'll be bought off. He was here, right? So
maybe he knows somethin'. And now get your tight little
ass home.''

Sugar May eased away from him, scared, her big brown
eyes wide as the old man creaked up onto the platform. She
didn't dare push for singing tonight, but she'd push those
two dumb bastards that made a show of themselves. She'd
most certainly tell on them.

Nick Bartello crashed out on one of the many beds in his
hotel room, without even undressing or removing Fryer's
leather thong with the animal bones from around his neck.
He liked it, it reminded him of his hippie days. He hadn't
noticed he'd had a tail on him from the moment he left
Fryer's bar.

Edith Corbello, Juda Salina's sister and weighing two hundred pounds, was asleep in front of the TV set. The house
was one of a run-down, one-story row, with a sagging felt
roof and maybe ten feet of battered frontage facing the
street. There was a veranda all right, tiny, the front railing
missing half its posts, but even on fine evenings Edith rarely
sat out—there wasn't much enjoyment in looking across a
vacant lot full of weeds at the raised section of the I-10's
concrete underparts, or the trash stuck on the barbed wire
around a disused warehouse, or the slack utility cables slung
right in front of the house; she just stayed put and dreamed.
Edith woke with a start when Sugar May nudged her.

"Fryer is blazin' Mama. Willy and Jesse went into the
bar tonight threatenin' him and waving a gun around. He
also said there was some guy asking questions about Anna
Louise Caley, an' he said this one didn't look like he'd go
away easy.''

Edith Corbello eased herself onto her big flat feet, her
swollen ankles spilling over on her heels. She was wearing
dirty old slippers, about the only thing her bloated feet could
get into.

"I swear, I'm gonna teach them both a lesson. I'm gonna
scare the fuck out of them both.''

"They were stoned, Mama,'' Sugar May added, almost

gleefully, and received a swipe to her head from Edith.

"An' you should be in bed, go on, git out. *Out!*"

Edith shuffled to the door and into the dark hallway. She passed the closed door to her "company" parlor, making her way down to the back of the stifling hot kitchen. She looked in. The place was filthy, grease on the walls and floors, littered with old takeout cartons and empty beer bottles and stinking of decaying food and cigarettes. She pulled the cord of a rickety ceiling fan and pushed open the screen door to the yard. Willy and Jesse were flat out, one on a hammock and the other on the backseat of an old wrecked car. For her size she moved fast, picking up a broom, and with one swing she brought it down first on Jesse's head and then sideswiped Willy, so that he fell out of the hammock with a scream.

"I'm gonna fix you both good, I warned you. What's this about you going down Fryer's place, shooting more'n your yapping mouths off?"

The broom swished again, catching Jesse in the eye. He howled as Willy tried to dodge it, but she clipped him hard on the top of his head, and he sank to his knees, holding on to his head with the flat of his hands. Her breath heaved in her chest, her eyes bulged and the sweat streamed off her body.

"Pair o' you git in that kitchen and make it presentable, then you come see me in the front parlor. You're gonna have to make good with Fryer or so help me God I'll put a snake in your guts, an' you know I don't make empty threats. *Move!*"

She sank onto the old car seat, tossing the broom aside. Since Raoul had left she'd had her hands full with those two, and sometimes she just got so angry with Juda. All that money she was making, while she was still living in a pile of ramshackle rooms with four kids. She wished she had never set eyes on that rich bitch Elizabeth Caley.

CHAPTER

11

Lorraine was woken by a shaft of sunlight, diffused and softened by the gathered muslin curtains, coming through the doorway to the bathroom and the balcony beyond. For a moment she was unsure where she was until she saw Robert Caley, already showered and shaved.

"What time is it?" she murmured.

"Seven." He walked to the closets, just a small towel around his waist, and selected a shirt, suit and tie, tossing them onto an elegant spoonback chair. Lorraine sat up and blinked. He turned and smiled.

"When you sleep you look like a ten-year-old, but for that scar. How in God's name did you get it?"

Lorraine drew the sheet around herself. "Oh, some bar someplace. I'd better get back to my room."

"No hurry. You want me to order some breakfast?"

Lorraine squinted up at him. "You think that's wise?"

He laughed, dropping the towel to pull on his briefs; he was completely relaxed about his nudity.

"Maybe not, but you can call from your room, then we can eat together." She sat up, watching him pull on his trousers. "I have a meeting, ten o'clock."

Lorraine swung her legs from the bed and he came toward her, bending down to kiss the top of her head. He leaned over and traced the scars on her back, then on her arms. "How did they all happen?"

Lorraine drew away from him. "Well, at some point I

didn't care too much about living. They're the self-inflicted ones, the others—''

He cupped her face in his hands. ''Wherever you've been, my darlin', is past. You're with me now.''

She looked up into his face, trying to figure him out. ''I was there, though, Robert—like it or not, I was a drunkard.''

He kissed her, holding her tightly. ''But you're not now. You're my lovely Lorraine, and last night is one I will remember for a long time.''

''Me too,'' she said softly, wishing he would get back in the wide sleigh bed again, wanting to hold him naked, wanting him to make love to her again. For a moment she felt that he wanted it too, but his phone rang and he eased away from her to answer it.

''Hi, Phyllis. No, no, I'm already dressed. How is she?''

Lorraine picked up her robe from the floor and slipped it around her shoulders. He had his back to her.

''She is? That's good. Well, tell her I'll call later.'' He turned to face Lorraine as he pressed line 2 to pick up a waiting call. ''It's Phyllis, says Elizabeth is fine, maybe another week.''

He returned to his call, his manner changed. ''When? It was set for eight this morning . . . what? Shit, okay, no, I can make it. Call him back and tell him I'll be there, and thanks, Mark.''

He replaced the receiver and sighed. ''Lloyd Dulay wants me to meet him at his place, so I'm going to have to move fast. Will you leave me the number of your hotel so I can call you?''

She nodded. He finished dressing and put on his shades.

''Talk to you later.'' He kissed her cheek and closed the door behind him.

Back in her own suite, Lorraine sat on the balcony. What the hell did she think she was doing? She must have been out of her mind; no matter what the night had been, or meant, she couldn't help feeling depressed and listless. She called down for a pot of hot, strong black coffee, and drained three cups and smoked two cigarettes before getting ready to leave.

Lorraine walked back into Robert Caley's suite. To her surprise it had already been cleaned and the bed made up.

There was no indication of their night together: it was as if it had never happened. She crossed to the escritoire to leave her hotel and phone number, pulled the lid down to write, and then saw a stack of documents left neatly in order and a file with CASINO DEVELOPMENT printed on it. She wondered if Caley had forgotten it in his hurry to make the meeting; she opened the cover and saw the site for the proposed casino underlined three times: the Rivergate Convention Center.

Lorraine picked up the file and returned to her own suite. She began jotting down notes. Some of the information blew her mind. Two hundred thousand square feet of gaming area, two hundred tables, six thousand slot machines and a projected five and a half million annual customers. Lorraine was filling up the pages, salaries estimated at $107 million. The sources of funding listed were as mind-blowing: $170 million equity, almost $500 million in bonds, a further $140 million bank credit, and on it went to mount up, the grand total well in excess of $800 million. The document listed the hard costs, including the parking structures, gaming equipment, state taxes, city taxes, interest, cash load preopening, finishing fees and expenses. She noted that the expenditures totaled as much, if not more, than the sources. Finally listed was the projection of revenue, ending up with a profit margin target of around $120 million.

Detailed on the following pages were the proposals of what seemed to be the rival consortium, Doubloons, consisting of nine Louisiana residents, nine wealthy men clearly eager to make themselves even wealthier; no wonder Caley was so strung out about whether he or they would be awarded the concession. Lorraine noticed that the cost in excess of $40 million had been incurred in securing leases on the site where the casino was to be completed, and wondered if Caley had borne all of these himself. If he had, then he not only must be very wealthy but, as he himself had implied, was stretching himself to the very limit too.

Lorraine returned the file to his room and could not resist opening up every drawer in the desk. She found his real estate license, his New Orleans office address, details of new hotel developments, mostly in the riverfront area, and one of the hotels that was jointly owned by both Robert and

Elizabeth Caley. Contrary to what he had said about his
wife's having nothing to do with his business, her name
appeared on numerous deeds. But most shocking to Lorraine
was a folded document in the name of Anna Louise Caley.
It was secured with a seal and a red ribbon, and contained
details of Anna Louise's trust fund. Using the letter opener,
warming it over her lighter, Lorraine worked on easing the
seal up without breaking it until it came away from the
paper. The thick yellow-papered deed was deeply creased
and brittle and she opened it with care. She gasped: there
had never been a mention at any time, verbally or in any
statement she had seen, of a trust fund for Anna Louise
Caley, and the amount was a staggering $100 million. The
trust fund was to be managed by her parents until Anna
Louise became twenty-one, and should she fail to live to
that age, then the fund would automatically revert to Elizabeth Caley.

Rooney had put on a suit he hadn't worn in a while, and
had been surprised that it fitted him, but those few pounds
he had lost had made him look and feel better.

"My, you look snazzy," Rosie remarked as he walked
into the restaurant across the street from the St. Marie, and
he flushed.

"Remember our deal? No diets while we're here."

"Sure, and I'm game—while we're here, we can eat anything we like."

Rooney clapped his hands and grinned. "Right, let's go,
they got pancakes here that are delicious, and Nick and Lorraine will be down in a second."

Hungover, dressed in the clothes he had slept in, dark
shades on, Nick listened as Lorraine recounted her findings.
Watching Rosie and Rooney eating pancakes with syrup,
Lorraine realized she was hungry. She hadn't eaten anything
since dinner on Caley's private plane. She ordered scram-
bled eggs and smoked salmon, which made Nick feel even
more ill.

"How did you get your hands on all this?" Rooney asked
with his mouth full.

"I stayed at the same hotel, in the same room Anna Louise disappeared from. When I went in to thank Mr. Caley,
he had already left."

" 'Went in'?'' Nick asked.

"Yeah, there was a connecting door, I had the key. Caley had a breakfast meeting with Lloyd Dulay."

Nick poured himself more coffee. "So you stayed in the room next to Caley's?"

Lorraine nodded. "Yep. I questioned the staff, which was the reason I accepted his offer, so quit with the snide remarks, Bartello. What is that shit you got around your neck?"

"It's a gris-gris." He leaned close to Lorraine. "What's that on your neck, sweetheart? Get bitten in that fancy hotel, did you?"

Before Lorraine could answer, Nick took off, and she inched up her collar. "Mosquito bite. I must have given one little bastard a real night out."

"I'll give you something for it," Rosie said at once. She had brought a first-aid kit with every conceivable thing they could require.

"It's nothing, just forget it."

Rooney was scratching his ankle, now sure he had been bitten by something too.

"I think the same little bastard just got me. Heat's like a blanket an' still only January. What this place must be like in the peak of summer, God only knows."

"Well, hopefully we won't be here more'n a few days," Lorraine said, a little sharp, as she was not getting much response from anyone to her findings. In fact, they seemed to accept it all, as if they knew it already—Robert Caley was still their number one suspect!

"I'm out of here, see you later—we'll meet up in my room. It makes me feel like Snow White or something, by the way, Rosie—it's got about five beds."

Rosie was getting rattled by all the complaints about their hotel rooms.

"Listen, if you think you can do better, go ahead, but it's Mardi Gras, there wasn't much choice."

"Don't get pissed, I was just mentioning it."

Rooney sniffed.

"If we get short of cash, we can all bunk in together or maybe make a few bucks rentin' them out. You want some more coffee?"

Lorraine drained her cup and nodded. "I'll be right back." She set off toward the restroom, and Rooney signaled to the waitress to order a fresh pot of coffee.

"Where's Nick?"

"Getting cleaned up, I don't know," said Rosie, still irritated.

"What's the matter with everyone this morning?" Rooney asked, puzzled.

"I was in a perfectly good mood when I came down for breakfast," Rosie snapped back.

"Now, don't get all steamed up about Lorraine. We've all mentioned that we got enough beds for a basketball team."

Rosie banged the table. "Well, we can check out, one of you can try to find accommodations that can take all four of us at the same time. I spent enough time trying to get the best deal I could, but not so much as a thank you—it makes me sick."

Rooney reached over and patted her hand. "Come on now, no one minds, and you never know, one of us might get lucky."

"What's that supposed to mean?" she glowered.

"Have a few friends call in! Just a joke, sweetheart."

"Well, I don't find it funny, it undermines my confidence. You might all have been doing this investigation work a long time, but I haven't, and you make me feel inadequate."

"Then I'm sorry, Rosie, but, you know, you could take it as a compliment—cops always get at each other, joke around, it's the way we interact. Treat you any different and you should worry."

She flushed and suddenly smiled. "That right?"

"Sure. Now, did you want another coffee?"

Rosie nodded.

She felt a lot better—in fact, she always did when she was with Rooney. He was restoring her confidence, especially as a woman, in more ways than she had ever hoped possible.

At the turn of the century the Dulay home, an amalgam of Victorian gothic turrets and towers and an incongruously Mediterranean-looking front portico, might have been thought a vulgar, ostentatious hybrid, but it had cost a king's ransom to build, and Lloyd liked to let people know that there was nothing shabby-genteel about his family; they had had money then, and they had money now.

Robert Caley drove along the allée of specially trained oaks through Lloyd's extensive grounds—the formal garden, the wilderness garden, the kitchen garden, the cut-flower garden, the water garden—which the Dulays had lain out on several acres of prime site near the agreeable cool of parks and country clubs between river and lake shores, and which glowed like green velvet even when every other yard of ground in the state was a bleached gray-brown. He rang the door, and a uniformed maid ushered him past several waist-high bronzes of the Dulays' favorite dogs and horses into the breakfast room. Caley never ceased to marvel at both the crassness of Lloyd's taste and the boldness of its execution: the modeling of plaster- and woodwork throughout the house was overall heavy, and Lloyd had decided to offset the darkness of the breakfast room's paneled ceilings by commissioning modern murals around the walls, in which neoclassical nymphs and satyrs peeped through more thick foliage. There was something lascivious in the painting, and Caley wondered whether the young Creole goddess, attired in French maid's costume and at this moment pouring coffee at the mahogany table, might perhaps have been the inspiration for one of the voluptuous nudes to which she bore a striking resemblance.

There was only one place setting at the table, where Georgian silver-covered dishes faced a large, abstract sculpture in colored Perspex, which served as an epergne: Lloyd fancied himself a collector of modern art, but his reforming zeal had not yet encompassed the two hundred feet of glazed chintz fussily swagged, draped and festooned across the room's huge picture windows by his grandmother, nor the fifty pounds of early Anglo-Irish glass hanging from the ceiling, the chandelier's enormous pendants almost touching the plastic structure beneath. The effect was grotesque.

"Just coffee," Caley said, and the maid acknowledged him with only the smallest of nods of her beautiful head with its wide cheekbones, pale coffee-colored skin, delicate nose and large, slanting almond eyes.

The heavy door burst open and Lloyd Dulay strode in. He stood at six feet three and, despite being in his seventies, ramrod-straight, his shock of white hair combed back from his high forehead. He was a formidable man, and beside him Caley felt small in comparison.

"Sit down, boy, sorry to change the meeting place but I had a round of golf this morning that hadda continue. I made five birdies, *five*. Thank you, Imelda, honey."

Dulay touched the maid lightly with his big wide hand, and she smiled, eyes downcast, almost too demure, too beautiful. Caley knew she was probably Dulay's mistress; he was famous for keeping them "in house," and perhaps in this case, no display to his guests.

"How's Elizabeth?" Dulay asked as he removed the cover from one of the dishes and forked a large portion of Charentais melon and berries onto his plate.

"She's fine, Lloyd, be out soon."

"I sincerely hope so. Carnival wouldn't be the same without her, and we got some fine entertainment this year."

Lloyd went on to discuss the floats, the big parties and masked balls that different krewes—the local name for Carnival organizations—planned to hold, the new King of Carnival and the young society girl who would be presented as his Queen. Then, seated in his thronelike Carver chair and gesturing expansively, he eulogized about the time his own daughter was presented as a maid of Rex, his voice booming around the vast cavernous room.

"Saffron looked more beautiful than ever that day. I tell you, Robert, that girl could have had her pick of any man falling at her pretty little feet, begging her for a dance. You know, I even offered her, *offered*, ten million dollars if she got herself married for long enough to give me an heir. That is one of the blights of my life."

Caley chewed his lip. He couldn't recall how many times he'd sat opposite this bully of a man, forced to listen to his loud adulation of his whore of a daughter. He even wondered at times if he wasn't in some roundabout way hinting that Caley should fuck his daughter—which Robert and almost everyone else had—but if he knew her reputation, Dulay never gave so much as a hint. He just seemed to enjoy the sound of his own raspy voice, and not until he had finished his fruit, sausage patties with a variety of savory confits and old-fashioned Southern biscuits did he fall silent.

As though summoned by telepathy, Imelda reappeared and cleared the table, and again Caley saw that big hand stroke his little "in house" woman. He was sure that if he didn't have a legitimate heir, he most certainly had a number of illegitimate kids. Rumor had it to be around ten or eleven.

Dulay looked over the cigar box held out for him by Imelda. He chose one, sniffing at it with his big hawk nose, then she clipped the end, brought to the table an antique silver perfume bottle remodeled into a lighter, and slipped out. Not until the cigar smoke rested like a halo above Dulay's head did he focus his beady, ice-blue eyes on Caley.

"The Mayor's meeting with the governor and some of the legislative leaders in Baton Rouge sometime this week. Way I see it, he ought to save himself the trip—what we got to worry about is right here in New Orleans. Some people just seem to want to stand in the way of change until it rolls right over them, though it seems like there might be something in all this federal-law stuff. Or so my attorney is bleatin'."

"That's bullshit, Lloyd, and you know it. They're just trying it on."

"Robert, you're not hearing me. It's the delay. Don't you see, the more they delay granting you the go-ahead, the longer it drags out—and no matter how much you kick against it and say it's not you they're turning up their noses at, nobody's gonna believe it."

Caley sat back. Even in the chill of the air-conditioned room he could feel the sweat break out on his body; he knew that Dulay had brought up the zoning objections purely as a pretext to cover some move of his own.

"So are you pulling out?" he said nervously.

"Hell, no, I am right behind you. But you are gonna have to give me some proof that it's not just me in deep in this."

"Right now, Lloyd, the only person in deep is me. It's my own money that's bought those leases. So far you haven't put in so much as a cent."

Dulay stared hard at him and his eyes seemed to shrink. "No, Robert, you got my name attached, and here that means something, understand me? My name carries a lot of weight in these parts.''

''I know, I know . . . sorry, but right now, Lloyd, I'm being squeezed, you got to know that.''

''Sure, I do, nobody likes their balls held in a vise, but at the same time you're gonna be the man who makes the most, so unless you want to carve up your interest—''

''I don't.''

''Maybe not now, not today, but perhaps you should give it some thought. If you're gonna go belly up, then nobody's gonna back your development, even if the land you got is worth something.''

''More than something, Lloyd.''

''Right, right, but can you keep afloat?''

''Depends on how long. What's friend Siphers doing in Baton Rouge?''

Lloyd shrugged. ''They have to go through some sort of little pantomime of discussing the Doubloons proposal— crease the pages before they toss it out.''

''You're sure the governor is going to toss it out?''

Lloyd pushed back his chair. ''Sure. This is your show, Robert. You're the one who made the commitment and got ground broken people said couldn't be broke. A bunch of guys trying to jump on your bandwagon will just find they fall off on their ass.''

''So when do you think we might get a yea or a nay?''

''Oh, any day now, Robert, and you'll be the first to know. As you know, the governor is a personal friend,'' Dulay said silkily.

There was something in his manner just a shade too smooth to trust, but Caley was too tired to press the old man further and stood up, forcing himself to smile.

''I'll look forward to it, Lloyd.''

''You count on it,'' Dulay said, and gestured toward the door. The meeting was over. He paused as they walked out into the huge entrance hall with its bronze menagerie. ''They found your little girl yet?''

Caley shook his head. ''No, but Elizabeth has hired a new agency. They'll maybe get some results, they seem very capable.''

Lloyd glared. ''Capable? Holy Jesus, Robert, she's your

daughter! You just hired *capable*—I'd leave no stone unturned if it was my little girl, I'd hire the best this country
has.''

''We did,'' Caley said flatly.

Dulay held out his arm and it felt like a dead weight on
Caley's shoulders. ''You sure you can keep going? Money-
wise?''

Caley nodded, and the big man hugged him close. ''I feel
for you and my lovely Elizabeth, she must be going through
hell.''

''She is.'' Now all Caley wanted was to get out, but the
big man's arm held him like a vise.

''You call on me, Robert, I mean it. You're like family
to me and that sweet child keeps me awake at night. What
do these agencies think might have happened?''

Caley stepped aside. ''That she could have been abducted,
you know, kidnapped by the opposition, maybe to stop me
from opening up.''

''Bullshit, they're too big to play that kind of game. Jesus,
I know every man on the Doubloons board, lot of old
friends, some I was in knickerbockers with, and I can tell
you every man is a gentleman.''

''Why didn't you kick in with them?'' Caley asked quietly.

Dulay shrugged and walked into the marbled hallway. ''I
wasn't asked . . . and I like to be asked. I'm not a man that
barges in on anybody's deal, they gotta come to me. With
my kind of capital I don't get into anything without being
shown a little respect.'' He towered above Caley. ''You've
always shown me respect, Robert, and for that reason alone
I'm with you on this deal. You're a man that's climbed up
from nothing and I admire you. I also care about that wife
of yours—we go back a long ways, and I look forward to
seeing her soon as she arrives. My house is yours, you know
that, Robert.''

Caley looked back at the huge house, riding like an ocean
liner above the smooth lawns, and Dulay's empty words
rang in his ears. ''My house is yours, you know that,
Robert.'' What a joke! Dulay was squeezing for a much
bigger chunk, it was obvious, squeezing and waiting like a

shark to step in and offer to bail him out for a percentage that Caley could see—sixty-forty, and the sixty wouldn't be his but Dulay's.

The chauffeur headed back to the hotel. Caley closed his eyes, thinking of Lorraine and the previous night. No wonder he felt worn-out. But he wanted to see her again, needed to see her, because at the moment he knew Dulay was shifting the ground under him, and it felt as if he was going to go down.

Nick rejoined the others at the black iron courtyard table, washed, shaved and wearing clean clothes. Rooney was making notes on the back of an envelope. "I'm going to have a chat with this cabdriver's brother."

"Really? Can you fill me in, I mean, what cabdriver and who's his brother?"

Rosie leaned forward. "We used him last night, Nick, drove past Caley's proposed site for his casino, and this guy was full of it. He said his cousin, not his brother, was a cop, said they're all corrupt."

Lorraine was sitting with her eyes closed, face tilted to the sun.

"Okay, I think I'm gonna go back to the bar I wound up in last night. This old trombone player sort of warned me off."

"Off what exactly?" Lorraine asked without moving.

"Anna Louise Caley."

Lorraine turned to face him. "Go on."

Nick shrugged. "That's it, he just said to get the hell out, and thinking it over he's got to have a good reason and a better one than . . ." He leaned forward, frowning. " 'Murky waters'—he said something like that, roots go deep . . . I dunno, just got a feeling he knows something. And you, what you gonna do?"

Lorraine yawned. "Well, maybe start interviewing Caley's business associates and, er . . . what's her name? Anna Louise's friend. I think that'll more than take up my day." She checked her watch. "So what d'you say we all meet back here about six tonight?"

Rosie looked at Bill, who was still scrutinizing his notes.

"Anybody want me to do anything? If you don't, I'm gonna go to the Voodoo Museum."

Rooney tucked the envelope into his pocket and got up. "I'll rent a car, drop you off there if you like, Rosie."

"Oh, thanks. See you all later."

Lorraine held up her hand. "Just a second, before you scoot off, Rosie, will you get me appointments to meet all Caley's business partners and Tilda Brown?"

Rosie nodded. "Sure, I'll do it right away. You arrange the car, Bill, and I'll meet you in the lobby."

Lorraine watched them go off, easing between the tables. "They're getting very friendly, aren't they?"

Nick rocked in his chair. "Yeah, hadda terrible meal out with them. Rooney gettin' all coy and a bashful Rosie are hard to take."

"You serious?" Lorraine said, laughing.

"Yeah." Nick watched her, wanting her. He instinctively knew she'd had a lot more than just a dinner on the plane with Caley.

"What did you get from the staff at Caley's hotel?" he asked.

"Not much. Only one thing that's not on any report was that the maid did not turn down Anna's bed at around eight to half past because there was a DO NOT DISTURB sign on the door. Which could mean she'd already left, or—"

"Nice suite, was it?"

"Yes, it was." She wanted to take off his shades, see his eyes, because he had that irritating smile.

"You fuck him?"

Lorraine picked up her purse and her note pad. "What you think I am, Nick?"

"I'd sure take a chance like that, but then chance'd be a fine thing, right?"

"You said it."

She edged past his chair and he caught her hand. "No offense."

"None taken, Nick, but back off about me and Caley, it's starting to get on my nerves."

Nick got up and walked with her. "Just being cautious, sweetheart—he is our main suspect, right? Even more so now with that little legacy you found." He took off his shades. "You know, maybe Caley had been dipping into the trust fund. It must be like a red-hot carrot, one hundred million bucks is fucking hot."

Lorraine felt dizzy. "Yeah, I thought of that, and I was wondering if there was any way we could find out."

Nick slipped his arm around her shoulders as they went into the lobby. "You could ask him."

Lorraine sighed. "Yeah, but then he'd know I went through his papers. I don't want to frighten him off if we're right—"

"That is some mosquito bite you got, you should get calamine lotion on it." She turned angrily toward him and he pulled her close. "Don't bullshit me, I know what it is. I don't care if you fucked him or not, just so long as you don't start to—"

"Start what?"

"To care. Because I don't want you to get hurt, you mind if I say that?"

She rested against him; it took him totally off guard and he held her a moment. "Also, I have to admit that it makes me jealous as all hell. Not that there's any hope for me but—"

She smiled up at him. "You never know, Nick, when you're all washed up and smellin' cute you're not a bad-looking guy. Just not . . ."

"Your type?"

She laughed softly. "You would have been once, like Lubrinski was, but, Nick, you'd be hell on any woman who cared about you. I know your kind, you love the chase, but when it's over you're bored and on to the next."

"Ah, you got me figured out, huh? But you know, me and Tiger, we're looking to set up a place, one with a back-yard so he won't piss on the carpets, and with the right woman—"

"I'm not the right one, Nick, and we're wasting time."

She saw the hurt look pass quickly over his face and then he gave her that smile of his. He kissed her lips before he sauntered off with his lopsided walk in his beat-up cowboy boots.

As she unlocked her room at the St. Marie, Lorraine wished she hadn't been so dismissive because Nick, like

Jack, didn't come out with those kinds of words easily. In many ways she was attracted to Nick, it was hard not to be, but it wasn't anything she would allow to happen because what she had said about him was the truth—Nick would never settle down, even with his "backyard" routine. He was and always would be a loner, like Jack.

She sat on the colored synthetic bedspread and looked up at the bubbled wallpaper and air vent clogged thick with dust; after last night it all seemed ugly and depressing, and although it was still only eleven o'clock, she felt tired out. That awful feeling in the pit of her stomach that Caley was involved in his daughter's disappearance wouldn't go away, and even after a night with him, a wonderful, special night, she couldn't help being logical. She was able to subjugate her emotions toward Caley, and allow the professional judgment to take over.

There was a sudden tap on the door and Rosie peeked in, carrying a sheet of paper.

"I've listed those I could get hold of and those you'll have to maybe see tomorrow. I got a car booked for you with a driver at a real low cost because some of these are quite a ways apart, and Tilda Brown's place is twenty-odd miles out of town."

Lorraine glanced over the handwritten notes. "So it's Tilda Brown first, then Lloyd Dulay? Okay, I'll get cracking."

The phone rang. It was Robert Caley.

"Hi, you free for lunch?"

"Ah, ten minutes ago I was, but I'm just on my way out."

He sounded disappointed. "How about dinner?"

"Can I take a rain check on it?"

"Sure. I'll be back at the hotel early evening—maybe go out to the house, so just give me a call."

"Will do."

There was a moment of silence, both wanting to say some kind of endearment, but neither did. Rosie hovered nearby, listening as she pretended to check her notes. She wondered who the call was from, because Lorraine was suddenly acting coy and she was blushing.

"Talk to you later."

"Yes, about six-ish," she said, and the phone went dead.

She replaced the receiver and looked at Rosie.

"Who was that?"

"Robert Caley," Lorraine said dismissively.

"Oh, you seem to be getting along very well."

"That's the idea, Rosie—you get along with somebody, you get more information from them, they talk more freely."

"Mmmm, I'm sure they do. So, you going out with him this evening or are we having a case update? Only I got to let Nick and Bill know."

Lorraine brushed her hair. "I just said I would call him, Rosie."

"Okay, I'll make a note of that, shall I? We'll meet down in the lobby."

"Fine, see you later."

"Okeydokey." Rosie started for the door.

"You and Bill seem to be getting along pretty well too," Lorraine said nonchalantly.

Rosie had her hand on the door handle, her back to Lorraine, and her whole posture suddenly became defensive. "Yes, well, I make it my business to get along with him. We're partners after all, and like you said, you get a lot more out of people if you get along with them."

"But Bill's not a suspect," Lorraine said, amused.

"Maybe he's not, but as someone learning the business, I need some guidance to keep up with someone as experienced as you."

"Ohh, that was a bit near the knuckle, Rosie." Lorraine laughed.

"It wasn't intended that way, but you can get real nasty if I make the smallest mistake, so all I am doing is making sure I don't make any more."

Lorraine was suddenly concerned. "Hell, Rosie, you know me well enough that if I snap at you, you know you can come right back at me."

Rosie smiled. "Yeah, well, sometimes I just get the feeling you don't think much of me, but I won't forget what you just said."

Lorraine crossed the room and put her arms around her friend. "You just always be honest with me, Rosie. Jesus, we all make mistakes."

"No!" Rosie smiled again, assuming a look of mock surprise, which made Lorraine laugh again as she crossed back over to the dressing table.

"I'm glad you and old Rooney get along, he's a good man. He was a good cop too—bit rusty now, or maybe it's just that he's not as hungry as he used to be."

Rosie's cheeks went pink. "You undermine his confidence, Lorraine, like you do mine. He and Nick are working hard, we all are. We're all after the same thing, and there's nobody not pulling their weight."

Lorraine accepted the put-down gracefully, to some degree impressed by her friend—Rosie was more centered than she had ever known her.

"Yes, I'm sorry, you're right. See you later."

Rosie opened the door. "Take care, and check in with us, because we're all backing you to the hilt."

The door closed, and Lorraine frowned. Rosie was different these days; maybe it was working alongside Bill, maybe it was her diet boosting her confidence. Lorraine stared at her own reflection.

"Maybe," she murmured to herself, "you should start straightening out as well."

She touched the bruise of the love bite on her neck, and could not prevent the warm feeling that began in her groin flooding right through her body until she hugged herself. She was happier than she had been for a long, long time.

Tilda Brown's family home had been built on the lake in the 1970s, a low white ensemble of rectangles and cubes with a nod to tradition in the form of modern reworkings of traditional architectural features, square columns and vestigial balconies barely six feet off the ground, which reminded Lorraine of the wing stumps of some flightless bird. Still, it clearly hadn't been lack of money that was responsible for its boxy blandness, and money was still much in evidence: a European convertible and a shiny new Range Rover were parked outside, and a gardener was working outside. The large, well-tended yard adjoined the levee, and Lorraine told her driver, a sullen black boy of twenty, to pull up a couple of hundred yards away so she could walk around the back.

"Wait for me, okay?"

"Yes, ma'am, you got me booked for the day."

From the levee she could see a tennis court and pool, each with floodlighting and a flanking cubist pavilion: by the pool a blond teenager lay stretched on a chaise longue, and Lorraine went around to the front of the house before the girl—Miss Tilda, she presumed—looked up and saw her. She rang the doorbell, and a maid in a pink housedress opened the door.

"Come along in, Mrs. Page. Miss Brown is poolside and she says to ask if you'd like a cool drink."

"Thank you."

Tilda Brown had a perfect, all-over golden tan, her waist-length blond hair silky and well cut, and she wore only the smallest of bikini briefs and top.

Feeling the heat, Lorraine was relieved when Tilda got up from her chaise longue and suggested they go to the small air-conditioned pool house, further shaded by large palms. She sat in a chair made of stainless-steel "wicker," its cushions covered in what seemed to be hot pink Spandex, and motioned Lorraine to its twin.

"It's real hot already," Tilda said, smiling, "but I got all goose pimples, coming in from the sun. You mind if I just fetch a wrap?"

Lorraine returned the smile. The maid appeared to serve homemade lemonade, and Lorraine had drunk half her glass before Tilda returned, draped in a long silk kimono, wearing large dark sunglasses with thick white frames and smelling of fresh flowers. She was very nervous, her little hands shaking as she poured herself a lemonade.

"Can you tell me about your relationship with Anna Louise?"

"Sure, she's my best friend. We both come from here—I mean, not that she lives here full-time like my family, but we first met when we were real young, you know, six or seven years old. Then we didn't see each other for quite a while, maybe five years, but I got to go to UCLA and we met up again, and it was like no time had passed at all. It was nice to be made so welcome at her home because I sometimes got so lonely."

"So you knew each other really well?"

"We did, and I miss her."

Lorraine asked if she could smoke, and Tilda shrugged, fetching a small chrome ashtray. "You had an argument the day before she left LA," Lorraine said as she lit her cigarette.

"We used to argue a lot, Mrs. Page, we didn't always agree on everything even though we were best friends."

The girl flicked her silky hair over her shoulder with an immaculately manicured hand, the nails lacquered oyster-pink to match those on her toes. Lorraine envied the Tilda Browns of this world, their ability never to perspire. This was money in front of her, and young as Tilda was, one could tell she had never wanted for anything in her life.

"Can you tell me what the argument was about? It'd be the morning of February fourteenth last year."

Tilda's eyebrows furrowed. "Well, you know Anna Louise was a good tennis player and she used to get impatient with me because I was not in her league. Even when we were just warming up she'd do these smashes and I just used to get so angry because it wasn't a competition. But with Anna Louise . . ." She hesitated.

"Yes, go on, Tilda."

"Well, Anna Louise was competitive in everything and I just got tired of it. I said to her that I wasn't going to play with her anymore and she threw a tantrum, and believe you me, Mrs. Page, she could get so angry sometimes, say such horrible things. I had just had enough, so I said to her that unless she apologized to me I was not going to travel home with her, no way. I would prefer to travel alone than with somebody as bad-tempered and mean as she was being towards me. Well, she just refused to apologize and so I went in to tell Phyllis that I wanted to leave right away."

"Just like that?"

"Yes. Phyllis arranged for Mario to take me to the airport and she also got me my ticket. I called my mama and papa and they collected me here. I said I didn't want to discuss it, but that I was not going to stay with Anna Louise ever again."

Lorraine drained her glass and Tilda immediately refilled it. At last she removed her big white-framed sunglasses.

Lorraine wanted to see her eyes, to try to ascertain just how good a liar Tilda Brown was going to be.

"I never saw her again. And I have felt so guilty. The last time we were together we were fightin', had those cross words with each other, and if . . . if she won't ever be coming back, then . . . It just gets worse, and sometimes I cry about it because we would have made up—no doubt about it, we always did."

"So she didn't call you when she arrived here with her parents?"

"No, she didn't, but I wish very dearly that she had."

Lorraine sipped the ice-cool lemonade, wondering how to play it. Tilda seemed to be the genuine forlorn best friend and at one point even had tears in her gray-blue eyes, but she never looked directly at Lorraine and she was exceedingly nervous.

"On the night Anna Louise arrived in New Orleans, where were you?"

"At home. I had a dress fitting, and I ate supper with Mama and Papa before going to bed, 'bout ten o'clock."

"And she never came around to see you, to make up to you?"

"No, but like I said, I wish that she had. All I do now is pray that she is still alive, because I will make up to her for that silly tiff we had . . . and it was so silly."

"Do you know somebody called Polar?"

Tilda frowned. "You mean like polar bears? No, I never heard of anyone with that name."

"How about Tom Heller?"

"Oh, I know him, he was at college with me."

Lorraine was becoming irritated by her singsong voice. She decided she had waited long enough. "You ever go to the Viper Room with Tom?"

Bingo, the cheeks flushed bright pink. "I beg your pardon?"

"The Viper Room . . ."

The baby eyes blinked and the blush deepened as Lorraine drew out the picture of Anna Louise being fucked by the guys at the Viper Room.

"Oh, my goodness . . ."

"Mmm, oh, my goodness me. That was taken the night

before your little tiff, wasn't it? You were upstairs, weren't you, in the private section of the Viper Room?''

Tilda crumbled fast. She bent her head and started sobbing, begging Lorraine not to tell her parents. If her family were ever to know she would be in such trouble.

Lorraine passed Tilda a tissue from a box, covered in the same pink synthetic fabric as the cushions, and the weeping girl blew her nose. ''I am so ashamed.''

She continued to sob for a while, then quieted down. ''Anna Louise used to take pills from her mother. The first time we took them we just acted silly, but then she started to take them real regular, you know, and she'd make me drink vodka, she liked vodka. Then we'd go clubbing and . . . I can't tell you how ashamed I am . . .''

''No need to be in front of me,'' Lorraine said, encouraging her to talk.

''I don't remember what we used to do or what I did—I just used to blank out.''

''But you both used to get screwed, right?''

She nodded, and down came the tears again. ''I guess so.''

''The morning you had the little tiff was after you had been out clubbing with Anna Louise, so you were probably a bit hungover, weren't you? So was the 'tiff' really about tennis or was it something more important?''

Tilda sighed. ''Oh, it was just awful, she could be such a bitch about things. She wanted to make sure we had our stories straight so her parents wouldn't find out. We were down by the tennis courts and you're right, we weren't playing. I had such a headache, I was feeling sick, and Mr. Caley came by on his way to work. When he stopped and asked if I was feeling unwell, I just started to cry. I know what we did was bad, but she could be very insistent, you know? She'd make threats that if I didn't do what she wanted, then she'd tell my parents.''

Lorraine waited as she dried her tears and then sat back.

''He was so kind, Mr. Caley, sat me down and asked if I was sick, if there was something wrong. He even gave me his handkerchief . . . and I just cried and cried because I couldn't tell him what I was crying about. He sat with me until I stopped crying and said that if there was something worrying me it was always best to share, that if ever I wanted to talk to him then all I had to do was call. He was so worried, so kind and thoughtful, more like a friend . . .''

"Was Anna Louise sitting with you and Mr. Caley?"

"Er, no, she had gone into the pool house, said she was going to have a swim and . . .''

"And?" Lorraine asked impatiently.

"Oh, Mr. Caley left. He gave me a real nice kiss on the cheek and said he had to go into the office. Then she just flew at me."

"Who did?"

"Anna Louise of course. She began hitting and kicking me, real crazy. She used her tennis racket and hit me real hard, and then she got me down on the ground and was clawing and scratching at my face and pulling out my hair. She was on top of me, pushing my head into the ground.''

"Did she think you had told her father about what had happened at the Viper Room—was that why she attacked you?"

"Yes, she said she had seen me with her father. She wouldn't listen to me—she said she was gonna make me sorry. I hit her back and then she spat at me, right in my face, saying she would tell my parents, tell everybody that I was making a play for her father. I was so shocked . . . I was speechless.''

"But he was just being kind and fatherly, right?"

"Why, yes, of course, but she was crazy about him."

"Wait, wait, what do you mean, crazy about him?"

Tilda had her hands clenched at her sides. "She was obsessed by her daddy, she talked and talked about him, that no man ever lived up to him and that . . .'' Tilda turned away and up came the flush, her cheeks burning bright red.

"Go on, Tilda, and what else?"

"She said they were lovers, that they were in love."

Lorraine lost it for a moment, she was so taken aback by what Tilda had said. "She actually told you that she was having a sexual relationship with her father, Tilda?"

"Yes, yes, that is what she said."

"Did you believe it?"

Tilda twisted her fingers, pulling at a ring. "I just had to leave, Mrs. Page. I ran into the house and asked Phyllis to get me a ticket, I never wanted to see her again.''

Lorraine's heart was thudding. "You didn't answer the question, Tilda, this is very serious. Were Robert Caley and his daughter lovers?''

Tilda licked her lips and turned away, her voice strained, hardly audible. "I don't know, but he was just friendly to me, really and truly, he never made any advances.''

"What about her other friends?''

"She only had me, I was her only true friend. She couldn't tell anyone else about things, everybody thought she was so wonderful, they didn't really know her. And no one liked to stay at the house because of Mrs. Caley acting weird, you know, all boozed up and sometimes so out of it it was just plain embarrassing.''

Lorraine stayed for another half hour, carefully taking Tilda back over her entire statement to the police and the reasons why she had never before admitted the truth about her argument with Anna Louise that morning. It boiled down simply to her being afraid it would get out that she, like Anna Louise, used to go clubbing, stoned and drunk. Tilda did not seem to realize the importance of the question of whether Robert Caley's relationship with his daughter had sexual overtones or not. When pressed by Lorraine for proof, she became agitated and tearful.

"Was Anna Louise just infatuated or do you believe there was more than a father-daughter relationship, Tilda? Did you ever see them together?''

Tilda refused to look at Lorraine, chewing at her lip. Lorraine patiently told her that if what she had said was true it could be the reason behind Anna Louise's disappearance, the reason she might have just run away and might still be alive but afraid to return. What Tilda finally came out with made Lorraine feel wretched.

"She told me they slept together, that he had put her on birth-control pills because he was afraid she would get pregnant.''

By the time Lorraine got back to her driver she had left Tilda Brown looking like a rag doll: her face was puffy from weeping, her nose red from wiping it, and even her little rosebud lips looked chapped and ugly. Lorraine instinctively believed Tilda's reasons for not admitting what she and

Anna Louise had argued about. She had also been given yet
another reason why Robert Caley, even more than before,
was their main suspect. Lorraine needed a drink, a real one,
and she was afraid she'd stop and get one, so she ordered
the driver to take her on to Lloyd Dulay's mansion. Her
initial shock on being told about Robert Caley and Anna
Louise made her whirl through a spiral of emotions. Having
slept with Caley the night before made her want not to believe it, but why would Tilda Brown lie? And gradually her
feeling of betrayal and foolishness turned to burning anger.
Robert Caley most certainly had a motive to get rid of his
daughter, and she was going to prove it.

Nick swore. He knew he'd got off the streetcar a couple of
stops too early, and he studied his own route map, ignoring
the neat bundle of street maps and locations Rosie had given
him with telephone numbers of restaurants, taxi companies,
etc. He didn't like carrying around anything more than he
needed, or anything that he couldn't stuff into his back
pocket. He was near the new Convention Center, on Lafay-
ette, looking out for Francis X. Roper's Investigation
Agency. He had an old buddy who used to work for them;
it was a long shot and he'd not seen or spoken to Leroy
Able for over ten years, but worth a try.

Nick got the brush-off from Roper's agency, a surpris-
ingly smooth-looking place, when he eventually located it.
The receptionist, a red-haired spitfire with green-rimmed
glasses, gave him an appraising look that'd have stopped a
streetcar dead in its tracks, never mind Nick, and she
snapped that she did not know of any Leroy Able—she
made even the name sound distasteful. This was a high-class
agency dealing with fraud cases and working closely with
the police. She seemed to give a lot of weight to the word
"police."

"You maybe got a forwarding address?"

"Check the telephone directory."

"You got one?"

She pursed her lips and pushed a big yellow directory
across her pristine desk. Nick thumbed through it, taking
covert glances around him at all the posters and advertise-
ments the company displayed—missing persons, domestic

undercover security work, installation of video cameras, surveillance work. Every case, a poster proclaimed, was the firm's top priority.

"You busy?" he asked, as he checked down the As.

She was about to reply when the telephone rang, and she snapped the name of the agency into the phone, listening with one eye on Nick and suddenly assuming a sweet voice for the potential client on the other end of the line. "Yes, sir, we have a full-time staff of six investigators, all licensed and highly trained, and we have our own camera equipment, which includes a variety of long-range lenses and high-powered binoculars. Our teams also carry handheld radio communications and cellular telephones. I can make an appointment for you, just one moment, please." She reached for a large date book as Nick jotted down Leroy Able's address. Whether he was still in business was something he'd find out.

He thanked the woman with green-rimmed glasses, who appeared not to even notice his departure, and headed for Magazine Street in the warehouse district. When he found Able's address, he double-checked he was at the right place, as the ground floor seemed to be a boxing gymnasium.

Nick went up the stairs into the gym, peering through the double door. "Anyone know a Leroy Able?"

"Top floor" came a bellow from a stout boxer well into his fifties, slamming the hell out of a punching bag.

Leroy was thumbing in leisurely fashion through *The Times-Picayune*, a cup of coffee from which rose the unmistakable smell of New Orleans chicory in front of him, his feet up on his desk.

"Hi, Leroy Able around?" Nick asked.

The paper was slowly lowered. "Who wants him?"

"Old buddy, shit, it's you, isn't it? Leroy?"

Leroy slowly took his cowboy boots off the desk and stared hard at Nick.

"Nick Bartello, LA Drug Squad, last saw you 'bout ten years ago, maybe more."

"Oh, yeah? Well, I don't have a good memory for faces—what you say your name was?"

"Shit, man, Nick, Nick Bartello."

"Oh, yeah, yeah, recall the name now. Siddown, want some coffee?"

Nick was a little fazed by Leroy; he didn't show any recognition at all. "I went to Francis X. Roper's place, I reecalled you mentioned working for his agency."

Leroy handed Nick a paper cup of black coffee and perched on the end of his desk. "You know what I hate? People who start talking with a Southern accent ten minutes after they get to New Orleans. What's this reecall crap, Bartello, you wop?" Leroy cuffed Nick's head and gave him a wide grin. "You had me wondering there for a second, man, it's the gris-gris around your fucking neck."

Nick fingered the leather thong and the bones. "I dunno what the shit it is, was given to me last night down some cruddy bar."

Leroy fingered the bones, raised his eyebrows. "Well, you must have got well and truly loaded—this isn't tourist shit, this is the real McCoy."

Nick shrugged. "So, how's life?"

Leroy eased back into his swivel chair. "Ah, not bad, making some dough, of late mostly for the dental board, you know, carrying out medicative investigations."

Nick laughed as Leroy leaned back and let out a big loud bellow, showing his splendid white and gold-capped teeth.

"Yeah, man, long way from the LA Drug Squad, but at least I don't have a leg full of lead. And I'm my own boss."

"So you do know who I am," Nick said, reaching for his coffee.

"Yep, just was worried for a second I owed you dough. I don't, do I?"

Nick shook his head, and looked around the office. Leroy's joke about the dentist wasn't right on the level. His office was in good repair and looked like the business was coming in.

"You want a job?" Leroy asked, seeing Nick's curious looks.

"Nope, I'm on one, that's why I'm in New Orleans."

"Oh yeah, and what's that?"

"The Anna Louise Caley girl, she disappeared eleven months ago."

Leroy nodded. "Yeah, I know the one, lot of private eyes

in on it, but me? I stayed clear: I stick mainly to salvage myself.''

"But you must have heard about it?''

"Sure, like I said, it was pistol-hot at one time, but as far as I know they all came up with zilch. Word was the girl must just have flown the coop—they do down here, you know, especially around Mardi Gras. Kids flock here, get laid, get stoned and move on with some drifter. City draws them like a magnet.''

"This one's different, she's rich as hell.''

Leroy leaned on his elbows. "Rich kids, Nick, are just like everybody else. They like to get stoned and laid, preferably with a little dash of danger thrown in, and then it's back to Mama and Papa, who welcome them home with open arms.''

"But she's been gone eleven months.''

"Then I'd say she's dead.''

Nick got up and paced around the office. "Yeah, I think so too. Question is who killed her, and if I find out I get a nice bonus.''

"Well, I'd like to help, man, but like I said I got this dental case.''

Nick smiled. "So what's putting you off, huh?''

Leroy hesitated, and suddenly became serious. "You want it on the level?''

"Sure, I do, I want whatever you've got that'd help.''

Leroy ran his hands through his iron-gray curls.

"Okay, the Caleys and the types you're dealing with are high-powered money people. Elizabeth Caley is a big star around these parts, so you'd get a lot of people coming forward with bullshit just for the rewards they offered. I think it was twenty-five thousand bucks. I know that to date something like twenty people have said they seen her, and you chase it up and find it's nothin' and then . . .'' Leroy rocked in his chair. "Money runs out and you find you spent half your fee gettin' diddly-squat results. So for the time being I'm sticking to salvage and dental.''

Nick drained his coffee. "What d'you know about an old black jazz player goes by the name of Fryer Jones?'' Leroy stared as Nick flicked the bones at his neck. "He gave me these.''

"Fryer Jones did?"

"Yep, last night."

"He's famous where he hangs out, around the French Quarter and ward nine. All the young kids wanna hang out at his bar, play a few sets with him and the old guys—he used to be one mean trombone player. They drift there, score some dope, maybe play a few numbers. He uses kids like most use toilet paper, but the cops leave him well alone. If he's not openly dealing on the main drag, he's out of their hair, out of the main tourist routes, an' that's all this city cares about." Leroy rubbed his thumb and finger together to indicate money, then he leaned back. "I'd say Fryer must be worth quite an amount by now. No kiddin', he's been running that bar for decades, got a string of little girls whoring for him, all in the name of jazz, brother! But if you want my honest opinion, he's a piece of shit, because it's not all singing the blues that holds them to that stinking bar—it's what you got around your neck too."

Nick touched his bones. "What?"

Leroy shook his head. "You don't know, do you? Gris-gris is supposed to ward off evil voodoo spells, and old Fryer used to have a few connections in that field. In fact, I think he may even be related to one of the Salina sisters."

Nick tensed up. "Hold it, Salina?"

Leroy nodded. "Yeah. One was called Juda, the other . . . er, shit, can't recall right now, but she married. They were real high priestesses. Word is that . . . now I remember her name, it's Edith Corbello. She has a daughter, Ruby, 'bout eighteen, she works in a hair salon. She does some modeling on the side and some new black krewe that's getting together for the Carnival has put her up as their queen."

Nick hitched up his jeans. "Wait, wait, you're going too fast for me, man. There's a Juda Salina in LA, reads tarot cards, that kind of stuff?"

"They do a lot more than tarot readin', Nick. If it's the Juda that's related to the Corbello family, she's almost like royalty in some areas—and I don't mean for the tourists. These are supposed to be the real thing, related to the big voodoo queens they had last century, and they can put the fear of God into people. Like I said, it's more than booze and drugs gets the kids hanging around those people, and if you got your head screwed on right, you'll stay well clear of Jones an' anyone who has anything to do with the Salina sisters. I tell you, you wouldn't even get me through the door of their place and I wouldn't go to Fryer's unless I had a good reason.''

Nick felt uneasy, and his leg was beginning to hurt from all the walking. He rubbed it hard with the flat of his hand. ''I saved the fucker's life, so maybe he owes me.''

Leroy lit a cigarette, the smoke drifting from his aquiline nose as he looked hard at Nick.

''Pack up and go home, Bartello, don't you go getting involved in all this shit. Like I said, you'll come out with nothin'.''

Nick moved painfully down the stairs, past the gym now full of heavy grunts from kids sparring and thwacking the punching bag. It was strange, and it had always worked that way, but the more he was warned off something the more it fed his adrenaline. And he didn't believe in all that voodoo shit anyway.

CHAPTER
12

Lorraine sat on a wide and slippery banquette, richly up-holstered in vermilion silk damask printed with gold fleurs-de-lis, while Lloyd Dulay lowered himself into a matching chair opposite. Lloyd had decided to receive Lorraine in the drawing room to impress her with the full splendor of his house; his improvements to this room were limited to covering one wall with floor-to-ceiling mirrors, in which two Hepple-white chairs were reflected as though standing in an airport lounge. Golden scrolls and swags were everywhere visible—the drapes, of course, were a mass of corn-colored fabric tied back with chocolate-box bows, and ornate gilded plasterwork adorned the fireplace, the huge overmantel mirror and the fire screen, which stood in front of two artificial logs on a stand. The central ceiling medallion extended for six feet of plaster wheatears, garlands and rosettes, and an-other splendid chandelier hung like a huge gilded lily be-neath. A number of modern abstract paintings were suspended by taffeta ribbon bows from the picture rail, and every surface in the room was cluttered with lamps, knick-knacks, bibelots and bulky arrangements of both dried and fresh flowers. Lorraine hated the place and she was uncomfortable, her mouth dry and the thought of a drink coming persistently to her mind, but she forced it out of her thoughts.

"You wanted to see me, Mrs. Page, on a personal matter?"

"Yes, Mr. Dulay, I did."

He nodded his mane of white hair and pointedly looked at his watch. "Then get to the point, I have people for lunch."

"I am investigating the disappearance of Anna Louise Caley."

"Are you, now? Well, I wish I had a million dollars for every one of the so-called agents I have spoken to. Quite truthfully, I don't think there is anything I can add that would be of any use at all. I have business dealings with Robert Caley and I have known his lovely wife for more than thirty years, so I have known little Anna since she was knee-high to a grasshopper."

She loathed him, his loud voice, his condescending, imperious manner. His vast house made her cringe because it was the very reflection of the man—big, loud and heavy. She felt there should be a family crest over the doorway that read: "I have billions of dollars, so fuck you."

She pushed on. "Everyone I have spoken to about Anna Louise says the same thing, that she was naive, shy, beautiful. Tell me what you thought of her."

He closed his eyes. "She was all those things, and affectionate, sweet, with a smile that would break any man's heart. I loved that little girl, Mrs. Page, I loved her."

"Did Robert Caley love his daughter?"

For a fraction of a second he was thrown. "Why, yes, he was her father."

Lorraine met the tiny, cold blue eyes. "What do you think of Robert Caley?"

Dulay laughed, but she knew he was confused. "Why do you ask?"

She held his nasty stare and he was the one to look away. "Maybe if he was fucking his own daughter she had reason to disappear!"

The huge man rose out of his seat. "If you were a man I'd knock you right through that wall."

"But I am not, I am just investigating the disappearance of a young girl, sir."

He towered above her. "Lemme tell you this, Mrs. Page. If I thought for one moment that what you have just said could be true, I'd get a gun and shoot the bastard myself."

"If you also discovered that Anna Louise was not as sweet or naive as everyone makes out, how would that make you feel?"

"I don't follow you, Mrs. Page."

She took out the photograph, slowly, and his eyes narrowed with suspicion.

He scooped it up in one massive hand and held it up to the light, his eyesight, unlike his presence, not being so strong. "What the hell is this disgusting thing?"

"A photograph," she said sweetly.

"I know that, woman, but where in God's name did you get it? Because this isn't the little girl I knew, this is . . . Dear God, it breaks my heart."

"Maybe Robert Caley isn't the man you know either, so what can you tell me about him?"

He was really shaken. "Does Elizabeth know this exists?"

"Yes."

"And Robert?"

"No."

He shook his big head, slumping back into his chair. "She was as precious to me as my own beloved daughter. Dear God, why did she subject herself to this disgusting show?"

"Maybe because she was abused, angry, I don't know. All I am hired to do is find her, dead or alive."

"Is she dead?"

Lorraine looked away. "I hope not."

She could hear the clock ticking on the mantel as he continued to stare at the photograph. At one point he withdrew a printed silk handkerchief and wiped his eyes.

"I know that Anna Louise has a large trust fund."

His head jerked up, the photograph forgotten.

"Mr. Dulay, I am looking for motives for Anna Louise's disappearance. And that is why I am asking you about Robert Caley. The trust's assets amount to one hundred million dollars."

"Do they?" he said softly.

"I am also aware that right now, with this casino development, Mr. Caley is stretched to his financial limits and—"

"Mrs. Page, I said before that if Robert Caley harmed a hair on that little girl's head I'd get a gun and shoot him, not just for myself but for Elizabeth. That said, I do not believe for one moment that the man I have known for twenty-odd years would have any such inclination towards his own daughter. The thought is sickening, degrading and unjust. He's not a great man, but he's a hard worker and has earned his money the hard way. I am one of a number of advisers who take care of Elizabeth's money and investments, and a trusted family friend, so much so that I feel that I must make sure you leave this house with no aspersions cast on Robert Caley's name."

Lorraine retrieved the photograph, slipping it back into the envelope. "Do you know that Elizabeth Caley has a very serious drug habit?"

"No, I won't believe it." Lloyd got up and stared arrogantly into the mirrors behind Lorraine's head, as though finding confirmation of his beliefs in his own image. The purpose of the mirrored wall was more than clear—it allowed Lloyd to enjoy the sight of his reflection as well as the sound of his own voice.

"I can give you the address of the clinic she is in right now." She waited as he sat down, his face concerned and confused. "I am sorry if what we have discussed disturbs you, and obviously I must ask for your total—"

"I would never divulge what you have told me, Mrs. Page, not to anyone, so help me God. I am stunned, stunned . . . shocked, because if what you say is true it means that those nearest and dearest to me are nothing but liars."

"Not necessarily." She smiled.

"What?"

Lorraine snapped her briefcase closed. "Perhaps they chose for you not to know. As an investigator, it is my job to find out what lies beneath the surface."

"Isn't your job, Mrs. Page, to find Anna Louise?"

She nodded, walking to the door. "Yes, Mr. Dulay, it is, but if during my attempts to trace her I uncover certain discrepancies or illogical statements, then I have to follow them through. If you have nothing to add or nothing that can help me, then I thank you for your time."

"Robert Caley is a good man," he said lamely.

She turned at the door. "Yes, I think he is, but I have to make certain that he is in no way connected to his daughter's disappearance so I can eliminate him as a suspect.''

He rose slowly from his chair, moving toward her. ''Is he suspected by your agency?''

''Everyone I meet is a suspect until I get to the truth, Mr. Dulay. If there is any way you could find out for me if Mr. Caley has been using his daughter's trust fund, I'd be very grateful if you could let me know. May I call you again?''

Dulay agreed. He didn't say good-bye as Lorraine closed the door behind her and found her own way out. The big man sat in a dazed, uncomprehending state, feeling outraged and betrayed. He decided there and then that he would withdraw from the Caley development. He wanted to confront Robert Caley to his face, but first he wanted to know if the bastard had touched a cent of Anna Louise's trust fund. He more than anyone could check it out—the hundred million dollars had been his.

Lorraine felt used up and disgusted with herself at the same time. She knew that what she had just done was wrong and unprofessional. Part of her didn't know why she wanted to put so much pressure on Dulay, but perhaps in reality it was a roundabout way of putting it on Robert Caley because of what Tilda Brown had said. She hated him to be under suspicion, wanted him to be innocent. At the same time she was sure he was guilty, but of what? She refused to believe that it was now more than likely that he had murdered his own daughter.

Rosie at last found the sign for the Voodoo Museum on Dumaine and entered the building nervously. She found a group of eight other people, mostly women, standing in a small reception area buying a variety of charm powders, novelties, dolls and candles offered for sale, while they waited for the tour to begin. Behind the young woman at the desk was the portrait of an imposing woman dressed in the costume of the last century. She wore a kerchief on her head and gold hooped earrings; her skin was a rich yellow-brown with just a hint of copper, her eyes a fathomless black. Even in painted form her gaze seemed to penetrate the years, and her presence dominated the room. When the tour guide appeared, it was to this painting he first drew their attention.

"This, ladies and gentlemen, is a portrait of Marie Laveau, the most powerful queen of voodoo this city has ever seen, called the Popess of Voodoo by the time she was forty years old because she was consulted by the gentlefolk of that time, as well as by her own people, and even by royalty, so that her reputation was known all over the world. Her powers were legendary, and when she walked in the streets the crowds would stand silent and hold up their children to catch sight of her: it was as if they knew people would still be talking about her for a hundred years after she died. She held her rituals near the Bayou Saint John, and people said they saw her walk on the water; she could make the sun go dark and call down the spirit of the storm, and she could call up the spirits of love, and, of course . . ."—he stopped and smiled—"of destruction too."

Rosie looked into the ageless eyes of the great sorceress: she felt certain she had seen the face before, and she racked her brains to remember where.

A hush had now fallen on the gaggle of tourists as the guide led them down a narrow passageway in which hung the portraits of a number of voodoo queens, none, however, of Marie Laveau's preeminence; some she had been taught by, and then vanquished or eclipsed. The guide stopped in front of a portrait of another light-skinned young black woman in a formal, old-fashioned dress, with black ringlets knotted at the back of her head and arranged in front of her ears; these eyes were cruel.

"This, people say, is Marie's daughter—Marie the Second, if you want to call her that—said to be more drawn to the darker side of her powers than her mother. People said they saw Marie Laveau up to 1918, 1919, and it was more likely that it was Marie number two they saw, though there are people who say Marie her mother never died: you go rap on her tomb and she'll hear you."

"Did Marie Laveau have any other family—like, are there any of her relatives living today?" asked one of the group with interest.

The guide laughed. "There's a lot of voodoo practitioners say they can trace a connection to the bloodline of Marie

Laveau, but the strongest claim is that of the Salina family—
there are two sisters who were both practitioners at one time,
and those of you who are staying for Carnival will have the
opportunity to see a daughter of the family, Ruby Corbello,
who will be queen of a new black krewe that has been
formed this year.''

The guide ushered them farther down the passage to a
room from which issued a rhythmic and strangely tranquil-
izing drumbeat; the group stepped hesitantly inside to find
themselves surrounded by an eerie collection of carved
masks and statues, some decorated with beads and jewelry,
and with dishes containing offerings of various kinds and
lighted candles arranged in front of them. One corner of the
room was separated from the rest by old iron cemetery rail-
ings: inside were tombstones and animal and human bones,
which made Rosie shudder despite the guide's explanation
that for a religion believing in communion with the departed
ancestors, signs of death were not to be feared but cherished
for protection. He pointed out one glass case of drums and
other shamanic instruments to facilitate the journey to the
spirit world, and another containing a wide variety of bones,
dried animal claws and skins, roots, powders, beans and
barks: each one of these, he told them, was a mojo, and their
combination by a skilled practitioner yielded a gris-gris, a
powerful protective amulet often worn in a sealed bag
around the neck. In the final corner of the room was a large
number of small statues and dolls, for the most part crudely
made of a handful of straw or dried grass tied around two
crossed sticks and covered with a few scraps of material,
with tiny, oddly fierce skulls and faces then painted on.
Some of these, the guide said, were to enhance fertility; he
said nothing about any other use.

The sweet smell of incense greeted them at the door of
the next room. Here the masks and statues were brightly
painted and seemed joyful and celebratory after the shadows
next door. Richly worked hangings and religious paintings
showed many signs of Christian influence, and images of
Catholic saints were pinned up over a cloth-covered table
on which stood more candles, statues and a bottle of rum.
In front of them a picture of the Crucifixion faced a small
prie-dieu, and the guide proceeded to explain how voodoo

was not a set of evil spells but a religion, which had been the only link with their own culture black people had been allowed to retain in the days of slavery, and which had sustained the people through those harsh times. It saw God latent in the whole of creation and later had blended easily with Christianity, the loas, or individual spirits, becoming identified with the angels and saints.

Marie Laveau herself, he went on, had attended Mass regularly at St. Louis Cathedral, had friends among the clergy and had done much charitable work among condemned prisoners and during the fever epidemics. Nonetheless there was a frisson of unease when the guide indicated that the small wooden structure in the corner housed a python named after Marie Laveau's famous snake, Zombi, symbol of the bridge between spirit and material planes, and a few members of the group craned their necks to peep nervously through the glass panes.

The tour was officially over, and Rosie stepped closer to the altar while other members of the group looked at the snake or examined the old tree-stump into which Marie Laveau's followers had dropped prayers and petitions, and saw four more of the disturbing dolls arranged on a rack above the candle flames. The presence of a world she did not understand, but which still lived in the city around her, filled her with awe and a touch of fascination, and she bought some souvenirs and a booklet describing the career of Marie Laveau before she left. The beautiful and commanding face seemed to haunt her, provoking a persistent feeling of déjà vu, but perhaps Marie Laveau had made everyone who had ever seen her feel that they had always known her, that in her the mysterious and the familiar met.

Rooney sat sweltering in his rented car. He'd been parked outside the designated meeting point for over half an hour, and felt a little uneasy to be sitting in the tough downtown waterfront area with a rental firm's sticker in the back window, someone obviously off his home turf. He was about to give up the wait when he saw the patrol car cruising slowly behind him. He adjusted the rearview mirror to watch his contact approach. He shook his head. Men, and cops in particular, come in all shapes and sizes, but he had never seen one that resembled Harris J. Harper.

"You Rooney?" Harper said at the car window. Close up, his face was as weird as his fat, wobbling body. He must have been one of those beautiful babies with an upturned nose, rosebud mouth and bright blue eyes, because whereas the rest of his body had grown, his face had remained the same size, his cheeks puffed out, and his layered chins gave him the unfortunate appearance of having no neck whatsoever.

Rooney nodded, and Harper waddled his way around to the passenger door. When he sat inside the car it felt as if the springs would give way.

"You been waitin' long?"

Rooney nodded. "Yep, since noon, but that's okay."

"Could do with a beer, huh?"

"You said it."

"Okay, Captain Rooney, you follow me, I know a bar a block away, just stick on my tail."

"Thanks."

Harper eased his blubbery body out and then leaned in. "Er . . . five hundred bucks okay with you?"

Rooney hesitated. "Hope it's worth it, that's a lot of dough."

Harper shut the door and patted the top of the car. "Be worth it, Captain, be worth it."

Rosie continued. "Voodoo is a religion as serious as any other. There's a lot of occult, kinda dark stuff that's got associated, but that's not the point. It is a way of connecting with positive, spiritual parts of experience, and is very natural, an important part of a lot of people's lives—"

"It's all bullshit," Nick said, yawning.

Rosie leaned forward. "I don't think so. Everyone thinks it's a lot of evil stuff about killing people and turning them into zombies, you listening, Nick?"

"Yeah, it's rivetin', Rosie."

"What making someone a zombie actually is, is a form of sanction against people who committed some very serious crime, like murder maybe—"

Nick rolled his eyes. "Give me the good ol' electric chair anytime, baby."

Rosie looked at him in irritation. "I won't tell you if you mess around. The priest could give them a kind of nerve poison that would produce a state a Western doctor would think was death, and the person would be what they called 'passed by the ground'—buried and then dug up again. That's why white people call zombies the walking dead."

Nick looked up and saw Lorraine heading toward their table. "Here comes one now."

Rosie looked up. "What?"

"A zombie. It's Mrs. Page."

Lorraine slumped into a seat beside Nick and Rosie in the shaded garden of the hotel.

"Listen, we maybe need to rethink a few things," Nick said. "I paid a call to an old pal, used to be in the drug squad with me, Leroy Able. In fact, I haven't been in contact with him for more'n ten years but we used to get along . . ." Nick drained his beer before continuing. "Okay, you know there are high priestesses in the voodoo church, they are pretty powerful women, and the top of the heap in the voodoo pile is always, you will be pleased to know, a woman. It's a big deal, Lorraine, they are like royalty down here and very powerful."

"I've been to the Voodoo Museum," Rosie began, but Lorraine cut her short. Neither of them had given her a moment even to say hello.

"Christ, Nick, what has this got to do with our case?"

He snapped, "I'm gettin' there, all right? There are two sisters who are real big-time, very dominant with the potions, whatever the hell they do. Rosie's got some stuff from the museum you can read for yourself. According to Leroy, Juda Salina and her sister are the top dogs."

Lorraine was stunned. She reached for a Coke can and shook it—empty. She looked over the table for something else to drink. The thirst had started.

"Why didn't you tell me that?" Rosie asked.

"I was getting to it, Rosie."

"Juda Salina's sister, Edith Corbello, still lives here in a real low-grade area, though she's not so active now. Remember you wanted Raoul checked out? Well, he is Edith

Corbello's son, Juda Salina's nephew. There are two other boys, called Willy and Jesse, and two daughters, the youngest called Sugar May and, last but not least, Ruby Corbello, hairdresser, wanna-be model, who is going to be a queen in the Carnival this year.''

Lorraine now really did need that drink—her mouth was dry, and her head throbbed. "Okay, now let's piece all this together because my hair's standing on end, Nick—oh, and can you pour me some water?''

Rosie poured a glass of water for Lorraine, her attention on Nick.

"Just forget all this voodoo crap and look at Juda Salina. She had a hold on Elizabeth Caley, knew her from here, they even brought her back here to try and help trace Anna Louise.'' Nick lit a cigarette and passed it to Lorraine, then lit one for himself. He had seen the way she had gulped down the water Rosie had passed to her, noticed that her hand was shaking visibly as she drained the glass. "All along we've been looking for a motive, a reason—what if it was blackmail? I mean, you found those pictures of Anna Louise, you dug up stuff on Elizabeth Caley—''

"Wait, wait, Nick, not so fast. You suggesting the motive all along was blackmail and it went wrong?'' Lorraine frowned, rubbing her temples as she tried to assimilate everything that was being said to her.

"Yeah, led by that fat bitch Juda Salina. She's got enough family down here to move a body, she may have even gone to them . . .''

Lorraine dragged on her cigarette. "I better see this— what was her name—Corbello? Any more water, Rosie?''

Nick took her hand. "A second, I don't believe in all this shit, right? An' my pal Leroy said he doesn't, but what he does believe is that these people are dangerous, not with the spells and that crap but they'd kill you soon as spit in your eye. And he warned me to go very carefully because they got a whole army. They beat them drums and you're never seen again.''

"Like Anna Louise Caley?'' Lorraine said softly, her hand already reaching for the glass of water Rosie was pouring for her.

"Exactly, but this moves Robert Caley into second position now because we got something outside, something that maybe makes more sense, nothing to do with his casino or his money—''

"Drugs?'' she asked, gulping the liquid.

"Could be. We know Anna Louise boozed and got stoned with her little friend Tilda Brown. Maybe on that night she disappeared she went to the Corbello woman's house to score and saw something? Say that Juda Salina, who we know she went to see, was drug-pushing, not just here but in LA.''

Lorraine ran her hands through her hair. It was wringing wet—she was soaked in sweat. "Shit, Nick, I think you're right, we've been on the wrong fucking track all along.''

Nick nodded. "And I don't think Elizabeth Caley's involved either. Maybe she's just one hell of a good customer and we know she needed to score drugs, so the link is Juda Salina and her family.''

Rosie left the table and made her way out of the courtyard: Lorraine hardly seemed to notice that she had got up. "Where are you going?'' Nick called after her.

"Going to get some more refreshments if it's all right with you,'' she replied, without even turning around.

Nick stubbed out his cigarette, looking sidelong at Lorraine. "What's up, sugar?''

"Nothing's up, Nick, maybe I'm just tired.'' She hunted for another cigarette in her purse. Nick tapped another out of his own crumpled pack, lit it and passed it to her as before.

"I hate this brand, like smoking something from out of the refrigerator,'' she said, none the less dragging hard on the cigarette, her foot tapping nervously against the table leg.

Nick acted as though nothing were out of the ordinary. "Been a tough day, huh?''

"Nothing I can't deal with.'' She reached for a can of Coke that Rosie had left, but knocked it onto its side and the dregs spilled over the table.

"Shit,'' she snapped, dabbing at the tablecloth, and now Nick gripped her hand.

"You're all stressed out, just take it easy.''

Lorraine bowed her head, holding on to Nick's hand.

"I want a drink so bad sometimes, Nick, it drives me nuts. It comes over me and I just can't think straight, or maybe I'm thinking too much. . . ."

He moved a strand of her hair gently away from her cheek and leaned close to her.

"Just hang on in there, Rosie's bringing some more Coke an' I'll get you some more of your cigarettes."

"Thanks." She liked the strength of his hand, didn't want to let it go, but she glanced up and saw Rosie on her way back with another bag of Cokes and potato chips. Rosie banged it down and yelled, "Ah, look what you've done to my book, I was reading that and you've got Coke all over it! Honestly!"

Lorraine leaned across the table and picked up the blue paper booklet, shaking Coke off it. As she did so, she noticed the picture of Marie Laveau on the front.

"What's this?" she asked Rosie.

"She's Marie Laveau, the most famous voodoo queen ever."

"Why is this so familiar?" Lorraine said, almost to herself.

Rosie took the booklet. "Well, I felt the same thing, like I'd seen it before, her face."

"The turban, the robes . . . give it back to me, Rosie." Lorraine was up on her feet, walking up and down. "Shit! I don't believe this, it's staring us right in the face, Rosie."

"What you talking about?"

Lorraine slapped the photograph down. "This is Elizabeth Caley. She's got this painting in her drawing room, it's from a film."

"No, it isn't. That's from a painting of Marie Laveau, I got it from the Voodoo Museum, but you're right, she's the spittin' image of her."

"*Swamp*," Lorraine said, clapping her hands, congratulating herself. "The film was called *The Swamp*—it was the first movie Elizabeth Seal made, wasn't it, Rosie?"

"Maybe it's on video," Rosie suggested.

"Good idea, let's see if we can get it. She's a big number around here, so you never know. Attagirl, Rosie, this is really good."

"Thanks." Rosie smiled.

"I mean it, you're doing good—make an investigator of you yet!" Lorraine stood up and gave Rosie a hug, beginning to feel better herself. "If it's okay with you, I'm going to take myself off for a snooze. I'm exhausted, maybe take a shower."

Rosie put the pamphlet away in her purse as Lorraine touched Nick lightly on the shoulder. "I'm okay, Nick," she murmured. "Don't keep looking at me. I just need a couple hours' rest."

Nick shrugged his shoulders as she walked away.

"What was that about?" Rosie asked.

"Nothing," Nick replied.

"Oh yeah? She looked pretty strung out to me—you think I should go up and sit with her?"

"Nope, maybe get on to tracking that video. I'll hang around here, wait for Bill."

Rosie gathered her things together and looked at him sidelong. "Maybe you'd like to babysit her ladyship? She looked like she needed a friendly shoulder."

"Well, I'll be right here. And leave the Cokes, huh?"

Left alone, Nick sat toying with the chilled can of Coke, wishing he could go up to Lorraine's room and lie next to her—and not just as a comforting friend.

The Crawfish Bar sat on a dingy corner of the wharf district, a peeling clapboard building with windows covered in rusting wire mesh. It had been an old grocery store, and you had to buzz the door to get inside; it was clear they didn't want any casual trade. The place was almost deserted, and Rooney and Harper sat on two stools at a counter against the back wall under the television, the commentary of the basketball game masking the sounds of their conversation.

"I'm not sure if I'm gonna like these," Rooney said, looking at his plate of boiled crawfish and the ugly black plastic dish, virtually the size of a trash-can lid, which had been slapped down to take the heads and shells.

"Sure you will. These little critters are known as 'mud bugs' because they live in the freshwater streams, and this place, lemme tell you, pal, serves the freshest in the whole of New Orleans," Harper said as he tucked a napkin under his chin. Rooney stared disbelievingly at what looked like toy lobsters to him.

"Right, now, you follow me. First you grasp the head between thumb and forefinger of one hand like so . . ." Harper demonstrated, dangling it in the air, and Rooney dutifully followed suit. Harper was more interested in his lunch than in talking, saying they should eat in and down their beers before they got to business. So it was at least half an hour before he volunteered any information, and not before his five hundred bucks were stuffed inside his wallet.

"So what you need to know, Bill?"

"What you came up with on the disappearance of Anna Louise Caley."

Harper shrugged his fat shoulders. "Sweet diddly-squat!"

"That all I get for five hundred fucking bucks?" Rooney snapped.

Harper gave a furtive look around. "Depends on what else you want to know . . ."

"Any dirt on Robert Caley?"

"No, sir. Well-respected man, got his real estate license, hadda wait awhile even though he is married to Elizabeth Seal, but he didn't give any bribes, just applied as a resident of New Orleans through the right channels."

"But he's not exactly a resident, is he?"

"You kiddin' me? They got palatial residences, three, maybe even four. Rich as Croesus. Mind you, rumor was while back now, more'n twenty—five years, that she, Elizabeth Seal, and a big tycoon by the name of Lloyd Dulay were an item, and he kind of added to the lady's fortune."

"He's one of the partners in Caley's casino development, isn't he?" Rooney asked.

"Yep, a couple of heavy hitters on his side. I'd say it'll go through eventually. Just a question of time."

"You ever hear any rumor 'bout Elizabeth Caley having a drug problem?"

"What, you kiddin' me? No fucking way."

Rooney sighed. "So, can you give me more details on how your investigation was set up? There was a big reward out and quite a few claimants, right?"

"True, but by the time we shifted through their so-called eyewitness reports it was all bullshit, and a number of 'em had been set up by a few officers trying to get their hands on the reward—''

"What do you think happened to her?"

Harper wiped the sweat from his face. "The girl picked up some drifter, they got into an argument and he killed her. There was only one arrest, old jazz player by the name of Fryer Jones, somebody said they'd seen him talking to her out in the Quarter."

Rooney frowned. "You had an arrest? But that's not in any report back in LA."

"Well, it wouldn't be, would it? LA is LA, this is New Orleans, and things happen a little bit different down here. You might not even find a report on Fryer Jones in our department either."

"Why?"

"Because nobody likes to get on the wrong side of that old buzzard. He's very influential, and we got people here with heavy superstitious minds. Fryer's real clever at twisting minds to suit himself."

"I don't follow, how strong was the case against him?"

Harper shrugged. "Just someone thought they had seen Anna Louise Caley talkin' to him. Like he's not far from the hotel, not in the same kind of district, mind you, but his place is no more than a ten- or fifteen-minute walk away. We got nobody else to verify the eyewitness's report and he was found floatin' in the river 'bout five months back, so like I said—''

"You think he was murdered because of his report against this Fryer?"

"Quite possibly, but there again he was a junkie so he coulda easily tripped and fallen into the river."

"So no charges were brought?"

"Nope. Fryer denied seeing Anna Louise Caley and he had 'bout twenty witnesses that said he never left his bar that night, so we let him go." Harper checked his wrist-watch. "I'm on duty."

"You think he'd talk to me?"

Harper hitched his pants over his belly. "Up to you, but I wouldn't go near his bar alone or at night, it's kinda off-limits. We don't bother him and he don't bother us, and like I said, he's a man I keep my distance from because believe it or not, that voodoo crap really fucks with your head, know what I mean?''

Lorraine felt better after she had taken a shower and two aspirin, and not until she was wrapped in her bathrobe did she check the messages that had come in for her. There were four messages to contact Robert Caley and one to call Lloyd Dulay. She stared at Caley's name, wanting to call him but afraid even to hear his voice, so she called Lloyd Dulay, who was not at home. She was just about to lie down on the bed when there was a rap at her door.

"It's me and Bill," Nick called.

She sighed, not wanting to see them.

"I was just going to take a shower," she lied as she opened the door.

"Go ahead, I'll join you." Nick grinned.

Rooney was not amused. He was hot and sweaty, his feet felt like swollen balloons, and he sat on a straight-backed chair as Nick slumped down on the single bed.

"Well, you can both hang on until we've talked a few things through," Rooney said with a touch of irritation. "Right, this cop had some very interesting information."

"I hope so, you coughed up five hundred dollars for it." Nick yawned, his face twisting as he rubbed at his leg. "Christ, I hate this city—my leg is driving me nuts, it's the damp."

Rooney flicked out his notes. "Can we get down to business?"

The phone rang. Lorraine looked at Nick. "Can you get it? If it's Robert Caley, say I'm not here, and if it's reception, will you tell them to hold all calls?"

"Sure." Nick reached over and picked up the bedside phone, pleased by the fact that she didn't want to see Caley. "Mrs. Page's room."

"I interviewed this cop, right?" Rooney went on, "And he told me that the bastards down here had made an arrest."

Nick gestured to Lorraine. "She's right here." He covered the phone.

"Who is it?" she whispered.

"Something to do with Tilda Brown, it's the cops."

She pulled a face and took the phone, inching onto the bed beside Nick.

"Lorraine Page speaking." She listened, then her body straightened. "Yes, I did, today, yes. I'm sorry?"

Rooney and Nick were all ears; just by her body language they knew something was up.

"Yes, of course, I'll come right away. Oh, then I'll wait outside the hotel."

Lorraine replaced the receiver. "Tilda Brown hanged herself sometime this afternoon. They want to interview me, they found my card in the pocket of her robe, they know I was there this morning—"

"Shit," Nick said softly.

Lorraine was really shaken, pressing her hand to her forehead. "They're sending a squad car. . . . Oh, shit, goddamn it! The stupid, stupid girl."

Nick reached for her hand. "Come now, get yourself together. If you want I'll come with you."

She eased away from him. "No, no, stay here, talk over everything we've come up with. Oh, God! Why did she go and fucking do this, why?"

"Come on, you can't blame yourself, Lorraine," Rooney interjected.

Lorraine headed for the bathroom and then turned. "No? I really grilled her, I even showed her that fucking picture of Anna Louise and . . . I didn't have anything to do with it? Who you kidding?" She slammed the bathroom's inadequate louvered door.

Nick looked at Rooney. "Maybe go to my room, leave her alone for a while."

Rooney sighed. "Okay, but I need a beer or something, this heat is wearing me to shreds."

"I'll be right with you." Nick waited for the door to close before he got up and walked to the bathroom; he didn't knock, but walked straight in. Lorraine was standing shaking, gripping the washstand with both hands, tears streaming down her face. She didn't even have the energy to tell him to leave, and he prized her hands loose, then drew her close, holding her tightly as she rested her head on his shoulder.

"Sshhh, don't fight me, you just let it all out. It'll make you feel a whole lot better, believe me, I know."

She clung to him, and he scooped her up in his arms and carried her into the bedroom. He laid her down on the bed, and as he had so wanted to do earlier, lay beside her, holding her in his arms, and even kissing her gently as she wept. She needed him, though she didn't want him as badly as he wanted her, but even being close to her gave him hope, still more when she leaned on her elbow and looked into his face.

"You're one of a kind, you know that, Bartello?"

"Yeah, it's been said before."

She smiled, and he wiped her cheek with his finger. "That's my girl. Now, do you want me with you?"

"No, I've got to straighten myself out, I've made enough mistakes already, Nick."

She took him by surprise when she cupped his face in her hands and kissed him on the lips, sweetly and platonically, but he was thrown into turmoil nonetheless. He was wise enough—and had enough self-control—not to push things any further, but the kiss had given him more hope than ever before.

"You got me, Mrs. Page, you know that, don't you?"

She drew away from him, already disciplining herself to get moving and face the police.

"Did you hear what I just said?"

She turned and looked at him in the way he adored, her head on one side and her hair falling across to hide her scar. "Maybe, Nick, I ain't worth having!"

He laughed as he sauntered to the door, and walked out without looking back. "I'll be the judge of that!"

By the time Lorraine was dressed, two little white message envelopes had been posted under her door. She picked them up as she left for the waiting patrol car.

"I was here this morning with a group," Rosie said to the young man who had taken over the later shift at the Voodoo Museum; he seemed graceless in comparison to the smiling young woman who had been at the desk earlier.

"If it's lost property we ain't found nothing today," he said, without even looking up from his newspaper.

"It isn't. I want to make inquiries about a video," Rosie

persisted, passing over the Page Investigations Agency card.

"This isn't a video store, ma'am." He didn't even glance at the card.

"I know that, but it's a particular video, an old film called *The Swamp*, starring Elizabeth Seal as Marie Laveau, and none of the video stores have it. I know the film was made, I've seen the portrait of Miss Seal as—"

The paper snapped shut. "I think you must be mistaken. Elizabeth Seal is white, Marie Laveau was colored. If you want another guided tour . . ."

His eyes bore into Rosie, frightening her, but she didn't back off. "They use makeup, you know, and . . ."

"And you didn't hear me right, ma'am, you got the wrong information. And if you don't want a tour, then you should leave."

"Thank you, I'll have another tour."

He sullenly took her money for another tour ticket and ignored her as she moved past him and said she would wait for a guide inside. She stood in the dim, scented room for some minutes, but no one joined her. She waited on, her heart beating. Then came the soft drumbeat, and she wondered if the young man had turned on a tape.

Rosie stepped into the hallway and looked at the portraits of the queens, but it was Marie Laveau's image she saw constantly in her mind's eye, the glowing face, the eerie, pitch-dark eyes. She physically jumped when she heard someone behind her, not the young guide but a tall, austere-looking black man with iron-gray hair. He wore a smart gray suit and a white shirt with a stiff collar and tie. He held Lorraine's card in one large, finely made hand.

"Are you Mrs. Lorraine Page?" His voice was quiet and deep.

"No, I am her assistant, well, partner, my name is—"

"Please come through," he said, gesturing to the room at the back.

Rosie was so scared she was hyperventilating. She was sure it was much darker than it had been, and the drumbeat was becoming unnerving.

"What precisely are you investigating?"

Rosie shifted her weight from foot to foot. "Well, that is

really a private matter, but we have been hired by Mr. and Mrs. Robert Caley.''

"What for, precisely?'' the man asked, keeping his eyes fixed on her face.

"Er, they had a daughter, her name was Anna Louise Caley and she disappeared eleven months ago from here. Well, not exactly here here, but from her hotel in New Orleans.''

"Mmm, yes, I recall reading about it,'' his deep voice rumbled. "So what has this film to do with . . . Caley, you said?''

"Yes, it's just that Mrs. Caley used to be Elizabeth Seal.''

"Ah, yes, so she was, the film star, a very beautiful woman.''

Rosie felt more confident and stepped closer. "Her first film was called *The Swamp* and there is a painting in her home, almost identical to the portrait of—''

"Queen Marie Laveau.''

"Yes. And we, that is Mrs. Page and I, and Captain Rooney who is also part of the agency, well, we would like to see the film.''

"Why?''

Rosie licked her lips. "Er, I don't know, to be honest, it's just that we are trying to piece together backgrounds, that sort of thing, and it was such a coincidence, me being here and seeing the painting, that's all really.''

"Mmm, that's all. But you see, it isn't quite as simple as that.''

"I'm sorry?''

He leaned forward, the candlelight illuminating his handsome features. "Let me try to explain something to you. Queen Marie is a very special part of our heritage. We are proud of her, we worship her, she brought hope and faith when there was none. We took great exception to this film you referred to. It was a betrayal of our faith, a typical Hollywood commercial vehicle that was a distortion of the facts. This film is dismissed, disowned, and no one in New Orleans, in the state of Louisiana, will acknowledge its existence.''

"So it was about voodoo, this film?''

He stared at her and then shook his head, smiling. "Let

us say it was an attempt to portray our great queen and it was an insult to her memory. To begin with, they cast a white woman in the role; Elizabeth Seal may have black blood in her veins but she is ashamed to admit it, even though she has for many years been a generous benefactor to our cause." He gave a formal bow. "So if you will excuse me."

"Are you saying that Elizabeth Caley—"

"Is a believer and a very generous and caring woman. Please pass on my condolences to her regarding her daughter. Good evening."

"Thank you very much," Rosie stuttered, still unsure if she had heard correctly. But she didn't wait around. The drumbeats were in time with her own heart and it scared the hell out of her.

Lorraine sat in the stifling, overheated office in the New Orleans police department. A female officer was taking down her statement. A wiry detective sergeant sat behind a cluttered desk, his chair creaking at every twist of his body.

"So you do not know of any reason why Miss Tilda Brown would have taken this tragic course of action?"

"No. As I have already said, I was there for no more than three quarters of an hour, going over, in fact, your previous inquiries, whether or not Anna Louise Caley visited her on the night she disappeared, routine questions—"

"Did she seem perplexed or upset?"

"Yes, she was Anna Louise's best friend, so she obviously got upset." Her brain was ticking over at ninety miles an hour, deciding not to mention the photograph or the insinuations regarding Anna Louise and her father being lovers.

"Well, it's a tragedy, but who knows what goes on in a youngster's mind?" said the sergeant, his chair creaking ominously.

"Yes, who knows?" she repeated, and then hesitated. "Are you sure it was suicide? Did she leave a note?"

He frowned. "We have no indication any other party was involved."

"So there was a note?"

He nodded. "I am unable to disclose its contents, as it

was personal to her parents. She was their only child."

"But it was suicide?"

"Yes, it was. She was wearing only a silk kimono and she had taken the belt, tied it to a curtain rail, stepped up on a small dressing-table stool and kicked it away. There were no visible signs of violence on her body other than the marks left by the belt. Her mother found her, and is under sedation. As I said, she was an only child."

Lorraine stopped at the hotel reception, said that although she was in she wanted no calls and did not want to be disturbed by anyone—that included her associates also staying at the hotel.

There were more white envelopes with telephone messages posted under her door, but she stepped over them. She hadn't even opened the ones she had taken with her. She felt drained and didn't want to face anyone, talk to anyone, even Robert Caley, because she blamed herself for Tilda Brown's death. She wanted to go over everything that she had said, everything Tilda Brown had said, because somewhere there would be a clue as to why a beautiful eighteen-year-old girl with everything to live for had gone to such tragic lengths. Maybe there was even a clue to Anna Louise Caley's disappearance.

CHAPTER

13

Nick had put away more than a few beers with Bill Rooney. They had traded notes, discussed the new findings, and Rosie joined them with her notes about the meeting at the museum. They'd continued to discuss their developments over supper together in a nearby bistro. All three felt that Robert Caley was no longer their main suspect and they should concentrate on the Juda Salina, drugs and voodoo connection, especially after hearing that Fryer Jones had actually been questioned by the police regarding Anna Louise Caley's disappearance.

It was after ten when they got back to the hotel. Rooney and Rosie were tired out but Nick was fully alert; he had always been a night owl. When they were told that Lorraine was in her room but had requested not to be disturbed, it irritated the hell out of Nick, but the other two were thankful.

Nick went up to his room, paced around and drank a quarter of a bottle of vodka he had bought before he decided to go and see Lorraine. He tapped on her door and waited, then looked quickly up and down the empty corridor and took out his own room key. He'd been in more than enough hotels, and he wondered if, as was often the case, the security aspect of the keys left a lot to be desired. He was right—his key fit, and he opened Lorraine's door.

He stood looking at her, slowly unscrewing the cap from the bottle and taking a long slug. She lay on her belly, one arm hanging over the side of the bed, the other tucked under her pillow, and the sheet thrown back to the base of her back. He padded closer, sitting on the bed opposite to drink her in, wanting to lie naked beside her more than anything he had ever known. Lorraine slept soundlessly, her lips slightly parted, and even in the dim light he could see the scars on her arm and back. With the alcohol, his inhibitions relaxed more and more, until he tucked the bottle down beside the bed and ran his palm gently along the curve of her spine; she stirred, and slowly turned to face him as she woke.

"Nick?" she murmured, still half asleep.

"Yeah," he said softly. She turned over, reaching unhurriedly for the sheet to cover her naked breasts.

"How the hell did you get in?"

He smiled. "Oh, I huffed and I puffed an' I blew the door down."

"You're drunk," she said, yawning.

"Not yet, but I couldn't stay away from you."

She sat up, drawing the sheet closer. "You'd better go, this is crazy, Nick."

"I know, but like I said—I couldn't keep away."

Lorraine sighed; she didn't need this, and it was beginning to irritate her. "I need to sleep, Nick."

He stood up, suddenly almost boyish. "I know, I'm sorry, I always was a dumb bastard, but . . ."

She flopped back, looking up at him. "But what?"

He hitched up his jeans, avoiding her eye.

"But what, Nick?"

He laughed softly. "Do you think I could have just one kiss, just one, and then I'm gone."

"You're nuts, you know that, don't you?"

"Yep, but that's all I want—well, it isn't, I'd like a whole lot more, but maybe this isn't the time for you and me to dive between the sheets."

"You'd better go," she said again, but she was smiling. She couldn't help it, he was getting to her, she knew it, and maybe so did he.

"Come here, Bartello, an' the deal is—"

"One kiss," he said, almost jumping across the bed to sit close to her and wrap her in his arms. She reached up and kissed him on the lips, and as the sheet fell away from her breasts he bent his head to kiss her nipple.

"Nick, that's enough."

He moaned, tracing her breast with his tongue, and then drew the sheet gently back over her.

"Good night, princess. I love you."

She watched him limp to the door, half turning for a last look at her, and then he was gone. Sometimes he was so like Jack Lubrinski it made her want to weep, but he wasn't Jack, he was Nick Bartello, and as she snuggled down she felt the warmth of his love, and although she didn't want to admit it, it felt good.

Back in his own room, Nick found it impossible now to sleep. He was still restless by eleven, so decided he would go back to Fryer's bar, see what else he could pick up. It was almost twelve when he passed through the silent lobby, where only the night porter was on duty. Like Rosie and Rooney, the other, mostly elderly guests had all turned in, it seemed.

Robert Caley sat with a bottle of Scotch. He had been drinking since around seven and had now almost drunk himself sober. The only woman he had cared about in so long not only didn't return his calls but had betrayed him to such an extent he didn't know whether he wanted to kill her or himself. Lloyd Dulay had been around like a man possessed, accusing him of fucking his daughter and telling him with pleasure that the governor had told him privately that there was no question of Caley's being awarded the license to operate the casino. An official public announcement would be made shortly, but the governor had indicated that he considered a broader distribution of ownership to be appropriate, and he, Lloyd, had had no hesitation in accepting the invitation to join their number that had been extended to him by Doubloons. Finally, Dulay said grimly, he figured that Caley had walked himself into one hell of a mess, and if he used one cent more of his daughter's trust fund to bail himself out of it, he would find himself in court.

"Who did you get all this crap from?" Caley had snapped angrily.

Dulay had hesitated, and then looked Caley straight in the face. "The investigator, Lorraine Page."

Caley was stunned. The accusations had been like blows to his heart. Why, he kept on asking himself, why was she doing it? How could she lie in his arms one night and the next day systematically try to destroy him, unless that had been her intention all along? He just couldn't believe it. The booze helped numb the pain, and the more drunk he became, the more he convinced himself she wouldn't have done this to him. But when call after call to her remained unanswered, he began to get angry at himself for being a sucker, angry that maybe all his adult life he had been just that, a sucker.

The anger built when he received a cable saying that Elizabeth had discharged herself from the clinic and had ordered Edward to stand by to fly her to New Orleans. Caley called Phyllis in LA to be told that Lloyd Dulay had called to speak to Elizabeth. Phyllis had given him the clinic's phone number.

By twelve Caley was drunk, hurt and bewildered—and also facing bankruptcy. But he kept on calling Lorraine, needing to speak to her, to give her the chance of explaining to him, because he still could not believe that she would betray him. Nothing else mattered to him, not the money, not even Anna Louise, just that Lorraine, the woman he had fallen totally and stupidly in love with, had used him. Even when he received a call from Elizabeth, he felt numb. She sounded calm and distant, and angry. She refused to tell him why she had discharged herself, merely stated that she would not be coming to the hotel but would be going straight to their home in the Garden District.

Caley knew that Dulay must have said something to her, but he didn't have the energy to argue on the phone, preferring to see her face-to-face. He did, however, ask if Lorraine Page had also contacted her at the clinic. Elizabeth seemed surprised. Then he heard the fear creep into her voice.

"Has she found out something?"

Caley sighed, dragging on a cigarette. "Maybe, but I don't think it has anything to do with Anna Louise—"

"What, then?" Elizabeth asked, her voice wavering.

"You're the one with the secrets, Elizabeth. I'm just the

dumb bastard that went along with everything.''

There was a lengthy pause. "You think we should stop payments?''

"We? *We?* You're the one who instigated this investigation, Elizabeth, not me. You hired her, you fire her. She's only on it for two weeks, isn't she? Just stop the payments."

Again there was a long pause and he could hear her rapid breathing, knew she was suffering a panic attack, but this time he didn't care, this time he wasn't on hand to sort it all out, carry her to bed.

"There was a bonus," she said softly.

"What?'' he asked, lighting another cigarette from the stub of his last. "What are you talking about?''

Again there was a pause and then he heard a deep intake of breath. "Don't be angry with me, but I offered to pay a million-dollar bonus if they found Anna Louise.''

He closed his eyes. She was crying, and he felt like weeping himself. "Well, that's your business. I'll see you at the house." He replaced the receiver before she could reply, then pressed for the desk and gave instructions he was not to be disturbed.

Caley lay on the bed, inhaled deeply and let the smoke drift slowly from his lungs. A million-dollar bonus! No wonder she made love to him. A man who felt foolish and betrayed, a man who felt as inadequate as he now felt was dangerous, because if Lorraine Page had walked in at that moment he would have taken her by her throat and squeezed the life out of her.

Lorraine was in a deep, dreamless, exhausted sleep. She had pushed away the sheet and lay curled up naked, her body glistening with perspiration. But nothing woke her, not the red blinking dot on her telephone as the calls came in, one at midnight, one at a quarter past, and the last at one-fifteen.

Juda Salina woke, her massive body soaked in sweat. She could feel the horrific restriction on her throat and knew that what she had seen a few days before was now happening.

"Raoul," she croaked, and then screamed out, *"Raoul, get in here."*

He stood bleary-eyed at her bedroom door. "Yes? What you want?"

"Water, get me some water."

It was going down, it was happening, and there was nothing she could do to stop it. What she had seen, what she had felt, she would have to go through, and it made her angry that she was an open avenue for such pain. But that was her God-given power, and as much as she hated it, she had to give way and let it happen. It was the will of the spirits, she had been chosen, and there was nothing she could do to stop it.

Raoul passed her a glass of tepid water and she gulped it down, her fat hand shaking as she drained the glass. He hovered, waiting. "You sick?"

She shook her head and lay back on her mound of pillows with a sigh. "No, I'm not sick, we'll still be going."

"You want some more water?"

"No, maybe just sit with me awhile, talk to me."

He sat on the edge of her bed, his short cotton wrap tied tightly around his waist. "All be buzzin' back home, starts any day now, and Ruby is all jumpy with nerves."

Juda sighed again. "You talk to your mama?"

He nodded. "Sure, said she'd whacked Jesse and Willy with a broom, they been getting drugged up at Fryer's bar, and Sugar May's a handful, wants to be a singer, so she hangs out there too. It's making Mama go crazy with worry."

Juda nodded her head. "Ruby's got a beautiful face and a lovely tight body, but I don't think she has the knowledge. That's why I think she's gonna be okay. But when we get home you sit your brothers down and you tell them they should keep away from Fryer Jones. If they don't, they're gonna get hurt bad, and the same goes for Sugar May."

She closed her eyes and he chewed his fingernails, his foot tapping against one of the bed legs.

"You don't do those drugs anymore, do you, Raoul?"

"No, Aunty Juda, not now I'm working for you."

"That's a good boy, they no good for you. Stop that tapping on the bed, Raoul, gettin' on my nerves. You're a real jumpy boy lately, so if you can't sleep, make yourself some of that tea I get for Mrs. Caley."

"That'd take an elephant out," he said, still chewing his nails.

"Well, I've had to increase the strength over the years. . . ."

He uncrossed his legs and then promptly recrossed them, his foot tapping into the dark night. He couldn't stop it, his whole body was twitching, and he needed to get back to his pipe, had just been smoking up when she'd called out to him. If she'd looked close into his eyes she would have seen for herself: Raoul had advanced; he was no longer rolling the ganja, he was using crack now, and most nights. As soon as he saw she was asleep he would slip out to the clubs, and be back before she woke, back before she knew he'd been out to score.

Nick headed toward Fryer Jones's bar, hands stuffed into his jeans pockets, cigarette dangling from his mouth. He heard the car backfire, like a gunshot, and he automatically ducked, turned and sidestepped to the wall. *Crack*, it backfired again, and then he heard the loud, screeching music as an old broken-down Camaro careered toward him.

Willy was high, his brother Jesse hanging out of the window, yelling, "I said it was him, it's him, Willy! Pull on over now."

Nick sighed with irritation, not in any way scared by the two stoned kids, but his hands were out of his pockets and he was looking up and down the road, making up his mind which way to go, to see if there was anyone who'd witness what he knew was going to go down.

"Eh! *You motherfucker, you!*"

The old Camaro lurched to a standstill just a few yards ahead of Nick. He moved closer to the wall, fists clenched, ready to thrash them both, knowing that if it came to it he'd go for the .22 stashed in his boot.

Willy crashed the gears into reverse and the Camaro screamed backward. He hadn't intended to mount the pavement, he just misjudged the curb. Jesse was still hanging out of the passenger window, swearing and cursing at the guy who had beaten the hell out of them the previous night. Only tonight he was on his own, no old bastard Fryer Jones around. As Nick moved to one side to avoid being crunched by the car, his leg gave way. He stumbled and had just straightened up when Jesse came at him, screeching, doing a farcical kung fu side-kick. Nick grabbed his foot and twisted it, throwing Jesse off balance and making him fall on his hands and knees.

"Get the shit, Willy, get him!"

Carrying a baseball bat, Willy ran at Nick and swung wildly, striking him on his forearm as Nick protected his face. His leg buckled again, giving Jesse a few moments to get back on his feet. He grabbed the baseball bat from his brother, and as the two of them closed in on him Nick ducked and dived and took off, heading toward a lit-up bar. He ran as fast as he could, hampered by his bad leg, needing a moment to get his pistol out of his boot. But the kids were on his heels, Jesse swinging the baseball bat in a frenzy. He clipped Nick on the shoulder but he kept on running. Just before the safety of the bar he stumbled again. Willy moved in front of him and Nick saw the knife come out. He held up his hands, gasping for breath. "Hey! Come on, just take it easy, huh . . . ?"

Nick saw the alley right across the road and dived between them both, but not before Jesse took another swing with the baseball bat. This time it hit Nick just on the left side of the head above his ear, making him reel. He could see the neon sign of a liquor store and was trying to make it there, hoping there would be someone around to help. His breath rasped in his chest, the shooting pains in his leg were crippling him and his head thudded, but he made it right up to the doorway. The door was locked. He jammed his finger on a security buzzer and hurled his body against the door.

"Open the door, open the fucking door."

The two boys were grinning, one swinging the bat, the other opening the switchblade. They had him cornered; the alley was a dead end and there was nowhere to run to. Nick was trapped.

Raoul still sat by his aunt's bed, his whole body twitching now, and he was desperate to get back to his pipe.

"You still need me to stay with you?"

She didn't answer. He stood up and leaned closer, sure she was sleeping, when she scared the hell out of him. She sat bolt upright, her hands clutching at her throat, and started retching. He backed away, not that he hadn't seen this before, his mama often went into spasms and he hated it, just like he hated the way all his life people had come to their run-down house and started screaming and shouting in that dark front room, the kids banished to the backyard.

She twisted and turned on the bed, making it creak and groan from her weight. At one point part of the bed actually lifted as she rolled to one side. He saw it then, the old wooden box, and became even more agitated, frightened by her grunting and moaning. Saliva trickled down her fat chin and frothed at the corners of her mouth, but all he could think about was the box, because he knew what was inside it.

Nick Bartello couldn't run anywhere. He'd tried to reach his hidden .22 but the baseball bat had swung down on his arm and he'd felt the bone crack. He was defenseless but he remembered their faces, so young, the two arrogant black kids he'd given a whipping at Fryer's bar. When they hemmed him in he still put up a good fight, but he knew it was the end, and with the pain in his leg he didn't have a chance to defend himself. He curled up as they kicked at him, putting his hands up to protect himself. Then one of the boys leaned over him and he saw the blade close up, saw his whole life as it ran before him. Lorraine's face was the last image he saw as they cut his throat, giving him one last kick to turn his body over.

Fryer Jones was in his usual seat at the bar. Willy and Jesse Corbello walked in and drew up stools next to him. Fryer held on to his trombone as Willy threw the gris-gris necklace on the bar.

"This yours, Fryer?"

He picked it up, felt the blood still sticky on the white bones, and he sighed. "Boys, you just done somethin' bad, these were mine, given in good faith."

"You not given us what you promised, you old bastard, and besides, you gonna do the same for us as we done for you, right? We been here all night, man, never left your bar," Jesse said, and leaned over to get himself a beer.

Willy opened Nick Bartello's wallet. "Who gives a fuck? Nobody saw us anyway, we was cool. Hey! Drinks on the house, we just scored a few bucks."

Fryer eyed the boys and kissed his teeth. They were running out of control, getting into bad trouble, just like their crazy brother Raoul. He looked at the gris-gris he had given to that poor bastard. He picked it up, tipped his beer over it, washing the blood away with his gnarled thumb, then hung it around his neck.

"Think I'll play a set," he said to no one. He eased off the barstool and wended his way back to the mirrored stage. As he passed two thickset black men playing bid whist, he murmured, "Thrash 'em hard, they gotta be taught a lesson from somebody, and they're getting outta hand, way out."

The two young boys were sitting on the barstools, laughing and joking, guzzling their free beer, confident they were running the show, confident no one would touch them. They were the Salina sisters' boys.

"Where's Nick?" Lorraine asked as she joined Rosie and Rooney at the breakfast table for waffles and cream.

"I dunno, but we all had an early night," said Rooney, squinting over the menu. "I called his room, no answer."

Lorraine sat down and brought out all the small white envelopes with her messages.

"How did it go last night?" Rosie asked as she signaled for the waitress.

Lorraine began slitting the envelopes open. "They haven't got the exact time Tilda Brown hanged herself, but they think about two or three hours after I left." There were fifteen messages from Robert Caley, one saying his wife was arriving in New Orleans. Dulay had called four times, and Nick twice. She noted the time of the last call. "I would say Nick is sleeping one off, seems he didn't take such an early night." She tossed the message over to Rooney.

Rosie had been studying the menu and turned to Rooney. "Maybe we should cut down on all this sugar. I know we had a deal, but I don't know about you, I felt a lot better before we made pigs of ourselves here."

He nodded. "You order for me, then."

"Okay, maybe just some fresh fruit."

"Fine," he said, and then flushed as he caught Lorraine looking at him and smiling.

"What you looking at me like that for?" he said defensively.

"Because it's nice to see you two getting along so well."

"I noticed you and Nick were real friendly too," Rosie put in, afraid that Lorraine disapproved of her friendship with Rooney, or thought it unprofessional.

"Hell, don't be so defensive, Rosie. And you're right, I'm getting on really well with Nick, he's okay, but that doesn't mean we're up for a double wedding or—"

Rooney gasped. "Who's talking about weddings? Me and Rosie are just on the same diet."

Rosie brought her menu up quickly to cover her face, not wanting Rooney to see that his remark had upset her.

"So," she said expressionlessly, "it's fruit all around, is it?"

Juda Salina eased her bulk into the shower, calling out for Raoul to put the coffee on and bring around the car to take them to the airport. It had been a bad night, but it was over, the dark cloud had lifted. It came down like a blanket fifteen minutes later when she kicked open the kitchen door and there was no coffee on the stove, just Raoul's sleeping bag left in the middle of the floor. And it got darker when she went back into her bedroom, because just sticking out from under her bed was her precious box. Fat as she was, she got down on her knees fast and dragged it out. It was never this close to the edge, she was no fool. In fact, she slept feeling it through the mattress and the bedsprings on purpose so nobody would ever steal it from under her at night.

She screamed out loud when she realized all her savings were gone, every single dollar, more than one hundred fifty thousand dollars. Money to put toward Ruby's float, her Mardi Gras gowns, money for her sister, her kids. Her savings, all gone.

At first Edith Corbello thought it was one of her clients screeching down the phone; it was a while before she realized it was her own sister.

"Hush now, Juda, hush now, I can't understand a word you're saying."

Juda eventually gasped out that Raoul had stolen everything she possessed, all her life's savings; everything she'd worked so hard for in order to come back to New Orleans and live in style was gone.

"No, no, honey, you got to be mistaken."

"I am not mistaken, he's even taken my car, my car, Edith, that little shit's got my fucking car." Juda gripped the bed tightly, gasping for breath, her massive bosom heaving. "I never done evil work, Edith, you know that, but so help me God, I will on Raoul. I'll fill that boy full of stuff to eat his guts alive, he's gonna wish he never saw the light of day!"

Juda slammed the phone back on the hook. She slumped into a chair, put her head in her hands and wept. How many times had she been told by Mrs. Caley to put her money in the bank and she had always refused? Through her tears she ranted and raged against Raoul. She didn't even have enough money to go home for Carnival, wouldn't see Ruby crowned.

Eventually the tears and rage subsided into a deep depression, and she sat as if wedged into the chair. How could he do that to me? she said to herself over and over, and then looked at the ceiling. How come the spirits talk with me and I don't know when my own blood is stealing from me?

She wiped her face with a tissue and sniffed, and picked up the phone again. Maybe *she*'d help her out, like she'd helped *her* for all these years.

Phyllis answered, stunned to hear the plaintive voice at the other end. "Juda? Mrs. Salina, is this you?"

"Yes, Phyllis. Something terrible has happened and I need to speak to Mrs. Caley."

Phyllis pursed her lips; she was going to enjoy this. "I'm sorry, Mrs. Salina, but Mrs. Caley is not at home."

"Can you get her to contact me?"

"Well, if she calls home I will tell her you rang."

Phyllis was sure the horrible creature was crying, and when she thought of all the years she had been treated like a piece of worn carpet by the big fat woman, she enjoyed her moment of power.

"You know, Phyllis, I've been a good friend to Mrs. Caley, we go back a long time, so, please, I'm asking you, if she calls home, tell her to contact me. This time it's me that needs her and I need her bad."

"As I said, Mrs. Salina, I will relay the message to Mrs. Caley. Good-bye."

She replaced the phone as Peters walked into the hallway.

"Who was that?"

Phyllis followed him into the breakfast lounge. "That wretched fat woman, Juda, wanted to speak to Mrs. Caley. I said I would relay the message, but somehow I think it might just slip my mind. I've always hated her, she's a blood-sucking leech and Mr. Caley loathes her as well."

Phyllis sat opposite Peters as they ate breakfast together, and Peters stared from the window.

"Nice to have the place to ourselves, isn't it?"

"Are you all right, Mrs. Caley?" Edward asked, and Elizabeth dropped the magazine.

"Shouldn't you be at the controls?"

He smiled. "It's on automatic pilot, Mrs. Caley."

She turned away. "You are paid to fly this plane, Mr. Hardy, not the automatic pilot. Please stay in the cockpit, you know how nervous I am about flying."

Seated at the far end of the plane, Mario looked up from his book. Edward flicked him a glance and returned to the cockpit.

"Can I get you anything, Mrs. Caley?" Mario asked.

"No, nothing, thank you."

She picked up the magazine again, the glossy pages blurring before her eyes. The models in their glamorous poses and gowns only reminded her of the last trip with Anna Louise, and she could hear her voice: "I like this one, Mama, what do you think?"

She had replied that she simply adored it, not even really looking at it. Just watching her daughter had pained her; she was so young, so very pretty, with her whole life ahead of her. She was envious of Anna Louise's youth, her athletic talent. She took after her father so much it sometimes unnerved Elizabeth just to look at that fair hair and bright blue eyes.

Elizabeth sighed. The secret of Anna Louise's parentage didn't matter in this day and age, nobody would care, but when she had been Anna Louise's age, and coming from where she did, it had mattered a great deal. She closed her eyes and thought back over her life, knowing without doubt that if she had it to live over again she would not have become involved with the movies—or that movie. It had destroyed her, made her dependent on Juda Salina and her kind, and somewhere deep inside she yearned to be free of it all. Perhaps that was why she took so many drugs, gambling with her own life. She longed for freedom, for air, for sunshine, the sun she was afraid to let touch her milky-white skin—not because it burned, but because it turned a rich, dark shade of brown.

Elizabeth's beautiful slanting eyes brimmed and tears spilled as if in slow motion down her cheeks. She'd used the ability to cry on cue often in her film career and had been proud of it, but now there was no "action," no cameras. The tears were for her own empty, silly, frightened life.

All the diners had left the breakfast room, leaving Rooney, Rosie and Lorraine the only people still sitting around their table.

"Okay, let's get the day started," Rooney said, pushing his chair back.

Lorraine stubbed out her cigarette. "Try Nick's room again, Rosie. If he's not back, shove a message under his door, tell him where we'll all be so he can make contact."

"Will do, and you take care."

Lorraine smiled. "Yes, ma'am . . ."

"Listen, about this video—"

Lorraine walked toward the exit, her arm loosely around Rosie's shoulders.

"What about asking Lloyd Dulay? He's known Elizabeth all these years, and as you're going to see him, I just thought . . ."

"Good idea, I'll ask him, Rosie."

Rooney was standing by the lobby desk. He turned as the

women approached. "That bastard's not in his room, he's been out all night."

"Well, he's probably with some hooker someplace," Lorraine said, slightly irritated, as she headed for the elevator. Her reaction surprised her, she was jealous, but concealed it immediately. She smiled and told Rooney to let Nick sleep it off, but not for long. They had work to do.

Edith Corbello found Jesse out back on the old car seat. He had been severely beaten, his nose and right arm broken. He was bruised and crying in agony, but when she asked who had done this to him, he just whimpered that he had fallen down the stairs.

She had just started to clean her son up when she heard the front door closing and footsteps shuffling down the corridor.

"That you, Willy? *Willy, get your ass in here!*"

She believed that Willy had beaten up his brother, and when he came into the kitchen she was sure of it. Both his eyes were black, his nose was bleeding and he had a lump on his forehead the size of a mango. She would have slapped him hard, but he could only just about walk.

"I had enough of you boys fightin' each other, I'm gonna get Fryer here to sort out the pair of you. I can't handle you no more, and it's time he took some responsibility."

"It was Fryer that done it," Willy said, and Jesse kicked him so hard that he howled in agony. He had so many bruises to his body it was hard to miss one.

"You tellin' me that bastard did this to you both? *Yes?*"

Jesse shook his head. "No, Mama, we done it to each other, honest, we just started foolin' around and . . ."

Edith glowered. "You git your brother to a hospital right now, you both lookin' all beat and your sister about to be crowned. I'm wiping my hands of you both. I am ashamed, you hear me? *Ashamed!*"

Edith banged out. She wanted to weep; what with Raoul gone and Juda screaming at her, it had been a bad day and it wasn't even nine o'clock. But she knew it would get worse, a whole lot worse, when she had to tell Ruby that there was no money for her gown, already half stitched up and nearly finished.

Ruby was lying on her bed, in the best bedroom of the tiny run-down house, with a treatment pack on her face. She was being photographed tomorrow for one of the hair-trade papers, just a promo for the salon where she worked, but it was a start. When she heard what her mama had to say, she got off the bed in a rage. "You tellin' me Raoul stole all Aunty Juda's money, he *stole* it?"

"That's what she said, and she don't even have the money for the plane ride for the parade."

Ruby screamed with rage; she was damned if her crazy crackhead brother was going to stand in her way out of this house and away from everyone in it. She sobbed and clawed at the walls with her nails, her tears making trickles on her white mask until at last she hunched up in a corner like a little girl, the fight gone out of her.

"Ah, Mama, what are we gonna do, what are we gonna do?"

Below, Sugar May listened up and grinned from ear to ear. Served that mean stuck-up bitch right. Ruby Corbello always got everything she wanted, never had to wear anyone's cast-off clothes like she did. She skipped out of the house in delight as an old yellow cab drew up to take Jesse and Willy to the hospital.

Edith sat on her daughter's bed, near to tears herself. She felt worn out by it all.

"Maybe ask Leroy, Ruby?"

Ruby shook her head. "With a wife and two kids he needs his money, Mama. There ain't no fortunes to be made in the kind of investigation work that's on his level. You know who the only one with money is, you know."

Edith shook her head. "I'm not asking Fryer, I wouldn't ask him to spit in a jam jar."

"I didn't mean Fryer," snapped Ruby. "Why don't we ask her lady friend, one who's been paying out all that money for years? We ask her direct, she's rich, isn't she?"

Edith shook her head. "No, we don't cross Juda's territory, Ruby. That Mrs. Caley is her wages and it's her money been keeping us all. I wouldn't go behind Juda's back."

Ruby stood in front of her mother. "I know you done things for money, things you've always been against, I know that, Mama."

"You shut up now," Edith said with a warning slap.

Ruby dodged aside. "I saw you making it, Mama, I saw Juda coming here for her so-called tea. I know."

Edith hit out again. "You saw nobody come in here, girl, *you hear me*? You say one word about that business to anyone and I am warning you—"

Ruby stood her ground. "No, Mama, I am warning you because my day is gonna be the best day in my life and nobody will mess it up for me."

Ruby ran out of the room and Edith covered her face. She heard the front door slam hard and crossed to the window. There was Ruby striding down the street, arms swinging, still with treatment cream all over her face. It was a terrible morning, like some kind of train running out of control. And there was more to come.

As she made her way heavily down the narrow staircase, Sugar May passed her with a rolled-up newspaper. She swatted a fly with it.

"If that is today's paper, Sugar May, don't you go screwing it up like that before I've even cast my eye over it."

The young girl chucked the paper at her mother. "I'm gonna run away, I'm gonna find Raoul and share in all his millions." She stuck out her tongue, and her mother used the same paper to hit her across the side of the head. Sugar May just laughed and ran out.

Halfway down the front page was an article headed FORMER DEBUTANTE COMMITS SUICIDE. Edith sank onto the stairs, her eyes popping out on stalks as she read the detailed article about the suicide of Tilda Brown. She felt as if there were a noose around her throat, getting tighter and tighter, taking the breath out of her body.

Ruby knelt in front of the high white tomb in the First St. Louis Cemetery. On the ground in front of it she had drawn the ve-ve of Marie Laveau, the swirling hieroglyph that would invoke the spirit of the voodoo queen, and now she drew another cross to add to the hundreds already on the monument, pressed her hand flat against it, and knocked on the tomb. She was so intent in prayer to the dead priestess's spirit, straining every fiber of her being, that she did not hear Leroy Able's soft-footed approach. Her face was still streaked with white cream, and for a moment Able thought he was seeing a woman risen from the tomb, and he froze.

"Ruby?"

She turned around.

"I thought you didn't believe in all that." It had been one of Edith's great griefs that her older daughter seemed to have no time for her heritage, sneering at it as a lot of superstitious African rubbish that would keep her in the ghetto and foil her plans for going to New York and being the new Veronica Webb.

"Well," said Ruby gruffly, embarrassed to have been seen. "Can't do no harm, I don't reckon. Something terrible has happened. Raoul run off with the money for my gown and it's half stitched, I only got two more fittings."

"Come out of sight here, quickly now, the place is full of tourists coming around looking at the graves. Hurry up, get out of sight."

Ruby let Leroy draw her away from Marie Laveau's tomb to a less frequented part of the cemetery where the brick-oven tombs of people too poor to afford a private sepulcher lined the perimeter walls. She took the handkerchief he offered her and sank down to sit on the ground, cleaning her face and stretching her long slender legs out in front of her. She had changed since the last time he saw her, and her beautiful oval face, deep slanting black eyes and waist-length wavy hair had begun to look more and more like those of the great queen; she could have been her daughter, or Marie Laveau herself come back to life and youth a second time.

"We'll find the money, Ruby, everyone will give towards the gown, you don't have to worry about that. The krewe won't let you go without. You're just being a silly girl."

She sighed. "Maybe, but things are bad at home, Leroy, really bad, and my brothers are all messed up. Even my sister is going to get herself in trouble, she hangs out at that shit bar, they all do."

He bent down and stroked her soft hair. "But you don't?"

"No," she said softly.

"Because you're different?"

"You know I'm different. I have more in front of me than that neighborhood or this whole damn city—least I had till Raoul fucked things up, but there's nothing I won't do to get that money and have my day. I even told Mama to call up . . ."

She bit her lip and turned away. He frowned. "Call who?"

Ruby shook her head. "I said too much."

"No, Ruby, you haven't said anything at all. Who did you tell your mama to contact?"

Ruby kept her head down. "Mrs. Caley."

Leroy stood up, towering above her. "No, you don't do that, you hear me? Since her daughter disappeared there've been police inquiries, private-investigator inquiries, and they're still going on, you hear me? You stay away from all that. I mean it, Ruby, you don't ever get involved."

She looked up rebelliously. "But what about my gown, Leroy? If we don't pay Alma Dicks, she won't finish it."

He drew her to her feet. She seemed so light, so fragile. "Your gown will be ready, Ruby, and you will be the most beautiful queen Mardi Gras has ever seen."

She smiled. "Wanna see something, Leroy?" She began to move her body sinuously. "I can do the snake dance, Leroy, like Mama used to do." She twisted her hips and rolled her head. She was as lithe, as hypnotic as a serpent, and he wanted to reach out and draw her into his arms, but she danced toward the high tombs and suddenly she had passed between two of them and was gone. It was as if she had never been there. Leroy sighed. He had changed in so many ways since he came back from LA. It was not just the responsibility of having a wife and two children; he had come back and found his roots, rediscovered himself and his beliefs, but sometimes it was hard to lose that other Leroy that would fuck anything that swayed in front of him in a skirt. And being confronted by beauty such as Ruby Corbello's was a real test of his faith.

Nick Bartello's naked body was in the morgue, his clothes folded into paper bags. They found no identification on him, and as his pockets had been stripped, it was surmised that it had been a mugging, even though he didn't look like a tourist from the main routes, more like a drifter coming in for the Carnival. There were a lot of Nick Bartellos found and never identified, and they would have left it that way but for a tattoo on his left forearm: a shield, the LAPD badge.

Leroy Able was back in his office and back in his public persona when he got the call. When the sergeant asked if he'd been contacted by any old buddies, he frowned and leaned his elbows on his desk. "Nope, why do you ask?"

"We got a stiff found early this morning, an' you was in the LAPD, weren't you?"

"Yeah, why?"

"Well, this guy's got a tattoo of a shield, no other ID found on him. He's also got a couple of bullet scars in his right leg."

Leroy hesitated. "You want me to take a look?"

"Found him up in an alley two blocks from Fryer's bar, wouldn't you know!" The fat officer waddled ahead of Leroy, who came up to his elbow. "Throat slit and he'd taken a beating, no witness, no nothing."

The sheet was drawn away from Nick's face and Leroy stared down. He breathed in. "Nope, sorry, never set eyes on him. You know these old hippies get tatted up, don't mean anything too much."

Lorraine had time to study every bonbonnière, trinket tray, hand-painted lampshade and china parakeet in Lloyd Dulay's cavernous drawing room; Dulay had kept her waiting for over an hour, and she was furious when he eventually strode toward her, hand outstretched.

"My apologies, but I was kept waiting at the airport, I was there to meet Elizabeth Caley. Then I had to drive with her to the house, and it was hard to get away."

"That's all right," she said coldly.

He sat on the scarlet-and-gold sofa, stretching out his long legs. "Even harder when we talked about Anna Louise's trust fund . . ."

She stared. "Really?"

"Yes, down by near forty-two million."

She coughed. "Robert Caley?"

He made an expansive gesture with his huge hands. "Couldn't be anyone else. He knows I know, and I also pulled out of the casino deal—the man is nothing but a thief. He didn't deny it and I wanted to beat the hell out of him. He wanted to do the same to me when I told him I knew about him and Anna. He denied it, swore to me he had never touched her. I don't know if he was telling me the truth or not."

She licked her lips. "You think he might also have killed her?"

"What?"

"If what you say is true, and Robert Caley has used Anna Louise's trust fund, do you think he might have anything to do with her disappearance?"

"You didn't say that at all, Mrs. Page."

"No, well, I'm asking it now."

He got up and rubbed at his shock of white hair. "He wouldn't need to kill his daughter to cover it up. She probably wouldn't find out."

"If the casino deal went through."

"Yes."

"But if it didn't?"

He shrugged. "I can't give you an answer because I truthfully don't know."

"Could you tell me just how much money Elizabeth Caley is probably worth?"

He crossed the priceless Bessarabian rug to stand by the windows. "She's always used the best financial advisers to invest her money—I know because I am one of them. . . ." He remained with his back to her. "Elizabeth had a very substantial inheritance, so I would estimate her fortune to be somewhere in the region of two hundred million, perhaps more."

Lorraine blinked: she had not been in any way prepared to hear a figure like that.

Dulay turned toward her. "You know, Robert also had access to a lot of that, from what I can gather, but he's a stiff-necked bastard. Wanted to make it on his own. 'Course, she was always bailing him out." He gestured dismissively. "I guess Elizabeth will bail him out of this fuck-up he's got himself into right now."

"Is that possible?"

"Is what possible?"

"For him to be bailed out, as you say?"

He looked at her as if she were a stupid child. "Well, yes and no. The way the wind's blowing, he's not going to get any casino license, but I guess whoever does will have to negotiate with him for the land. If Elizabeth gives him something just to tide him over, maybe he won't have to sell at an undervalue because he needs the cash."

She was taken aback again and looked away, not wanting him to see her confusion, but he was not looking at her. He was fiddling with a gold chain tucked into his waistcoat. "I'm going to tell you something that is highly confidential, Mrs. Page, and as such I want you to swear it will not go further than this room."

She folded her arms. "Well, I can't really do that, if it has any criminal connection—"

"It doesn't."

"Then you have my word, Mr. Dulay."

He sat down heavily again.

"If there was anything going on, it would not exactly be incest."

"I'm sorry?"

"I said, Mrs. Page, it would not be incest. I am referring to what you suggested yesterday, that Caley was having a sexual relationship with Anna Louise."

"I don't understand."

"Anna Louise is not Robert Caley's daughter. She's mine, Mrs. Page, which is why I was able to find out about the trust fund, because the funds in it were mine too. Anna Louise is my daughter, not Robert Caley's."

"Does he know?"

"Of course."

"Did Anna Louise know?"

"No."

She took a deep intake of breath. "You confronted Robert about the trust fund, and he admitted it, but you said you were not sure if he was having a sexual relationship with Anna Louise?"

"If you want it word for word, I said that if he was abusing my daughter, I would shoot his head off his shoulders, and he said, and I quote, Mrs. Page, that if I was ever to make such a disgusting accusation again, then the head would come off my shoulders!''

"But did you or did you not believe him?'' she asked quietly.

"Yes, I suppose I did, because he was very shocked. In fact, he went through a range of emotions I didn't honestly think he was capable of, but in the end he was just violently angry.'' He leaned forward in his chair, his small, hard eyes boring into her flushed face. "Maybe check out all the facts before you throw dirt, Mrs. Page.''

She stood up and snapped back at him. "If I had been given the facts maybe I would not have needed to. I am just trying to do my job, Mr. Dulay.''

He stuffed his hands into his pockets, and as she was already walking to the door he followed. Suddenly she stopped.

"Do you have a video of Mrs. Caley's film *The Swamp* I could see?''

"Good God, whatever do you want that for?''

"Just part of my job, to know everything I possibly can know about my clients.''

He went to an antique fruitwood cabinet in the corner of the room and slid the doors apart: this was where he kept his video library.

"She won't be happy about this—it's a terrible film, cheap, shoddy, but she is wonderful.'' He handed her the video.

Lorraine put it in her briefcase. She was shaking and angry with herself. She had jumped so quickly to such disgusting conclusions she was ashamed of herself. If she had been unable even to return Robert Caley's phone calls the previous evening, the thought of facing him now made her cheeks flush with shame, so she pushed it to one side, refusing to dwell on what she would have to do to repair the damage.

She ordered her driver, the same one as the day before, to take her back to Tilda Brown's house.

"You know, Bill, I'm getting worried,'' Rosie said as they sat at a sidewalk café near the French market.

"Me too, it stinks. They pick up this bastard, an anonymous tip says they saw him talking to Anna Louise Caley and—''

''I'm not talking about Fryer Jones,'' Rosie said.

Rooney looked at his watch. ''He always was a horny son of a bitch.'' But it sounded hollow even to him.

''Why hasn't he called in?''

''I don't know, do I?'' Rooney snapped and then patted her hand. ''Sorry, sorry. Look, tell you what, say we give it to one o'clock, when Lorraine's due back at the hotel. If Nick hasn't shown up then we'll start looking for him.''

''Like where? This is a big city.''

Rooney downed his third café au lait. ''Start with the cop shop, if they haven't got him banged up or on a slab—''

''What?''

He wiped the froth from his mouth. ''Morgue, Rosie, start at the lowest point and work upwards. I know one thing for sure, until that two-bit shit shows up I'm not going near that bar of Fryer Jones, and I hope to God Lorraine doesn't take off without coming to us first. If you look at the list of so-called eyewitnesses that give that trombone player one hell of a tight alibi, half are made up of Juda Salina's relatives, including Raoul Corbello.''

''I tried to get in touch with Juda—it was busy for almost an hour, then no reply.''

''What about Edith Corbello?''

Rosie's cheeks went pink. ''She's not in the phone book, I was going to try other ways when you came back.''

Rooney stood up. ''Well, let's go back to the hotel and have another try. Right now, until Lorraine gets back, we got nothing else to do.''

Mrs. Brown's sister, Helen Dubois, came into the drawing room, a modern interior of metal and glass and bare boards polished to shine as though lacquered, the walls covered in severely tasteful beiges and oatmeals the better to display a collection of fashionable yarn paintings and primitive art. In this stark setting, the plump, distressed woman looked all too human and out of place. ''I am afraid neither Mr. or Mrs. Brown can see you, Mrs. Page. They are still very shocked, and my sister is under sedation.''

''Yes, I'm so very sorry, please pass on my sincere condolences.'' Lorraine took her time gathering up her purse and her briefcase. "The police called me in to give a statement—I was here earlier in the day, I interviewed Tilda."

"Yes, I know."

"I can't help thinking that maybe it was something I said that may have sparked off . . ."

"We won't ever know, will we?" Mrs. Dubois said sadly. "But the police said Tilda left a note."

"Yes, but it didn't give any reasons."

"May I ask what it said?"

Helen Dubois took out a handkerchief and pressed it to her eyes. "Just 'May God forgive . . . Tilda.' "

They walked toward the front door, Lorraine really taking her time as they passed more Mexican-looking textiles and a jardiniere of desert flora in the hallway. "Mrs. Dubois, do you know why I was here, why I came to see Tilda?"

"Yes, I believe you wanted to question her about Anna Louise Caley."

"Could I see Tilda's bedroom?"

"Why?"

Lorraine hesitated, trying to think of the best way around it. "Well, for one, Anna Louise may still be alive—it is a possibility—and she and Tilda were very close friends. After yesterday's tragedy, I would pray to God that I did not leave any stone unturned in my search for her. At the same time, even though I cannot think of anything, maybe I did inadvertently say something . . . I have a terrible feeling of guilt, Mrs. Dubois, and I just think if I could perhaps sit a moment in Tilda's room, rethink everything we discussed, perhaps I will have more of a clue as to why she did it, and it would give some comfort to her poor parents."

Mrs. Dubois hesitated, looked up the open-tread wooden staircase. "I don't know."

"Is the police cordon still in place?"

"No, no, they took it down about two hours ago."

Tilda's bedroom had a feel similar to Anna Louise Caley's— large enough to accommodate a turquoise sofa on back-tilted metal legs, a dresser, a cheval mirror surrounded by more Mexican-looking embossed metal, and a king-size bed. All but the sofa was white, and the room seemed strangely bare, characterless, but the exigencies of decorator taste had been relaxed to permit a fitted white carpet and a wall of built-in closets on each side of a door that led to a spacious bathroom. The room showed few signs that the occupant had been only in her teens.

The carpet was marked near the window by a number of dust footprints, more than likely from the police and the medics who had removed the body, and some faint, washed-out brown stains, already dry, which could have been coffee or perhaps, as is usual in suicides by hanging, Tilda's bowels might have opened and the mess been cleaned up. There was no other sign that anything untoward had occurred in the room; even the curtain rail Tilda had hanged herself from remained in position, and the dressing-table stool, covered in white fabric with silver upholstery buttons like outsize sequins, was back in place in front of the triptych mirrors.

Mrs. Dubois stood in the open doorway, pressing a handkerchief to her eyes to try to stop herself from weeping.

"You don't have to stay with me," Lorraine said softly.

"Thank you." Mrs. Dubois turned away, just as Lorraine saw the white bear resting on the pillows of the bed. "Oh, just one thing, Mrs. Dubois." Lorraine picked it up, sure it was similar to the white fluffy bears she had seen lined up on Anna Louise's bed. "Do you know where Tilda got this bear from?"

Mrs. Dubois swallowed, her brow puckering.

"It's just that Anna Louise had the same bears, and I wondered who gave it to Tilda."

Mrs. Dubois shook her head. "I really don't know, it's been there quite a while, I think. I recall seeing it before . . . it's a polar bear, is it?"

"Polar," Lorraine said softly.

"Yes, that's what she called it, Polar."

Mrs. Dubois began to weep again and excused herself as Lorraine replaced the bear on the pillow. As soon as she was alone she drew back the covers and felt beneath the pillows, the sheets and the mattress, getting to her knees to look beneath the heavy woven cotton bedspread, but there was nothing hidden in the bed or underneath it.

Lorraine made a slow tour of the neat bedroom, sitting at

the dressing table and opening each drawer. Some contained underwear, lingerie, all very expensive items folded with tissue paper placed between the garments. Even the rolled-up tennis socks were lined up like balls. In the closets, Tilda had as extensive a wardrobe as Anna Louise's and rows of shoe boxes. Lorraine bent down, wondering if she would get lucky twice, that any personal mementos might have been hidden in the same way Anna Louise kept hers, but she found nothing other than shoes. She recalled the room she herself had had as a teenager, full of junk, books and magazines, cards stuck and pasted to the shabby wallpaper, and all the pictures of the rock stars and movie stars she'd had the hots for. But it was clear that in Anna Louise's and Tilda's rooms their parents' decorators' taste predominated, and they had hardly a knickknack of their own, apart from the somehow pitiful stuffed animals. Even the display of cometics and perfumes was more fitting for a much older woman; Tilda's creams in the immaculate bathroom were for dry skin and wrinkles, intensive moisturizers, serums and chemical peels. Nothing was used—everything down to the toothbrush looked brand-new.

Lorraine sighed. A girl had hanged herself inside this whiter-than-white innocent room, but there was no sign of the tragedy, no sense of who Tilda Brown was. She closed her eyes, trying to remember their conversation. According to Tilda, Anna Louise was jealous of anyone's being shown any affection by her father; had Robert Caley given the girls the white polar bears? Was that the reason she used the name Polar on her secret messages? Was that who the Valentine cards and birthday gifts were from? Did Robert Caley use the name Polar?

Lorraine picked up one of the tennis rackets stacked neatly in a row in the closet Tilda had set aside for her sport and ski equipment. Even if Robert Caley did sign himself Polar, what did that matter now? Even if he had been sexually abusing Anna Louise or having willing intercourse with her, she was not his own flesh and blood.

Lorraine leaned forward and replaced the racket alongside the row of others. She glanced at one racket, whose cover bulged slightly on one side—perhaps a pair of socks? Lorraine drew back the zipper and felt inside. Her fingers touched a package of some kind and she took it out. The newspaper-wrapped package was about eight inches long, string wrapped tightly around it. Lorraine sat on the dressing-table stool, carefully untying the knot, then unwinding the string. She put it to one side and placed the package on the mirrored dressing table, moving aside mother-of-pearl-backed combs and brushes.

The paper, she noted, was dated February 15, the year missing where the newspaper had been torn across. It was also dirty, stained with what looked like mud, some of the print smudged. She eased the paper away from the contents and almost dropped it, springing up from the stool with shock because of the horrible smell. Urine and human feces were caked around a doll, whose trunk, arms and legs were made of crudely stuffed and tied sacking wound around with wool. It had a white dress, equally crudely hand-stitched, made from what looked like an old piece of T-shirt. The head was cheap plastic, like the head of a Barbie doll, and glued onto the face was a picture of Tilda. An ordinary dressmaker's pin was stuck through the left eye of the doll, protruding right through the back of the head. When Lorraine turned it over, there were two or three long blond hairs and what appeared to be dried specks of blood attached to a tiny, pinkish-brown fragment of skin tied to the torso with crossbands of wool.

"Mrs. Page," called out Helen Dubois, and Lorraine quickly rewrapped the doll and put it in her briefcase just before the door opened.

"I think perhaps you should go. Mr. and Mrs. Brown have the chaplain coming to arrange the funeral, and—"

"It's all right, I was just leaving."

The driver started the engine as soon as he saw Lorraine emerge from the house. She sat back in the hot, stuffy car, slowly rolling down one of the windows. She could smell the doll in her briefcase, so she pushed it away from her. She didn't want to take it out, didn't want to handle it again unless there was soap and water handy. She washed her hands as soon as she got back to her hotel room, over and over again. Then she dried them, sniffing at them, and stared at the wrapped parcel.

"Lorraine? Are you in there?" It was Rosie.

Lorraine let her in, turning straight back toward the bed. "You will not believe what I found at Tilda Brown's place, it's already stinking up the room, and . . ."

Rosie was red-eyed from weeping, clutching a big white handkerchief. "Lorraine . . . I've got something to tell you."

She knew something was wrong when the big, bulky figure of Rooney walked in behind Rosie and quietly closed the door.

"What is it? What's happened?" She could feel her legs shaking.

Rooney didn't mean it to come out so bluntly, but there was no other way. "It's Nick, he's dead, Lorraine."

Her face drained of color. She looked at Rosie, back to Rooney, hoping it was some kind of a joke, but she knew it wasn't by the expression on their faces. She felt for the side of the bed and sat down, trying to keep calm and steady.

"How did it happen?"

Rooney helped Rosie to sit down. "He was murdered, throat cut. The cops found him in an alley early this morning, no wallet, no ID on him, and he was taken to the city morgue. They haven't done an autopsy yet."

Rooney gestured helplessly. "The only identifying mark was a tattoo of the LAPD badge on his arm—lot of them had it done when they were rookies."

"Yes, I know," she said softly. "Jack Lubrinski had one, wasn't on his arm, though—it was on his butt."

Lorraine's lips trembled and she clenched her teeth, needing to be alone. "You mind giving me a few minutes by myself, just want to be on my own for a while."

Rooney nodded and took Rosie's arm. "Sure, you give us a call when you want us." He knew intuitively that it was better to leave, but Rosie hung back.

"Just go, Rosie. Come on, sweetheart." He pushed her toward the door and closed it behind them, leaving Lorraine still standing motionless, her hands clenched by her sides.

Rosie turned on him in the hall. "God, she's a cold-hearted bitch, imagine even talking about that guy Lubrinski. I mean, Nick, Nick's . . ." Rosie began to sob and Rooney put his arm around her and supported her down the corridor.

"She didn't show any feelings about him at all." Rosie wept, but Rooney knew different: he'd been a cop too long not to recognize that look on someone's face, often followed by a joke or some casual comment, anything to conceal the blow to the heart. Lorraine would weep for Nick, he knew that, but not in front of anyone else. She would try to come to terms with Nick's death in her own way, the way he knew too, privately—you never wanted to show anyone the pain.

Lorraine splashed cold water on her face, still dry-eyed and shocked, still not really registering the fact that she wouldn't see Nick again. She whispered his name, over and over again, half questioningly, as she patted her face dry, and then walked into the bedroom and looked first at the bed where she had been sleeping when he woke her, then at the bed opposite where he had sat. She lay down on her own bed, curled up facing the empty one, wanting to reach out to him as though he were still there.

"Nick?" she whispered again. "Oh, Nick . . ." she repeated, and then the tears came, her face crumpling like a child's as she wept for Nick Bartello, lovely and crazy as he had been. She wept until she was exhausted, cried out, and then sat with her head in her hands.

It was then she caught sight of the bottle of vodka he had left. It had fallen on its side and rolled just under the bed. She stared at it, unable to look away, and it drew her like a magnet until she got down on her knees to retrieve it. She held it in her hands, examining the bottle, almost caressing it, and then slowly unscrewed the cap. Just one drink: she just needed the one to get herself back together and be able to work. Just the one and she'd be able to put the bottle away. She was sure of it.

CHAPTER
14

Rooney arranged for Nick's body to be sent home when the autopsy was finished. He had called Nick's sister to tell her the news, and she had been silent and uncommunicative but had said she would bury him and gave Rooney the address in downtown LA. Not until the end of the call did she ask how he had been killed. Her voice broke just a fraction when Rooney told her.

"Lenny was always getting himself into trouble."

"Lenny?" repeated Rooney, confused.

"Yes, he called himself Nick, but we, the family, always use his middle name, Lenny, well, Leonardo. Er, just one thing, Mr. Rooney—we can't take his dog."

"That's okay, I'll see to the dog." They had nothing more to say to each other, so he paid his condolences and replaced the phone.

"I'll take care of Tiger," Lorraine had said quietly. Rooney had nodded and then excused himself. She knew he needed to cry, and he did, leaning up against the elevator, returning later to force them all to get on with the job.

Lorraine drank from a can of Coke, seemingly more preoccupied with getting the day's work started than discussing Nick, and her apparent lack of emotion confused and worried Rosie. Rooney had warned her to leave Lorraine alone, and not to ask her questions, but Rosie couldn't stop looking at her: Lorraine's face was chalk-white and her eyes redrimmed, but that apart, she seemed almost overbright.

"Rosie, will you quit gawking at me all the time," she snapped.

"I'm just wondering if you are all right."

"I'm fine, Rosie—now how about we get back to the reason we're all here?"

They discussed the hideous, rotting doll, and then Rosie wrapped it in two newspapers and stuffed it into a drawer. Lorraine did not have any energy to interview anyone, but she knew she would have to speak to Elizabeth and Robert Caley. They also discussed the importance of Fryer Jones's arrest and release, and his implication in some way with the disappearance of Anna Louise, but Rosie and Rooney would not allow Lorraine to go alone to his bar. Nick had been murdered a few blocks from there, and if there was a connection they would have to find out. Nick's stupidity in going off alone made them angry, as now they had no idea where he had been or who he had spoken to. But their anger did nothing to ease their grief.

Rosie pulled a face at the smell coming from Lorraine's briefcase as she withdrew the video of *The Swamp* and knelt down to slot it into the video recorder she had persuaded the receptionist to lend them from the lounge downstairs.

Lorraine drew the curtains and perched on one bed as Rooney and Rosie sat on the other. She saw him give her a gentle pat and lean in close. "You all right, darlin'?"

Rosie nodded, returning his pat of comfort, making Lorraine feel excluded, but she ignored it as the film began. It was faded like some old sixties Technicolor film. Even the old Columbia Studios logo was fuzzy and the music was sliding badly. The pre-film script made them all lean forward.

"This film has carefully researched the life and times of the voodoo queen Marie Laveau, who arrived in New Orleans in the early nineteenth century."

The film was tedious; it took a long time for the actual plot to unfold. Despite the faint picture and blurred lines across the print, Elizabeth Seal was certainly a great beauty, and her dance with a live snake was the high point of the first twenty minutes.

"They really did a good job of her makeup, she really

does look black," Rosie murmured. The film rolled on, the plot at times very confused. Even though the film spanned more than one generation and everyone else became gray and wizened, the star remained looking about twenty throughout. Even when they laid her body in her coffin she looked young and beautiful, whereas the real Marie Laveau had lived into her eighties. It really was a Hollywood-style distortion of the facts.

At the end the credits began to roll, and Rosie picked up the control to switch it off when Lorraine shouted, "Wait, wait! Roll it back, Rosie, *stop*!"

They looked at the last section of the artists' credits, and under the group heading of SNAKE CHARM DANCERS were two very familiar names, Juda and Edith Salina, and under the group of VOODOO PRIESTS they found the name of Fryer Jones.

Rosie turned off the TV and opened the curtains, while Lorraine picked up a fresh can of Coke and opened it on her way to the bathroom. There, she poured part of its contents down the toilet, and then topped it up with Nick Bartello's vodka before returning to the bedroom. She sat down, drinking from the can, her foot tapping.

"Well, I've got my energy back. I want to talk to Elizabeth Caley this afternoon—"

Rooney puffed out his breath. "You want me with you?"

"No. We need to get to Juda Salina's sister—you got an address, Rosie?"

"No, not yet, I was about to when . . ." She was about to say Nick's name but covered fast. "She's not listed in the phone directory but I got a directory of clairvoyants, voodoo advisers and experts from the museum. She may be in that, I haven't checked."

"Do it, but you don't go near her until I'm back. From now on we stick together, report in frequently, and if we move on, we give time and location."

Rooney looked pissed, and Lorraine turned to face him. "Bill, I handled the Caley situation badly. In an interview with Lloyd Dulay, I said things I shouldn't have without checking the facts first. So I have to see him alone and apologize."

"Okay, you know what you're doing."

"Not always, Bill, and I was out of line with Caley."

"Well, you got results."

"Yes, I did." She hesitated. "Nick gets murdered, Tilda Brown commits suicide. I got those results all right because I was angry and tired out, tired because I had been up all night screwing Caley."

"What, are you serious? You fucked Robert Caley?"

"Yes, yes, I did."

"I don't believe it," Rosie said, astonished.

"Well, it's true, and it was a dumb move to make, but . . ." She gave a glum smile, and lifted her shoulders in an apologetic gesture. "Couldn't help myself. So the next day I was so determined to find out if he was a suspect or not, I went at it like a bat out of hell."

"Nick was right, then? He suggested you do it, and it got results."

Lorraine turned away. "No, Bill, Nick was wrong. I didn't fuck him for information, I did it because I wanted him. Now excuse me, I need a shower."

She closed her bathroom door, and Rosie snatched up her notes, her face set rigid. Rooney reached for his jacket and made for the door.

"That's it, is it?" Rosie said angrily.

He turned, surprised. "What?"

Rosie put her hands on her hips. "We just accept it, say nothing? She sleeps with our client. The guy hired us, Bill, and she gets fucked by him. Oh, that is really very professional, really good work. Gets laid so hard that the next night she crashes out early and Nick goes it alone and gets killed?"

"Rosie," Rooney warned, glancing toward the bathroom.

"I don't care if she does hear me, I am disgusted, disgusted!"

"Don't be."

"Why the hell not? Now she's going to see his wife— what if she finds out, what do you think will happen? We'll lose that bonus. I am through taking orders from that slut."

Rooney opened the door and walked out into the corridor. "Come on, Rosie, she got the information on the trust fund and she might not have if she hadn't gone through that connecting door.'' He stopped and turned back with a half-smile. ''We don't have one, do we?''

''I beg your pardon?'' Closing the door with a bang, she caught up with him at the elevator. ''Was that a half-assed come-on, Bill?'' Rosie glowered.

''Hell, no. It was just a joke.'' He stepped into the elevator. ''I wouldn't make an indecent proposal to you, Rosie, I have more respect.''

The elevator door closed, and he pressed for their floor. They stood in silence as the elevator stopped and they stepped out into the hallway. Rosie's door was first, and she was determined to open it without even looking at Rooney, but he placed his big hand on the handle.

''Unless you wanted me to?''

She looked at him, refusing to allow herself to smile. ''I haven't had an indecent or a decent proposal made to me for a long time, Bill, but right now, with Nick gone, I don't think I am ready for either. See you later.''

She turned the key and entered the room. Not until the door was closed behind her did she allow a small smile to break through. The old buzzard's really got the hots for me, she said to herself gleefully.

Lorraine dressed with great care, with the fan running overhead so she wouldn't break out in a sweat before she'd finished admiring herself. She had one of her new suits on, a silk shirt, high-heeled sandals and a single strand of cheap but good-looking pearls. She picked up her briefcase, having washed everything inside and just about managed to get rid of the smell of the doll.

In reception, she passed Rooney, who turned and gave her a smile. ''Looking good.''

''Thanks. Was that you or Rosie who slammed the door?''

''Me, getting worried you might have blown our million. Do you know if Mrs. Caley has found out?''

''If she has, I'll sort it out. You won't lose because of me, Bill. I know what I did was unethical, but at least I didn't lie. Saying I'm sorry I did it would be a lie too. I liked him. Liked him a lot.''

Rooney turned away. "What about Nick? You liked him too?"

"You know I did."

"Then we split three ways now, huh?" he said sadly.

"I guess so. What's that you've got there?"

He held a folded sheet of paper. "A list of Nick's possessions. His clothes, he had nothing else. His cowboy boots, his wallet and driver's license were missing."

Lorraine sighed. Her heart sank, but then she remembered something. "What about the necklace? That gris-gris thing he had around his neck, that listed?"

"Nope, but we don't know if he was wearing it or if it was also stolen."

"Well, check his room and I'll come right back here as soon as I'm done at the Caleys'."

"They know you're coming?"

"No, best to keep an element of surprise! Mind you, they might refuse to let me in, but I doubt it. They must know by now about Tilda Brown—it was in the papers." Lorraine started for the doors, and stopped. "Bill, the newspaper wrapped around that voodoo doll. It had a date on it, February fifteenth, but no year. Could you check with the newspaper printers and see if they can date it by some of the articles? It's just too much of a coincidence, the date. Anna Louise disappeared on February fifteenth, so if it was last year's paper it means Tilda Brown kept that thing for a long time."

She strode out through the heavy front door to meet her driver. Rooney remained staring at the pitiful list of Nick Bartello's possessions, and he couldn't help hearing his friend's voice and that smoky laugh he had had. "No coincidences, Billy Boy. Never believe in them, just good detective work."

Rooney sighed, a lump in his throat. He couldn't actually remember if it had been Nick or Jack Lubrinski who'd said that. They had been so alike and now they were both dead. Rooney became aware of his own mortality and was scared; no son, no wife, but maybe, just maybe a future with financial security beyond his meager pension. And maybe there was also Rosie.

Elizabeth hurled the pot of Lancaster neck cream at Caley's head, but it missed by yards and smashed against the wall of her bedroom in the beautiful Garden District mansion in which she had grown up.

"How could you, how could you fucking do this to me?"

Caley sidestepped the brushes and the silver-backed mirror that followed, and waited until she hurled her body down on her velvet daybed, her arm resting against her brow in classical fashion.

"Go away from me, I hate you!"

He applauded. "Bravo, none of your performances deserved an Oscar more than this one, Elizabeth."

"Fuck you!" she screamed.

"Why don't you just calm down? Why work yourself up into such a state that you're gonna need to call your dealer for something to space yourself out into oblivion? That is what you usually do, isn't it?"

She dived across the room and glared. "Calm down? You have stolen, *stolen* from your own daughter's trust fund!"

"Correction, she's not my daughter."

"You were paid to treat her as one!" Her face was red with anger, but even as she said it she wished she hadn't as she saw the pain on his face. She immediately resorted to tears. "How could you steal from Anna Louise, Robert, and why? You know if you ever needed anything I always gave in to you in the end, you know that. So why?"

He sat sullenly, hands clasped in front of him. "Because I was sick and tired of coming to you for handouts. Sick and tired of playing the same charade, of forever needing you to bail me out. I didn't want to touch one more cent of your fucking money. I just wanted for once to stand on my own two feet, prove that I could do it. Maybe get back my self-respect. That's all there is to it, I didn't want to ask you."

She smiled. "Why not? You have for the past twenty years, and it's not that I don't have enough, for Chrissakes!"

He felt exhausted even trying to explain, but he felt he owed her that much. "Because I knew it would work. I knew it, and it would have made me independent. Don't you understand? It would have been my own show, not yours, not even associated with you."

She smirked. "But you couldn't pull it off, could you? Just like you could never have gotten the time of day from any one of your so-called partners without me—without my being who I am."

He sighed, shaking his head bitterly, and his voice had an undercurrent of sarcasm. "True, everything I am is because of you, you've given me everything. What do you want me to do, kiss your feet? Jesus God, Elizabeth, I've been on my knees too often, taken too much of your shit to do it again."

."My shit? You think I like being married to a failure? You think I wouldn't have liked someone I could lean on? Someone who would take responsibility?"

"What? *What did you say?*"

"I need, I always have needed—"

He was hardly able to contain himself. "You and *your* needs are all I have been taking care of since the day I agreed to marry you, and that, as you fucking well know, was also part of the deal, taking you on, your drugs, your booze and Lloyd Dulay's illegitimate child. *Don't you tell me about your needs.* When have you ever, *ever* at any time considered mine? Huh?" He dragged her toward him, scaring her. "Yes, look at me, Elizabeth, you look real good, because whatever I was paid to marry you, whatever contract you had me sign to keep my mouth shut, had to do with Anna Louise. Now she's dead, so that contract is now null and void."

She tried to wriggle away from him, but he gripped her wrists, pulling her toward him. "Yes, *dead*, she is dead, and you just won't face it."

"She isn't, she isn't, how can you say it? You don't know for sure."

He wanted to slap her, but all he did was release her, moving as far away from her as possible. "It's been nearly a year, Elizabeth—if she's not dead, where in Christ's name is she?"

She started to cry, and he began to walk out but she screeched at his back. "Juda said she felt her presence, she told me."

He stopped and pointed his finger. "That goddamned woman is nothing but a leech."

"Takes one to know one, Robert."

He took four fast steps toward her and backhanded her across the face. She stumbled, and then he went after her again, this time gripping her by her hair.

"You have spent thousands on that fucking fake bitch. Even when I barred her from the house you still saw her, you even took Anna Louise to her, a fat, stinking pig of a woman who just greases your vanity to get what she wants. Well, how much did she make from you for her so-called psychic feelings on Anna Louise? How much, Elizabeth?"

"Nowhere near as much as you have taken in one week, never mind twenty years. Juda and I—"

"Oh please, not that again, not the old friend from the past, because it makes me puke. She's a con artist, and what kind of vise she's gripped you in for twenty years is beyond me, unless it's blackmail."

"Don't be ridiculous."

"Ridiculous?" He sat down, shaking his head. "You don't have a life, Elizabeth, you spend your days and nights in a drunken or drug-induced haze, and Lorraine Page . . ."

He hesitated. Just saying her name hit him hard. "Mrs. Page told me you were now injecting a drug that could give you a thrombosis. Do you even remember me getting you in the ambulance, this time, to save your life? How many more clinics, Elizabeth? How much more punishment can that body take, how many more times can it be surgically put back together again? Well, it's no longer any concern of mine."

"What do you mean?" She looked scared.

"It's over, I quit. I want a divorce," he said calmly and matter-of-factly.

"I'll have you arrested for using Anna's trust—Lloyd will call the police."

Robert Caley laughed. Deep inside, he felt good for the first time in days, perhaps years. "Really? Well, go ahead, and you know what I will do? I will tell everyone you lied to me, that Anna Louise was not my child. I'll demand they give Dulay blood tests, and that means the very thing you are so terrified of, Elizabeth, your blood will be tested too.

The gloves will come off, and if you want it dirty, it will be dirtier than you ever believed. I will expose your drug addiction and your freak friendship with that fat bitch.''

"Stop it!"

He smiled, now ticking off on his fingers. ''I will give details of your plastic surgery, the face-lift, the body tucks, the liposuction. So much for your big-star status! The only place you are still a star is here. Out in the real world you were forgotten fifteen years ago.''

"Stop this!"

''No, Elizabeth, you stop this sham right here and now because there's no need for it to continue. Without Anna Louise, there's nothing. Consult your lawyers, but there will be no contest.''

''Don't do this, Robert. I mean it, don't do this or you will be sorry. I'll make you so sorry.''

''Will you?'' He was walking out now, smiling all the while. ''You've made me sorry, Elizabeth, from the day we married. Now I'm going to make you pay for it and you *will* pay for those twenty years. Believe me, that megafortune is going to be sliced right down the middle.''

''I'm warning you,'' she said furiously.

''No, I am warning you, because this time I mean it!''

She glared, her mouth a thin tight line. ''You do, and I will fight you, tell them you even had sex with your daughter!''

''That deserved a punch in the face, Elizabeth, but I will never strike you again. You will never hold that against me, and as you know, she was not my daughter.''

''You adopted her.''

''I gave her my name. I also loved her like a daughter, and she loved me. You can't take that away. There's nothing you can do to harm me. It's over. Good-bye.''

''She was a cheap slut, you didn't know that, did you? The precious *daughter* you loved so dearly was a cheap whore.''

''Don't do this, leave her alone.''

Elizabeth smirked. ''Ask Mrs. Page, get her to show you the photograph of your beloved sweet daughter.''

He walked out, closing the door quietly behind him, and she stood in a blind fury, wanting to scream after him, kick him, punch him, scratch his eyes out. But she walked to the window and looked out, her arms and hands clenched around herself. Her voice was hardly audible.

"I will make you bleed, Robert Caley. So help me God, I will make your life a living hell, just like mine."

Lorraine stared out of the car window at the rows of gracious colonnaded houses that the new American arrivals in New Orleans had built for themselves in the Garden District when cotton, sugar and slaves had begun to make them rich: street after street offered the same vista of dazzling white columns, black ironwork fences and the dark green of shade trees and glossy clipped shrubs. Much of the area dated from the decades before the Civil War when the natural wealth of the whole region had poured into New Orleans, and it was as though the magnificent Italianate and neoclassical houses had been erected to show the world that the South was an empire to rival any that had been seen on earth.

"Nice area," said the driver. He was slowly warming to Lorraine; he liked the fact that she never felt the need to patronize him because of his race or involve him in some inane conversation, and that she didn't hide her moods. He liked it that sometimes she was really attractive as a woman and sometimes she was not. Tonight she was. She looked sexy and classy, and it made him straighten up in his seat. When they arrived at the tall, double-galleried mansion on one of the most exclusive streets in the district, he was out of his seat fast to hold open the passenger door. Lorraine held her hand up for a moment, took a swig from a can of Coke, which she had brought with her, then tucked it back against the seat. The soft drink was laced with vodka, and she had already bought another bottle back at the hotel.

"Okay, just hang in there, pal, 'cause I don't know if they are gonna let me over the doormat." She looked up at the great white house, framed between two chestnut trees behind an austere spearpoint fence, and straightened her jacket.

"Right, ma'am, I'm here—no place else to go, ready and waiting."

She turned and stared at him for a moment. "What's your name?"

"Frankie, short for François."

She touched his shoulder lightly. "Keep your fingers crossed, François."

He liked it that she didn't call him Frankie; François sounded cool.

Missy, one of the Caleys' maids, ushered Lorraine into the drawing room.

"Will you please wait just one moment while I inform Miss Elizabeth you are here. I think she is resting awhile."

"Thank you, and would you stress that it is very important that I speak to her?"

Elizabeth hung up the phone and smiled; she hadn't even had to persuade Juda—she agreed instantly. She then called Edward to tell him to return to LA immediately and collect Mrs. Juda Salina—it was imperative that she arrive as soon as possible.

She felt more confident now—she'd get Robert put into his place, she'd make him pay. She smiled at her reflection in the large gessoed and gilded mirror above her bureau, and the feeling of compressed rage lifted until she was almost light-headed just thinking about taking revenge. Robert Caley was no more than a cheap con man, he'd been one when she met him. He was very attractive—that had helped—and he'd taken the bait even faster than she had believed he would. But it had had to be fast because she had already been three months pregnant, and neither she nor Lloyd, who was already married, had wanted any scandal. And after Caley had signed the prenuptial agreements and the various other deals for a considerable amount of money, Lloyd and Elizabeth had toasted each other with chilled champagne.

"He's a good find, Elizabeth," Dulay had said admiringly.

"Well, we didn't have too much choice."

Dulay had leaned over and patted her belly. "Con men are easy enough to control. Never let him handle the purse strings, my darling, I'll always oversee all that, and I'll get trust funds set up for you and my baby."

"If it's a boy, Lloyd, what then?"

"Screw the scandal. You get rid of the creep, I'll get a

divorce, and we'll get married." They had toasted each other again.

They had even decided that they would call him Louis if it was a boy. She had wept when a girl was born, and Anna Louise was named after the son Lloyd had wanted so badly. But he had been true to his word and made watertight financial settlements, hiring advisers to handle the money and trust funds, for both herself and Anna Louise. But his visits grew further and further apart, until she saw him only once a year at Mardi Gras. Anna Louise never knew who her real father was because Caley had kept his side of the bargain, had brought her up as his own, and was named as the father on the birth certificate.

Missy peeked in. "A Mrs. Page downstairs asking to see you, said it's important, ma'am."

Elizabeth frowned, irritated at the interruption of her daydreaming, but then felt guilty. "I'll be right down, Missy, just powder my nose."

She opened one of the drawers of her satinwood bureau and stared at the rows of pill bottles, then she slammed it shut. "Now don't, Elizabeth, don't get it started all over again," she said sharply to her own reflection. "Just stay calm."

Lorraine waited downstairs, looking around her at the double parlor whose elegant proportions and furnishings exhaled restraint and grace as unmistakably as those of the Dulay house screamed for attention. Whatever impulses Elizabeth had toward movie-star glamour she had kept in their place in the Los Angeles house, while here little had changed since the inventory taken by her great-grandmother. The ceiling frescoes painted shortly after the house had been erected had never been covered, while the Russian carpets, the piano and music box, and the delicate chairs and side tables had been part of the young bride's dowry: curtains that fell straight and plain to the floor did not try to compete with the magnificent plasterwork of the cornices, and for fifty years the walls had been a deep and quiet Nile blue. The two fireplaces were unashamedly empty of dried flowers or fake logs; above one hung a family portrait, above the other a Corot.

It was a quarter of an hour before Elizabeth Caley came into the room, looking stunningly beautiful in a cream silk suit.

"Mrs. Page. I am so sorry to have kept you waiting."

Lorraine smiled. "That's all right, really."

"Now, what can I offer you? Champagne, or wine, or maybe a real Southern sloe gin?"

"I don't drink, Mrs. Caley."

"Oh, well, maybe an iced tea?"

"That would be fine."

Elizabeth rang for the maid, drew up one of the chairs and sat opposite. "You wanted to see me?"

She was bright-eyed, not a hair out of place, groomed and manicured and more confident than Lorraine had ever seen her before.

"You look very well," Lorraine said quietly.

"Thank you, I am. Ah, refreshments."

Missy passed them both tall fluted glasses of iced lemon tea, with slices of lemon and lime. It was refreshing, bittersweet.

"Mmm, delicious," Elizabeth said, putting down her glass. "Cigarette?"

Lorraine took out her own pack and lit Elizabeth's first before her own.

"Have you any results, any news?" She could have been asking about a movie contract from an agent; she showed no emotion whatsoever. She was clearly in control of herself.

"Well, I have certainly been kept very busy." Lorraine opened her notebook and took out her pen. "You know the polar bears on Anna Louise's bed, did you give them to her?"

Elizabeth's eyes widened in surprise, but knew it was not a frivolous question. "No, I think Robert gave her three or four. She used to call him Polar because sometimes he can be very frosty, you know."

"Did he also give one to Tilda Brown?"

Again, Elizabeth seemed slightly fazed by the question. "I really don't know."

Lorraine looked at her directly. "Did you hear about Tilda Brown?"

"Yes, I did. They were the first people I called on when I arrived. Tragic, just terrible."

"Yes, it is. I interviewed Tilda, just to go over her original statements, but she confirmed that she never saw Anna Louise."

Lorraine paused while Elizabeth sipped her iced tea, patting her lips with a folded white linen napkin.

"Do you know a man called Fryer Jones?"

Elizabeth blinked and then shook her head. "No, I don't think I do."

"He was the only person the police arrested for questioning—an eyewitness said he saw him on the night of the fifteenth talking to Anna Louise close to his bar near the French Quarter, not far from your hotel."

"I didn't even know they had arrested anyone." She sounded surprised.

"Well, it wasn't publicized because they released him the same evening. He had a number of alibis from people who stated he didn't leave his bar the entire evening. There was a Jesse Corbello, his brother Willy, and young sister Sugar May, plus . . ." Lorraine passed the handwritten sheet Rooney had jotted down from the police files. "Do you know any of these people at all?"

"No, no. I'm sorry, I don't."

"Do you know Edith Corbello at all?"

"No."

Lorraine seemed to be concentrating on her notebook, but she was watching Elizabeth closely; she had hardly given the list a glance. "But you know Juda Salina."

Mrs. Caley was tensing up now, small signals of her unease showing. Her knees pressed close together, her arms twitched slightly. "Well, you know that I do."

"She is Edith Corbello's sister. They used to be known as the Salina sisters."

Elizabeth suddenly gasped. "Of course, yes, I do recall her. I don't know her, but I remember Juda mentioning her sister—she's married to Fryer Jones, I think."

Lorraine looked up, taken by surprise. She paused a moment before continuing. "There is also another son, Raoul Corbello, he was working for Juda in Los Angeles."

"I don't recall the name."

"And also a second daughter, she's eighteen, Ruby Cor-bello. She is about to be crowned."

"Not debutante of the year, surely!"

"No, she is queen of a new black krewe in the Carnival—it's apparently a great honor, and a big ceremony."

"Yes, yes, it is. More tea?"

"No, thank you." Lorraine picked up her glass; she had only taken a few sips, and watched Elizabeth pluck at something on her skirt. "And what about Lloyd Dulay, do you know him?"

Elizabeth's head shot up and she stared wide-eyed at Lorraine. "Of course I know Lloyd, he's a dear old friend."

"Anna Louise was his daughter," Lorraine said flatly.

Elizabeth looked away, her cheeks flushed. "You have been busy. I hope you have been equally discreet—that is a very personal and private matter. Did he tell you or did Robert?"

"It will remain private, Mrs. Caley, I assure you, and Mr. Dulay told me himself."

"Good heavens!" She sighed and then said she felt tired, and if Lorraine had no further questions, would she mind if she excused herself?

"I saw your film *The Swamp* and I enjoyed it very much."

Elizabeth laughed, a little theatrically. "Oh, goodness me, where on earth did you see it?"

"Mr. Dulay kindly lent me a video. I noticed in the cast list that both the Salina sisters and Fryer Jones were in the film—not large parts, basically extras."

"I didn't mix with the extras, Mrs. Page."

"But you saw a lot of Juda Salina."

"Yes, but not during the filming. We met up years later at some function here, and if you don't mind my saying so, I really can't see how that old film has got anything to do with your tracing my daughter. Good heavens, I was almost her age when I made it, so it was a long time ago."

"Do you believe in voodoo, Mrs. Caley?"

Her hand flapped. "Oh, really, I can't answer that, no, no, I can't answer that."

"Did your daughter?"

"I very much doubt it, she was a very sensible girl."

"So are many of the thousands of worshipers here. Do you know if Tilda Brown believed in it?"

"Tilda? I wouldn't know, but then one never knows what children get up to."

"She was hardly a child, she was the same age as Anna, almost nineteen. . . ." Lorraine wondered whether or not she should mention the doll. She knew Elizabeth was lying; her tic had become far more pronounced as she brushed her skirt one moment, then picked at the flecks of the raw silk, then scratched with her long red fingernail.

There was a long pause, and then Lorraine went for the kill. "I found a doll in Tilda Brown's tennis racket case. It was a disgusting, stinking, handmade doll encased in excrement and urine. It was made, although crudely, to resemble Tilda, and even had a cut-out photograph of her face stuck onto the head. Human hair and, I think, possibly blood was matted on the top of it and there was a long pin sticking through the left eyeball out to the back of the head."

Elizabeth Caley stared at the toe of her sandal, very still now. There was another long pause before Lorraine continued, "Because of their distress, I have not been able to discuss my findings with Mr. and Mrs. Brown, but my partners are taking the doll to the mortuary, hopefully to get samples of Tilda's hair and blood to see if they are a match."

"This has nothing to do with Anna Louise," Elizabeth said sharply.

"Perhaps not, but do you know what that doll represents? According to a book I have on the voodoo culture, it is a terrible curse. It is, Mrs. Caley, a death doll."

Lorraine flicked through one of the handbooks Rosie had bought from the museum. She found the page and pressed the book further open. " 'Put hair of the person you want to affect in the side of the doll, use black pin where you wish to induce pain,' you will see a diagram—"

"No, I don't want to see it—take it away from me, please."

Lorraine closed the book. "This might have no connection to Anna Louise, but on the other hand, I must—"

"Stop this right now, and do not for pity's sake show the Browns anything so repellent. It is just appalling that you should even think that poor little Tilda would have—''

''She wouldn't have made the doll for herself. Somebody must have made it and given it to her. Maybe whoever did is guilty of manslaughter at the very least!''

''No, she committed suicide.''

''I know that, Mrs. Caley, but Tilda was Anna Louise's best friend, and I am simply trying to ascertain if they played around, went to any ceremonies.''

''No, absolutely not. No.''

''But you are very close to Juda Salina, at one time a high priestess, as was her sister. Edith Corbello is apparently less active now, but still runs a spiritualist group and a practice similar to her sister's in LA. Juda Salina doesn't mention the voodoo connection, but hands out leaflets to her clients advertising that she is a psychic medium, reads tarot cards, specializes in trances and hypnotism, spiritualism and . . . voodoo. I have a copy of her leaflet—''

''No, I do not know anything about this.''

''But as Anna Louise went to Mrs. Salina on a number of occasions with you, might she not have seen this? And being young and impressionable she may have started messing around with the occult.''

Elizabeth pushed her chair back, scraping the beautiful antique rug. ''I do not want to repeat myself, Mrs. Page, but this has gone far enough. I do not wish to discuss this element in any way whatsoever. In fact, if you believe Anna is dead, then I see no point in your continuing.''

Lorraine stood up. ''No point? I am trying to find out if your daughter was murdered and at the same time who is responsible. She has been missing for eleven months.''

''I *know* that!''

''So why say there is no point in pursuing this angle?''

''Voodoo is *not* an angle, Mrs. Page, it is a way of life, and you probably would not understand the complexities of it. It is taken very seriously here and is not, as you have implied, similar to the occult or black magic. It is not used for curses or evil, but the reverse, it is practiced as a safeguard against sickness and is spiritually uplifting.''

''I am trying to learn, Mrs. Caley, and if you have any information I would be grateful.''

''What do you mean, information? I don't have any information, why do you think I hired you? And as I did hire you, Mrs. Page, I am now dismissing you. I will fully reimburse any costs you have accumulated to date, but I no longer wish you to continue this investigation."

"I am sorry, but I can't walk away from this."

"Of course you can. You're only hired, you have no personal ties to keep you."

"I'm afraid I do. You see, my partner was murdered working on this case, so I have strong personal reasons why I would like to bring it to a conclusion."

Elizabeth hesitated, but did not ask any further details about the murder, dismissing it. "You seem to have forgotten what that conclusion was, Mrs. Page."

"Not at all. It was to find your daughter, dead or alive."

"But you have not found her."

"And my time is not up. I still have over a week to go, we have an agreement."

"And I am paying you off, finished. Phyllis will send you a check. Now, if you will excuse me."

"One million, Mrs. Caley—you can pay off the final week now or whenever, but the contract still stands."

"Don't be silly, it was a verbal—"

"No, it wasn't. We have it in writing, one million dollars. So even if you did pay me off, I wouldn't leave, not until I had covered every possible avenue. I'm sorry."

Elizabeth's hands were clenched tightly, her face set in a hard, furious glare. "You don't know what you are getting into, Mrs. Page."

"One never does on a case, Mrs. Caley. That's what makes it so interesting, the unexpected twists and turns."

Elizabeth's voice was hushed, threatening. "You might just get something totally unexpected here, and believe me, you will wish to God you had walked away."

Lorraine felt drained as Elizabeth Caley left the room, her footsteps echoing on the black-and-white checkerboard tiles of the hall as she called out, "Missy, Mrs. Page is leaving, show her out!"

The maid appeared at the door.

"No need, Missy, I know my way out."

Lorraine replaced her notebook in her briefcase and

turned as the door slammed shut and Robert Caley stood
there.

"You've got a fucking nerve coming to the house."

She snapped her case closed, her legs shaking at seeing
him so unexpectedly. She took hold of herself and looked
up, meeting his eyes. "I owe you an apology. I said things
I shouldn't have without verification. I am sincerely sorry."

He stuck his hands into his trouser pockets. "Sorry? You
bad-mouth me to my partners, you pass around scurrilous,
disgusting accusations about myself and my daughter, you
remove details of private papers from my desk and—"

"I have said I am sorry."

"It's not good enough. I want a formal letter of retraction
sent to Lloyd Dulay."

She blushed and could not meet his eyes. "But you were
using Anna Louise's trust find illegally."

"You don't back off an inch, do you, Mrs. Page? That
million-dollar bonus must be a big incentive."

"Maybe as big as your daughter's trust is to you?"

"Touché!"

Lorraine picked up her briefcase. "I am not scoring
points, Robert."

"Aren't you?"

She sighed. "No, I am not. I am trying to do my job,
that's all."

He was so angry he wanted to throttle her. "Does that
include fucking someone for information the way you used
to for a drink?"

She wanted to say that it had meant so much to her, she
wanted to drop her briefcase and go into his arms. Instead
she froze him out, her eyes without a flicker of emotion, so
direct and cold it was he who broke the moment, turning
away from her.

"Did you give Anna Louise toy white polar bears?"

He shook his head in disbelief. "What?"

"She had a row of white bears on her pillow—you gave
them to her?"

"Yes."

"And your nickname, or pet name, was Polar?"

"Yes, yes, it was."

"Did you also give one of the same white bears to Tilda Brown?"

"No."

"Do you recall how many you gave to your daughter?"

He had to sit down. She was snapping out the questions as if he were some suspect held on a rap in a police station.

"It's important, Robert, how many?"

"Five, for her thirteenth, fourteenth, fifteenth, sixteenth and seventeenth birthdays. I then said there was no more room for them. They were to mark her teenage years, for her diaries."

"Her diaries?"

He rubbed his head. "Yes, the bears unzip, they have a sort of secret pocket where she used to keep her yearly diary."

Lorraine could feel the buzz. "Did the police ever see them?"

He shook his head. "No . . ."

"Why not?"

"They weren't there. Maybe she outgrew them, I don't know."

Lorraine's buzz went flat fast. "Shit! Okay, now can you try and remember if on that flight, the one on the fifteenth, Anna Louise carried or packed one of those bears?"

"I have no idea."

"It's very important, Robert, think." He shook his head, and she came closer. "When you went into her bedroom at the hotel, did you see one of the white bears?" He sighed, and she moved even closer. "Shut your eyes and think, Robert. You said her purse was in the sitting room and her new dress was laid out in the bedroom, so you must have looked at the bed."

"Why? What's so important?"

She was close enough to bend down and touch him, but she remained upright. "When I went into Anna Louise's bedroom in LA, I found four bears lined up on her pillows. Four, Robert, not five, *four*."

He reached out, not looking at her, and stroked her calf, her leg so slim he could almost slip his hand right around it. "No, there wasn't one in the hotel." He eased her around to stand in front of him and leaned forward, his head pressed into her crotch. "Why did you not even answer one call, Lorraine, why?"

"I wanted to, Robert, but I was too guilty. I was all out of kilter that day, tired from being with you. And I suppose when Tilda hinted about you and Anna, and Dulay told me about the trust fund, maybe I was jealous, or plain angry, but I have no excuse, I should not have said the things I said without . . ."

She could feel his breath, his lips pressing through her skirt, but a part of her mind was working by itself. She remembered Phyllis saying she packed the day they left, or was it Elizabeth?

"I have to go, Robert."

He dropped his hands and rested back in the chair, looking up at her. "What's so important about the bear?"

She had picked up her briefcase and was already crossing to the door. "Tilda Brown said Anna Louise did not see her on the fifteenth, but what if she was lying? What if the bear was a peace offering, because they'd had such an argument? It was over you, Robert, do you know that? Your daughter was jealous of the attention you gave Tilda."

He stood up, hands wide. "Jealous? She was jealous of little Tilda?"

"On that day, before you went to work, you passed Tilda on the tennis courts, remember? You kissed her because she was crying, and Anna Louise saw it."

"It was harmless, I swear before God!"

"I know that, but Anna Louise didn't, and I think it sparked off a jealous rage, which resulted in—"

"Tilda leaving . . ."

She nodded, then looked at the phone. "Can I make a call?"

She didn't wait for an answer, dialing the Caleys' home in LA. Phyllis answered, and before she could even inquire how Lorraine was, she was asked if she recalled seeing Anna Louise packing, on the fifteenth. Phyllis fell silent.

"Phyllis, are you still there?"

"Yes, I am, I'm thinking. You see, I never did any packing or anything like that, but I remember Mrs. Caley asking if I'd check to see if Anna Louise had packed any nice dresses, as she would be invited to a lot of parties and—"

Lorraine interrupted. "Did you see what was in her bags?"

"Well, yes, and so did Mrs. Caley, they were full of T-shirts and sneakers."

"Anything else?"

"I don't think so. They had a bit of a tiff about it later because Mrs. Caley told Anna to go and repack. But I never saw what was in the bag and I don't think Mrs. Caley did. Was it something important?"

Lorraine said it wasn't, and thanked Phyllis. As she replaced the receiver, Missy appeared at the door.

"I've brought all your cases down, Mr. Caley."

Lorraine frowned. He waited until Missy had gone and then said quietly that he was moving back into the hotel. "Can I call you?"

Lorraine went up to him and kissed him. He slipped his arms around her and they were embracing when Elizabeth Caley appeared in the doorway. Lorraine caught sight of her watching them and quickly broke away. "Shit!"

He now saw Elizabeth hurrying back up the stairs. "It's all right, I'm leaving her. It's true. I've had enough, I am leaving for good. Come on, I'll walk you to your car. You going back to your hotel?"

"You're leaving her?"

"Yes, I should have done it years ago."

Robert kissed Lorraine again as she got into the car. "Maybe have dinner tonight?"

"Yes, I'd like that."

She smiled up at him, wanting him to kiss her again, and he touched her cheek. "Elizabeth said something about a photograph, you showed her a photo of Anna Louise. Did you?"

"Yes, it was taken at a nightclub."

"Do you have it with you? Is it something I should see?"

She hesitated. She had it with her but decided against showing it to him now. "I'll talk about it with you tonight."

He kissed her again and shut the car door, watching her smiling and waving to him as François drove off.

François flicked a look at Lorraine from the rearview mirror, and smiled. "Well, they certainly let you over the mat!"

She laughed, a big, loud bellow.

He was getting to like this lady a whole lot. "Back to the Saint Marie?"

She leaned back on the seat and closed her eyes. "No. Tilda Brown's."

She felt guilty about feeling so good and couldn't help smiling. Robert Caley was no longer a suspect and he would also be free if he left Elizabeth. And she looked forward to spending another night with him. Lorraine drained the last of the vodka and Coke, reassuring herself constantly that she was in control: the craving had stopped—she didn't crave the drink, she was just slaking a normal thirst. Everything was under control.

Elizabeth Caley watched the car drive out from behind the old lace curtains of her bedroom. She didn't know how she was going to deal with everything and she needed Juda badly. It was all falling apart, and the pills in the drawer drew her like a magnet.

Lorraine sat forward, chewing her lip, flicking through her notebook to her early jottings. They had all said it, how odd it was that Anna Louise actually ordered that dress, the one she saw in *Vogue* and then had been so determined to get. She had called from the plane to ask Phyllis to get it for her. So maybe she had not repacked anything at all after her conversation with Elizabeth, but put the polar bear inside her bag. Lorraine knew she was making erratic assumptions and wild guesses, but maybe all the fuss about getting the dress sent out had a reason, because everyone had been in a good mood when they got to the hotel the night Anna Louise disappeared.

Lorraine was so intent on working everything out to a rational conclusion that she did exactly what she had agreed not to do: she forgot to call in to check with Rosie and Rooney and inform them she had left the Caleys' and was now on her way to Tilda Brown's home. Something else she had no intention of telling them was that she asked François to stop at a liquor store, where she bought herself a six-pack of Coke and another bottle of vodka. It was all right, she told herself, nobody would know, and as long as she kept doing the top-ups in the can, no one could even suspect. It helped too, it helped a lot to forget Nick Bartello's voice, his smile, made it all go away. Most of all, it made her feel certain she was in control.

CHAPTER

15

At first Mrs. Dubois refused to let Lorraine into the house; preparations were being made for Tilda's funeral, so it was hardly a suitable time for either of her parents to speak with Lorraine.

"I just need to go into Tilda's bedroom. Please, Mrs. Dubois, it is important, or I would not intrude at this very sad time. I think when I was last here I left my key, it may have fallen from my purse. It'll take no more than two minutes."

Mrs. Dubois agreed and asked the maid to show Lorraine upstairs.

The maid remained by the door as Lorraine started to search the room, itching to get to the bed and to the white polar bear, still left on Tilda's pillow. When Mrs. Dubois called for the maid to help her with something below, leaving Lorraine alone, she picked up the bear immediately. It was too light, and she knew there was nothing inside, but she found the hidden zipper and checked just in case. She was disappointed, not even bothering to pretend she had been looking for a key when the maid returned, tapping on the open door.

"Thank you, no luck!" she said, walking toward the hovering maid; the girl seemed nervous. "How did you get along with Miss Tilda?" she asked.

"Fine, ma'am, just fine, but she kept to herself. I just used to clean her room, press her clothes. She didn't act up

or nothin', not like she used to. I been asked to show you
out because Mrs. Dubois is busy."

"How do you mean, not like she used to?" Lorraine
asked, still very casual and friendly.

"Well, the maid before me was fired, they didn't get
along, an' I was told by Mrs. Brown that I was not to in-
terfere with Miss Tilda's personal things. She didn't like me
even tidying up her room, but then she was real neat and
tidy."

"When was she fired, the maid before you?"

"Oh, last year, I only worked here since then."

Lorraine kept on smiling. "What date would that be?"

The maid really was eager for Lorraine to leave, looking
down the stairwell to the hall below. "Well, I was interviewed mid-February, 'cause Ruby had already left."

"Ruby?" Lorraine followed her down the wide staircase.

"Yes, miss, the previous maid here was a girl called Ruby
Corbello. She got a job in a hair salon after she left."

"Thank you very much."

One minute depressed, the next Lorraine was buzzing
again, and to the maid's relief hurried out without even asking to speak to Mrs. Dubois.

Lorraine sat in her car thinking it was too much of a coincidence, then she sighed. Maybe it was the lead she needed.
She checked her watch and told François to take her back
to the hotel, realizing how late it had got and remembering
her own instructions that they should all keep in touch.

Rosie and Rooney sat at the garden table in the courtyard
of the St. Marie with their cups of frothing café au lait.

"I dunno, she tells us to call in, and then she goes her
own way. I mean, where is she now? Mrs. Caley said she
left over an hour and a half ago," Rosie said, irritated.

Rooney looked at his watch and said nothing. He'd done
what Lorraine had asked, checked at the morgue, but there
had been no gris-gris necklace on Nick's body or listed
along with the rest of his personal possessions.

"Maybe he didn't have it on," he said.

"What?"

"The necklace."

"As far as I can remember, he was wearing it when we last saw him, he kind of liked it. I miss him, Bill."

"Yeah, me too, he was a good guy."

They sipped their coffee in silence, then Rosie took out her note pad.

"What we going to do about Edith Corbello? It's a shame to waste time. I got her address, but her phone number's not listed, so we'll just have to turn up."

Rooney pushed his coffee aside. "You're right. I'll leave my notes under Lorraine's door and we'll go see this Mrs. Corbello. Might as well be doing something!"

Lorraine found the torn pages from Rooney's notebook under her door. She sat on the bed, reading the scrawled writing. No necklace was found on Nick Bartello's body. There was also a brief outline reiterating what the cops had said about Fryer Jones and his alibis. In brackets he added that Fryer Jones was married to Juda Salina. Coincidences! Lorraine underlined Raoul's name, remembering him from LA.

What Rooney had not mentioned was the fact that he and Rosie were going to see Edith Corbello. He had been going to, but Rosie suggested they just go ahead and see what they could come up with and tell Lorraine later. Lorraine waited around for a while, got a sandwich and Coke and sat outside in the garden. She checked over her notes, wondering what she should do next, deciding not to follow the Ruby Corbello lead until she had talked to Fryer Jones.

François was a little apprehensive about taking Lorraine to Fryer Jones's bar. He watched her in the rearview mirror, drinking the Coke and topping it up with vodka, but she didn't seem in any way intoxicated.

"I'm not a tourist, François. But you wait right outside, and if I'm not out in half an hour, you come in and get me! So just take me there!"

"Okey dokey, we're on our way."

The cab drew up outside the tiny dilapidated house in the old Irish Channel.

"You sure you want this address?" the cabbie asked.

"Yep, but if you wait you got a return fare," Rooney

said, passing over the money and an extra ten-dollar bill.

"Sure, be right out here for you, sir."

Rooney and Rosie looked at the battered front door, its glass panel broken and blocked out with a piece of board. The top four panes of a French door had also been broken at some time and replaced with an almost opaque frosted glass, so that it was impossible to see into the house. Rooney took a few steps down the alleyway between the house and its neighbor and saw a broken fence enclosing a yard out back with old wrecked cars and a string hammock strung between two leafless trees. Bits and pieces of rusted car engines were scattered among ripped tires, inner tubes and bursting bags of garbage.

"If we got the right address, you leave the talkin' to me," Rooney said, hitching up his pants.

"You said that three times already," Rosie said petulantly.

"Fine, then make sure you do, no interruptions."

The doorbell didn't work: Rooney banged on the front door and it creaked open.

They stood on the porch and waited before knocking again, peering into the dingy hallway.

"Yeah, what you want?" Sugar May called out from the kitchen.

"Mrs. Edith Corbello?"

"She's busy right now, you got an appointment?"

Rooney looked at Rosie and said quietly, "Okay, now we do as I said, see what we can come up with." Rosie nodded as Rooney, smiling broadly, looked toward Sugar May. "Hi, there. We just came, on Fryer Jones's recommendation—we don't have an appointment," he said.

Sugar May wrinkled her nose, strolling down the dark, dirty hallway. "She don't like being interrupted. You have to wait, see what she says."

Sugar May pointed to a room off the hall and disappeared back into the kitchen.

Rooney and Rosie sat on a sagging sofa whose broken springs bulged beneath them. The carpet was threadbare, cigarette butts ground into the pile, and there were beer stains on every available surface. The doorway had an old beaded curtain tied up.

"What a dump," Rosie said quietly, then turned as a high-pitched scream from the room down the hall made her sit bolt upright.

In the room was a table covered with a cloth, a mirror propped up behind it reflecting a figurine of the Virgin and a picture of Marie Laveau on the wall behind. Incense and three blue candles smoked in front of the statue, surrounded by saucers of rainwater, a dish of bread and apples and others of special grasses and oil.

Edith had made the young girl lie on a cot while she bathed her head with an infusion of herbs; now she pressed down on the girl's temples with both hands, her eyes shut tight, chanting to invoke the spirits' healing powers.

The girl's head wobbled at the pressure of Edith's strong hands pressing down hard on it. It felt as if her neck was going to break, and it was worse pain than any of the blinding headaches she'd been having every month.

"Oh my, we got tension in here. We got such tension. Sit up now, girl, and put your head forward so I can feel your neck."

The young girl moaned, and Edith closed her eyes, rubbing and kneading the vertebrae down the girl's neck until she felt a click. She twisted the girl's head quickly and there were two more loud clicks. Edith smiled.

"Yes, that got it, you feelin' easy now, honey?"

Rosie looked at Rooney as the moans stopped and a soft laugh could be heard, but he was immersed in an old magazine.

"Listen to this. 'Voodoo came with the slaves from West Africa in the sixteenth century and in New Orleans the name of Marie Laveau is legendary. She is said to have been the daughter of a wealthy planter and a quadroon girl. She was part Indian, and she married a Jacques Paris, who mysteriously disappeared after the marriage, when she began calling herself Widow Paris.' Holy shit! 'Marie Laveau had fifteen children and she lived in Saint Anne's Street between North Rampart and Burgundy Street. She is said to have eliminated all other queens by her powers of the gris-gris, literally voo-dooing them all to death. And today the doctors of respectable medical schools have consulted voodoo doctors for treatment of paranoid schizophrenics.' ''

Rooney was about to continue reading from the magazine when the door farther down the hall opened, and although they couldn't see who was coming out, they heard the deep throaty voice of Edith Corbello.

"Don't you worry yourself about payin'. Get well, and get employment, and then you come back and see me, Tulla."

Sugar May yelled from the kitchen. "Hey, Mama! You got clients in the front room, you hear me, Mama?"

Edith Corbello walked in to see Rosie and Rooney, and whatever they were expecting didn't quite add up to the large, stout woman in an apron and old slippers, frizzy graying hair surrounding a big, round, sweating face.

"Yes?"

Rooney stood up. "I am Bill Rooney and this is my friend Rosie."

Edith sighed. "Mmm, what you be wanting?"

"Can we talk to you? You are Edith Corbello?"

"Sure, I am, but I don't see strangers. Who sent you to me?"

"Fryer Jones," Rooney said.

Edith nodded, and walked back to her room. "Come on in, but I got an appointment in fifteen minutes."

The room was darkened by old drapes drawn across the window, and besides the bed and the altar table, it contained a large old trunk and a row of hard chairs. Even in the dim light, it was noticeably cleaner and more orderly than the rest of the house, and there were a variety of masks and pictures on the walls.

"Sit you down, get a chair for yourself," Edith said to Rooney. Moving behind the desk, she opened the trunk, took out cards and a stack of leaflets. "These my prices."

She passed two leaflets that were torn at the edges and the print faint. They listed rituals, consultations and readings that would reveal the future, as well as healing bathing with a long list of oils and herbal remedies for health and vitality. All the treatments offered cost between twenty and fifty dollars. Underlined in red pen were the items that would be extra to the cost of the session—herbs, teas, candles and incense, plus any necessary home visits.

Rooney opened his wallet and laid out two fifty-dollar notes.

"You want a reading?" Edith said, indicating the deck of tarot cards.

Rooney leaned over to Rosie and held her hand. "We need advice."

"You come to the right place." Edith stared at Rooney and did not touch the two fifty-dollar notes.

"Well, Mrs. Corbello, Rosie and I, this is Rosie . . . we want to get married."

Rosie almost fell off her chair, and turned to Rooney with her mouth open. He planted a kiss on her cheek.

"We're in love," he said.

Rosie remained speechless: Bill needed to have no further worries about her interrupting, as his words had put her in a state of shock.

"Mmm." Edith folded her hands over her big belly, looking from one to the other, and smiled, but her eyes remained suspicious and wary. "A lot of people want the same thing, marriage. If you want this lady, and she wants you, where's your problem?"

"I'm already married."

"You get a divorce."

"She won't give me one."

"Ah, so you got a troublesome wife?"

"That's right."

"Mmm, mmm, I been one of them." She chuckled.

Rooney released Rosie's hand. "I have offered her a good settlement and she has refused, point-blank, and she won't move out of the house, and we got no children. She is just refusing to release me out of spite."

"That's sad—children make a house into a living thing, they also wreck it something bad." She chuckled again.

This wasn't what he had expected. There were no evil spirits or drumbeats, just a big woman who seemed, if anything, amused by him. He was unsure how he should approach what he was working his way around to asking, when Edith leaned toward him.

"You are not impotent, are you?" Edith said, and started

to flick the tarot cards with her big, raw hands.

"No, I am not, most definitely not. But I feel like I am with a wife that won't give me a divorce. I got to wait, maybe two years or even longer, and then she—"

"How long you married to this other woman?"

"Er, twenty-five years."

"Long time. An' she been a good wife?"

"Yes."

"So, she no longer good, huh? Because she is no longer wanted?"

"Yes, that's right. So, what we were thinking about, what we've been told is that you might help us?"

Edith nodded her head, and stifled a yawn, her hand resting on the tarot cards that she only brought out for the types like these that came to her, white tourists.

Rooney coughed; the room was stiflingly hot and claustrophobic. "If this voodoo works, like we've been told it does, then we're here to ask you to do something for us. Voodoo is what we want."

"Mmm, mmm." Edith stared at Rosie and after a moment she asked, "Don't you talk?"

"I agree with Bill, he is speaking for both of us," Rosie said sweetly.

"Does he now? And so, Bill, what is it you want exactly, huh? Voodoo covers a mighty big area, you want to tell me specifically what you are wanting from me?"

"My wife to die, Mrs. Corbello, can you do that? Make us one of those voodoo dolls that make people—"

Edith slapped the table hard and she gave them a wide grimace. "You want me to make you a voodoo doll? Make your wife afraid of her shadow? Make her think she is cursed? Make her so frightened of the spirits that she lies down and just wastes away? All her limbs to go stiff and her thoughts twisted so she gets to be like a zombie? Huh? That what you are asking me for?"

Rosie began to get scared and looked at Rooney.

"Yes, now if that is more than fifty dollars, I am prepared to pay," Rooney said.

Edith leaned back in her chair, her big hands clasping the arms. "You believe that I can do this for you?"

"Can you?" Rosie asked.

"You want this doll too, do you, Miss Rosie cheeks?"

Rosie nodded, and then almost fell backward out of her chair as Edith let the lid of the trunk bang back down, scattering the cards on the bare floor. For a second they both thought she was going into a trance as she rose up on her feet, her big body looming over the pair of them.

"Get out of my house, pair of you, *get out right now*!"

"But Mrs. Corbello . . ." Rooney said.

She moved toward him, her finger digging him in the chest. "You know my name, but you don't know me and I don't know you. You take your evil thoughts out of my house and you *take your money with you*!" She threw the two fifty-dollar bills in their faces and yanked open the door. "Sugar May, *Sugar May*! These two people are leaving, an' they are never coming back."

Rosie and Rooney were shoved out onto the doorstep by the little girl in pigtails and rubber flip-flops. The broken front door slammed hard after them and then swung back open. It was no wonder it didn't have any glass left in it.

"Well, I left the talking to you!" Rosie said as she walked down the path.

"I just tried it on," he said grumpily. "I tried it on because of that doll Lorraine found. I mean, maybe we could have gotten her to talk."

"We? You did all the talking, Bill Rooney, and it didn't work, did it?" Rosie said as they looked up and down the street for the taxi driver. He had gone, and she shrugged. "He must have seen us coming, Bill. That was a nice tip you gave him, ten bucks more than the cab ride," she said, and linked her arm through his.

"Never mind, we can walk," he said, feeling dumb and inadequate; he had blown it and wondered if he had lost his touch. That really got to him. "We should've waited for Lorraine," he said.

"We did, and she didn't show," snapped Rosie. She was getting sick and tired of having to wait for Lorraine, but nevertheless they made their way back to the hotel like two naughty schoolkids who knew they were going to get bawled out.

Edith was at the upstairs window, watching the two squat bodies walking down the street, furious at Fryer for sending people like that to her. She opened her dressing-table drawer and took out the telephone. She always hid it because she hated it, loathed the intrusion of its jangling ring, especially when she was working.

The telephone rang at the side of the dingy bar by the door leading up to Fryer's room. The barman was just coming on duty and picked it up. "Fryer's."

"You get that bastard on the line," said Edith in a fury.

"What bastard are you referring to?" he asked, grinning.

"Zak, you son of a bitch, this is Edith and you know it, so you get him to the phone. You tell him he never sends me over scum like I just had to deal with. They had cops written all over their big fat faces, and I knew he didn't have no wife, she's already buried six feet deep. He could get me in a whole lot of trouble."

Zak placed the handset on the bar, saying he'd just go check if Fryer was around.

"I know he's there, that son of a bitch don't ever move his ass outta there!" Edith shouted down the phone.

Zak moved up the narrow staircase, shuffling his feet on the bare boards. "Eh! Man, Fryer, it's Edith on the telephone, she's all steamed up about you sending some cops to her place."

"What?"

"Just repeatin' what she's yelling on the telephone. She's mad as hell."

The door at the top of the stairs inched open. "Tell that fat bitch I never sent nobody over there. She's raising bad spirits like she's raising bad fucking kids."

Zak shrugged as the door closed and returned to the bar.

"Hi, Edith," he said into the phone.

"You get that lazy son of a bitch to talk to me," she yelled.

Zak took a deep breath. "Fryer said to tell you that he would never waste your precious time sending nobody to you you didn't know or trust like a brother. He's not feelin' so good right now, but said he'd call you later. If you need him to come over he'll drop whatever pressing things he's got on, because you are a very important woman in his life."

"May God forgive the lies that spew out of your lips,

Zachary. That no-good son of a bitch probably never even lifted his hungover head." She slammed the phone back down.

Zak laughed, and then turned as the door opened at the far end of the bar by the main street entrance. Lorraine Page squinted to adjust to the darkness and then slowly began to walk the full length of the room. Zak never took his eyes off her as she hitched her skirt up and sat on a high barstool.

"Diet Coke when you're through checking the price of my suit," she said softly, and flipped open her pack of cigarettes. "You got a light?"

Edith stashed the phone back in the drawer. She hadn't paid a bill for years. The boys had done something with the wiring on the telephone cables outside their house and connected their line to someone else's. Nobody called in except maybe Juda. Nobody ever made appointments over the telephone because Edith wasn't listed in the book, and she never paid any taxes on her earnings, meager as they were. A bit of thieving never bothered her. What did was strangers coming to her parlor, especially strangers that smelled like cops and asked for bad work. She'd have it out with Fryer. All the years she'd known him, he'd never understood, never believed in her. That was his problem, he wasn't a believer in public but in private she'd scared him a few times, even if he refused to acknowledge it.

Juda traveled luxuriously in the Caleys' private plane, and their car was waiting at the airport to drive her straight to their mansion. She wondered what Elizabeth needed her so badly for and felt tired just at the prospect of having to deal with her. But she would have to, she always had to pay for the "luxuries," and this was heavy—first-class all the way.

Missy opened the imposing front door, looking scared.

"Oh, Mrs. Salina, I sure am glad you're here, she's acting up bad. She's crying and shouting up there, she's thrown her tray at me and she's in such a rage. Mr. Caley packed all his things and walked out, saying he's never coming back home."

"All right, Missy, don't you get all excited now, make

us a nice pot of tea, the kind Mrs. Caley likes, and bring it straight on up.''

Juda began to walk slowly up the gently curved staircase. Her legs pained her, her feet were swollen from the flight, and she clung to the banister rail as she heaved her body up stair by stair.

''She got some medication in her bedroom, Missy?''

Missy looked up fearfully. ''I don't know what she got up there, Mrs. Salina, but she's acting crazy, saying there's people there with her and there's things inside of her. Got me to shut up the shutters, then open them again. She makes me shiver, she does.''

Juda could now hear the furniture being hurled around, and Elizabeth's hoarse voice talking loudly to herself.

''Get away from me, stay away from me, *don't touch me*!''

Juda took a deep breath before she opened the bedroom door. Elizabeth Caley was disheveled, her long hair loose as she staggered from bed to window to bureau, the beauty and dignity of the room making her behavior seem even more grotesque. She appeared to be half dancing, half trying to control the body spasms that made her look as if she was working up to some kind of fit. Spittle formed at the side of her mouth, but as soon as she saw Juda she sighed with relief, stretching out her arms.

''Thank God, Juda, help me. Please help me, they've come for me. They're here again, the snakes are inside me again.''

Robert Caley unpacked his clothes, almost high on his own adrenaline. He'd done it, he'd finally done what he should have done years ago.

He called Lorraine at her hotel but was told she was not in her room, and then checked with the desk downstairs to make sure the adjoining suite was still retained for her. He called Lloyd Dulay and asked to see him. He wasn't going to grovel, not ever again. Doubloons had not been awarded the gaming license; it had gone to a huge gaming conglomerate from another state that no one had even known was in the running. Clearly the governor had made some new friends, but he hadn't forgotten his old ones either—the land, of course, was still Caley's, and the governor had announced that Caley, Doubloons and the new group should get around a table and hammer out a partnership agreement. Caley's financial future was safe.

Just hearing the tone of Caley's voice, Dulay didn't argue, agreeing to see him that evening. Caley then called his other partner, arranging to meet with him the next day. He felt confident, knowing he now had enough on Lloyd Dulay to ensure that he wouldn't make any trouble. It felt good. But the one person he wanted to share his newfound freedom with was still not at her hotel. He left a message at the St. Marie, saying he wished to see her urgently, and left his cell phone number on which he could be contacted at any time that evening.

Lorraine was beginning to feel uneasy as a few more people entered Fryer's bar and sat as far away from her as possible.

She had asked to speak to Fryer, but the barman had said he was resting. She smoked four cigarettes, getting more and more edgy and impatient as she waited for him: she eyed the rows of liquor bottles, needing another drink, but disciplined herself not to ask for one, telling herself again and again that she didn't need it. The telephone rang and the barman asked the caller to hold, and disappeared through the doorway at the end of the bar. She heard him call up to Fryer and a gruff voice yelled down.

"Shit, man, what you wake me for? Tell him to come by tonight."

Lorraine moved off her stool and walked the length of the bar. "He's awake now, okay? So I am going up to see him whether you like it or not."

Zak reached for the phone to speak to the caller, at the same time looking at Lorraine. "Don't you go up there, miss."

"You try and stop me," she snapped back, and disappeared.

Fryer Jones had one hell of a hangover, more than his usual; and he sat up, angry at the yelling from below. He leaned over his bed, picked up a bottle of bourbon, and took a long swig before he flopped back on his dirty stained pillows. The door opened, and Lorraine looked in.

"Mr. Jones, my name is Lorraine Page."

"What?" he grunted, and then eased up on his elbow. She stepped into the room but could hardly see him in the darkness. He could see her and he liked what he saw. "Well, come into my parlor, said the spider to the pretty pushy broad with a briefcase in her hand and all."

There was an overpowering smell of urine, tobacco, stale booze and body odor. A ragged curtain hung over the small window behind Fryer's single bed; a broken armchair with stuffing coming out of it was stacked with sheets of music, brown with age. The walls were covered with posters, old photographs and masks. Shelves hung lopsided with books and magazines.

"You wanna sit?" Fryer asked, scratching his crotch. He was barefoot and his denim shirt was open to the waist, the thick leather belt of his dirty jeans unbuckled and the fly half open, but he behaved as if he were seated in some luxurious boudoir, and added an elegance to his gestures that lifted him above the squalor.

"Sit down, miss. What you say your name was?"

"Lorraine Page, Mrs." She passed him a card and looked hesitantly at the only chair that was not under a mound of rubbish. The rocking chair was covered by a knitted shawl, and as she sat down it creaked ominously, moving backward so that her feet left the ground before she rocked forward uneasily and put her briefcase down beside her.

"*Mrs.* Lorraine Page," he said softly, and then flicked the card away. "Uh-huh, a private investigator."

"Yes, Mr. Fryer, I have been hired by Elizabeth and Robert Caley to trace their daughter Anna Louise." The rocking chair creaked again and she held on to the arms, trying to keep still. She couldn't help noticing that one of the posters, peeling off the damp wall, was from the movie *The Swamp*. It was a garish picture of Elizabeth Seal with a snake entwined around her body, arms reaching up to the sky.

Lorraine opened her briefcase and took out her notebook. "You mind if I ask you a few questions?"

"For a lady that walks into a gentleman's bedroom with a whole lot of purpose in her stride, I'd say I don't have much option. Why don't you set that nice tight little butt you got next to me?"

"I'm fine where I am, Mr. Fryer."

He smiled, and then let out a rumble of a laugh. "I guess you are, Mrs. Page, but I don't see as how I can help you in your investigation." He saw her glance at the old movie poster. "I was in that movie, *The Swamp*, the one your eyes keep straying to, with your employer, Mrs. Caley."

"Yes, I know. And you were arrested on February sixteenth last year and questioned regarding the disappearance of Anna Louise, Mrs. Caley's daughter."

"I was, but I was released with no charges. I also had a full bar of customers who all stated that I never set foot outside my establishment the entire evening."

"Yes, I know, but most of them were your own relatives."

He eased his legs over the edge of the bed to sit upright, staring down at his toes. "Is that so? Well, maybe you should talk to the police about that, because they got a list as long as your lovely legs that says not only my relatives was drinking and making music in my bar that night, but a lotta mah friends."

"Did you see Anna Louise Caley that night, Mr. Fryer?"

He reached for some papers and a tobacco pouch. "No, but some motherfucker says he saw me talkin' to that poor child, and in this town, Mrs. Page, there are a lot of them. Motherfuckers. But when the police of this mighty fine city take you in, you do not argue, you got no option. They beat you up on the way to the cells, they beat you up in the cells, and they beat you up some more just for somethin' to do when they release you. It's a kind of custom we got in New Orleans."

He sprinkled tobacco, or what she presumed was tobacco, onto the paper and licked it. Her eyes were becoming accustomed to the dark, dingy room, and to him; there was a kind of magnetism to Fryer Jones. He seemed not to care she was there, he was so laid-back and casual, his deep, throaty, smoky voice quite attractive.

"But you were held until the following morning," she said.

"That I was, but they had to check out that what I was

saying was true, and it was the truth, Mrs. Page. I never saw Miss Caley that evening. In fact, I ain't seen her for a long, long time. Maybe four or five years.''

"But you knew her?"

"Sure, I did, and I knew her mama."

"Mrs. Caley says she does not know you, Mr. Fryer."

"Well, she don't, I know of her, maybe she knows of me. Don't make us friendly now, does it?''

He lit up and inhaled deeply. He took three more deep drags, letting the smoke swirl into his lungs, sucking it in with a loud breath before he sighed, releasing it. And then to her astonishment he held it out to her.

"You want a hit?"

"No, thank you."

"How about a drink?"

He brought out his bottle of bourbon.

"No, thank you, I don't drink."

He laughed, watching her, and then gulped down two big shots before he screwed back the cap. Lorraine took out her cigarette pack and, as she had forgotten her lighter, had to cross to him for a light. He struck a match, looking up into her face.

"Oh yes, you got nice eyes too, I like the way you look. Like the way you hold yourself, Mrs. Page, you are a classy lady, mmm, mmm.''

Lorraine returned to her precarious perch. "You were married to Edith Corbello?"

"Close, but not quite right. I was married to her sister, Juda Salina.''

Lorraine chewed her lip. He dragged on his joint, his eyes mocking her as she tried to think how she should lead up to what she wanted to ask him, thrown slightly by the fact that Elizabeth Caley had given her incorrect information.

"So you are married to Juda Salina?"

"Yes, ma'am. We met on that movie, best money I ever earned in my life. They hired a whole bunch of us for bit parts. We was due to film for 'bout a week, but it got to two and then three, man, I was sitting around for more'n a month. They paid for it, though, paid well. I got this bar outta the proceeds, I never earned such easy money.'' He chuckled again.

"And Juda and her sister?"

He nodded, his face almost obscured by thick smoke as he dragged again and again on the joint.

"The Salina sisters was brought in because of the problems, you know, to kind of quiet things down. It was gettin' outta hand, but I didn't care, I was being paid. None of us had employment." He lay back, smiling at her. "You know, it's hard to believe but those two sisters were beautiful, man, they was glorious to look at. But then nature has its way, and they blow up and get so bloated it's hard to believe that once they was a force. A beautiful force, yess, yess, I didn't know which to fuck first."

He stared vacantly at a spot on his filthy, stained ceiling and sighed, rubbing himself.

"She was beautiful too, Elizabeth Seal," Lorraine said softly.

"No, Elizabeth Seal was just a pretty little thing. I used to feel for her, locals was against her, she was white and she was rich, and she was not Marie Laveau. Never could be, so they thought. Marie Laveau is a goddess, she is worshiped in these parts, and to get a pretty little white girl to play the part was creatin' bad feelings. Real bad feelings." He curled up his legs and lay on his side. "So they bring in the Salina sisters to kind of calm the waters, you know, to act as spiritual advisers, because folks here think they are related way back to Marie Laveau, and if they give their blessing, well, it's theirs to give."

Fryer looked at the burning stub of his joint and dropped it into the filled ashtray at his bedside. "I am getting very stoned. It's age, takes less and less now. Do I have another drink? Yes, I think so. You sure you won't join me, Mrs. Page?"

He drank from his bottle again, and replaced the cap, then started to make another joint. "You know why Elizabeth Seal is crazy, Mrs. Page?" he asked, his attention on his joint. Lorraine's was on the bottle: she wanted a drink badly now.

"No, I don't."

"You want for me to tell you?"

"Yes."

"Then come and sit near old Fryer, come on, sit close."

"I'm fine where I am," she said.

"Are you now? Well if you say so, but I have never had a woman complain. I may be old, but my snake never lets me down."

"Tell me more about Elizabeth Seal," she interrupted him.

"Then will you sit by my side?"

Lorraine shrugged, wanting to get him to talk, not ramble. "Maybe I will."

"Ohhh, then lemme think. Elizabeth Seal. Well, she was a girl with big hopes, big dreams, and they was all falling down because she was beginning to wonder if the film would ever get made. There was a whole lot of trouble, folks gettin' drunk and not turnin' up for work, an' if an' when they did they started fighting. Then Juda found out something about Elizabeth, don't know how, but Juda could find out anything. Nobody ever had secrets from the Salina sisters."

"Found out what?"

Fryer chuckled, taking much longer to roll up the joint, as his movements were so slow. "Marie Laveau was a woman of mixed race, and Juda finds out that little Elizabeth Seal has black blood in her veins. Way back obviously, but it was there, like a sleeping cobra. So Juda gets paid a lot of money and she gets everyone together and says they got to stop the threats, stop the curses."

"What do you mean?"

"Hell, they had been laying coffins and conjure balls outside her trailer, beatin' the drums so she couldn't get any rest, making that child's life a nightmare with their chanting and their curses. It was rumored they'd even done some kind of sacrifice so that she'd be unable to walk or talk, or speak the shit-filled lines they was calling the script. And then one night a whole bunch of the motherfuckers took her out to the swamp, saying they was just wanting to show her rituals. Well, they done a lot more."

"Like what?"

Fryer hesitated, taking yet another hit from the bottle, and Lorraine could see from his difficulty in screwing the cap back on that he was getting drunk as well as stoned. He rocked backward and forward for a moment, sucking his teeth.

"She was what they call a zombie, you understand what I am saying? They had scared her so bad she was wild-eyed and stiff, no life inside her. Scared the shit outta me, scared everyone that saw her, 'cause they was supposed to be taking care of her. She was no more than fifteen, sixteen maybe, and it didn't look like she could work no more. And . . . oh yeah, they got this big scene all set up and they was runnin' this way an' that, wonderin' if they should get a doctor in to see her."

"I don't follow."

Fryer licked his paper and rolled up another joint. "Then they brought back the Salina sisters, and paid them even more money. Miss Seal was locked up with Juda for two days. Then Juda got to a meeting, well, all the black people, called us into an old church, and they locked them doors, and Juda stood up on the pulpit and she screams and she goes into a kind of fit, and she tells everyone they done a bad thing, a very bad thing. She says Elizabeth Seal had every right to be Marie Laveau because she was as much black as she was. And she held up her picture, and her voice went real quiet and she says . . ."

Lorraine had to wait as he puffed his joint alight.

"Look on the face of your queen, look on her face and tell me if you don't see the likeness." He began to chortle, curling his legs up again. "I said to myself, I'm gonna have a piece of that beauty. She was so good, so powerful, an' she shut every mouth up, made them get so scared. She says every hex laid at Elizabeth Seal's door is gonna come back doublefold on them. They screamed and hollered, man, they screamed that church down. Like the windows shook from their yelling like crazies themselves."

"Was it true? Was what Juda was saying the truth?"

He turned on her and his face suddenly became angry. "Who knows what is truth and what ain't? Those two sisters was being paid more'n me, more'n any of us, on the condition they got that film moving. I dunno what is true an' what ain't." He sighed. "All I know is that the only scene in the film that's any good is that little girl dancing with the snake. She sure as hell didn't look white, didn't act white, and from then on Juda and her sister stayed in her big fancy trailer until they finished the film.''

Fryer opened his bottle again and drank. His big black eyes were becoming unfocused.

"What do you think happened to Anna Louise Caley?''

He lifted his hands up. "Hell, I don't know, but I'd say something bad. A girl don't disappear around here unless they want to, or something bad took place.''

Lorraine opened her briefcase. "I want to show you something.''

He rubbed himself and leered at her. "I'll show you something if you come and sit by me.''

Lorraine took out the voodoo doll wrapped in a towel.

"I found this at Tilda Brown's, she was a friend of Anna Louise's. Do you know what it means? More important, do you know who would make something like this?''

Fryer stared at the doll nestled in the towel. He sniffed and sat back. "Where you say you got this?''

"Tilda Brown, she committed suicide. This was hidden in her room.''

Again he sniffed, and then covered the doll up. "Mrs. Page, I am not a believer but I don't play with this kind of thing. You get it outta here, and you go with it. Go on, get out, *get out*!'' He sprang from the bed, scaring her, pointing his gnarled finger at her chest. "Take that shit outta my place. I don't believe, Mrs. Page, but that's not to say that I don't get uneasy, understand me? I don't meddle with them, and they leave me alone.''

"No, I don't understand.''

He leered at her. "No, I don't expect you do, no white does. You all try to take it apart, try an' understand, but you never will. Just as black is black and white is white. You want some advice, throw that thing away, burn it because—''

"Because what, Mr. Fryer? Why don't you tell me what this thing is?''

"I'd need a lifetime, honey.''

Lorraine picked up the doll, rewrapping it carefully. "I have only a few more days to try and trace Anna Louise Caley. I need all the help I can get.''

He pointed at the doll. "Somebody is trying to frighten

someone. Whoever gave that to that little girl wanted her to
hurt long and bad, so bad that destroying it would make it
worse. That is one bad, bad thing.''

She snapped her briefcase closed. ''Maybe that's what it
did, frightened a young eighteen-year-old girl into taking her
own life.''

''I seen worse.''

''What could be worse?''

Fryer pulled the poster down from the wall. ''What they
did to Elizabeth Caley, slave to the drums, slave to the
drums.'' He sat down on his bed and picked up his trombone. ''You know, it's all about being a slave. I am a slave
to this instrument, it dominates my life, I am only a whole
man when I am playing. Losing myself, feeling the sounds,
like that little Elizabeth Caley feeling the earth beneath her
feet and dancing herself into a trance until she felt the blood
she had denied flowing like juices, and she could dance. Do
you dance, Mrs. Page?''

''No, no, I don't think so.''

''That's sad. But then you have a sadness to you. I feel
something from you, Mrs. Page, sit by me. Come on, now,
share a drink with me.''

She did, not wanting to, but drawn to him and to the
bottle. He unscrewed the cap, wiped the bottle neck with
his sleeve and passed it to her, no longer being sexual toward her, just kindly. The bourbon hit hard on the back of
her throat, warming her, and she smiled at him as she took
another swig.

''You know when they brought the slaves here, they
dragged them from their roots and their religion by their
chains. They buried their dead in big open graves with cats
and dogs. They were confused and frightened, seeing their
loved ones without food and water to travel to the other
side. They were fearful because they believed that if the
dead did not have food and water for that journey, their
souls would forever walk the earth. And superstition,
brewed with fear, is a powerful weapon.''

He replaced the cap on the bourbon and picked up his
battered trombone.

''You give that thing you brought here to someone who
is not afraid, it means nothing but a bad smell. But if you

give it to someone who believes, it burns the nostrils and it becomes a terrible thing, a curse. Do you understand what I am saying?''

She was trying to follow what he said, wondering if Tilda Brown would have known what it meant to receive such a hideous curse. ''Do you think that Juda or her sister could have made it?''

He stared at her, and she had to look away from his dark, unfathomable eyes. ''No, no, they would never abuse what they believe is a gift from the spirits. They do good work, Mrs. Page, not bad.'' He touched the center of her forehead. ''They have the sight right in there, they can see the past and the future.''

''But you don't believe?'' she said softly.

He closed his eyes, his hands stroking his trombone. ''I have seen them working themselves up into trances, plucking out evil, healing pain. But I never wanted to be a part of it, because I could never be. I'm not like them, my soul is young, my soul lives in my music and I am a happy man. I never wanted all that pain, never could deal with it.''

He pursed his lips and blew two low blasts on his trombone. Then he looked at her with a smile, his gold teeth gleaming in the faint light. ''Find the maker of the doll, Mrs. Page, and you'll have the evil, or stay beside me and we'll make sweet music.''

Lorraine smiled back, unafraid of him, liking him, and he knew it because he laughed.

''That's my evil, I am a ladies' man. I sure do love the ladies, and I can tell you, I have had many, and not one went away unhappy.''

She stood up, laughing with him. ''You sure about that?''

''No, I ain't ever sure about anything but this.'' He held up his trombone. He didn't look up when she walked out, but started to polish the instrument with the edge of his shirt, seeing his grizzled face looking back at himself. He knew he had said too much, but that was always the way with him when he was stoned. He rested back on his pillow, and frowned.

Something scratched at his neck and he slipped his hand beneath the pillow to feel the necklace. He hadn't worn it since the boys had returned it covered in sticky blood. It had unnerved him, scared him a little, and he would never wear it again. But he sure as hell wanted it close when he slept because it could have been his throat those crazy kids had cut open. It had been given to him by Juda. She had loved him then and never wanted any harm to come to the man she cared about. She'd even warned him never to part with it, as it warded off any evil coming his way. So far he'd been lucky, unlike that poor limping son of a bitch.

Lorraine was walking very unsteadily by the time she got back to François, but she had another drink on the way back to the hotel, telling herself she'd sleep it off—once she got some black coffee inside her she'd be fine. She was feeling pretty laid-back now, smiling, but as they got closer to the hotel her mood began to plummet, and she hurled the Coke can out the window, swearing and muttering under her breath. François saw it all in the rearview mirror, saw her run her hands through her hair and lurch from one side of the seat to the other as he took the corners, not even at speed.

"Maybe you shouldn't drink no more, Mrs. Page."

She leaned forward, her face contorting with anger.

"Fuck off, who the fuck you think you are, tellin' me what to do? Just drive the fucking car, that's what you're paid for, you son of a bitch."

"Sure, lady, we're almost there."

He saw her stumble as she walked toward the hotel, saw her stop, smooth down her skirt and put on dark shades. She looked as if she was taking deep breaths before, straight-backed and head held high, she walked into the courtyard and disappeared behind the palms.

Lorraine found Rosie and Rooney sitting under the palms in the hotel courtyard.

"Where the hell were you two?" she snapped.

"We could ask the same of you," Rosie replied angrily.

Lorraine sat down, kicking off her shoes. "Working, that's what I've been doing."

"Well, maybe we have too," Rosie said, prodding Rooney under the table for him to say something.

Lorraine leaned her head in her hands and told them briefly what she had been doing, then stretched her arms above her head, yawning. "Fryer's right, we got to find out who made that doll." She signaled to the waitress. "You want another beer, Bill, or are you drunk enough already?"

Rooney looked away, pissed off by Lorraine, but by no means drunk. Rosie watched Lorraine carefully; she hadn't been sure at first, but now she was, she could smell the drink. Lorraine scanned the terrace from behind her dark glasses, her voice just a little too loud.

"Ruby Corbello is first on my list tomorrow. She was sacked from the Browns' same day as Anna Louise arrived in New Orleans. Maybe, just maybe, she got the diary out of the polar bear, and that diary is very important. It might be all we've got, it might also give us a clue as to who gave her that doll. And we have to find out when she got it. Did you check out that newspaper date, Bill?"

The waitress appeared and Rooney was thankful; he hadn't checked it out, and judging by Lorraine's mood there would have been trouble. She ordered black coffee and a sandwich.

"So, Rosie, you get the Corbello address?"

Lorraine listened and lit a cigarette, her foot tapping on the table leg in mounting anger as Rosie told her what they had done.

"I don't recall telling you to fucking go and see Edith Corbello, or make up some stupid story about wanting a doll made. Jesus Christ, I've never heard anything so dumb! Gonna make it tough for me going there now. Why? What made you do it, Bill? I'd have thought you, of all people, would have known better. You're supposed to be the professional, for Chrissakes."

"You mean like you?" Rosie said quietly.

"What?"

"I can smell it, Lorraine."

Rooney frowned, looking first at Rosie, then at Lorraine.

"I had some liqueur chocolates." Lorraine laughed humorlessly, too loud. She peered over her shades. "You fouled up, Bill."

"Sorry." He shrugged.

"It's not good enough!" Lorraine snapped.

Rosie was getting really uptight. "We waited here for you, and when you didn't show, as we had agreed, and we found out you'd left the Caleys' house, we didn't know what to think. So don't you get uptight with us, it's you that should have come to the hotel and told us what you were doing.''

"Piss off, Rosie, go on, just fuck off, will you? You're getting on my nerves.''

Rosie pushed back her chair.

"I'll do just that, and maybe when you've sobered up we can have a proper conversation, like professionals.'' She marched off. Rooney looked after her, then back at Lorraine.

"She's talking bullshit, so come on, what's the matter, Bill? Lost your tongue as well as your touch?'' Lorraine asked sarcastically.

Rosie was still within earshot and spun around. "Leave him alone," she snapped.

"Oh, you talking for Bill now, are you? Well, tell me, Rosie, did he find out about the newspaper the doll was wrapped in?''

"Shit, I knew there was something," Rooney said uncomfortably, noticing that people at other tables were beginning to look at them.

Lorraine stared at him. "You search Nick's room for the gris-gris?''

Rosie looked at him and then at Lorraine. "We should get her back to her room, Bill—''

"I asked him a fucking question," Lorraine cut in. "Well, did you find it or didn't you?''

"No, no, I didn't.''

Lorraine slapped the table. "Why don't you go up there right now and search? They'll be renting it out any day, they might already have, so ask reception if they found anything.''

Rooney pushed his chair back. "Right, whatever you say, but keep your voice down. Everybody's looking at us.''

Rosie stepped closer to him. "Don't take this crap from her, Bill, she's drunk. Can't you smell it? Look at her!''

Lorraine had now got to her feet, knocking over her chair as she pointed at Rooney. "It is what I say, Billy, and I wish the two of you would stop fucking it up. From now on, please just do what I tell you to.''

Rooney walked away from the table. He seemed depressed and heavy, and Lorraine knew it, but let him go. She hadn't finished, and she couldn't find her shoes. Now she turned on Rosie. "You know, you got to stop playacting at this investigation business. It isn't a game, it's serious!"

"Oh, is it? That why you fucked Robert Caley? That was very professional! Now get yourself together and get up to your room."

"At least I got developments, which is more than I can say for you two, bumbling around like amateurs. You've both just tipped off Edith Corbello."

"But you said Fryer Jones—"

Lorraine slapped the table again, this time with the heel of her shoe.

"Rosie, I don't take everything he said as gospel. He's a stoned old bastard I wouldn't trust as far as I could throw him. What I do take very seriously is that Rooney, as my backup, *just blew it*."

Rosie pursed her lips. Sometimes she really loathed Lorraine, but before she could say anything, the waitress brought the coffee.

"He fucked you yet?" Rosie blushed. "Oh, come on, what's all this? Being coy doesn't suit you, Rosie, and the sneaky little glances that pass between you both, plus the pats and the sniggers, get on my nerves."

"Maybe you're jealous," Rosie snapped, meeting the curious glances of their fellow guests as Lorraine sat down again and reached for the coffeepot.

"Where's my sandwich? I ordered a ham and cheese sandwich."

The waitress tightened her lips and said it would be right there. Lorraine slurped at her coffee.

"I'm jealous, *jealous*? Got to be kiddin', Rosie. But you didn't answer my question. Has he? Can he?" She laughed, adding sugar to her coffee and spilling it down the front of her shirt. Rosie leaned close.

"That is my business, not yours, and you should apologize to him for speaking to him the way you did. In fact, you should take a good hard look at yourself Lorraine, because what you are is a hard-nosed, drunken bitch."

The slap came so fast it made Rosie stumble back. She clenched her fist to give one back but controlled herself. She could hear people murmuring all around her: everyone was staring at them. "Now you'd better apologize to me, because we don't need you."

"No, just the cut of the million bonus that I'm doing all the work for. Don't worry, Rosie, we'll split it three ways, as agreed. That's if we get it."

Rosie couldn't stop herself: she punched Lorraine in the shoulder, having meant to hit her face but missing. Lorraine took the punch and then slowly fell off her chair to the floor. Rosie made no effort to help her get to her feet.

"Yes, *if*. Anyone blowing our chances was you falling for Robert Caley."

Lorraine took hold of the table to help herself up; she was beginning to feel sick.

"But even if we don't get the money, it won't matter to us, because we've got something else going for us, and it's something I doubt you will ever have. We're getting married, Lorraine."

Rosie walked away, leaving Lorraine holding on to the edge of the table. Everything was spinning, blurred and unfocused, and as the waitress returned with her sandwich Lorraine passed out.

Rooney saw Rosie standing by reception and walked over to join her.

"I carried her up to her room—well, me and the bellboy. She's out cold," he told her.

Rosie nodded and passed him a computer printout of their account. "She's been putting it on the bill, look at it. Vodka, bottles of it."

"Shit," Rooney mumbled.

"We're going to have to dry her out, maybe try and find a meeting," Rosie said impatiently, taking her anger toward Lorraine out on Bill. "Why did you let her talk to you that way?"

"Well, in some ways she was right, and, I mean, I knew something was wrong with her."

"I could smell it as soon as she sat down," Rosie fumed.

"Well, I guess we just let her sleep it off and talk to her when she's gotten herself together."

"What if she doesn't get herself together?" Rosie snapped.

Now it was Bill's turn to turn on Rosie. "Then I take over and I mean take over, because I've had just about enough of her crap. I'm not prepared to lose my cut of the one million, even if she is." Before Rosie could apologize, Rooney had walked out, letting the swinging doors into the lobby bang behind him.

Lorraine had been violently sick and now had a headache to end them all. She had soaked a towel and packed it with ice, and was lying flat out on the bed, hardly able to raise her head from the pillow. She sighed, not knowing why she'd been so hurtful, so cruel. She'd make it up to Bill and Rosie tomorrow. Tonight she was too tired.

She tried, too, to digest all that she'd been working on that day: she must find out who made the doll. Find that out, and she'd know who gave it to Tilda Brown. She winced at the noise as the door opened suddenly and Rosie barged in and banged down a tray of sandwiches and a pot of black coffee.

"You are going to sober up," she said, pouring out a cup. "You are going to get in that shower, drink all of this coffee, eat these sandwiches, and you are then going to accompany me to a meeting. I got an address and there's one in an hour's time."

Lorraine began to cry, sniffing and wiping her face. "Leave me alone, I'm not feeling well, it's just something I ate."

"Yeah, liqueur chocolates, you said. Lies won't work, Lorraine, I know you were as drunk as a skunk—in fact, the whole hotel knows. I'm surprised they didn't ask us to leave. Now, *sit up*."

"No."

Rosie hauled Lorraine to her feet and shoved her fully clothed into the shower. Lorraine howled as the jets of ice-cold water hit her, yelling that she would kill Rosie, knife Bill Rooney, twist his testicles off. Her threats became more and more ludicrous, but eventually she stopped trying to fight Rosie off.

Afterward, Rosie helped her into a nightdress and forced

her to finish the coffee and sandwiches, refusing to allow
Lorraine to go to sleep until she had promised that she
would attend a meeting the next day and sworn on the hotel
Bible that she would not touch another drop of alcohol and
that she would call Bill or Rosie if the thought even entered
her head. Lorraine was apologetic now, weeping like a chas-
tised child.

"I didn't mean to do it, Rosie, I swear before God I
didn't. It was just Fryer offered me something at his place,
I thought it was Coke. I give you my word I won't touch
another drink, all I need is sleep, please."

Rosie sighed, cleared up the mess in the room and
checked that there were no more liquor bottles. By the time
she was through, Lorraine was drowsy, and Rosie sat beside
her on the bed for a moment.

"You also got to apologize to Bill, you hear me? He
really liked Nick and he took his death very hard. So first
thing tomorrow you make up with him—me, I'm used to it,
but he isn't. You were downright rude."

"I'm sorry." Lorraine's voice was like a child's.

"Yeah, you should be, with all we got at stake." Rosie
stood up, and Lorraine held out her arms.

"Give me a hug, Rosie, please, I feel so bad about this."

Rosie hugged her, then gave her a warm smile as she
fluffed up her pillows. "You sure test your friends, Lorraine
Page."

"But I'm a lucky lady to have them," Lorraine answered
softly.

Rosie left her, thinking she was sleeping, but sleep
wouldn't come. Eventually Lorraine got up and looked at
her messages—several of them were from Robert Caley.
Part of her wanted to call him because if he asked her to
she would go. It wasn't enough to be hugged by Rosie, by
a friend; she wanted to be really loved by someone—by
Robert Caley. Why could Rosie and Rooney find comfort
with each other when she could find none? But she kept on
making lame excuses why she shouldn't call Robert Caley.

She opened her briefcase, taking out the soiled towel and
opening it to stare at the grotesque doll. Someone had stuck
the photograph of Tilda Brown's face over the plastic doll's
head. Someone had glued blond hair to the cloth body, cov-

ered it in excrement and urine, and then that someone had taken a long thin pin and pierced it right through Tilda Brown's face. That someone had to have access to a photograph. That someone had to know the curse would terrify anyone who believed in spiritual evil and its powers. Lorraine wondered if that person might be Elizabeth Caley, or even her missing daughter, Anna Louise. It might perhaps be Juda Salina or Edith or Ruby Corbello, or even, and she didn't want to accept the possibility, Robert Caley.

The unease remained as she got ready to go to bed. The telephone's ringing made her physically jump, but she didn't answer. When it stopped she called down to reception; the call had been from Robert Caley. She closed her eyes and felt it again, the warm rush of feeling she'd had when he had kissed her again, told her that he was leaving his wife. She was falling in love with him, and it scared her. She couldn't help remembering the pornographic magazine, the Valentine cards she had found in Anna Louise's bedroom, all from Caley using the nickname Polar. Who had taken the diaries, if there were any, from Anna Louise's polar bears? He had said none had ever been found. But he knew their hiding place, so he knew that if Tilda Brown had a diary it would have been hidden in the same place. Round and round in her mind went all her suspicions until she felt like weeping from tiredness.

"Please don't let it be him," she whispered.

CHAPTER

16

Rooney had had to wait for more than an hour as the printers took away the shreds of newspaper wrapped around the voodoo doll. It was almost eight when eventually a small crumpled man with ink stains on his hands and apron emerged from a back room, holding a full sheet.

"You know there is a price for this?"

Rooney nodded. "How much?"

"Well, I've had to go back into the files and double-check the photographs for you—say, fifteen bucks."

Rooney smiled, he'd expected to be asked for a lot more. "Sure, that sounds fair to me."

He took out his wallet and laid out fifteen dollars. The printer pocketed it, and gave a furtive look around; he had, as he'd said, gone through a lot of back issues, but it was on his employer's time.

"Okay, this newspaper issue was out on February fifteenth last year, 'cause of the casino pictures and the—"

Rooney interrupted, taking the sheet. "That's all I wanted to know, thanks."

He stood outside the printer's, folding the single sheet of last year's paper into a small square. The evening was hot and clammy, and he was sweating all over, so he trudged down the street until he saw the streetcar, and stepped up inside. He sat on the bench seat close to the entrance, hoping for a bit of a breeze, but the air was hot and sticky. He ran his finger around his collar, not sure if it was the heat that was getting to him or the fact that he had made up his mind to propose to Rosie.

Shaved and showered, he tapped on her door. She opened it, wearing a big bath towel around her plump body.

"How did it go?"

"Well, it was the date we all wanted, Feb. fifteenth last year. Can I come in?"

"Sure." She stepped aside, drawing up her towel. "I just had a shower."

He sat on the edge of one of the many beds in her room, waiting as she dressed in the bathroom. He told himself he was a lonely old fool, and tried to make himself back out of what he wanted to ask Rosie.

"You divorced?" he blurted out as she returned.

She looked surprised. "Yes, I told you, years ago. Why?"

He took a deep breath. "No reason," he said grumpily, unfolding the newspaper printout and passing it to her.

"That's a lie, there is a reason." She was looking at the double-folded center piece. "What?"

"You want to get hitched to me, Rosie?"

"You bet I do."

"What?"

She sat next to him and took his big hand. "I said yes, I do . . ."

"Shit, you do?"

"Yes . . . you worried about that?"

"Hell no, that's what I wanted you to say."

There was a moment of silence and they slowly looked into each other's face.

"So, we're engaged?" she asked coyly.

"Yeah, I guess we are," he said flatly. It had all gone as he had hoped, but a fraction too fast.

"We'd better tell Lorraine," Rosie said, and he hesitated.

"Maybe don't rush it, wait until we both get used to the idea, okay?"

She nodded, smiling. "I meant about the newspaper article, Bill!"

Lorraine was deeply asleep when Rooney called to tell her the newspaper date coincided with the day Anna Louise had arrived in New Orleans. She refused to go and dine with them, saying she needed a good night's rest. It was after nine and she couldn't get back to sleep for a long time. She thought about going to see Robert Caley but decided against it. Instead she tossed and turned, pushing him from her mind, going over what had happened during the day—with the exception of her lapse back into drunkenness.

She got up, feeling restless, and began to pace the room. She came to the conclusion that only one person could have hated Tilda Brown enough, and that person was Anna Louise Caley. But how in the hell could she prove it without either of them being alive? And Tilda Brown's suicide must not be given priority over tracing Anna Louise, unless they were linked. And Lorraine intuitively knew that they were . . . but how?

She wanted a drink and searched around the room for any bottle that Rosie might have overlooked, still convincing herself that she was in control, and that the problem had been caused by the bourbon at Fryer's bar, not the diluted vodka she had been drinking all day. She knew, though, that she was going to have to be a lot smarter, as Rosie and Rooney would be watching her every move. She couldn't call down to reception for a bottle, as she was sure that Rosie had found out about that, perhaps had even warned them not to send anything up to her room, and she didn't have the energy to leave it.

She didn't realize that energy had nothing to do with it; but she was moving into another phase of the addiction— that of fear. She was afraid of leaving the hotel room, afraid of facing Rosie and Rooney, and her confidence in her ability to analyze the case was wavering badly. The more she sorted through her notes, running over details, the less confident she became, not knowing what the next move should be. It was later, when the sweats began, that Lorraine knew she needed something to get her back on her feet. She called down to ask the receptionist to see if her driver, François, was outside the hotel, and if so, to have him directed to her room.

It was over half an hour before François was tracked down, and by the time he had seen Lorraine, agreed to buy her a bottle of vodka and brought it back to her, more than an hour had passed. She called down then to reception for a six-pack of Coke, assembling everything she needed, but didn't open the bottle immediately. Just knowing it was there was enough: she'd be all right now.

But still sleep eluded her as she continued to turn the case over in her mind for hours, and she eventually fell asleep planning to see Ruby Corbello first thing next day. In the morning, she told herself, everything would be all right again.

Robert Caley left the city that night and drove up the coast to a casino in Gulfport, Mississippi, where he and Dulay had often played in the private rooms. High-stakes gamblers rarely bothered with the riverboat casinos in New Orleans, but once the casino in which he would now be a partner was open, all that would change. A lot of things were going to change for him now. By nine-thirty he had lost more than ten thousand dollars, but that didn't matter now: he was going to be rich. There was no limit to demand for gambling, and he knew he would never have to worry about money again. Dulay came in after ten o'clock, and it felt good to see him smile warmly, falsely, a cigar clamped in his mouth. Even Dulay had not succeeded in cutting him out in the cold because the leases that had been such a liability had turned out to be his salvation.

"Hey, Robert, how are you doing?"

Caley smiled. "Fine, I'm doing fine."

"Well, looks like we're both in the money . . . after the announcement, I mean." Even Dulay's polished manner betrayed a trace of awkwardness. "We're all on the same side now—the way it ought to be, hey Robert?"

Caley smiled; the man was a snake. There was no reason why the Doubloons group should have been cut in on the deal, but, clearly, pushing the governor's golf cart was a useful skill. Still, it felt good to come out a winner, and he was sure, very sure, that at long last he had played with a full deck.

"Yes, Lloyd," he said with equally false graciousness. "It seems like we are. You'll excuse me now, I was just on my way out."

He checked his watch, wondering if Lorraine had called. He wanted to see her, wanted her to know and to celebrate with him. He drove back to New Orleans, thinking of the new world they would share. He wanted her tonight, because it was all going to be different now—he was dependent on no one, he was free. He had been trapped for years, caught in Elizabeth Caley's secret nightmares, but that was over. Besides, they were nightmares he had never understood or cared to find out about.

Caley called Lorraine but was told she wasn't taking any calls, so he left a message to say he had returned to his hotel and had arranged for her usual suite to be waiting. He called again at midnight, but the message was the same—Mrs. Page was not to be disturbed. He let the receiver fall back onto the cradle, confused. He would wait for her to come to him, he would make no further calls.

Early the following morning, before Rosie and Rooney had even come down to breakfast, Lorraine had left the hotel. She had got herself dressed and out with just a couple of shots of vodka and half a pot of coffee: she'd been shaking badly and had a hell of a hangover, but at least she was able to get out of the room. She sat in the parked car, looking out of the window at the Corbellos' house.

"Wait here, François."

She knocked three times before the door was opened.

"Hi, I'm looking for Ruby Corbello."

The young girl was wearing a barely decent slip dress and rubber flip-flops.

"You from the festival organization?"

"No, but I need to speak to her, and if necessary I can pay." Lorraine took out a twenty-dollar bill.

"She's getting her picture took for a magazine this afternoon. She's not seeing nobody unless it's press."

"I'm a reporter," Lorraine lied.

"She's in the back room."

The girl skidded past Lorraine, snatching the bill, leaving the door wide open.

"Ruby? Ruby?" Lorraine called out.

"Who wants her?" came a high-pitched voice.

"I'm from the Mardi Gras press organization," Lorraine called.

Ruby Corbello had a sheet wrapped around her when she

came slowly down the narrow staircase. She was stunningly beautiful.

"Who are you?"

"My name is Lorraine Page, can I speak to you?"

Ruby glided down the last steps and hung on to the newel post, suddenly kittenish.

"I don't want mah picture took until I got makeup on."

Lorraine looked at the room off the hallway. "Can we talk?"

Ruby nodded, gathering the sheet around herself. "Sure, but no photographs until I'm wearing my gown."

She indicated the old worn sofa, and posed beside it. The torn sheet could have been draped by Yves Saint Laurent; anything on this girl would have looked classy.

Lorraine opened her notebook. "You used to work for Mr. and Mrs. Brown as their maid?"

"Uh-huh, yes I did, but I don't no more, that is all behind me now."

Lorraine smiled. "Tell me about Tilda Brown."

"Miss Brown?" Ruby asked, irritated.

"Why did you leave the Browns' employment, Ruby?"

Ruby's perfect face puckered. "Why you wanna know? They been saying things about me, huh?"

Lorraine sighed. "Well, in a way, and if I am to do this profile of you for the newspapers—"

"I didn't get fired or nothin' like that, I left. I walked out because that young woman was crazy and I wanted me a proper career."

"You mean Tilda?"

"Uh-huh, she was always jabberin' at me and she made my life a misery, because she believed she was so high-and-mighty. But she wasn't that high or that mighty. I know that, I know all about Miss Tilda Brown."

"Do you know she committed suicide?"

"Uh-huh, I know."

"Why do you think she killed herself?"

Ruby shrugged, and perched on the edge of a chair. "I don't know."

"Do you know Anna Louise Caley?"

"Mmm, I met her, and they was as alike as two peas in a pod, she was another Miss High-and-Mighty."

"Did she come here?"

Ruby threw back her pretty head and laughed. "Lordy, no, those white girls wouldn't dare come here."

"Did Mrs. Caley come here?"

Ruby drew back. "What? You joking me? The famous Elizabeth Caley come here? No way, ma'am."

Lorraine chewed her lip, wondering how she should play it. Ruby tossed her thick hair over her shoulder, as if ready for a movie camera.

"I was told you were fired from the Browns' residence for stealing."

"*What?*" She jumped up and danced around, asking over and over who had said that about her. Then she stood in front of Lorraine and pushed her face close. "Who dare say that about me?"

"I can't tell you, Ruby, but I have to ask everything because if we are going to put you on the front page of the newspaper, we have to be sure that there can be no repercussions. You are one of the queens in this year's Mardi Gras, and the whole of America will be watching."

Ruby slumped into a chair. "I done nothing wrong, nothing at all, and it was by accident anyway 'cause she was cheekin' me."

"What was?"

"That I found it."

"Found what?"

"Tilda's diary. It was in this silly toy she had on her pillow, you know, a bear. I felt something inside it, so I looked."

Lorraine felt her knees tremble as she leaned forward. "You have Tilda Brown's diary?"

"Hell no, I don't have it."

"But you did."

Ruby nodded, sucking at the end of the sheet. "She screamed at me and accused me of a whole lot of things, like her jewelry was missing and I never took nothing, I swear on the holy saints I never stole nothing, but her parents just told me to go. I got angry and I went up to her room, I didn't mean to steal nothing, just mess it up maybe, and then I found the diary. I was gonna give it back."

"When was this exactly, Ruby?"

"Day she come back home."

Lorraine took a deep breath. "You were fired on the day Tilda came home, that would be February . . ."

"Fourteenth, Saint Valentine's Day. Yeah, she fired me day she got back. An' I remember it was that day because I had so many hearts sent to me and even Errol Bagley sent me a little posy of flowers, an' I said to her that I was going anyways. I believe she was jealous of me, an' all my cards an' my posy of flowers because she didn't get nothing at all."

"Ruby, are you sure it was the day before Anna Louise arrived in New Orleans?"

"I don't know when *she* came—all I know is I wasn't working for Mr. and Mrs. Brown no more. They give me a week's salary! One week! They should've given me a month's."

Lorraine asked Ruby how long Tilda had owned the bear, but she couldn't recall exactly, only that it had been a while. When she asked what Ruby had done with the diary, she became evasive, flopping back and sprawling in the chair, chewing at a corner of the sheet. She wouldn't look at Lorraine.

"Did you read it, Ruby?"

"Sure, I did, most of it anyways."

"What did you do with it?" Lorraine asked again.

Ruby slunk lower in the chair. "It wasn't nothing bad, nothing illegal, and we hadda put a down payment on my dress for the ceremony. My gown is costing almost one thousand dollars, you should make a note of that."

Lorraine scribbled in her notebook, worried that she was pushing too fast for information, so she asked a few questions about the style and cut of the gown, and gradually Ruby became more eager to talk.

"It's blue handloom silk and it's got gold stitching all over it. I'd show you, only it's at the dressmaker's still."

Lorraine smiled encouragingly, feigning interest. "It sounds as if it's going to be magnificent, Ruby."

"Yes, yes, it is, and, and I got shoes to match!"

"Can I see the diary?"

Ruby was already floating around the room, the bedsheet

trailing. "Oh, goodness me, why you keep asking me about that thing? I don't have it."

"Who has it, Ruby?"

Ruby stared from the window, examining the fresh lacquer of her nails for smears. "I don't know about that, don't know nothing at all. Why you asking me about that diary? He said no one would ever know, so who been talkin' to you?"

Lorraine's blood went cold, because she knew who Ruby was talking about. "How much did Robert Caley pay you for it?"

"Two hundred dollars," Ruby said quietly.

"Do you remember when he gave you this money?"

Ruby nodded, and then sighed. "Next day, I went to his hotel. He had just arrived at the hotel and was going for a swim. Be the day after I was fired, I guess."

Lorraine took a deep breath. "Was it last year, February fifteenth?"

Ruby nodded.

"How did Mr. Caley know you had the diary?"

She pursed her lips and stared blankly.

"Did you know Anna Louise disappeared the same night?"

Ruby nodded. "He told me not to tell anyone I called him, and I didn't."

"You called him at the hotel?"

"Sure, yeah. Well, not exactly. There's a bellboy there I know, Errol, he's got this crush on me and he sent me the posy of flowers I just told you about. Anyways, I asked him to give Mr. Caley a message, that I was outside waitin' and needed to speak to him on something important."

"What time was this, Ruby?"

"Oh, 'bout six. See, I knew they were coming. Miss Tilda was supposed to travel with them but she came back a day early."

Lorraine's head throbbed trying to keep Ruby on track; trying to assimilate it all and piece it together was draining. She took a deep breath and smiled again at Ruby, who was growing bored by now.

"Why would he pay you so much for Tilda Brown's diary?"

Ruby yawned, and stretched her arms above her head. "I guess he didn't want his wife to find out."

"About what?"

Ruby giggled. "Him and that Miss High-and-Mighty was screwing. Mr. Robert Caley was banging Miss Tilda Brown, that's what!" She put her hands over her mouth and shrieked with laughter like a little girl. She thought it was so damned funny.

Lorraine sat with her head resting against the seat of the car. François looked at her, presuming Lorraine had been at Edith Corbello's house for a reading.

"Love not going smooth, huh?"

"No, François, not smooth at all. Can you stop at the next liquor store?"

As they drove off, Edith Corbello trudged past with two big plastic carrier bags full of groceries. She'd been out shopping to get supper in for Juda and half expected to see her when she went into the house.

"Ruby, is Juda here yet? Ruby?"

Ruby's head appeared over the broken banister rail. "If she was here, Mama, she'd tell you herself."

"She didn't call or nothing?" Edith asked as she trudged into the kitchen and dumped down her heavy bags.

"No, she didn't call, but I just had a long interview with the lady from the noospapers, they're doin' a profile of me for the front page."

Edith turned as Ruby sauntered in and posed in the doorway. "You see a reporter half naked, girl?"

Ruby rolled her eyes to the ceiling.

Edith sighed and began unloading the groceries. "If that's the clean sheet for Aunt Juda's bed, get it off and make up Jesse's room like I told you! Go on, get up those stairs."

Ruby sauntered out as Edith continued stocking up the old humming fridge. She was hot and exhausted, and one look around the dirty kitchen made her want to weep. She was going to have to spend hours cleaning up the house. Juda was real particular, and as she was paying for most of their keep, Edith always had to get everything nice and tidy. But it was becoming such an effort. What with trying to control her boys, and Ruby and Sugar May never helping out, the house was falling down around their ears.

Ruby walked in just as her mother's head rested on her bosom as she fell asleep. She banged the table, making Edith's head shoot upward with shock.

"I got these from under Jesse's pillow, Mama, he's been thievin' again. It's somebody's wallet, drivin' license and—"

Edith snatched the leather wallet and flipped it open.

"If it had any money in it, it's empty now," Ruby said.

Edith saw the old worn ID with Nick Bartello's address, and thudded to the back door, kicking it open.

Jesse was sprawled in an old moth-eaten hammock, writing on his arm cast with a felt-tip pen. He hit the ground hard when Edith kicked him out of the hammock.

"You get your butt in that kitchen right now, an' bring your no-good brother with you."

"Why? What I done, Mama? I just been sleepin', you near broke my other arm, for Chrissakes."

Edith waved the stolen wallet under his nose. "I warned the pair of you not to do no more stealin', an' so you'd better get in that kitchen or I'll call the cops."

"I found it," Jesse said, backing away.

"Oh, did you? Then you won't mind me callin' up the police then, an' sayin' so, right? Right?" She boxed his ears and he ran like a scalded cat, shouting for his brother.

Ruby was furious, standing with her hands on her hips. "They get into trouble, Mama, and then it's gonna get in the papers and with me having my big day it's just not fair. They're gonna spoil everything."

Edith turned on Ruby, wagging her finger. "Nobody is gonna do anythin' to ruin your crowning, Ruby Corbello."

"Only maybe herself," Fryer said as he sauntered through the back gate and stood there, squinting at Edith.

Ruby shrieked. "I never done nothing, Fryer Jones, an' you're a fine one to talk, letting Sugar May drink in that bar of yours an' she just a kid. Next thing she'll be strippin' off like them whores you got working for you."

"Get your butt inside!" Edith stormed, shouting for her to finish cleaning up the bedroom for Juda. A very disgruntled Ruby slammed into the house. Edith sat heavily on the steps outside the back door and stared at the old wallet.

"They're out of control, Fryer, I get tired out just waking up in the morning these days."

Fryer leaned on the rail, looking down into Edith's face. He reached for the wallet and flicked it open. "This is bigger trouble than you ever had, Edith. Your boys killed this guy."

"No, no, they wouldn't do that!" she said firmly.

Fryer squashed in beside her and put his arm around her shoulders. "They did, Edith, they were high and shooting their mouths off down in my bar, and Jesse had a gun. They get up to all kinds of things when you're sleeping, but we can take care of it. You're gonna let me handle it my way."

Edith nodded. Fryer helped her to her feet and they went into the kitchen. Ruby was flinging dirty dishes into the sink.

Fryer opened a beer sitting at the rickety table. "We burn that wallet for starters. As far as I know, nobody saw them do it an' the police don't know nothin'. I'll say they was in my bar all night if they come askin'. They already had one good thrashin' from me, now I'd better give them another."

Edith nodded as Fryer eased his old leather belt from his trousers. Ruby ran the tepid water into the sink. The pipes gurgled and clanked as she halfheartedly rinsed the dirty dishes, trying not to chip the varnish on her nails. Edith seemed weighed down by it all, fanning herself with an old newspaper and staring out of the window.

"They're comin' through the back gate now," she said flatly.

Fryer fingered the beer-bottle neck. "There's a private investigator going around askin' all kinds of questions, she been here?" Edith shook her head. "Well, you be warned about her, she's been hired by the Caleys to find that girl of theirs. Tall blond woman, kind of fancy-looking, with a scar down her cheek."

Ruby dropped a plate, it smashed to the floor. Fryer turned a baleful look on his niece. "You know anythin' about this woman, Ruby, called Lorraine, Mrs. Lorraine Page?"

Ruby held on to the sink. "No, I not seen her."

Edith picked up the broken plate and tossed it into the garbage pile as the two boys appeared in the doorway.

"Right, then, Edith, and you, Ruby, get out the kitchen."

• • •

Ruby was scared, tucking in the sheet on the small bed, listening to the thrashing being given to her brothers, as they howled like dogs. It went on for at least fifteen minutes.

Edith had begun to vacuum with an old upright machine that billowed more dust out of its packed bag than it sucked up, but it covered the screams of her boys.

The brothers were wiping their eyes with their shirtsleeves as Fryer eased back his old belt into his trousers.

"I'll keep my mouth shut, but you got to pay me, that's the bargain, boys. As from now, you work for me. You clean up my bar and you do like I tell you to or I will take this to the police." Fryer held up Nick Bartello's wallet. "First you start with your own kitchen, I want this sparkling and swept, not a thing out of place, you hearing me?"

They nodded their heads like glum children.

"From now on you both working for me until I say you're free to go find employment somewhere else."

They began to carry out the garbage as Fryer opened another bottle of beer. He'd burn the wallet but he wouldn't tell the boys.

Sugar May appeared with a carton of chocolate milk, teetering on a pair of high-heeled silver shoes. She sniggered as her brothers began getting out the brushes and mops and fetching buckets.

"What you find so funny, Sugar May?" Fryer asked.

Sugar May giggled. "I heard the whoopin' and hollerin' like squealin' pigs."

"You did, did you? And where you been this morning?"

Sugar May shrugged. "Oh, walkin' around."

Fryer looked at her shoes. "Uh-huh, you been strolling around in them platform soles, have you?"

She flicked her hips and drained her chocolate milk, sucking on it loudly before she tossed the carton toward where the rubbish bags had been.

"Lemme see those new shoes of yours, Sugar May." Fryer held out his hands, and Sugar May balanced on one foot and swung the other up into his crotch. "You steal these, Sugar?"

"I did not, I bought them."

"Where d'you get the money to buy leather shoes of this quality?"

"I got it from a reporter lady that came to see Ruby—she gave me twenty bucks, and that's God's own truth."

Fryer watched as the skinny girl sashayed to the door, the shoes making her feet look ridiculously large.

"When did this reporter lady come here?"

"This morning. You ask Ruby, I'm not lyin'."

Fryer drained his beer and pointed the bottle toward Sugar May. "You go help your mama clean up the house, you got company coming, your Aunty Juda's arriving for supper."

"I don't make any mess, so why should I?" she said, pouting in the doorway.

Fryer stared at her, and then wagged his finger. "Because I am telling you, an' if you don't you'll get just as bad a thrashing as your brothers. You want that?"

She was about to get lippy with him, but something about his mood made her change her mind and she teetered back to the sink to finish what Ruby had begun.

Fryer passed Edith, now vacuuming in the hallway. "Ruby upstairs?" She nodded. "No need to worry yourself about those boys of yours, Edith, they'll behave well for a while." He moved slowly up the stairs, then leaned over the banister rail and looked down at her big, sweating body. Hard to believe she, like her sister Juda, had been as beautiful as Ruby.

"Growing old is a tough business, right, Edith?"

"Uh-huh, sure is when you got two boys unemployed. Ruby don't give me nothing much."

"But you're still working, aren't you?"

"Sure, but you know, Fryer, half the poor souls that come here ain't got a pot to piss in. They all as hard up as we are."

Fryer wasn't hard up, he had money, just hated to part with it, but he dug into his old torn jeans. "Edith, go get some nice fresh flowers for Juda and maybe a new dress for yourself." He tossed a thick wad of money down the stairs, which landed in the hall, and Edith switched off the vacuum cleaner.

"You're a good man, Fryer."

He continued up the stairs. "No, I'm not, Edith, I never was and I never will be, but I ain't no sucker either."

Ruby was halfheartedly clearing junk off the dressing table, taking the opportunity to stare at her own reflection. She glared when Fryer walked in, closing the door behind him and slipping the bolt across.

"Don't go sitting on the bed, I just made it," she said sullenly. Fryer sat squarely in the center, and never took his eyes off her pretty, angry face.

"You had a visit this morning, Ruby. Woman said she was a reporter, is that true?"

"Uh-huh, gonna put me in the papers."

"Well, you might get into the papers, Ruby, but not the way you think you're gonna be in them. Be a big picture of you being arrested, maybe in handcuffs."

Ruby was about to snap back at him, but she didn't. She wasn't afraid of Fryer Jones the way her brothers were; he was nothing but a dirty old lecher who had pawed her since she was a little tot.

"So, Ruby, you want to tell me how much you were paid for that doll you made?"

Ruby's mouth fell open. "I never made nothing."

Fryer smiled, resting back on his elbows on the clean white pillow. "Yes, you did, child, but you had better tell me who you made it for, not that I don't already know."

"If you know, why you askin'?"

He sat up and now his face was angry. "Because you played with fire, honey child, and you might have to pay for it. You tell me, and from the beginning, just what you been up to, Ruby Corbello, or do you want me to beat it out of you?"

"You lay one finger on me and I'll make you regret it."

He couldn't help laughing. She was so beautiful when she was angry, she turned him on just looking at her. She reminded him of Juda, that same fire in her loins, those same wondrous snake-colored eyes. He turned away from her, and sighed, but he got up fast when she tried to get out of the room. He dragged her back to the bed by her hair, throwing her down hard, and he leaned over her.

"You got death on your hands, Ruby."

She looked up into his face, unafraid. She began to un-
button her cheap white cotton blouse, licking her sweet full
lips.

"Want to play with me, Fryer?"

He placed his hand over her throat and pressed hard, making her gasp. "No, Ruby, I don't want to play, I'm here to
save your soul, so you tell Fryer what you've been up to!
And if you lie, then I'll squeeze the breath out of you."

Ruby rolled away onto her side, and he waited. She didn't
seem to care or worry about his threats, twisting a strand of
her thick hair into curls around and around her long slim
fingers.

"That Tilda Brown accused me of prying into her private
things when I done nothing but work like a slave for her
and her family. She had no respect for me and I told her
off, told her she was being high-and-mighty to the wrong
person. She said in that high voice of hers, 'Oh, am I? Well,
you just got yourself fired, Miss Ruby Corbello.' "

Fryer sat with his head slightly bowed, listening to her
soft voice rise and fall like music. He felt her body roll over
and move closer to him, her fingers no longer twisting her
curls but gently stroking his back. She told him, almost play-
fully, that when Tilda Brown's parents had taken their
daughter's side and asked her to leave she got angry and
went up into Tilda's bedroom. She hadn't planned to steal
anything, she had intended to piss over her nice frilly white
clothes. She giggled at the thought. But then she had found
Tilda's diary.

Fryer listened in astonishment as Ruby told him how she
had read the diary and knew she had something worth
money, so she had contacted Errol at the Caleys' hotel and
asked to have a meeting with Robert Caley in private. She
sighed, saying she now realized she could have asked for so
much more money, but at the time she had thought two
hundred dollars was a good price.

"I should have asked for thousands. I was dumb. He paid
me right there, told me never to say one word of this to
anyone, never to tell anyone I had a meeting with him, and
he wouldn't ever mention it to nobody."

Fryer still felt her fingers smoothing his back, making him
stretch upward, and she giggled.

"Go on, Ruby."

She explained that she had gone to the dressmaker's and asked for gold stitching on the dress, but the dressmaker had said that with just two hundred dollars they could only do the front of her bodice. "I wanted gold all over, Fryer. I wanted to shine like I was the sun."

She rolled away from him and he turned to face her. "Anyways, Errol had given me this cute little posy for Valentine's Day, so I went back to the hotel to thank him, and we were standing in the courtyard when Anna Louise Caley called down to me. She wanted me to see her in her room, said it was urgent."

She'd had a moment of worry in case she saw Robert Caley, having just given him Tilda's diary. So Errol had sneaked her in through the staff entrance and she had gone to Anna Louise's bedroom.

"I made a mistake, Fryer. You see, I thought maybe she'd seen the diary somehow and I started saying I had nothing to do with it, just like I promised Mr. Caley. But she got all crazy, Fryer, you ain't never seen anyone go so angry in your whole life. She was spittin' anger and asked over and over what was in it, and so I told her."

He gently touched her cheek with the back of his gnarled hand. "Go on, honey, then what did you do?"

She sucked on one of his fingers and smiled. "She wanted me to make a voodoo doll, she gave me a photograph and a little envelope with some of Tilda's hair, skin and blood. But I don't know, they was just funny little black bits and pieces."

Fryer could feel his heart thudding as her singsong voice described how she had come back home and sat stitching and making up the doll. She giggled like a child when she told him she had crapped and pissed all over it before wrapping it up in newspaper and tying it with string.

"She give me another three hundred dollars, Fryer, an' I saved it all up. That's what I been usin' for my gown, now I got gold all over the skirt."

"How did you get the doll to her?"

Ruby smiled, describing how Anna Louise had lowered some string and she had tied the doll to it and then Anna Louise had pulled the string over her balcony at the hotel.

Ruby had then gone home and never thought any more about it.

Fryer's head ached, and he moved away from the bed. When he saw her reflection in the dressing-table mirror, she was leaning up on one elbow, her miniskirt eased up around her crotch, her blouse half open and her legs spread wide.

"You must never tell this to another soul, Ruby. You hearing me?"

She cocked her head to one side. "I never told anyone but you, Fryer, I'm not stupid. But you know something kind of strange?"

"What?"

Ruby swung her legs from the bed and bowed her head. "Well, Anna Louise was full of hatred, she was all deep down angry. She said she wanted Tilda Brown to hurt bad, to cause her pain. When I was making up the doll, I got one of the pins from my dressmaker and I looked at this doll, and I closed my eyes and I let my fingers feel the little head and then I stuck that pin in hard. As it went in, I said, 'This'll hurt her bad.' I wanted to hurt her too for being so mean to me. Getting me fired like she did. So I did an extra twist just for me."

Fryer watched as the young girl lifted her head. As her hair parted from her face her eyes glittered, and he got the feeling he was looking into the eyes of a dangerous snake.

She whispered, smiling, "And then she hanged herself. Now, ain't that funny?"

Fryer walked into the kitchen, where the boys were now scrubbing the floor and Edith was frying up a pan of chicken. It all looked so ordinary, so domestic, so innocent.

"I'm going back to my bar now, Edith. You give Juda my regards."

"I surely will, Fryer, and Sugar May's out buying a nice bunch of fresh, sweet-smelling flowers for her room."

"That's good."

Edith wiped her hands on her apron. "You gonna come to the ball with us, Fryer? It's gonna be something special, and Ruby is gonna look like a dream when they crown her."

He nodded, knowing she would, and knowing just how much that dream had cost made him uneasy. He had always felt uneasy around the sisters when they were younger. All

their potions and their visions, all the trail of people coming
to them for guidance, weeping and wailing, treating them as
if they were royalty, and in a way they had been. Now Ruby
was grown, and contrary to what Edith and Juda believed,
that their powers had stopped with them, he knew they
hadn't. The Marie Laveau legacy would live on. Upstairs in
that tiny bedroom was proof, and it unsettled him, just as it
always had.

"You watch over Ruby, Edith. Maybe you and Juda sit
down and talk to her, make sure she don't abuse what God
given her. You make sure of that now."

Edith frowned, not fully understanding his concern.
"She's just a pretty girl, Fryer. . . . Fryer, why you actin'
this way?"

"I'm not actin' any way, Edith honey, just watch over
that child. Maybe it's time she learned to have some of your
big heart."

He had gone before she could ask him any more questions, and she went back to cooking the chicken, the beads
of perspiration rolling off her big, round face. Someone
rapped on the back door, and she banged down the slatted
spoon and crossed to the door.

The woman had a small child in her arms. She looked up
at Edith, her face strained. "Please, Mrs. Corbello, my youngest is so sick, it's some kind of fever."

Edith ushered the frightened woman into her altar room.
She was about to close the door when she hesitated and
called up the stairs, "Ruby honey, will you come on down
to me now?"

Ruby peered over the banisters. "I'm busy fixin' mah
hair, Mama."

"Well, you do that later. I want you down here with me."

Ruby blinked; her mama had never asked her to come
into the back parlor before.

"You want me in there with you?" Ruby said hesitantly.

"Uh-huh, come on, we got a sick child in here." Edith's
tone of voice was not going to take no for an answer.

Ruby came down the stairs, buttoning up her blouse and
straightening her skirt, a little frightened.

Edith was sitting behind her table, and the woman was
weeping, rocking the sick baby in her arms.

"How long has he not been feeding from your breast?"

"Days, Mrs. Corbello. He just gone all quiet on me and vomitin' up all night. Now he just lies still. I got him a bottle to try and feed him, but he won't take it."

Ruby watched as Edith took the child and unwrapped his blanket and eased off his clothes while the mother wept, rocking backward and forward in her chair. Edith beckoned Ruby to her side.

"Hold him up real gentle, Ruby, lay him flat on his blanket."

Edith walked out of the room and hurried into the kitchen. She put a pan of milk on the stove and examined the bottle, sniffing at it, then she boiled up a big pan of hot water to sterilize the bottle and the nipple. She turned as Ruby walked in, holding the child in her arms, with just the blanket around him.

"Mama, this little one's been bruised bad, all down his belly and his back."

"I know, we got to talk to her easy, see what she says. We'll use some herbs and oils on his hurt body and keep him cool. I'll need an iced cloth and fresh water."

"He should go to a doctor, Mama."

Edith busied herself at the stove, testing the milk.

"She got no money for a doctor and she scared what she's done to the child. She'd be arrested if a doctor saw that, that's why she's come to me. So do as I tell you, Ruby."

Edith talked quietly to the weeping woman as Ruby tended the baby. He was still listless, but the soothing creams lowered his temperature. The mother eventually admitted she had hit the child after days of sleepless nights when she could no longer cope with his crying. Edith examined her breasts and then told her that as she was dry of milk her child was crying for sustenance, and they must begin to encourage the baby to suckle from the bottle. She never admonished the woman, but was gentle and understanding throughout.

Ruby held the bottle to the baby's lips as the woman held on to Edith's hand and watched as her mama said she would ease her mind so she would be able to cope with her child. Her big hands massaged the woman's head and shoulders until her eyes drooped, and then she worked on her neck and back, a rough, hard massage. She then sipped from a cup of liquor, and Ruby's mouth dropped open as Edith hissed out the water in a spray, covering the woman's face and head. She drank and hissed the liquid three times before leading the woman to the cot in the corner of the room and helping her to lie down. She was in a deep sleep almost as soon as her head rested against the pillow.

Ruby looked down at the child. She said nothing, but Edith saw her gaze deep into the child's eyes—no trace now of the sneering teenager in her manner, but a quiet intensity. The child's eyes opened and he looked back at Ruby, not listless now, drinking in her eyes. Then suddenly his lips puckered and he began to suck from the bottle in Ruby's hand.

Ruby looked up at her mother as she felt the child's pulse, and it was as if this was the first time in many years she had really seen her—not overweight and irritating, but almost regal, someone to be admired, and it made Ruby feel humble and ashamed. She couldn't stop the tears filling her eyes. Edith kissed the top of her daughter's head and caught the tear that trickled down her cheek on her finger. For a second it was a shining clear crystal.

"They don't come for tears, Ruby, just your love and a little of your strength. Mine's fading now, but . . ."

"I'm strong, Mama, I'm strong." Even Ruby's voice had changed; it seemed quieter, more melodious.

Edith nodded. "I know you are, Ruby. You purify your heart, because maybe you are stronger than you know."

Lorraine was silent on the drive to Elizabeth Caley's home. François had tried to make conversation, but, receiving no reply, fell silent, watching her through the rearview mirror. She clutched a bottle inside a brown paper bag. He'd seen her go to open it on two occasions, and then stop. She acted like a woman who had just got bad news. She had, and it took all her self-control not to go and confront Robert Caley there and then, but even more not to take a drink. She had to find further proof of Robert Caley's guilt. Yet again, he was their number one suspect, and this time she would not allow herself to be sidestepped by her emotions. She wanted to nail him.

• • •

Lorraine stood in the hall at Elizabeth Caley's mansion. Juda Salina came slowly down the sweeping staircase. She was as tired out as her sister had been.

"Well, she almost did it for real this time. They been an' pumped it all out of her, and now she's sleeping like a baby."

Lorraine waited until Juda reached the bottom step. "It'd be a pity if your golden goose died, wouldn't it?" she said sarcastically.

Juda gave her a scathing look. "I earned every cent I ever made from her, Mrs. Page—believe me, I earned it."

Missy brought them some tea in the double parlor and then left them. Juda sipped her tea; she seemed truly exhausted and her thick makeup had run on her big, round face.

"I never thought I'd be seeing you again."

"Why?" Lorraine asked.

"No reason," Juda said, and then smiled to herself. "Powers dimming, get confused and too tired nowadays. Anyone close to you with the initial L?"

"No."

"That's good. I had a bad premonition about someone, I thought maybe it was you."

Lorraine shrugged. "Well, as you can see, Mrs. Salina, I am fine. Where is Robert Caley?"

"I dunno, maybe at his hotel, maybe not. I left messages but he never came here, so I guess he really don't care anymore."

"About Elizabeth?"

"Uh-huh, she thought maybe he'd come, you know, if I said she was in a real bad way, but I guess she done it once too often." Juda clasped the arms of her chair. "You know, Mrs. Page, it may be hard to believe, but Mrs. Caley is one sweet woman. Just, she got demons inside her. I've tried to help her for twenty years but they get so strong she just goes crazy and sometimes she frightens even me. Maybe she should let out who she really is, but she won't, she keeps it hidden away, so she has to use anything that'll ease the pain, anything that'll stop the demons."

Lorraine stared. "You keep them alive, Juda, don't you?

I know about her, I know she is too scared to admit she's got black blood, but I can't believe that is all there is to it!''

Juda smiled. ''Oh, you been talking to Fryer, he's the only one that knows. I'm right, huh? You been to see Fryer Jones?''

Lorraine nodded. ''He told me that he knew, but I don't know if he was aware that Anna Louise was not Robert Caley's child.''

''Oh, he knows. But, Mrs. Page, maybe half of what he said was just him piecing things together. Old Fryer likes to be in on things, always hated not knowing.''

''Were you, or are you, blackmailing Mrs. Caley about her past?''

Juda laughed softly, closing her eyes. ''No, Mrs. Page, I wasn't doing nothing like that, I wouldn't stoop so low.''

Lorraine half raised an eyebrow; if Ruby could contemplate getting money out of Robert Caley, she was damned sure that Juda or Edith had shown her the ropes.

''You don't believe me?''

''No, Mrs. Salina, I don't. What I have seen is your apartment and limo—are you telling me that fancy address on Doheny Drive is paid for from your business?''

Juda stared at Lorraine. ''She pays me, I admit that, and she pays me well, but it's not the way you think.''

''What is it, then, Juda?''

Juda sighed and looked away. ''Mrs. Caley was hexed, a long time ago. Because she played Marie Laveau in that movie she got to believe, and as a believer she needed me. That's all I ever been to her, someone she could talk to, someone who knew her secrets and could soothe her fears. She is a woman who is very fearful.''

''That's it? Elizabeth Caley was fearful, of what?'' Juda shrugged her big shoulders, refusing to look at Lorraine. ''What about Anna Louise Caley, Juda?''

Juda sipped her tea. ''She was obsessed with her father, nothing more to be said, she wanted him to herself.''

''Did he want her in a sexual way?''

Juda smiled, shaking her head. ''No, honey, the girl was just infatuated. He is a real handsome man, and a nice strong body to him, and Anna was just going through a stage in her young life. But she kept on coming to me, begging me to help her, wanting love powders and herbs and gris-gris bags. I just let the child talk.''

"Did you give them to her?"

Juda looked away. "I have to earn a living, but I never encouraged the girl, always told her that no good would come of it, that it wasn't natural for a girl to dote like that on her father."

"But he wasn't her real father, and you knew it. Did you tell her?"

Juda shook her head. "No, ma'am, the child didn't know, that was a big secret we all kept close. Mrs. Page, all I could do was tell her not to go after something that was unobtainable, but she was kind of crazy, you know. Asking for potions, things she'd been reading about, anything that would make him respond as a man to her. You got to remember Anna Louise spent a lot of time here in New Orleans when she was a little one, she was often at this place by herself for months. The help was black, she had a sharp mind, she took everythin' in, a real inquisitive little girl she was."

Juda sighed, and closed her eyes. "I told her over and over what she wanted was bad business and only evil would come of it, but you know, she kind of liked that. There was a side to that girl, a bad side. I hate to speak of it now, but there could be a look to her face that was mean-spirited and bad. She was spoiled, used to getting anything she wanted, but the one thing she couldn't get was her own father on top of her! It was sick all right."

"What do you think happened to her?"

Juda opened her eyes and stared hard at Lorraine. "If I knew, honey, I'd be in line for that one million dollars you are trying to get."

"How do you know about that?"

Juda sucked in her breath. "Honey, there is little connected with Miss Elizabeth Seal that I don't know about. Truth is, all I know is that child is dead, an' she's been dead a long, long while."

"Like eleven months?"

Juda nodded. "Yes, she's been gone a long time, I don't get any feeling that she is alive, so now you know. But I got to earn a living, I got a big family to feed, and sometimes it helped Mrs. Caley to have something to hope for.''

"Even if it was a lie?" Lorraine asked coldly.

"I wasn't going to be the one to tell her I felt no feelings, no heart, because I knew she'd start up those bad drugs again. All I did was try and keep her steady."

Lorraine rubbed her head. "So let me ask you again, what do you think happened to Anna Louise?"

"They didn't bring me down here until she'd been gone awhile. By then it was too late, I got no response."

"What about Ruby?"

Juda gave a tight-lipped smile, and suddenly Lorraine could feel that she was very tense.

"Well, Ruby is Ruby. She's my niece. Why you ask me about Ruby?"

"She worked for Tilda Brown's family."

"Mmm, mmm, she did. In fact, I got her the job. Anna Louise told me her friend was needing a maid, so I rang Edith, and Ruby called by their house. Be about three years ago. Work is hard to come by around here, a lot of unemployment."

"But Tilda Brown came to you, didn't she? With Anna Louise?"

Juda pursed her lips, the deep shiny lipstick running up the lines around her mouth like cracks in baked red earth. "Once or twice, I read the tarot cards, looked in her hand, but nothing serious. They was just young teenagers, it was harmless, and they paid me fifty dollars!"

"Did Tilda believe, like Anna Louise, Juda? I mean, they were close friends, they may have thought it was fun, or interesting. Did they both come to see you together always?"

Juda sighed. "One time Miss Brown booked an appointment by herself, encouraged by Anna Louise, I think. If anything, little Tilda seemed frightened, and when I next saw Anna Louise I said to her not to weave stories, that she was giving her friend nightmares. You got to understand, Tilda was born in these parts too, she would have been brought up by black servants, and children hear things, get things distorted."

Lorraine was tick-ticking again. She got to her feet and started to pace up and down.

"What kind of nightmares?"

"Oh, she couldn't sleep in the dark, silly things. She asked if somebody hexed you what you should do about it, that kind of thing."

"Who was hexing her?"

"I don't know. When I asked her she said she'd been reading some book, that's all."

"Did Anna Louise ask you to make something special for her, Juda?"

"Yes, I told you, love stuff."

"Not a death doll? A voodoo doll in the image of Tilda?"

Juda gasped, and clenched her hands. "No, no, and I would not play with that kind of thing, Mrs. Page. I would not be a part of it, no matter what money was offered."

"Really? No matter what money? Anna Louise was rich, she could have offered a lot, couldn't she?"

Juda stood up angrily, planting her big fat feet wide apart. "I don't have to sit here listenin' to you saying that stuff. I would never, so help me God, abuse what powers I have, not for a child, not for anyone. I don't play with darkness because if I do, I got to go into it too—maybe you don't or can't understand what I am, but it's not a gift I would wish on anyone, it's a vocation. I help people—I don't play with fire."

Lorraine raised her eyebrows. "You sure about that, Juda? I mean, you don't seem to be doing too badly. How about your sister? These powers you are supposed to have, do they weigh heavy on her?"

"You joke on, honey, we don't expect you whites ever to understand. When you do come to us, it's not for good, or for helping others. It's not for spreading joy or healing or loving, but for evil. That's the only time you people want to believe, when you want something from us, and it's been that way for centuries."

Lorraine laughed softly. "Come on, it's not us wringing the neck of chickens and drinking blood. Or was it newborn babies they used to slaughter for their joyful 'love thy neighbor' ceremonies?"

Juda pursed her lips, her whole face as shiny as her lipstick, her blue eyeshadow running into a smudge from her black mascaraed false eyelashes.

"You won't make me angry enough to say something

that'll go against me, Mrs. Page, because I have done nothing.''

''What? Don't kid me, you have withheld evidence, Juda. You have stated to me, and to the police, that Anna Louise did not visit you, nor did her friend Tilda Brown. You have also been blackmailing Elizabeth Caley for years. You say you haven't, but I don't believe you. But right now all I am trying to do is find out what the fuck happened to Anna Louise Caley, because I think she made *this*! And I think she gave it to Tilda Brown.''

Lorraine took out the voodoo doll wrapped in the hotel towel and thrust it at Juda. The big woman's large melonlike breasts heaved as she slowly unrolled the towel on a side table, her breath rasped and Lorraine saw that her black wig had shifted slightly, and her own short fuzzy gray hair showed through. Juda was drenched in perspiration, her curls wet around the nape of her neck and across her forehead. There was a dark V down the back of her dress, the underarms of her dress were damp, and her ankles were swollen, her feet puffy in her tight pumps. Lorraine watched as Juda looked over the doll, noted how she too sniffed it as she had seen Fryer Jones do, then pushed it away.

''This is not made by a professional voodoo practitioner: it's more likely to be a conjure ball here than a doll if someone wanted to do bad work. This is an amateur thing, disgusting. The pin's just a dressmaker's pin too, not the right kind. Whoever made this didn't know what they were doing.''

Juda flipped over the towel, covering the doll. ''I didn't make this thing, Mrs. Page, and I honestly don't know anyone who would. I'm getting old now, like Edith, we get real tired doing trances and rituals. They're all taken over by the young, me and Edith are tired old women now.''

''What about Ruby? Does she have the powers, as you say you have?''

Juda chuckled. ''I say I have them, Mrs. Page, and if you get off your high horse you kind of know I have them, and you are just that little bit scared yourself. Took a long time, Mrs. Page, but you are beginning to believe.''

''No, Mrs. Salina, I am not.''

Juda shook her head, took out a paper tissue from a

pocket and dabbed around her mouth. "I don't care either way, but maybe you should ask my golden goose, as you rudely describe Mrs. Caley, whether I am blackmailing her or not. You ask her, honey."

"Perhaps I will."

Juda put her hands on her wide hips. "I don't want to go back to LA, Mrs. Page, I want to stay here with my relatives. I'm one tired old woman and I pray what powers Edith and I have end with us, I think they do. Little Ruby don't have the sight, and you know something? I am glad, because sometimes the pain is so bad. We don't say what we feel when we have somebody crying at our tables, but we always know. Knowing is an affliction we were born with."

She came up close to Lorraine and pinched her chin in her fingers, staring into her eyes. "You're a clever woman, Mrs. Page, sharp-eyed like a pecking bird, an' you don't miss nothin' with those sharp bird eyes o' yours, but I can look at you and say you are hurting right now, hurting for some love, and it is tearing you apart. You been a woman with no love for a long, long time, and you ain't gonna find it in the bottom of a bottle."

Lorraine blushed and Juda laughed softly. "I'm right, huh, but you know what I don't understand—why can't I tell when my own nephew is gonna rob me of all my savings, eh? So what good is having this extra vision for every poor bastard that comes to me? How come I can't know things that'd warn me? Life is not easy, is it?"

Lorraine sat forward, not wanting to ask, but unable to stop herself. "What do you see for me, Juda, in the future?"

Juda laughed softly. "Honey . . . it'll cost you fifty bucks."

Lorraine went to open her wallet, but Juda put her hand on Lorraine's head.

"No . . . don't. You got to walk away, you make your own future, sweetheart, believe me. You don't want to know what's in store for you. Besides, I don't have the energy to get into it."

Missy appeared. "Mrs. Salina, she's askin' for you, she says you got to stay here, she doesn't want you to leave."

Juda nodded, and pointed to the door. "I'm keeping her alive, Mrs. Page, and if she pays me for it, who am I not to

take it? I got a niece set her heart on being a queen in a
fancy dress and a dressmaker asking for more money than
is decent. So if you want to go up and see her, you go do
it. I need to wash, freshen up."

Lorraine watched Juda walk to the door. She seemed
weighed down, not just by her bulk but by something else,
a sadness. And Lorraine remembered Fryer's saying that
once she had been beautiful.

Lorraine tapped on Elizabeth Caley's bedroom door.

"Juda, is that you?"

The voice was like a frightened child's, and when Lorraine eased open the door she saw the room was in semidarkness, the shutters closed. Even in the gloom it was clear
that Elizabeth's stricken face was as white as paper, so pale
that Lorraine was alarmed.

"It's me, Lorraine Page, Mrs. Caley. Are you all right?"

"Go away, I want Juda, I need Juda. I can't see anyone
else right now, go away. Juda, Juda!" Elizabeth was curled
up hugging the pillow, her voice barely audible. "Please,
please, get Juda, I need her—I am sick, very sick."

Lorraine took a couple of steps further into the darkened
room as Elizabeth moaned and then uncurled her body. Her
hands were clenched into fists, and she began to make deep,
guttural sounds, her body thrashing as if she was having a
fit.

"Juda! Juda!" she screamed, and her eyes rolled back
into her head, showing only the whites. It frightened Lorraine, who didn't know what she should do, but then Juda
appeared behind her. She'd changed into a big tentlike dress
and a blue silk turban, and was barefoot.

"I'm here, honey, rest easy now, Juda's right here."

Lorraine watched as Juda ran water over a cloth in the
bathroom and then dipped it into an ice bucket by the side
of the bed.

"You want to ask Mrs. Caley something? You go ahead.
You ever seen anyone act like this, huh? Take a good look,
Mrs. Page, these are her demons."

Lorraine looked over to the bed. Elizabeth moaned and
thrashed around the crumpled sheets, but Juda seemed unconcerned.

"She's been like this for thirty-five years. Started on that movie she made. They hexed this poor child, made her think the spirit of the snake was inside her, and sometimes it takes her over. Right now that's what is screaming out. Not the drugs or the booze, but her fears. This is what evil can do. This is what comes of playing with the spirits, Mrs. Page. This poor woman was cursed."

"I don't understand," Lorraine whispered.

"No, your kind wouldn't. Now, if you got nothing to ask her, leave me to calm her. This is what I am paid for, an' I do it because she can't trust no one else."

Lorraine took one more look at Elizabeth Caley and walked out. She closed the door behind her, still not fully understanding what was going on. But she didn't want to see any more because it was unnerving to see someone so out of control, as if in a fit. By the time she had walked to her car, that is what she believed was wrong with Elizabeth Caley—she was suffering from some kind of epilepsy.

Juda sat by Elizabeth Caley's bed, rinsing out the cloth and gently wiping her sweating brow. She would never cease to be in wonderment at Elizabeth's beauty, it always touched her soul, just as the demons inside Elizabeth wrenched and exhausted her. All those terrible curses laid on little sixteen-year-old Elizabeth Seal's head had created such agony, such fear, that she had lived inside it all of her adult life and there would never be an end to it. Juda knew that all she could do, all she had been able to do, was calm her and stop her from sinking into such a state of terror that it froze her mind and body. She eased that terror now, talking in a soft voice, whispering that it was going to be over any moment. Juda felt the evil, sometimes had taken it through her own body, just as she had felt the loneliness inside Lorraine Page. When she'd looked into Lorraine's face she had seen deep insecurity, and it made Juda feel compassion—not a lot, but some.

"Juda," murmured Elizabeth.

"I'm here, honey, like I always am, right up close, you can reach out and hold me, I won't leave you."

Juda felt Elizabeth's nails cutting into her palm as she clasped her hand tightly. Her body heaved as she retched, but there was no vomit; it was as if she was releasing something from inside herself, her mouth frothing and the spittle trickling down her chin as she heaved and her tongue hung out. Then she lay still and her hand slowly released Juda's. It was over.

Ten minutes later the wondrous eyes opened and the fear had gone. Juda saw the sweet, innocent smile of thanks.

"Everyone leaves me, Juda, but not you. I love you, Juda, I love you."

Juda kissed the perfect cheek. "I know. You're nice and calm now, no fears, nobody will ever hurt you, Marie. My own little Marie Laveau."

Elizabeth closed her eyes and sighed. "Tell me some more about her. Tell me how strong she was."

Juda smiled. "Well, you remember the day I first met you with that snake and you said to me, 'Juda, I can't let that thing wrap around my body.' And I said, 'Come on now, if Marie Laveau could, then so can you. What's more you're gonna dance with it, fall in love with it, feel its body inside yours,' and you said—"

"Dance with me, through hell and back."

Juda was rocking her gently in her arms. "That's right, honey, you showed you weren't afraid. You want to dance now, sugar, or are you too tired?"

Elizabeth eased away the bedcovers and, helped by Juda, stood up, her crumpled chiffon nightdress hardly hiding the outline of her glistening, sweat-soaked body.

"I want to dance, Juda."

How many times she had had to watch this she couldn't count, but she watched again as if it were the first time, still whispering encouragements as Elizabeth Caley stumbled around the room, her arms undulating like snakes and her thin white gown swirling around her. And Juda wanted to weep, weep for the exotic beauty that had once been Elizabeth Caley, who for one moment had allowed her real blood to shine through, caught on celluloid as the reincarnation of the greatest voodoo queen of all time.

It had not been Juda alone but many others who had sworn they saw Marie Laveau come to life for a few brief moments; the cameras had kept rolling, the director said nothing, none of the crew spoke as the big voodoo scene began to take on a life of its own and young Elizabeth Seal danced herself into a state of total exhaustion. It had not ended there, nor had it ended when Juda helped her back to her trailer. She had not come out of the trance, and Juda had been unable to stop the men from coming in, unable to stop them from encouraging her to engage in a night of debauchery. Even when the crew and director had packed up for the night and left, the "dancing" continued until the men had carried Elizabeth Caley into the swamps. Juda had been barred from going and Elizabeth was not brought back until dawn; she had been repeatedly raped, blood covering her gown and face. Whatever terrible things had been done to her left such a mark on Elizabeth Caley that thirty-five years afterward she was still living in fear and was sometimes transported back into the shadow world of that night.

Elizabeth Caley believed she was cursed for playing the famous Marie Laveau, and when she had been given the opportunity to admit she had the right to do so, because black blood flowed in her veins, she had refused, publicly denouncing the allegation as scurrilous lies. To this day she was still afraid that it would be proved, but as both her parents died shortly after the filming of *The Swamp*, there was no one who could betray her. Only the sun. Elizabeth Caley was not allergic to the sun. It did not burn her delicate, whiter-than-white skin—what it did was show her heritage. If this had been known in the days when Elizabeth was a star in Hollywood, she would have lost her contract with the studio. The birth of her daughter, Anna Louise, had quieted the gossip—the child's blond hair and blue eyes buried Elizabeth Caley's secret deeper, for Anna Louise took after her real father, Lloyd Dulay. Blond and blue-eyed, he was the man Elizabeth had loved for more than twenty years, but like everything else in her sad life, even that had been forced into secrecy.

CHAPTER
17

Rosie replaced the receiver and looked at Rooney.

"Caley's maid said she just left."

He sighed. "Well, maybe you're getting yourself all worked up over nothing, honey."

"No, I'm not, Bill, you didn't see the way she was. You don't understand, she's an alcoholic—one night off the wagon won't be the last."

"Hell, she was up and out before you or me, maybe she's more resilient than you give her credit for."

"Yeah, and maybe I know her better than she knows herself, Billy, and if you want to know, it's because I've got the same addiction. There's been plenty of times I've thought I could control it, you know, just a few drinks, it won't matter, but believe me, it matters, and I'm worried."

"You care a lot about her, don't you?"

Rosie looked at him in surprise. " 'Course I do. I mean, we may yell at each other, but underneath it all she's the best friend I ever had."

"Doesn't look that way to me. She's got a tongue like a viper—I know, because she's stung me with it pretty good."

Rosie sucked in her breath. "Same time, Bill, you and me are both here because of her. You and me could also have one hell of a nest egg because of her. You said it to me often enough, she was one of the best—well, when she was sober."

"I know, and maybe, Rosie, what I am facing is that I'm

not. She pushes me, and she can work stuff out and get on to it quicker than me, and I feel tired lately, you know? I don't know if it's just I don't have the incentive anymore, but I'm not a number one, never was . . . didn't really know it until now.''

"Yes, you were, and you still are—look at the way you got that cop to open up."

He gave a lovely chuckle. "No, Rosie, I belong to the old school, a dying breed, and you know something? I've even been scared to admit it to myself, but it's the God's honest truth—I've spent my whole life among the dregs of humanity, and I'd like to spend the next part breathing good clean air. I've done a lot of thinking about this."

Rosie suddenly felt frightened; was he saying that he wanted this new life without her? Her heart lurched in her chest as Rooney continued. "You may not be interested, but, Rosie, if we do get this big cash bonus, we should have us a good time, go on trips, maybe as far afield as Europe. I always wanted to see Vienna—that's somethin' else I never admitted to anyone." Rosie hugged him tightly. "Bill, I'd go anywhere with you, Vienna, China . . ."

"China?" he said, looking down into her upturned face.

"Yeah, I've always wanted to go there, don't ask me why. I'd like to go someplace exotic, stimulating, you know what I mean?"

He beamed. "China it is. But first, you think we should look out for a ring, you know, make this official?"

Rosie was brimming over with happiness and kissed him passionately in the middle of the hotel lobby, oblivious to the group of old ladies passing by. Nobody paid much attention—there were a lot of things more interesting to see in New Orleans than an old couple kissing.

Lorraine was parked just outside Tilda Brown's home, draining her second can of vodka and Coke and trying to think of the best way to go about things—whether to confront the parents and demand that they speak to her, or go to the back door and talk to the servants. She instructed François to head for the Browns' manicured driveway, and tried to get up the energy to open the car door, but she felt empty and tired out. Robert Caley was now in first place yet again as the prime suspect, and it hurt. Just as thinking about what Nick Bartello had said hurt, his death hurt, everything hurt. She couldn't get out of the car.

"You okay, Mrs. Page?"

"No, François, I'm not. I'm thinking about a nice guy who died, and another man who I thought was a nice guy but wasn't. If I go in there this afternoon, I have to come out with a result or I may not be allowed in again."

François leaned over the front seat. "You want some advice, Mrs. Page?"

She half laughed. "Why not?"

"Well, my advice is to come back tomorrow. You're not strong now, I can feel it. Whatever you need from this house can wait." She smiled and then agreed.

"Yeah, you're right. We'll come back tomorrow, François, and tomorrow I won't be drinking."

He gave that wide smile, half gaps, half gold.

"Okeydokey, Mrs. Page."

Juda stood in the kitchen and just smelling that big pan of hot chicken made her feel good. The small house was spick-and-span, cleaner than she had seen it for as long as she could remember. They had carried her bags into one of the boys' rooms and she had been touched by the beautiful, fresh, sweet-smelling flowers. The boys, wearing smart suits, and Sugar May, wearing a clean print dress, were laying the table for supper.

Edith had changed and was truly happy to see Juda, embracing her warmly, almost forgetting the terrible thing Raoul had done. They didn't speak of it right away because Ruby's dressmaker had arrived for a final fitting, so there was a lot of excitement emanating from the front room, Ruby screeching that nobody was to enter until the dress was fixed up.

Edith opened some beer, handing Juda a frothing glass.

"You able to stay awhile?"

"Maybe, all depends. I got to be on hand for Mrs. Caley, she was took bad last night again, but she's got the resilience of a wild bronco, that woman. I see her so bad, so bad, Edith, but she picks herself up again." Juda sipped her beer. Edith drew out a chair and sat opposite her sister.

"You know there is always a place here for you."

"I should sure as hell hope so, Edith, because I've been paying for this house since I can recall!"

Suddenly there was the muffled sound of the telephone, hidden in a drawer, and Edith looked at Juda in confusion.

"It's the telephone, I'll get it. I dunno who can be calling—you're the only one knows we got a number." Edith opened the drawer and lifted out the telephone, which was still ringing. "It's Fryer, maybe, he got the number."

She picked up the receiver gingerly. "Hello?" There was the sound of bleeps and static. "Who is this, please?" Edith said nervously, always afraid that one day the telephone company would call.

"Mama? I'm on a cell phone," came Raoul's voice. Edith had to sit down, her body breaking out in a sweat.

"Where are you, boy? *Where are you?*"

Raoul laughed and said he was calling her from his automobile. "I want to come home, Mama, but I ain't coming if I'm gonna get a whoppin' or you start hexing me. I know I done wrong, I know that, but I wanna come home see mah little sister crowned, Mama."

Edith passed the receiver to Juda. "It's Raoul, you deal with him, I am havin' nothing to do with that thievin', no-good boy."

Juda grabbed the phone. "He's speakin' from a phone in a car," Edith explained.

"An' I know whose money bought that phone," said Juda, her face turning red with fury. "This is Juda, you hearing me, Raoul Corbello? You get that snake ass of yours back here, and you bring me mah money—you got mah money?"

"I have, Aunt Juda, minus a few dollars, but I ain't comin' back if you're fixin' to do bad things to me. It was a madness that took over me, and I will return all I got left. All I want to do is be with my family and get your forgiveness and see my sister crowned."

"You all drugged up, boy?"

"Hell, no, Aunt Juda, I'm clean, I don't do drugs no more, not since they made me do somethin' as wicked as to steal from you, my own flesh and blood."

Juda pursed her lips. "You got a free and easy grease tongue, boy, but you come on home. You bring me my money, and maybe we'll sort this out real amicable, no whippin', but so help me God, if you disappear, then I'll set the devil hisself on you.''

''I'll be home soon, Aunt Juda, 'bye now.''

Juda slammed the phone down. She would have liked to have told him that she personally would whip him until he bled, but she wanted her life's savings back first.

Edith prepared herself for an onslaught about Raoul, but before it came there was a holler from Ruby that they should come and see her. Juda heaved herself up on her feet, and Edith reached out and caught her hand.

''She's changed, Juda, it happened so quick. You'll see, you won't hardly know the little girl you last saw running around.'' Juda drained her beer and carefully put the glass down.

''She's a good girl, Edith?''

Edith nodded, and linked her arm through Juda's. ''She looks just like we used to, Juda.''

Juda held on to her sister's arm. She spoke softly, not wanting Jesse and Willy to hear. The pair of them, dressed in their best suits like choirboys, were afraid to so much as take a Coke from the fridge without permission. Fryer's thrashing had instituted good behavior, for a while anyway.

''How much like us, Edith?'' Juda asked.

Edith stared into Juda's eyes. ''In every way. I didn't think so, but she helped me today and there was something there, I felt it.''

Edith pushed open the door, Juda just behind her, and both of them felt for each other's hands because of the emotion of seeing Ruby. Even the bad-tempered old dressmaker was close to tears, pressing against the far wall, smiling with pride.

Ruby turned slowly to face her mother and aunt. There was only one lamp lit and its radiance surrounded Ruby like a faint halo, the dress so richly embroidered in golden thread that it seemed to glow. The skin-tight bodice displayed the girl's slim waist perfectly, while the neckline, surrounded by exquisite garlands of embroidery, revealed the smooth brown skin of her bosom and throat. The cut, though, was modest, and the long blue sleeves were full-length, fastened with a dozen tiny golden buttons between elbow and cuff.

At Ruby's hips, the dress was gathered at the back in an effect that could have been worn only by a girl who was as slender as a gazelle, reminiscent of an old-fashioned bustle and train, the skirt almost filling the floor space of the room.

"Look, Mama, look." Ruby smiled, lifting the hem at the front to show the dress's silk lining and net underskirts, then her own delicate ankle and high golden shoe. She swished her skirts and the embroidery danced and sparkled like the gold of sunlight on water. Edith wiped a tear from her eye.

"There's a mantle too," Ruby cried, beckoning to the dressmaker, who unfolded a blue silk cloak, lined with the same golden silk, and fastened it on Ruby's shoulders with two scalloped golden clasps while Ruby reached behind her head and skillfully wound her long dark hair into a sleek knot.

"Here, girl, put these on before your headdress," said the dressmaker, unfastening the gold hoops that hung on her own ears. "Just try how they look with your hair." Ruby slipped the rings through her ears, her eyes cast modestly down.

"Oh, my, my, my," whispered Juda.

"You approve, Aunt Juda?" Ruby asked softly, and only then did she lift her eyes, the color of night, to meet her aunt's, and they were eyes that held secrets, that would see into nightmares and dreams.

Juda whispered, almost in awe of her niece, "Oh, I approve, I approve. Now you are ready to be a real queen, Ruby. You got a light inside your eyes now, child, you feel it glowing? Don't you abuse that now, honey, never abuse it, for it's very precious."

And then it was gone: the dressmaker fastened the headdress of tall ostrich plumes on Ruby's head and she was the laughing, posing, teenage Queen of the Carnival again. But Juda knew what she had seen, and looked at her sister, and they did not need to exchange a word—both knew that the sight was precious, just as they knew it would exhaust and weigh the young girl down. But they would be there when the darkness felt as if it was dragging her into oblivion, just as their mama had been, and their grandmama and great-grandmama.

• • •

Lorraine sat at the cheap veneered table in her hotel room, updating their information. There had been a note from Rosie and Rooney to say they had gone out to dinner, telling her the name of the restaurant and how to get there. There was also the number of an AA meeting, and a special note, underlined, from Rosie saying that if Lorraine had any sense she would go. Despite the suggestion that she should join them at the restaurant, the note made Lorraine feel excluded, and guilty about the fact that she had been drinking all day, but moderately, so that she was sure that even someone who knew her as well as Rosie could not have detected it. She hid the bottles she had bought—with so many beds to choose from, there were plenty of mattresses under which they could be stashed—before ordering some more cans of Coke, a hamburger and fries.

She finished her notes, making sure they were all neat and intelligible. Nothing must give her away, nobody must have any inkling that she was drinking again; she didn't even admit it to herself.

It was late, after midnight, and Fryer Jones rocked in his chair, looking from Juda to Edith, a half-smile on his face. Sometimes he'd forget which sister he'd married, and he couldn't be absolutely certain it wasn't both of them. He'd had them both on numerous occasions, which was the reason Eddie Corbello had taken off, and he was unsure which of Edith's kids were in fact his. He wasn't all that sure if he was actually divorced from Juda. He wasn't about to break their good-humored drinking session, as once again they refilled their glasses. Now they drank to the most powerful queen of voodoo, Marie Laveau, whose light was still shining now in Ruby Corbello's eyes. As the wine took hold, they determined in slurred voices that no one would ever destroy the past that belonged to their people. Juda and Edith touched glasses for yet another toast as Fryer got to his feet; he'd had enough.

"Good night, y'all. Watch over that little tinderbox Ruby, an' if she gets into trouble you call me. You two witches may not appreciate this, but I play a major part in this family."

He walked down the alleyway between the small crumbling houses, looking forward to playing some music, the way he always looked forward to it. He reckoned he had covered all his tracks, and Ruby and the boys, be they his or not, were safe. Soon he'd have his old cracked lips around the most kissable thing on earth, his trombone.

Lorraine plowed on through her notebook, checking back on information and jotting dates and names into a new book, and it was after twelve when she fell into bed. There had been no calls from Robert Caley, but she had told the desk to tell him she was not in her room. She was to be woken at seven in the morning, and a message relayed to Rosie and Rooney that she wanted a breakfast meeting at seven-thirty.

Lorraine was so exhausted she fell asleep as soon as her head hit the pillow, but she was awake before the wake-up call, already showered and changed. She checked her notes once more before heading down to the dining room. She had taken only a small slug of vodka from the bottle, and had then performed her usual routine, emptying out some of the Coke and then topping the can up. Nothing in her manner, she was sure, could give her away.

Rooney and Rosie were already seated, even though it was only seven-twenty-five.

"Morning, thanks for making it so early, we got to get moving."

"That's what we're here for, standing by, ready and waiting, boss," Rooney said, pouring her coffee.

Lorraine put down her can of Coke and opened her notebook, not even bothering with small talk.

"Okay, did you find that gris-gris necklace of Nick's in his hotel room?"

"Nope, not in his room," Rooney replied, and Lorraine chewed her pen tip.

"You sure he had it on when he went out?"

"No, I never saw him leave, but he had it on earlier in the day. In fact, he hadn't taken it off since Fryer Jones gave it to him." She made a note and then looked at him.

"Newspaper—you got written confirmation it was dated February fifteenth last year?"

Rooney nodded and pulled the folded copy of the page

from his pocket. "Means the doll was given to Tilda on that date or maybe the day after. Reason being, if someone was wrapping up something, they wouldn't use the fresh morning papers, but maybe the previous day's was lying around? So we more or less know when Tilda was given the doll."

"Mmm," Lorraine said, sipping her coffee. She flipped her notebook closed and picked up the menu, then tossed it aside. She had no appetite for anything but the can of Coke, and reached out for it again. Rosie looked quickly at Rooney, and then at the can. She interrupted as Lorraine began to outline the developments of the previous day in matter-of-fact fashion. "What did you just say, Tilda Brown was screwing Robert Caley?"

"Yes, well, she wrote it in her diary, may have been lies, but if he paid off Ruby Corbello, I doubt it. There must be some element of guilt, and more reason for Anna Louise to get so heated about seeing him kissing her, maybe she found out. I dunno, but I was wrong about the bear, she'd had it for months, so Ruby said, and it doesn't matter now anyway. I doubt the diary will still be intact."

Rooney squinted at the menu, and looked at Rosie. "Maybe you order? Nothing too fattening."

Rosie nodded and signaled to the waitress, who took their order for more coffee and fresh fruit.

"You not eating?" Rosie said, turning to Lorraine as the waitress moved off.

"Nope, nothing for me, coffee's fine."

Lorraine's foot kept kicking at the table. She listed on her fingers what she had discovered about Elizabeth Caley, and about Juda's involvement, breaking for quick sips of coffee and Coke before she continued.

"Ruby Corbello, Juda or Edith made that doll. Maybe even Fryer Jones? But one of them did, I'm sure of it. That doll was made to scare the pants off Tilda Brown. But Tilda didn't kill herself when she first got it, so what made her wait so many months and why didn't she destroy it?"

Rooney poured himself more coffee. "You think Anna Louise gave her the doll?"

Lorraine snapped. "Yes, obviously. Question is how and when she got it, and when did she take it to Tilda?"

Rooney scratched his head. "I go for the evening she

disappeared, maybe thought she'd be back in the hotel before dinner, and something happened to her either at Tilda Brown's or on her way back from there.''

"Yeah, right," agreed Lorraine, "I've been over and over what I said to Tilda on the afternoon I interviewed her and I still can't think that anything I said would have made her kill herself, or anything she said to me that gives me any insight. The only thing I said to her was that if Anna Louise had been having sex with her father, then that might have been a reason for her disappearance. Since then I've discovered that it wasn't Anna Louise having a relationship with Caley but Tilda, so maybe knowing that I would talk to Caley, she might have been scared it would all come out about them and hanged herself. Plus the fact I had the photo of Anna Louise at the Viper Room and she was scared *that* would all come out as well, because in her suicide note she wrote something like 'God forgive me.' ''

Breakfast arrived, and the waitress set up a trolley, placing a big bowl of fruit and another pot of coffee on it, and throughout the nervous tapping of Lorraine's foot never stopped.

"You interview the bellboy at Caley's hotel, Errol, scare him up a bit, Bill. He showed Ruby Corbello in, delivered a message for her, and he's not opened his little pillbox hat about that to me or to the police.''

Lorraine drained her can of Coke, then spooned some sugar into her black coffee.

"Don't you want honey?" said Rosie. "All you got to do is ask.''

"Sugar's fine.''

Rosie was watching Lorraine closely; maybe she was wrong, but somehow she was sure that Lorraine was drinking. She was searching her pack of Marlboro Lights as if she thought there was a stray one left inside, then suddenly threw the empty pack aside.

"You need a fresh pack?''

"Later," Lorraine said, her foot still kicking. "Okay, this is what goes down today. You stay well clear of Caley, Bill. I don't want to go near the hotel because I don't want to confront him yet! Okay, Rosie, job for you. Check all taxi

companies and see if they got a logbook of cab rides the
night Anna Louise disappeared.''

Rooney nodded and looked at Rosie. "We know they've
been questioned and they have come up with diddly-squat,
so this time give them the date, February fifteenth, the time,
about seven o'clock, and Tilda Brown's address. Maybe one
will remember if you say a purse was found and has never
been claimed, and a cabbie handed it in to lost property. Fat
chance in this place, but see what you can get, Rosie, say
you're looking for the guy to pass over a reward, I dunno,
make something up, but don't mention Anna Louise Caley
or anything to do with our case.''

Rosie nodded: she liked it when Bill let the old Captain
Rooney show, even though she had never known him when
he was on the force. Lorraine flipped over her notes as Rooney tapped her elbow and said, "Maybe I should see if the
police have searched Fryer's place for that necklace.''

"Yeah, good thinking. If they haven't, ask them to, or
maybe you take one of them with you. That guy you paid
the five hundred bucks to might help out, an' if necessary
pay him more. But don't you go on your own, Bill, it's in
a bad neighborhood.''

"You did!''

She nodded. "Yeah, I know, and it was dumb, but somehow I think they're such a bunch of male chauvinist bastards
around here I'd get away with it. Big guy like you might
not, and they got barmen in there like snakes, and a few
with muscles, so just do like I said, don't take risks.''

Rosie smiled and pushed her chair back. "Lemme go get
you some smokes, won't take a second. They got packs at
reception.''

Lorraine looked up at her and smiled. "Thanks, Rosie.''

Rooney started to peel an apple. "So, anything else on
the agenda? I mean, I know what I'm doing, what about
you?''

Lorraine frowned.

"We're moving,'' Bill went on, "but . . . you know we're
still no closer to finding Anna Louise Caley, no matter how
much information we've come up with. Getting as far as we
have has been time-consuming, and time is one thing we
don't have. Without that diary, without proof there was

some sexual thing going on between Caley and Tilda Brown, it'll be his word against yours, and that won't look good in a transcript of the investigation. Like 'When did you discuss this possible sexual motive?' "Oh, when I was being screwed by the defendant.' "

Lorraine sucked in her breath and turned away. "You hit below the belt sometimes, Bill."

"But all the same, you know I'm right."

Lorraine nodded. "Come on, Bill, it's not that bad, and maybe we'll get some joy with cabdrivers."

Rooney munched on the apple. "You think so? Well, have a look over the old case sheets, every cabdriver from every district was questioned and shown photographs of Anna Louise Caley. Nobody admitted picking her up, seeing her. It was the first part of the investigation by every private dick hired and all the cops, here and in LA. They got nothing. You want a slice of apple?"

Lorraine smiled and opened her mouth like a fledgling in a nest. "Sure, I like it peeled, always tastes different, doesn't it?"

Rosie had told reception that she wanted to collect something from Lorraine's room, and as the girl behind the desk knew they were all friends, she handed Rosie Lorraine's room key. Rosie was fast; she knew the places she used to hide bottles, so it didn't take her long to find Lorraine's hidden stash. She left the bottles where she had found them and walked out.

"One pack of cancer sticks," she said as she tossed the cigarettes on the table, and watched while Lorraine picked up her notebook and rose to go.

"We should talk some more," Rosie said quietly.

"I'm all talked out, Rosie, we haven't got the time to sit around gassing."

"You need to go to a meeting, Lorraine."

Rooney patted Rosie's hand. "Maybe let that go for a while."

"We can't let it go, Bill. We can't, can we, Lorraine?"

"Sure, we can. I got more important things on my mind right now, Rosie, and so should you."

Rosie picked up the empty can of Coke, smelled it, then

held it lightly in her hand. "Maybe you can pull the wool over Bill's eyes, and maybe even over your own, but you can't pull it over mine. I know Lorraine, and this . . . here, Bill, smell the can, it's been laced with vodka. One of the biggest myths in history is the belief that vodka doesn't smell—it does, believe me, it does."

"What's she talking about?" Rooney asked.

"Tell him, Lorraine, why don't you tell him how much you had to have to get yourself down to breakfast? Not that you ate anything."

"Get off my back, Rosie."

Rosie smashed the can down. "For Chrissakes, Lorraine, don't be such an idiot, you can't get away with it, you maybe think you can, but you can't."

"What the fuck is going on?" Rooney asked.

"Tell him, Lorraine, go on, tell him!"

"Leave me alone," Lorraine snapped.

"No can do, we've got too much at stake. She's drinking, Bill, she's started up drinking."

Rooney sat back. "Oh shit, this is all we need. For Chrissakes, Lorraine, are you out of your mind?"

Lorraine wouldn't look at either of them, but fumbled with the new pack of cigarettes, trying to unwrap it.

"She's got bottles stashed in her room," Rosie said flatly.

"Is this true?" Bill asked, sadness in his voice.

"Do you think I'm lying? I've just been in her room," Rosie snapped, and Rooney looked at her sharply.

"Rosie, do me a favor, just leave us a second, will you? I mean it, go on, go wait in the lobby."

Rosie pursed her lips, then pushed back her chair. "Fine, but I'm not waiting long. Like she said, we're running out of time."

Rooney struck a match and lit Lorraine's cigarette; she inhaled deeply.

"You need it that bad, huh?"

Lorraine let the smoke drift from her nose. "I need it, Billy, but it's under control, I promise. I just need something for a while, then I'll go to one of her fucking meetings."

"Can you control it?" He reached for her hand, but she withdrew it.

When she spoke her voice was low and husky. "Please

don't bring up that kid I shot, please don't. All I need is a stopgap, just to keep me steady. If I don't have it I'll fold, because I feel so bad inside.''

"Is it Caley?"

She nodded, then sighed.

"Yeah, it's him. I really liked him, Billy, and to be honest, I felt that maybe, just maybe I could have some love in my life. Then there was Nick—he was such a good guy. Sometimes it feels like whenever somebody is nice to me, loves me just a little bit, I foul it up, or it gets fouled up some other way, and I get so lonely—''

"You know," he said softly, "Rosie and me both love you. She really cares, and I just don't want to see you fuck up.''

She gave him that rare, sweet smile. "I promise that if you just let me get through this, at least until the time runs out on the case, I'll keep myself steady. In fact, I'll try not to touch the fucking stuff, I can't say more than that.''

Rooney nodded. "Okay, but if you do foul up, then . . .'' He sighed. "Don't destroy yourself, Lorraine, because you're too good, too smart, and you're one hell of an investigator, better than I could ever be, better than most I ever met.''

"Thanks. Now you go and talk to Rosie, we've got a lot to be getting on with.''

He leaned over and kissed her cheek. "Just promise me you'll talk to us when you need to, because we're here for you.''

She watched him walk away, ashamed, but unable to cry. She'd already done too much of that.

Rooney joined Rosie in the lobby as Lorraine shot past; she smiled, but didn't slow her pace.

"Any chance you telling us where we can reach you? Just in case we come up with something," Rosie blurted out, and Lorraine turned.

"I'm on my way to Tilda Brown's home and then I'll be back here, dunno how long it will take.''

The doors swung after her as she disappeared and jumped into her car. Rosie would have gone after her, but Rooney held her arm.

"Let her go, Rosie, let her go."

She glared at him. "I hope you know what you're doing, she's back on the booze, Bill."

"I know," he said sadly, tilting Rosie's chin up to make her look at him. "We can try to take care of her, but we can't stop her, she's got something inside her neither of us has."

"Oh yeah, well, let me tell you—"

"No," he said firmly, "let me tell you. She feels more guilt than either of us ever will, and if she needs liquor to get her through this, then we will just have to let it go and look after her as best we can—we don't have much time left as it is. She's aware of it all, Rosie, believe me, she knows, and I trust her."

Rosie shrugged. "Okay, but if she carries on this way, Vienna and China won't happen because she won't be able to function."

He straightened up. "But we will, and we got a lot to do, so let's get moving."

Robert Caley was now becoming angry at Lorraine's silence; it just didn't make any sense to him. Then he began to get a little uneasy as to why she had not called, so he tried to contact her again. As he was dialing her hotel number, there was a light rap on his door. He opened it, and the bellboy hovered.

"Yes?" Caley snapped.

Errol looked down the corridor and back at Caley.

"What do you want?"

"Er, can I come in, sir? It's just, someone's been asking me questions and I'm not sure what to say."

Caley sighed and opened the door wider. "What is it?"

Errol took off his pillbox hat. "I'm a friend of Ruby Corbello's, Mr. Caley, it was me that brought you the note that night last year."

"I don't know what you're talking about, what note, what night?"

Errol stepped from one foot to the other. "Night you first arrived last year, Mr. Caley, Ruby give me a note for you and I passed it to you and then you met her down by the pool, sir."

Caley took a deep breath, and reached for his wallet. "No, I don't recall ever speaking to you or Miss Corbello—in fact I have no idea who she is. Now, how much do I owe you?"

Errol licked his lips, peered to the half-open door. "You see, there was this guy stopped me on my way in to work and asked me about it. I said I never passed no note, and—"

Caley's eyes were like ice. "You didn't, and I never received anything that night. Now here's a hundred bucks, get out and stay out, or you'll lose your job. And when my casino opens I am going to need employees with good recommendations and experience, do you understand?"

"Yes, sir, thank you, sir."

Caley kicked the door shut after Errol, not too worried. If it ever came to it, it would be his word against the boy's. But he knew he would also have to make Ruby Corbello understand that she too had better keep her mouth shut. There was no diary—that had been destroyed immediately— but he just didn't like any loose ends, especially now when everything was looking so good. At no time did Caley connect the diary and Tilda to his missing daughter. She was gradually fading from his mind, and she hadn't been his own daughter anyway, but she had been useful.

Lloyd Dulay had not liked it one bit when Caley had said that if the accusations that he had had a sexual relationship with Anna Louise were not publicly retracted, he would sue, and obviously it would have to come out that Anna Louise was in fact Dulay's daughter. He was merely threatening, but Dulay had taken him seriously and suggested that if in place of a retraction of any stupid gossip he demonstrated full cooperation with Caley in the new partnership negotiations, that would be advantageous on both counts. On the one hand it would dismiss the allegations and prove they were simply ridiculous, because if a man of Lloyd Dulay's standing considered entering a business deal with someone he had accused of having sexual relations with his young daughter, then it couldn't be true. And on the other hand it would not be necessary to bring up the fact that Anna Louise was actually Lloyd Dulay's child. And he used the fact that poor Elizabeth was of such a nervous disposition he did not wish her to be put through some awful scandal in the papers.

Dulay had come around all right—and he hadn't taken much pushing.

Caley did not use his own driver, but walked a short distance from the hotel, then took the streetcar a few stops before flagging down a passing taxi to take him to Edith Corbello's.

Lorraine had returned to Mr. and Mrs. Brown's home. They had been talking quietly for almost half an hour, and it had been a testing, drawnout time. They could not remember when they had last seen Tilda with Anna Louise or with Robert Caley. As far as they knew, their daughter had no problems, none. That was why they were finding it so difficult to come to terms with her death.

"So during the time Anna Louise has been missing, you never saw anything faintly suspicious about Tilda's behavior? By that I mean, did she change? Did she become moody or uncooperative in any way?"

Mrs. Brown was so pale and washed out that Lorraine felt almost cruel questioning her. She wept constantly, wiping her tears away with a handkerchief, unfolding it to blow her nose, then refolding it again to wipe her eyes.

"Well, of course she was very, very upset. Anna Louise was her best friend, she was inconsolable about her, and for her to disappear like that was just dreadful for Tilda. They had been very close since childhood, and I think what made it worse was that they had argued the day before, so Tilda never had a chance to make it up with Anna Louise. That's what upset her most of all."

Lorraine looked at Mr. Brown, who sat straight-backed, his face bearing a pained, quizzical expression.

"Do you think Tilda did what she did because she was still upset about Anna Louise?" Lorraine asked, her voice hushed and sounding, even to herself, excessively conspiratorial.

"We don't know, we had thought she had gotten over it all, but she obviously had not, and quite possibly, Mrs. Page, your visit might have made her sink into a depression. We do not know, just as we really do not know why you came out to see her." He looked at Lorraine almost accusingly, and he was becoming agitated, his hands clenching and unclenching, though he tried to hide it by pressing them into his thighs. "We had interviews for many weeks after Anna Louise disappeared, and poor Tilda, on top of losing her dearest friend, was questioned more than anyone. What did you ask her, Mrs. Page? Why don't you tell us if she became upset, because we would dearly like to know, *need* to know what made our only daughter do such a terrible thing? She has broken our hearts."

Lorraine lied for a further half hour, making up chitchat questions and answers regarding her interview with Tilda about Anna Louise. It was all so emotionally tense that Lorraine felt they were draining her energy from her.

"I need to see any friend of Tilda's that she saw on a regular basis, and where she went. I need to build up a picture of your daughter prior to the tragedy."

Mr. and Mrs. Brown whispered to each other, and Mrs. Brown nodded her head. She then excused herself and left the room.

Mr. Brown sighed and looked toward the wall of glass through which the pool and tennis court were visible.

"We have tried to come to terms with it, Mrs. Page. We know Tilda was so worried about what had happened to Anna Louise. There were such stories about kidnap and rape, or even, pray God it is not true, that she might have been murdered. And as a result, Tilda kept very much to herself for the past few months, but my wife will give you details."

"Thank you."

He stared down at his shoes, and then bit his lip. "Although I do not see why you are taking such an interest. I believe Mr. and Mrs. Caley hired you to keep up the search for their daughter, and rightly so, but I do not understand why you would spend so much of your time on Tilda. In fact, I feel quite guilty that we are taking you away from your investigation to talk about Tilda."

Lorraine smiled. "Please, Mr. Brown, I think in the end it will only help me. You see, they were such dear friends, the more I find out about Tilda means I am also finding out about poor Anna Louise Caley."

"Ah, yes, I understand, well . . ."

Lorraine opened her briefcase and took out the doll, still

wrapped in the towel. He seemed not to be paying any attention, staring vacantly toward the window. She crossed to a dining table near the window, and unwrapped the doll.

"I didn't want your wife to see this because it is so upsetting, but I think you should."

He joined her at the table, and then gasped. "Dear God, where did you find this?"

"In Tilda's bedroom, hidden in a tennis racket cover."

His hands were shaking as he reached out, not to touch the doll but to hold the edge of the table.

"It was in my daughter's bedroom?" he said, aghast.

"Yes. As you can see, it has her picture on its face, and—"

His fist banged down on the table. "It must be one of the help, but why? Dear God Almighty, what would any one of them make this for? It's disgusting."

"It's a voodoo doll, Mr. Brown."

"I know what it is," he snapped.

"So you see why I am here. I know a girl who worked here, Ruby Corbello, was fired, and I think perhaps she made it out of spite, to frighten Tilda."

"I'll have her arrested."

"But I don't have the proof that she did, Mr. Brown. Also, the newspaper it was wrapped in was dated February fifteenth last year, the day Anna Louise disappeared, so your daughter had this doll for a long time."

He was staring at the doll, and suddenly his shoulders began to shake, and he sobbed, awful dry gasping sobs.

Mrs. Brown walked in, carrying a sheet of violet notepaper. "I've jotted down all the people I can think of."

Mrs. Brown straightened, trying to control himself, but he was obviously very distressed. "I'm sorry, so sorry, please excuse me, I'm sorry."

He rushed past his wife as Lorraine quickly covered the doll and looked after him. Mrs. Brown tried to touch him, but he hurried out, closing the door.

Mrs. Brown joined Lorraine at the window and sighed while looking out. "I think I know what upset him, they used to play in there for hours on end when they were children, Tilda and Anna Louise. We should take it down."

Lorraine looked out in the same direction as Mrs. Brown

but could see only a gardener clipping hedges and a small white building, the size of a shed, close to the bushes.

"My husband built that little playhouse for her and she would never let him take it down. She used to say she wanted to bring our grandchildren here to play in it when she got married, so seeing it must have reminded him. We loved our daughter so much, Mrs. Page."

"Yes, of course, I understand."

Mrs. Brown passed Lorraine the neatly folded sheet of notepaper. "These are some of the friends I know she visited, plus the pastor and group she went to church with. And this is her doctor and the girls she went horseback-riding with, and this is the list of the people she knew at college. I've put down their addresses and phone numbers, or the ones I recalled and were on the Christmas-card lists. Most of them came to her funeral—well, not the ones from her college."

"Thank you, I do appreciate this."

"She didn't go back to Los Angeles after Anna Louise disappeared, said she couldn't face it there. She said she wanted to be here, just in case she called, or made contact." Mrs. Brown drew out her sodden little handkerchief again. "She had been doing so well in college, it was such a shame, but she said she just could not think or concentrate until she found out what had happened to Anna." Mrs. Brown shrugged her shoulders.

"I'm sorry, it must have affected her deeply."

Mrs. Brown nodded. "Yes, it affected us all. Now, well, nothing will ever be the same again."

Lorraine slumped into the car and wound down the window.

"Jesus Christ, they say they don't know why their daughter fucking hanged herself when it's so obvious she was going nuts in that house because her best friend disappears and . . ." Lorraine leaned forward. "She doesn't go back to college. She stays home most of the time and is nervous and worried. She's got a fucking death doll in her tennis racket case. Holy shit, they must really have been blind not to pick up the fact their daughter needed professional help! And added to that, the poor kid had also been fucked royally by her best friend's father. No wonder she tied the knot. I think

I'd maybe do it under the same circumstances.''

François waited as Lorraine checked over Mrs. Brown's neat list of so-called friends. He had no idea what she was talking about, but he nodded his head.

"Okay, François, I want the pastor first. Then we've got to get to the first two addresses on this list.'' She passed him Mrs. Brown's note.

"Yes, ma'am, church it is. Pastor Bellamy is a mighty fine man.''

"You know him?''

"No, ma'am, but he's well known for preachin' a good sermon.''

Lorraine smiled. "Do you all lie, François?''

"Who do you mean by all, Miss Lorraine?''

She laughed. "Cabdrivers, François, cabdrivers. What do you think I meant, all blacks?''

He gave a big, gap-toothed grin that showed an inch of pink gum. "I didn't think a fine lady like you would make a racial remark like that. We hear and see things in a cab, Mrs. Page, but we say nothin'.''

"Unless there's money in it for you,'' she muttered.

"Unless there is money in it.'' He giggled.

They drove out through the front gates, Lorraine turning the interview over in her mind; she was sure it hadn't been the playhouse that had so disturbed Mr. Brown, but the foul-smelling doll she had shown him. She sighed. Maybe she shouldn't have shown it to him—it didn't do any good in the end, just added to their grief.

By ten-thirty Rosie had decided that the amount she was offering was too little. The first cab company seemed not the slightest bit interested in whether or not there was a possible reward for something left in a taxi maybe eleven to twelve months ago, which would entail hours of leafing through old record slips from the previous year. So she rethought her approach, and this time took a cab to the Hotel Cavagnal. She asked if they divided up the territory, cruised, or picked up fares by phone call, and was told that they did all three, so that was not much help. What was also not helpful was that the town was filling up rapidly as the preparations for Mardi Gras began in earnest. Bunting and flags were hung, large floral displays were being watered, and every shopwindow was being decorated. Posters of forthcoming events were being plastered on every available section of wall space, and the streets were beginning to throb with visitors arriving early for the parades.

Rosie got out at the hotel but did not go into the closed courtyard. Instead she walked a block up the street. Anna Louise had not booked a cab via the hotel—that they knew—so did she walk to the main intersection and flag one down? Rosie began to note all the different cabs passing back and forth. A few even slowed down and asked if she needed a ride. Eventually she flagged down a persistent one, which had passed her three times.

"You look like you're lost, ma'am," the driver said politely.

"Nope, not lost. I'm looking for a special taxicab. I'm from an insurance company, and whoever this driver is could be in line for..." She hesitated, wondering how much would be a good incentive. Then she stopped because she remembered Lorraine's saying in one of their note sessions that Robert Caley had seen his daughter's purse on the bed. So, did it mean she did not have any cash on her? If so, maybe someone from the hotel gave her a lift to wherever she went that night.

Rosie waved on her persistent cabdriver and looked around for a phone booth—she needed to talk to Lorraine.

She called the Browns' house to find that Lorraine had already left. She then called the hotel, but neither Rooney nor Lorraine was there. She returned to the Cavagnal and hovered outside for a while, trying to make up her mind what she should do and watching two bellboys carrying new guests' luggage into the hotel, departing guests' luggage out. For a smallish hotel there was a lot of activity. She heard one bellboy shout over to the other as he struggled with a set of Hermès luggage.

"The second-floor blue suite for those, Errol."

Rosie sauntered across to the sweating Errol, wondering if Rooney had already questioned him.

"Hi, I wonder if you could help me out?" she said, smiling warmly.

"Anything you need, ma'am," he said with a slight bow.

Rosie said that she was not a hotel guest, but needed to have a private conversation, and that she would pay for it. If he was unable to talk right that minute she could wait.

Errol pushed his pillbox hat up and gave a look around. "Well, what do you want to talk about?"

Rosie tried the direct approach. "Anna Louise Caley."

He threw up his hands, and shook his head. "Lady, I been asked about that girl more times than I can count. I don't know nothin' about her, and that is the truth."

Rosie looked away, something she'd learned from watching Lorraine. "Fine, it's just that I got five hundred dollars cash for a little bit of information."

"How little is this bit?" he asked, toying with what Robert Caley had said, what he'd given him, and what the future might hold. But a car drew up and he had to get back to work.

"I got a break in fifteen, why don't you come back?"

Robert Caley asked the cabdriver to stop about halfway down the street from Ruby Corbello's house. He paid him and told him if he wanted double his fare he should wait. He then walked down the road to the Corbellos'.

"Why, Mr. Caley!" Juda said, and it pained her to speak because she had such a hangover she could hardly lift her head.

"Mrs. Salina," he said, but without the surprise he felt at seeing her.

"Come on in," she growled, and he looked from the doorstep to see if anyone was watching, but there was no one.

Caley sat in the kitchen, refused any refreshment, mulling over whether or not he should ask after Ruby.

"My sister and niece, Ruby, are out visiting a sick baby. I am here alone, and it's good because it gives me an opportunity to talk to you straight."

He nodded, wondering how much she knew and if, like her niece, she was about to try to blackmail him. It was all becoming too much, too heavy, and he loosened his collar.

"I know you don't like me and you never have," Juda said, as she poured a glass of root beer. "But now I am asking you to help me."

"You want me to help you?" he said with a smile.

"Yes, sir. I've just lost my life's savings—my nephew stole it and I have come back here as penniless as I left over twenty years ago."

Here it comes, he thought, wondering how much she wanted.

"I want to stay on here, Mr. Caley. I don't want to go back to LA, I don't belong there, this is my home."

He looked at the stained wallpaper. This is going to cost, he thought to himself, but he would not show that he had any indication. He'd just act innocent.

"I can't take care of your wife no more, Mr. Caley. She drains me, she uses up everything I have, but I care for her and I don't want to let her down. I feel guilty. I feel that she is my responsibility, and that has been the rope that has hung around my neck. I used to feel that in some way I was to blame, but I no longer believe that."

"Are you asking for money, Mrs. Salina?"

"No, sir, not money, I don't want your money. I want you to get someone else for Mrs. Caley because I am tired out and I want to stay here, move back in with my sister. I want to sell my apartment on Doheny Drive. I don't want to go back there, Mr. Caley."

He coughed and ran his finger around his collar. "I'm still not sure I follow what you are asking from me, Mrs. Salina."

"No, maybe you don't, because you never took much interest, but you should know a lot from what Miss Elizabeth does. The way she behaves is because she can't help it."

"I'm sure she can't," he said brusquely, irritated by Juda, and then leaned across the table. "My wife takes drugs and alcohol like it's going out of fashion, she has an addictive personality."

"No, sir, she has a fear inside her that she is trying to get rid of. Now, you may not believe it, and you have that right, but she needs someone to control her demons. If she does not get help she will go out of her mind."

He smirked. "So you are saying that she isn't right now?"

Juda turned on him. "I am saying that you refuse to understand that your wife needs help, not from your clinics but from—''

''People like you?''

She pushed her face closer. ''Just what do you think I am, Mr. Robert fucking Caley?''

He didn't back off but leaned closer. ''You blackmail my wife and hold her in some kind of terror, that's all I do know.''

''You are wrong. I am forced into trying to control the terror, and what I am saying to you is that I can't do it no more. I am old and I am tired out. She is your wife, you fleece her more than I never even begun to know how, but that is not my business. Mine is to help her, because unlike you, Mr. Caley, I love her.''

''Do you?''

''Yes, sir, I do, but like I said, I am too old, so I am asking you to go back to her. I'll find someone she can hold on to to help her in the way she needs helping.''

''You mean someone who'll feed her drugs?''

Juda sat back, shaking her head. ''No, sir, I mean help her spiritually, that's the only help I have ever given your wife.''

''I am never going back to my wife, Mrs. Salina.''

Juda stared at him and she felt cold, icy cold. The chill moved from her big, bloated feet up through her body. ''Then why did you come here? To tell me that?''

He shrugged. He had come to see Ruby; all this was irritating and now all he wanted was to leave.

Juda stared at his handsome face; she saw his weakness and smiled. ''You will never have the woman you want, Mr. Caley. Your heart is frozen over by greed. I think you should leave, I don't want anything more to do with you.''

He eased back in his chair, about to stand up, when Ruby walked in. She gave him a nonchalant look, crossing to the fridge to take out a root beer for herself.

''Why, if it isn't Mr. Robert Caley,'' she said as she banged open a drawer for the bottle opener.

''You know each other!'' Juda said, surprised.

''Sure, we do, this is Anna Louise's daddy. Am I right?''

Juda looked from Caley and back to Ruby, who opened her bottle and drank it down thirstily.

"I used to work for Tilda Brown, Aunt Juda, you forgettin'? She was Mr. Caley's daughter's closest friend. Isn't that right, Mr. Caley?"

"Yes, that's right," he said, staring at Ruby, unable to fathom what was going on and how much Juda knew. From irritation he had slid into fear.

"Mr. Caley is opening up a big casino, Aunty Juda, gonna be a rich, rich man."

Juda watched her niece, then Caley. She was confused as to what the undercurrent was about, but she could sense it, and see the hold Ruby seemed to have over him.

Ruby sidled up to Caley and flicked her hips at him. He moved away.

"Mr. Caley is a very sexy man and he likes them young and fresh, 'bout my age, is that not so, Mr. Caley?"

He got up, moving as far away from Ruby as he could in the small kitchen. Juda could smell his fear, and she caught hold of Ruby as she passed her.

"Mr. Caley, would you wait in the hallway for a few moments if you please? I can see you want to talk to my niece."

Caley eased past Juda and went into the hall. The kitchen door slammed shut behind him as Juda kicked it closed.

"What's going on, Ruby?"

Ruby sat on the edge of the table, sipping her root beer and enjoying outlining what she had found in Tilda Brown's diary about Robert Caley. She gasped when the punch knocked her to the floor. Her soda bottle broke into fragments and she hunched up, terrified, as Juda picked up the damp dishcloth and began to swipe her with it so hard it made her eyes water. She covered her head, screeching, but then came the kicks and the slaps. It was as if Juda had gone crazy, and she kept up the onslaught until she had to sit down, exhausted. Her breath came in short, sharp rasps.

"You made that doll for Anna Louise Caley, didn't you?"

Ruby began crying, scared of her aunt.

"You shouldn't have done that, Ruby, you did a terrible thing, you raised up evil."

"He's evil, he was fucking that girl Tilda Brown."

Juda kicked her so hard she crunched into a tight ball.

She then ran the cold water and filled a tumbler full to the brim. Ruby didn't see her swallow, all she saw was this massive looming figure leaning over her and spitting out a jet-spray of water. She tried to inch away, but Juda grabbed her hair and then pressed her hands tightly around the girl's skull.

"You got evil in you, girl, an' I got to get it out."

Caley stood in the dank hall, waiting. He couldn't help hearing Ruby's screams and sobs, and the strange high but deep voice of Juda Salina calling out words that he couldn't make out. Eventually Ruby appeared, her hair wet and clinging to her face, and she was weeping.

"Mr. Caley, please don't go." She knelt before him and clasped her hands together. "I am sorry I came and asked you for money, I meant no harm, I have never meant any harm. I will never ask you for anything again, I give you my word. Please, don't you say anything about what I did, just as I won't ever repeat what was in that poor girl's diary."

Caley was nonplussed as Juda walked out from the kitchen.

"You go away from this house now, Mr. Caley, Ruby will never bother you again—she has more important things to do with her life. We want no money from you, we don't want anything from you."

"Is this true, Ruby?"

Ruby remained on her knees, nodding her head, and after a moment he left. Juda stood behind her.

"You never do anything that'll cause such pain again, Ruby, you hear me?"

"Yes, Aunt Juda," she whispered.

"You take in evil and it will possess you, do you understand? You got power, child, and it must not be used for the darkness, or darkness will seep into your soul and you will become its slave. You hear me?"

Ruby nodded, and then watched as her aunt eased her bulk onto her knees beside her.

"You ask forgiveness now, Ruby."

Ruby clasped her hands together. "What if we could get so much money, Aunt Juda, that'd help so many?"

"We don't ever want devil's money because he's sly and he always wants to be repaid. You must never be in debt to the devil. I've seen a woman who owes him, I don't ever want that to happen to you. You got a future ahead of you, but you have to obey the spirits and take care of our own, just like Queen Marie."

Ruby clasped her hands tighter, and whispered to Juda that she was afraid.

"We all are, honey, every living soul is frightened at some point in their lives, but you can help guide people through that fear. You got to respect that power, never abuse it; love it and it will do good. Mr. Caley will pay his own dues, you care only about your own, Ruby."

Errol was rubbing his head, his bellboy's hat in his hands. "I love Ruby Corbello, I have loved her since high school, but she don't seem to know I exist. Sometimes she walks past me on her way to Fryer Jones's bar, swishing her hips, smiling that smile. I know she's out of my league, I know that, but it won't stop my heart from fluttering like I was having some kind of attack. That is what she can do to me, make my heart beat faster than it should."

Rosie nodded. "I know how you feel, I felt that way about someone for a long time. In fact, I never would have believed he would love me, that's how low my self-esteem was, Errol, but, you know, two nights ago he asked me to marry him."

"You kidding me? Someone wants to marry you?" He was wide-eyed with astonishment, not realizing the insult. To his mind, Rosie was so far removed from his beautiful Ruby Corbello it was hard for him to accept that anyone could love the fat woman who sat beside him. It made Rosie laugh.

"I am telling you the truth."

"Maybe, Miss Rosie, it's different for you, you maybe don't understand about *desire*."

"Errol, you believe me. Fat, thin, ugly or beautiful, everyone finds their partner, and he or she becomes the most beautiful creature in the whole wide world," Rosie said with good humor.

"You don't understand, do you? You see, Ruby Corbello

really is the most perfect woman God created. She's a goddess.''

"That worked as a maid for Mr. and Mrs. Brown until she was fired for thieving, and now is sweeping up hair off some floor. Some goddess, Errol.'' Rosie paused. "All I want to know is if you somehow helped Ruby Corbello pass a package to Miss Anna Louise Caley, and if you knew what was in the package. You can be real honest with me because right now there are no police involved.''

Rooney returned to the hotel. He hadn't been able to contact his cop because he was on patrol duty, but was told to call after lunch when he would be back in the office. Nor had he had any joy with the bellboy, who'd been tight-mouthed, so it had been a pretty fruitless morning so far. There was a message at the desk for him to call Lorraine's room.

Rosie opened Lorraine's hotel-room door. She had a smug look on her face, so Rooney guessed she'd found out something, but she remained silent.

Lorraine came out of the bathroom looking worn-out. "Right, I'll start. My morning so far has been heavy, and pretty unproductive. Tilda Brown's father broke down when he saw the doll—and that was the high point. The rest has been downhill, but I've still got a few more 'close' friends to speak to. I hope they are more forthcoming than her local Bible thumper who said, and I quote, 'Tilda Brown was an example to every young teenager. She was joyful, enthusiastic and ready to help anyone in need.' That this joyful bundle tied her own dressing-gown cord to the curtain rail and hanged herself seems to have escaped him. Only one kid, part of the choir that Tilda Brown used to sing in, boy called Eddie Mellor, said she had changed over the past six months. She used to be much more outgoing and friendly, but she had hardly spoken a word to anyone, and seemed to him to be in a very nervous state.''

Rooney coughed. "You mind if I say something?''

"Sure, go ahead.''

"Well, we're hired to trace Anna Louise Caley, and you seem to have gotten sidetracked by this Tilda Brown girl.''

"You saying I'm wasting my time, is that it, Bill?''

"No, but we seem to be sidetracking, that's all."

Rosie told them how she had gone to the hotel and had questioned Errol.

"I did that too," Rooney muttered.

"I know, I'd hoped I'd see you there." Rosie beamed at him. "I just got better results than you, because me and Errol had a good long conversation. He admitted that he had passed a note to Mr. Caley, and he said Ruby Corbello had a conversation with Mr. Caley down by the pool. After Caley had gone back to his room Anna Louise saw Errol and Ruby talking in the courtyard; she beckoned to Ruby to come up, and Ruby asked him to smuggle her up the back stairs. This was, he said, around six o'clock. She was with Anna Louise for only ten minutes, and left the same way she had come in. And he said she was in a mighty hurry. Something we didn't know before is that Errol saw Ruby Corbello again later that night, the night Anna Louise disappeared, and it'd have been about seven-thirty, so she returned to the hotel."

Lorraine flicked through her old notebook. "The Caleys said they went down to eat around that time, in the hotel restaurant."

Rosie nodded. "Ruby, he said, was ducking and diving around the palm trees in the back of the courtyard. He's in love with her, and so he gets all angry because he thinks she's meeting up with one of the other boys working at the hotel. Errol follows her, and she's looking up at Anna Louise Caley, who is bending over her balcony. Which means she was still in her room at seven-thirty."

"Yes, and?" asked Lorraine impatiently.

"Well, by the time Errol got to the balcony, or was standing underneath it, there was no sign of either of them, and he was on duty, so he had to get back out front."

Lorraine sighed. "That's it?"

"Yep. Now, this is just supposition, but Anna Louise could have also used the service stairway, just like Ruby Corbello, to leave the hotel. That would mean she never passed the front desk, never took the elevator. It exits right around the back of the hotel near the garbage collection, and a car could have been waiting for her."

"Mmm," Lorraine said, frowning as she crossed to her

desk and searched around the top. "Need to know how long it takes from the hotel to Ruby Corbello's house."

Rooney and Rosie glanced at each other.

Lorraine was flicking through the maps and guides, chucking them aside, hunting for the street map she'd seen of the tourist attractions.

"If Ruby Corbello left that hotel at six-fifteen, then returned at seven-thirty, that gives her just over an hour to make that doll, wrap it up, and take it back to Anna Louise."

"Unless she made it at Fryer Jones's place," Rooney said.

Lorraine found the map and squinted over the small print. Then, tracing the route with her finger, she tapped impatiently on the table.

"Maybe she did make it at Fryer Jones's. If she didn't, it was quite a schlepp to her house unless . . ."

"Somebody drove her there," Rosie suggested.

"Yes, somebody drove her."

All three of them stood by the trash cans outside the staff entrance of the Hotel Cavagnal. Rosie was to take the route to Fryer Jones's bar and return, Rooney was to do the run to the Corbellos'. They both asked Lorraine the same question. "What are you going to do?"

"Talk to security. Okay, check watches and *move*!"

She was smiling as she watched them both charge off like kids at a sports-day event. She noted how many people came and went via the staff entrance. Then she slipped inside and walked down a narrow corridor. A small staircase led off to the right at the far end, and she moved up the stairs until she came to a door marked FOR AUTHORIZED PERSONNEL ONLY. Lorraine opened the door; standing with his back to it was a security guard. He didn't even hear the door close behind him as Lorraine continued up another flight of stairs till she reached Robert Caley's floor. She had seen no one, had not been stopped at any point, and she did a U-turn back the way she came. Again she saw no one, but when she opened the door to leave, a security guard turned, frowning. "You staff here?"

"No, I'm a guest," Lorraine said briskly, and gave the number of the suite she had used. He held up his hand, asked her name and dialed reception. When it was confirmed that the suite had been booked for Lorraine Page by Mr. Robert Caley, he apologized but warned her that she should not have used the private staircase, it was for staff only.

"I'm very impressed with the hotel security," she said, smiling.

He gave a small nod of his head.

"Is this exit covered at all times?"

"Yes, ma'am."

"Day and night?"

"Yes, ma'am."

"How many officers are on security?"

"Three, ma'am, we work in shifts."

"How long have you worked here?"

"Five years."

She nodded and kept smiling. "You were here, then, when Anna Louise Caley disappeared?"

"Yes, I was."

"I am employed by Mr. Caley to trace his daughter. You were obviously questioned, as I believe most of the staff were."

"Yes, I was."

Lorraine turned to face the staff door. "Maybe she left the hotel this way, that is why no one saw her leaving. Do you think it possible?"

He shrugged, not committing himself.

"You have to take the odd break, so it could have happened?"

"Guess so. Like you said, we take breaks, but usually we try and cover for each other."

She smiled, and turned to face the small yard. "Do cars ever park down here?"

"No, no parking allowed. If anyone parks here they get towed."

"But you could get picked up from here easily."

"Yeah, picking someone up is not parking, and some of the women working at night like to be met. There's a lot of drunk guys in the French Quarter."

"I'm sorry, what did you say?"

"The women like to feel safe."

"Is there a particular cab company they use?"

"Yeah, Gordon's Cabs—staff uses Gordon's Cabs."

Lorraine nodded. "But not the guests?"

He smiled. "No, ma'am, they not very luxurious. Just two brothers, one of 'em used to work here. You want their number?"

"Thank you," Lorraine said pleasantly, and passed him ten bucks. He pocketed it fast, then took out a ballpoint pen and jotted down a number on the back of a hotel card.

"Thank you, I'm expecting two friends shortly. A plump woman and a big, red-faced man. Could you tell them to come up to my suite?"

Lorraine walked out onto the street and then around to the front lobby of the hotel. She had been lucky that Robert Caley had booked the suite for her. She got her key from reception, asking if Mr. Caley was in his suite, and was very relieved to be told he was not. She then took the elevator to her floor. The room was wonderfully cool, and she sat on the bed and ordered some tea and cakes, then called Gordon's Cabs. There was an answering machine on, but she left no message, deciding she'd call again. Her eyes kept drifting to the closed door to the adjoining suite, her body remembering the night she had spent there. She walked slowly toward it, knowing she would have to face Caley sooner or later. It was locked, and she pressed her face against the white glossy wood door with relief. But she couldn't just forget their closeness, dismiss it, because it had been real. She had felt so loved that night. Then she felt scared because she remembered Juda's words about her being without love, and having been without it for a long time, and the sadness welled up inside her. That night had not had anything to do with love, it was lust, and she was sure that Robert Caley had used her because he had been protecting himself, covering his tracks so she could not unearth the truth of how he had killed his daughter. She stepped briskly away from the door. She had said it to herself earlier, now she said it out loud, pointing to the adjoining bedroom door.

"I am going to nail you, Robert Caley."

CHAPTER
18

Rosie had returned and was surveying the suite as the tea Lorraine had ordered arrived.

"My, this is very nice, I could move in here," Rosie said admiringly, looking from the hangings over the bed to the luxurious bathroom.

Lorraine poured tea for them both. "How long did it take you?"

"I walked there in forty-five minutes. If I'd been running I could have done it in less. Bar was jumping by the way, great music and a group outside drinking beer, kids mostly. This town's heating up, an' I don't mean the weather."

Rooney did not appear for another twenty minutes, and he was hot and sweating. He sank onto the bed with a moan, paying no attention to the decor of the suite.

"Fucking hot out there. Knock off ten minutes trying to flag down a cab, streets are crowded, and Mardi Gras's not even started yet. They got clowns walking around passing out leaflets, and there was a couple of jams, but I'd say if Ruby had a clear night she could get there and back in just less than an hour."

"Which does not give her long to make the doll," Lorraine said moodily.

"So she did it at Fryer's," Rosie said, passing Rooney a cup of tea.

"It wasn't exactly well made," Rooney said.

Lorraine sighed. "You know, we're just kind of grasping

at straws, trying to make the jigsaw pieces fit together.''

"You're trying to get her to Tilda Brown's house, right?''
Rooney said, and she nodded.

"But nobody saw her there either, just like nobody saw
her leave here, no cab company picked her up and she didn't
have a purse on her.''

"We've got a possible.''

"Possible what?'' Rosie asked.

"Cab company. The staff uses these two brothers for late-
night pickups, but they're not listed in Information, I've
checked. I think they're just two guys with a couple of cars,
so they're probably working without a license. You want to
check them out, Rosie? Maybe see them face-to-face. And
when you've finished your tea, Bill, call that cop and get
over to Fryer's. Check out the necklace and put a feeler out
about whether or not Ruby was there on the night of the
fifteenth.''

Lorraine yawned. She felt tired and depressed, as if they
were going around and around in circles. Time was moving,
they had only a week left, and they all knew it. Bill and
Rosie took off without complaint.

Lorraine hadn't meant to fall asleep, she'd meant to let it
all run by in her mind, sift through everything they had
come up with so far. She didn't hear the key turning in the
connecting door, which opened so silently she was unaware
that Robert Caley had walked into the room.

He stroked her cheek with one finger, and she woke with
a start.

"Hi! I was beginning to think I'd never see you again.''

She eased herself up, blushing.

"You never return my calls—do you know how many
times I have tried to see you, talk to you? In fact, the receptionist at your hotel knows me so well I don't even have
to say my name.''

"I'm sorry, but I've been caught up.''

He sat on a chair opposite the bed. He was wearing a
white collarless shirt and jeans, with the loafers she liked.

"I wanted to take you to one of the riverboats, I've
wanted to take you to a whole lot of places.''

"Well, I am here to work, you know, Robert.''

"Oh, I know that, but if you don't want to see me, why don't you come out and say so?"

"Things keep on getting in the way."

He cocked his head to one side. "How about dinner tonight?"

"I don't think so." She wouldn't look at him.

"You don't think so? Do I take it that you have other engagements? What do you mean, you don't think so?"

She chewed her lip. He stared at her, trying to fathom her, and then leaned forward. "It would be nice to celebrate with someone."

She looked up. "Celebrate?"

He nodded. "Casino development's going ahead. An out-of-town group got the license, but because I had the land I'm in as a partner. Dulay switched sides, but I've got him and his group eating right out of my hand. So the big bucks are going to start rolling in."

"How is Elizabeth?" she interrupted.

"I don't know. I told you the last time I saw you—I've left her. I've been here since then, waiting for you behind that connecting door!"

"Have you?" Lorraine eased her legs from the bed and pressed her feet into the carpet, staring down at her toes. She took a deep breath and slowly raised her head to meet his eyes. "You are a very good liar, Mr. Caley, one of the best I have ever come across."

"What?"

"You heard me, you are a liar."

He leaned back, turning his palms up. "What have I lied about?"

She eased herself from the bed and walked to the dressing table. He reached to touch her, but she sidestepped his outstretched hand. She began to brush her hair, keeping eye contact via the mirror. "What have you lied about? Well, let's try Ruby Corbello for one."

He leaned back again slightly but he didn't take his eyes off her face.

"She got a message to you, through the bellboy Errol, for you to meet at the swimming pool. That would be on the night of February fifteenth last year, and in case it has slipped your memory, that was also the night your daughter, or adopted daughter, disappeared.''

He looked away, showing no emotion at all.

"Ruby had a diary, didn't she? Tilda Brown's diary, and in this teenager's diary it gave explicit details of her sex life with you. *You*, Mr. Caley! So that kiss on the tennis courts wasn't quite as innocent as you made out, was it?''

He shrugged his shoulders and then leaned on his elbow, his hand partly covering his face, but his eyes were steady and didn't flinch from her angry gaze.

"What have you got to say to that?''

"Not a lot, Lorraine, but if you want me to go into details, then I will. Tilda Brown was not underage, she was eighteen years old. In fact, she made all the moves, and as you are more than aware of my wife's physical problems, not to mention her mental state, having a young, pretty and nubile girl creeping into your bedroom at night is hard to ignore, let alone the hard-on she gave me. So I fucked her. She liked it, I liked it, and there is no more to be said.''

"She also committed suicide," snapped Lorraine.

"I know, and I am deeply sorry about it, but I don't see that my sexual relationship with her can have anything to do with it.''

"Don't you?''

"No, I don't, but you obviously do. So if you have something to say, say it.''

Lorraine threw down her hairbrush. "Your daughter was fighting Tilda Brown for your affections, and you knew it. What happened, you get a kick out of that as well? As you pointed out to me, Anna Louise was not your daughter anyway, so were you also fucking her?''

"No, I wasn't. Just Tilda and a few other lady friends—you want their names?'' He sprang to his feet, and now she could see how angry he was. A small muscle at the side of his neck was twitching. "I lied to shield Tilda. She was already deeply distressed by Anna Louise's disappearance, and I wanted to protect her from further unnecessary questions by the police and investigators.''

"To shield Tilda or yourself?''

"Does it matter?''

Lorraine snapped open her briefcase and took out the towel with the doll in it.

"Unwrap it, have a look. I think your little blackmailing friend, Ruby Corbello, made that for your daughter to give to your girlfriend Tilda. Go on, open it, Robert. As you said, she was eighteen, she knew what she was doing. What you didn't say was just how long you had been having a sexual relationship with her. She was your daughter's childhood friend, wasn't she?"

He slapped her face, and she picked up the brush and swiped him across the cheek. He stepped back. "My, that was a nice left hook, but then you're a tough lady, aren't you? And you have the scars to prove it. A whore, a drunkard . . . I should have asked for a blood test before I fucked you, shouldn't I?"

"You bastard!" she snapped.

"Am I? And what are you? At least I know with someone as young as Tilda she's unlikely to be diseased."

She kicked him hard in the groin. He gasped and clutched at himself, leaning forward. "I can also take care of myself, Mr. Caley. You want to say shit to me, you'll get it back, which is something else maybe a young innocent kid couldn't do. Now look at the doll."

He was wincing with pain, still bent forward, as she flipped open the towel to show the voodoo doll.

"Do you know if Ruby Corbello made this for your daughter?"

"Of course I fucking don't, it's disgusting!"

"So are you. I found this in Tilda's bedroom, hidden in a tennis racket case."

He turned back to sit on the bed. "Anna Louise wouldn't do something as sick as that. Her mother, maybe. In fact, if you know who made it I'll order one for Elizabeth."

"You think it's funny?"

"No, I don't, I don't know what the hell to think, and with this burning fucking pain in my testicles it's tough thinking about anything right now. What the hell did you kick me in the nuts for?"

Lorraine rewrapped the doll. "You've gotten away with stealing from her trust fund. You're a thief, Robert Caley."

He laughed. "Bullshit, I'll be able to pay every cent back.

I've even offered to, but Lloyd Dulay wouldn't hear of it, and it's his cash, Lorraine. So who's stealing from whom?''

"You stole Tilda Brown's innocence.''

He threw his head back, laughing. "Did I? So what was that you told me about her and Anna Louise getting gang-banged at some club? Lorraine, you are thrashing around trying to find something, anything, to prove that I am . . . what? What are you trying to prove I am?''

"A thief.''

He laughed. "I admit it. Right, what next? Oh, of course, a child molester, right, that's the second thing, anything else?''

"A murderer, maybe.''

He straightened up, still nursing himself between the legs. "Who did I murder, Lorraine? Anna Louise, is that what you are trying to prove?''

She folded her arms.

"I didn't kill my daughter, I know no reason why she disappeared off the face of the earth unless it was to get away from her fucking mother, like I am doing. I admit I used Anna Louise's trust fund, but I had every right, I had given the best years of my life to Elizabeth, and to her daughter. I looked out for that child from the day she was born, and I had to be satisfied with that bitch doling out money as if I was a hired hand. It was me who built up her properties, worth almost nothing when I found them, now valued at millions. It was me who covered for her drinking, her drugs, me who saved her life, not once but Christ knows how many times, and I was never shown an ounce of respect. I have been cross-examined, interviewed, interrogated by cops and people like you, who in the end are all pursuing the investigation for money. But you, you win the prize. You're so desperate for that one million bucks my crazy wife offered, you will try anything, and I know why. You have only six more days to crack this case. You even fucked me to get more information. You, sweetheart, are the lowest of them all. Now get your stinking piece of evidence and get out of here before I throw you out on your ass, you whore!''

He was so angry he was panting, but she didn't back down. Instead she smiled at him.

"Takes one to know one, Robert." She threw a right upper cut, and he stepped back and let go with a body punch that made her gasp and totter backward, but she pushed herself off the wall, ready to go at him again. She walked into his fist, catching her right eye. He froze, not wanting to brawl with her, and that was his mistake. Lorraine brought her knee up, crunching him yet again, and then she punched him in the face so hard she felt her knuckles split open on his teeth. He sank to his knees, unable to make a sound.

She picked up her briefcase, shoved the doll inside and snapped it closed. She tossed twenty bucks onto his moaning, huddled figure. "That's for the tea."

She was shaking her fist—it hurt her more than his punch to her eye. As she opened the door the telephone rang. She hesitated and picked up the extension nearest to the door.

Rosie was so excited she was gasping. "We got lucky. Nicky Gordon picked up a girl outside the staff exit of the hotel. He had just dropped off a regular."

Lorraine interrupted Rosie, partly because Robert Caley was slowly getting to his feet, and partly because she was eager to know where the luck came in.

"Where did he take her?"

"Tilda Brown's."

Rooney laid the steak over Lorraine's eye, which was now really swollen.

"Hey, if you think I look bad, you should see the other guy."

Rosie was bandaging her knuckles, which were swollen, the skin split open. "You might have a cracked knuckle, Lorraine," she said.

"Bullshit, it's okay, I'm okay." Lorraine struggled up and staggered to the mirror. She took one look and felt as if she was going to faint; her right eye was closed and already dark bruising was showing above and below.

"Well, I look really good, didn't think it was this bad. Anyway, let's not waste any more time."

Rosie flipped open her book. "Reason he never reported it, or has never been questioned, is because he thought the girl was staff and she wore a head scarf and dark glasses. She came out of the staff entrance as he dropped Mimi Lav-

ette, a fifty-year-old chambermaid, off for the late shift. He
was doing a U-turn when we think Anna Louise waved him
down, gave him the address, and got impatient with him
when he had to double-check it. He got all nervous, even
talking to me, just for the so-called reward. You were right,
he hasn't got a taxi license, and judging from the look of
the vehicle I'd say that it's not taxed or insured either.''

Lorraine pressed the steak to her eye as the telephone
rang. Rosie answered, told the caller to hang on, and for a
moment Lorraine thought it might be Robert Caley, but it
was the cop, Harris Harper. He couldn't see Rooney until
the morning.

Lorraine suggested they leave visiting Fryer's bar until
the following day. Returning to Tilda Brown's home had to
be their first priority. She wouldn't let Rosie go with them
to the Browns' house. Two people questioning them was
one thing, but three looked like the heavy mob was in town.

Rooney and Lorraine went up the steps and rang the bell,
which echoed through the dark hallway. Lorraine peered in
through the glass as Rooney rang again. A maid turned on
the hall lights and opened the door.

"I urgently need to speak to Mr. or Mrs. Brown."

" 'Fraid they are not at home."

"When will they be back?"

"They is dining with friends."

Lorraine, Rooney and her driver François sat in the car
for over an hour. At last they saw the headlights of a car
heading toward them.

"Here they come, I hope."

They watched the car slow down and swerve past them
to take a left-hand turn into the driveway. Lorraine dug
François in the back. "Go after them, we don't want them
to refuse to let us in."

Mr. and Mrs. Brown turned, startled, as Lorraine got out
of the car.

"Mr. Brown, I'm so sorry, but I need to speak to you."

Half an hour later, Mr. and Mrs. Brown were still adamant
that Tilda, on the night of February 15, had remained in her
room watching her own TV. She had not eaten with them

but had had a tray sent up at seven-thirty. They had both gone up to say good night at ten-thirty. She had not left her room, no one had stopped by and no one had telephoned. All this had been stated over and over many times and Mr. and Mrs. Brown were tired and becoming irritated.

"Could I just go to her room, please?"

Rooney and Lorraine stood in the center of the dead girl's bedroom as Mr. Brown opened the doors onto the low, metal-railed balcony. Mrs. Brown had started weeping again, and her husband was angry at the intrusion, but Lorraine refused to leave. Rooney was embarrassed at the couple's obvious distress, and he was very uneasy. Lorraine looked bad, her bruised eye had swollen and was still closed.

"Maybe we leave it until the morning," he had said quietly.

"No. If that cabdriver was telling the truth, then Anna Louise Caley came here that night." Lorraine stepped out on the balcony and pointed to a narrow metal stairway leading down to the garden. "You don't have a dog, do you?"

"No, we don't."

She looked across the garden. "So if someone did come here at night and crossed the lawns, they could easily walk up to this balcony?"

"Yes, I suppose so, but why would they want to?"

"If they didn't want to be seen, Mr. Brown, and if they also knew the layout of the house, knew by looking up at this window that Tilda was here, someone could have come and gone?"

Mr. Brown pursed his lips and then suddenly turned to Lorraine. "What exactly are you trying to suggest? That my daughter had someone up here, someone she didn't want us to see?"

"No, Mr. Brown, maybe that someone did not want to be seen. Could you leave us alone for ten minutes? I'd appreciate it."

The Browns left Rooney and Lorraine alone, but it was quite obvious they did not approve, and said they would wait in the drawing room for ten minutes and no more. As the door closed, Lorraine turned to Rooney. "What you thinking?"

He sat down on the dead girl's bed. "Not a lot. So Anna

Louise came here and left. We got almost four missing hours before Robert Caley and his wife contacted the police, so she could have met with Tilda Brown, but after that God only knows what happened to her.''

Lorraine picked up the white polar bear, and tossed it back on the bed. ''If she left, she didn't take a cab, no record of her doing so, and the taxi she came in had already left. Bill, what if she never left here?''

''What?''

Lorraine walked out on the balcony and stared across the gardens. Just to her right was the playhouse, the place where the two girls had played as children, now locked up, and suddenly Lorraine knew. The hairs on the back of her neck prickled.

''I don't think she did.''

''What?'' It was Rooney's turn now.

''Come on downstairs, Bill.''

Mr. and Mrs. Brown sat in their drawing room in subdued but angry silence as Lorraine walked in, but before they could ask her to leave she pointed to the window with its expensive slatted blinds.

''The playhouse in the garden—I noticed it was pad-locked, can you tell me why?''

Mrs. Brown looked at her husband in confusion, but he only frowned in response.

''Did you padlock it, Mr. Brown?''

''Not that I can recall. Did you, honey?''

''No, I thought perhaps you had done it. Maybe Tilda did.''

He stood up. ''I didn't. In fact I avoid looking at the thing, it brings back such memories. Are you sure? Padlocked?''

Lorraine shrugged. ''Well, I saw the chain when I was here in daylight, maybe I'm wrong. Do you have a flash-light?''

Rooney plodded after Lorraine, Mr. Brown walked ahead with the light.

''Can you tell me what the fuck we're doing, Lorraine?'' Rooney whispered.

''You tell me. Everybody else on this street has security

cameras, they don't. They leave their gates open and put a padlock on a kids' playhouse? Doesn't make sense.''

The faint beam of the flashlight showed there was a padlock, and quite a heavy one.

''Perhaps the gardener is storing equipment in there?'' Mr. Brown suggested.

''Do you have bolt cutters or something we can get the lock open with?''

''Why?'' asked Mr. Brown.

Lorraine hesitated. ''I want to see what's inside.''

It was another ten minutes before they had prized open one of the links in the thick chain. Lorraine eased back the child-size door and stooped low to enter.

''Can you shine the light inside, please?''

Two chairs and a small matching table set with plastic teacups and saucers, and a tiny cotlike bed with two dolls tucked under a blanket were all that could fit inside.

''There's nothing here,'' Rooney said.

Lorraine took the flashlight from Mr. Brown and shone it around the house, then down to the plastic sheeting that covered the floor.

''Can you smell anything, Bill?''

Rooney sniffed, leaning in from the tiny door. ''Just mildew.''

''I'm rather cold,'' Mr. Brown said, standing outside, behind Rooney. Lorraine suggested he return to the house, and after hesitating a moment he walked away. She shone the yellow beam slowly over the interior, sniffing, until she got down on her knees and sniffed closer to the ground.

''Mildew, you sure?''

Rooney sighed, and bent low to get inside. He sniffed. ''Yeah, mildew, like moss or mold or something, but that's natural. It must be hot as hell when the sun shines inside here, it's all plastic and it'll sweat with the heat. What you doing?''

''Hold the goddamned light, Bill, I'm gonna pull back the ground-sheet.''

''For God's sake, Lorraine, why don't we come back in the morning?''

''Because we're here now, so do as I say.''

Rooney was on his hands and knees, shining the flashlight as Lorraine began to pull back the plastic groundsheet. She pushed the little chairs and table aside and, crawling on all fours, dragged back the sheet. She sat back on her heels, reached over to the table and took one of the small plastic plates.

''What you doing?''

''Digging, what do you think it looks like? Keep the light up, for Chrissakes, I can't see.''

Rooney crouched down, watching as she scraped the earth away from beneath the groundsheet.

''Ground would be dry in here. It was February, right? So if something was buried under this sheet it'd stay dry, and being inside, you said it stinks of mildew. Well, if a body was hidden under here we'd expect a lot of mold, same smell as mildew.''

Rooney held up the torch, then moved its beam to spread further over the tiny floor space, leaving Lorraine in darkness.

''What you doing?''

''Looking for droppings, rats'd be clawing their way in here if there was a body, and there's nothing, Lorraine. Plus they got raccoons in these parts, they'd have torn the place apart.''

She continued digging with the plastic dish, her hands and nails filthy, and Rooney shined the torch, watching. One inch down, two inches down, and still she shoveled the earth, making a deep hole. Then the beam from the flashlight began to fade.

''Batteries are running out,'' he said.

Lorraine began to scratch and dig the earth with her bare hands, and then she sat back. ''There's something here, come closer. For God's sake, get closer, I can't see. And it'd help if you gave me a hand.''

Rooney crawled toward her, the flashlight beam now just a faint yellow. ''What is it?''

''I dunno, I can't fucking see. You dig, I'll hold the light.'' She leaned back and took it from him as he began to dig harder. He used one of the plastic cups, scooping up the earth. Soil sprayed over Lorraine, and she brushed it aside.

"Shit! You're right, there *is* something." Rooney dug for a few more minutes and then squinted at the hole. They could just see a corner section of a black plastic trash bag. Rooney lifted up his hand; white maggots were clinging to it, covering the cuff of his jacket. "Aw shit, there's millions of them, maggots, fucking white maggots."

"Gimme the flashlight, I can't see a damned thing."

Lorraine passed the light over, and he shined it down into the hole he had sliced through the black plastic. As he carefully inched it aside they could see part of a skull in the yellow beam, the skin completely decomposed, but there was a portion of long blond hair and what looked like a headband.

"I think we just found Anna Louise Caley," Rooney said softly.

"We also maybe just got one million dollars," Lorraine added.

Rooney looked at her face, a black eye on one side and her scar running down the other. She looked like a prize-fighter coming up for round ten.

"You don't give in easy, do you?"

"Nope, but then life's not that easy. Least, mine isn't." She stood up, still having to bend, as the roof of the house was so low. "I'll go and see the Browns."

They were still there at dawn, as the police put up their cordons and arc lamps. It took two hours for the entire body to be dug up. The corpse was wrapped in four layers of black garbage bags, Scotch tape wound round and round the bags, virtually mummifying the body. All that was left were scraps of rotting cloth. The corpse had been buried almost a year, judging by the extent of the decomposition. Beetles and maggots were lodged in the eye sockets and the inside of the skull. There had been no terrible odor of death because all the gases had evaporated, and the mummification of the body, wrapped tightly with no air, had dried all the body tissues. There was little left as a means to identify the body, but the dental records and possibly the fine, almost waist-length blond hair. They would even find it difficult to determine what had caused the death.

• • •

By eleven o'clock the next morning the dental records had
been flown to the forensic laboratory from Los Angeles. The
body was formally identified at twelve-thirty. Anna Louise
Caley had died approximately eleven months ago. She had
been killed by a single blow to the back of her head, probably inflicted by a rounded, blunt-edged instrument.

Elizabeth Caley was informed at 12:45 P.M. that the body
of her daughter had been recovered at Tilda Brown's home.
She was also told that it had been discovered by Lorraine
Page and her partner, Mr. William Rooney. It was just after
two the same afternoon that Lorraine and François drove
back through the Garden District to the Caley residence.

"You want your bonus?" Elizabeth asked coldly. She
looked as elegant as ever, and Lorraine was impressed at
the woman's resilience.

"I will have all my reports typed up and sent to you,
either in Los Angeles or here, whichever you prefer."

"How did she die?" Elizabeth asked, lighting a cigarette.

"It's difficult to give you details at this stage, but she had
a deep indentation on the back of her skull."

Elizabeth inhaled. "They brought a headband—the police
asked if I could identify it as Anna Louise's. It wasn't hers,
it was mine."

Lorraine checked over all the receipts of their expenses,
which Rosie had meticulously kept and clipped neatly together.

"I will send our details of costs for the trip to New Orleans to Phyllis, unless you would like them left here? Mrs.
Caley?"

Elizabeth stared out of the long window at the fig orchard.
"Send them to Phyllis, she'll pay you."

Lorraine replaced the documents in her briefcase.

"Who killed her, Mrs. Page?" Elizabeth asked quietly.

Lorraine hesitated. "This is just supposition, because
without her statement obviously we will never know exactly
what happened."

"So what do you think happened?"

"Well, your daughter was very jealous of Tilda Brown.

Did you know Tilda was having a sexual relationship with your husband?''

Elizabeth arched one fine eyebrow, ''Well, I suppose he needed to get it someplace. It certainly wasn't from me.''

Lorraine looked away. Mrs. Caley sickened her—there seemed no emotion in her whatsoever, she was calm, almost sarcastic.

''Go on, please. I'm paying you for this, so I might as well hear what you have to say.''

''Anna Louise seemed to be very jealous because she was in love with her adoptive father, and the fight the two girls had before you and Anna Louise left Los Angeles was because your daughter had seen Tilda kissing or embracing Mr. Caley.''

''The cheap bastard,'' Elizabeth said bitterly, stubbing out her cigarette.

Lorraine licked her lips. Her head was throbbing, and her eye, although now less swollen, was still painful; moreover, she had been up all night.

''Go on, Mrs. Page,'' Elizabeth snapped.

''Well, after you arrived at your hotel that afternoon of February fifteenth, Tilda . . .''

Elizabeth crossed to the window and stood gazing out at the trees as Lorraine continued.

''I know that your husband met with a Ruby Corbello, a girl who used to be a maid at Tilda Brown's. She was trying to blackmail him.''

''What?''

''She had found Tilda Brown's diary and she wanted to get money for it. The diary contained confirmation that Tilda and your husband were having a relationship.''

''You read this diary?'' Elizabeth asked.

''No, I did not. I have not seen the diary, but your husband has admitted that he did meet with Miss Corbello, and she did give him the diary. He paid her two hundred dollars for it.''

Elizabeth laughed. ''Cheap at the price—silly child could have asked for a lot more. Go on, Mrs. Page.''

Lorraine told her that after negotiating for the diary with Robert Caley, Ruby had then been called to Anna Louise's room at the hotel, because, Lorraine thought, Anna Louise wanted to ask her to make a voodoo doll resembling Tilda, and when Ruby was seen back at the hotel later the same evening, she had probably come to deliver it. Lorraine noticed that Elizabeth's hand was shaking, but otherwise the actress remained impassive, gesturing for her to continue, and Lorraine went on to tell her that a cabdriver had recalled collecting a young woman from the hotel and taking her to Tilda Brown's house on the night of February 15 the previous year. Lorraine reached over and sipped some iced tea that had been brought in when she arrived. "That was the last sighting of your daughter, nobody ever saw her again. I think she knew Tilda's house so well that she did not enter via the front door but went up the staircase from the garden to see Tilda. Her parents have stated that Tilda never left her bedroom that night, so possibly they met at around seven-forty-five."

Elizabeth sat down, running her hand down her slim-fitting skirt, crossing her ankles. "Go on, please."

Lorraine sighed, her head really throbbing now. "How do we know what exactly happened? They were young, angry with each other, jealous, and both had been to Juda Salina on numerous occasions for tarot reading or whatever. Both girls, having been brought up here, were obviously aware of voodoo—Anna Louise perhaps because of your connections."

"My connections?" Elizabeth said sharply.

"You did play Marie Laveau, you even have a portrait of yourself in the role in the house in Los Angeles. So Anna Louise must have been aware of the voodoo culture. Perhaps they were both afraid of it, I don't really know, but I think Anna Louise wanted to scare Tilda, wanted to frighten her badly. Perhaps she showed her the doll and that started it, who knows, but they had fought before. In fact, when I interviewed Tilda she described how Anna Louise had struck her and punched and scratched her. So these two girls had fought before—perhaps that night they did again, and perhaps Tilda picked up something, a tennis racket maybe? And struck out at Anna Louise."

As Lorraine opened a pack of cigarettes and lit one, Elizabeth remained silent, head bowed slightly.

"Perhaps Anna Louise was leaving, facing the balcony,

and Tilda struck her from behind. There were stains on the carpet in that area, but after Tilda's suicide the carpet was cleaned, so we will never know if there had been blood there or not.''

Elizabeth looked blankly to the window.

''I think Tilda went down to the kitchen for some plastic bags right away because the body was wrapped very tightly soon after death. She then used reels and reels of Scotch tape to seal the bags around the body. She may have hidden it in her room, waited until the following morning, and could have dropped it over the balcony and dragged it to the playhouse. At some point she dug the grave, and buried Anna Louise, then put a padlock on the door and—''

''Left my baby rotting,'' Elizabeth said softly.

''Yes. Tilda did not return to college. She remained with her family, and from people I have interviewed I understand she became nervous and withdrawn, probably living in a state of terror that the body would be found. I think my visit to her must have scared her very much because someone new was making inquiries after all that time. I think I was the only one who had discovered not only the two girls' sexual permissiveness, but also their jealousy. Tilda became very upset when I interviewed her but did not give me any indication she had played a part in Anna Louise's murder.''

''Played a part? Dear God, she killed her!''

''I would say the surrounding pressures and the—''

''Please don't excuse the girl—she murdered my daughter.''

''Yes, she did.''

Elizabeth stood up, pressing her hands down her sides, then brushed one across the crease in her skirt. ''So, it's over.''

Lorraine also stood up. She swayed, feeling faint, and had to hold on to the arm of the chair.

''Are you all right?'' Elizabeth asked, looking directly at Lorraine for almost the first time since she had arrived.

''I am very tired.''

''What happened to your face?''

''Oh, I bumped into a door, it's nothing. But I would like to leave now.''

Elizabeth crossed to an escritoire and opened it. She sat

down on one of the delicate English chairs and drew out a checkbook. Lorraine picked up her jacket and briefcase.

"Do you still have the doll, Mrs. Page?"

"Yes, yes, I do."

"You didn't give it to the police?"

"No."

"Would you leave it here? I don't think it is necessary for it to be seen by anyone else."

Lorraine opened her case again.

"Why didn't you give it to the police, if I might ask?"

"Well, it is only circumstantial evidence."

"My, my, we are so professional, aren't we?"

Lorraine put down the doll, still wrapped in the hotel towel.

Elizabeth ripped out the check and blew on it to dry the ink. She then held it out at arm's length. "Your bonus, Mrs. Page."

Lorraine walked the few paces toward Mrs. Caley and took the check. She glanced at the amount: one million dollars.

"It won't bounce," Elizabeth said as she closed the lid of her desk. Then, without turning back, she picked up the doll and walked to the door.

"The maid will show you out, Mrs. Page. Thank you very much."

Lorraine remained standing, staring at the check as the *click-click* of Elizabeth Caley's high heels died away on the hall tiles.

Missy appeared and gestured for Lorraine to go with her to the front door. By now Elizabeth was almost at the top of the sweeping staircase, but she didn't look back as Lorraine left.

Elizabeth watched her depart in her car with her driver, and then let the curtain fall back into place. She crossed to the bureau. The headband was still in the plastic bag the police had brought it in, and she touched it with one delicate finger, before picking it up and tossing it into the wastepaper basket. She crossed to the bed, where she had placed the doll and slowly unwrapped it, staring down at the hideous face with Tilda Brown's photograph, the pin stuck through the doll's left eye. She picked it up, carried it to the old wide fireplace, bent down and set it on the bars of the empty grate. She emptied an entire bottle of nail-polish remover over it before she struck a match and set it alight. She stood there as the flames caught and burned it quickly; last to blacken and melt was the small plastic doll's head with Tilda Brown's face.

Elizabeth waited until all that was left were charred ashes and the acrid smell of burned plastic. She then went to her bedside and picked up Anna Louise's photograph and held it to her chest. She lay down, clutching the picture, her face impassive, but gradually her eyes filled with tears and they trickled down her cheeks, until she began sobbing quietly, saying her daughter's name over and over again, whispering that she was sorry, so very sorry.

Robert Caley had asked to see the body or what was left of it, but nothing had prepared him for the blackened, decomposed corpse. He was shocked and distressed, staying no more than a few moments. Like his wife, he wept for Anna Louise. He also asked for her forgiveness, knowing that in many ways he had been to blame. He was now on his way to accomplishing everything he had dreamed about, and he would without doubt be a very rich man, but he felt empty, drained and ashamed. Two young girls had died as a result of his foolishness and selfishness. The woman he could love had seen him for what he was, and he knew the damage was irreparable. Just thinking of her made him look toward the connecting bedroom door, and his heart thudded as it opened.

"Excuse me, Mr. Caley, but the manager has asked if you will still be requiring the double suite as—"

"No, no, I will also be leaving by tonight."

"Shall I tell the manager, then, Mr. Caley? Only with the Carnival coming up—"

"Yes, please, thank you."

The maid shut the door and locked it, and he packed his bags, wanting to get out as soon as possible.

The bellboy was carrying them to his car when Saffron Dulay drove up in her convertible Rolls Corniche.

"Honey, you're not leavin', are you?"

He looked at her as she slid out of the driver's seat and

sashayed toward him, arms held out for a hug. Golden-brown, golden-haired, she reminded him of Anna Louise.

"Daddy, give me a hug, give me a big bear hug and tell me you love me lots, lots and whole lots."

Caley wrapped his arms around Saffron; he was crying.

"Shush now, honey, I know, I know they found her," Saffron cooed, stroking his head.

He turned away, embarrassed by his tears, and she drew him close.

"Now, you're not leaving, are you? Not when I have come all this way to see you, and Daddy and you being in business together, you are not upping and leaving, you have to celebrate."

Saffron had already dismissed Anna Louise's death. That was over, that was all in the past. She saw him waver, hesitate, and she turned to the bellboy.

"Put Mr. Caley's bags in my car, would you?" She gave him that wide, frosty smile. "Hey, we are going to have a ball, it's just starting, it's Mardi Gras!"

She walked around to the driver's seat as his luggage was placed in the trunk, slipping on her dark glasses as she started up the engine.

"My daddy says you've gone and left that lush you been tied to for more than twenty years. That true, Robert?"

He nodded, getting in beside her, and like her he slipped on his dark glasses as they eased out into the traffic. They headed toward the Esplanade, Robert with his arm lying loosely along the seat, his hand stroking Saffron's slender neck.

"Oh yes, that is so nice." She laughed.

Caley smiled a sad smile, because he knew his life from now on would be filled with Saffrons. Money breeds money, breeds bastards.

Lorraine stared from the window of François's steaming hot car. She was sure Caley had not seen her, and she was glad, not because she looked bad, but because she might not have been able to hide her expression. Saffron's blond head was tilted back, laughing, Robert Caley's hand resting at the nape of her neck. A golden couple, seemingly with no remorse, no pain and no grief. She was more than glad, because it made her angry that she had been such a fool to have felt something for him, even for a moment. He was not worth it, not worth another thought, and whatever she felt would soon pass. He would soon be forgotten, just like poor misguided Anna Louise, whose skeleton lay covered in the morgue.

Lorraine walked in as Rosie snapped her last case shut on her pink frilled nylon bedspread.

"Right, that's me packed. You know they want us out as soon as possible because they're booked up?"

"How long did you book the room for?"

"Well, I did tell you we got a special rate so long as we leave before the hotel fills up. Mardi Gras is their busiest time."

"I know that," Lorraine snapped.

Rosie crossed to the writing table. "I did a provisional booking at a place way out of town in case we needed to stay on, but we don't, do we?"

Rooney barged in and dumped down his bags.

"So, how did it go?"

"Check's in my wallet, one million!"

Rosie whooped, and Rooney hit the flimsy wall with his fist. "Yes, yes. One fucking million."

Lorraine folded her arms. "So you're both leaving?"

Rooney frowned. "Well, we all are, aren't we? I mean, did you want to stay on for Mardi Gras?"

"Nope, I'm not crazy about the idea of being elbowed around the streets, but . . ."

"But what?" Rosie said as she opened Lorraine's wallet and took out the check.

"But, well, you think we're all done here?"

Rosie passed the check to Rooney.

"You mean we should see if it's good? I doubt if she'd bounce it on us," he said, squinting at the check.

Lorraine had that edgy feel, sort of shifting her weight from one foot to the next. "Nick's room booked, is it?"

"What?"

"I said, is Nick's room taken?"

"Yeah, well, we stopped paying for it," Rosie said, becoming suspicious.

"His body collected by his sister?"

"Yes," Rooney said, frowning.

"You know it was, we told you it was, he's probably buried by now."

"And forgotten, just like that? Forgotten like that pitiful skeleton in the morgue? Well, for your information I have not forgotten Nick Bartello, I have not forgotten him in any way."

"Shit, Lorraine, neither have we. If this is leading to us giving his relatives something from the one million, I don't mind," Rooney said.

"We don't need to give anybody else a cut of the one million," Lorraine said, slumping into a chair and leaning forward, her head in her hands.

"So what's up?"

She shook her head and then leaned back, closing her eyes. "What's up is some piece of shit killed Nick, and that shit, whoever he is, is just walking, and nobody is doing anything about it, that's what's up."

Rooney sighed, he could feel the carpet being tugged from under his big flat feet. "Lorraine, the cops have nothing, we got nothing. What do you want us all to do now, stay on here and start up another investigation?"

"I want us to finish off what we started. I said I wanted you to visit Fryer Jones's bar, I said I wanted his place searched with that cop you palmed five hundred bucks to, because some fucker got his necklace. Some bastard killed Nick Bartello, and I just want us to check out a few things before we all piss off back to Los Angeles and buy our own condominiums, okay?"

Rooney sighed, lifting up his hands to calm her. "Okay, just stay cool. I'll contact him right now, we can do it right away. But, Lorraine, if we come up with nothin', then I don't care what you say, I'm out of here. What about you, Rosie?"

Rosie nodded. "Yes, I'll leave with Bill."

Lorraine stood up. "Fine, but I might hang around until I am satisfied we gave Nick a run for his cut of the cash. So, we'll keep one room for us all—make it mine because I haven't started to pack."

Lorraine slammed the bathroom door shut, and Rosie sighed.

"When she gets into these moods, I could punch her, I really could. I mean, how can we come up with something if the police got nothin', huh? You tell me that? She just gets obsessive."

Rooney rubbed his chin. "If she wasn't so obsessive, Rosie, we'd never have found Anna Louise Caley or be looking at a check for one million. So we get off our backsides and do like she says because we got to keep her sweet. I don't want her suddenly saying she's got a right to a bigger cut."

"Are you saying she'd take Nick's share?"

Rooney dangled the check. "This is made out to her, Rosie. She's gonna have to put it in her account, then pay us our share, so I'd say we do whatever she wants us to do."

Rosie turned away from him. "You've got her all wrong, Bill. I admit sometimes she gets me real uptight—more than uptight—but I trust her, and we shouldn't even be thinking about who gets what."

Rooney felt a rush of emotion for Nick, his poor dead crazy buddy.

"You're right. I was wrong. Let's give her all the help we can. Some bastard out there killed him, and I want him. . . ."

Lorraine showered and changed but didn't feel very fresh or energized, just angry, and she knew it was connected to seeing Robert Caley. She glared at her reflection in the mirror.

"Hey, chill out of this one. Remember, he's not worth one more second of your time, so stop this!"

Rooney tapped and she opened up. "You got someone in here?"

"No, I was talking to myself."

"Oh well, this cop's downstairs, you want to talk to him?"

"Yep."

Rooney held open the door. All their bags were littered around the room. "Lemme warn you, he's no Burt Lancaster, he's kind of freaky-lookin'."

"Oh yeah?"

"Yeah, his neck is as wide as his ass!"

Harper sat with Rosie, well beamed herself; they made a good couple. He had a beer in his pudgy hand, and lifted half a cheek of his ass as Lorraine joined them. They were sitting under an umbrella on the blue-and-white plastic furniture of a cheap sidewalk café, its neon signs glowing weakly in the daylight. The pavement in front of them was thronging with people.

"This is Lorraine Page."

"Hi, how you doing?"

"Fine, thanks for coming over." She looked across at him over her dark shades. Rooney was right, the guy was obese.

"No problem, you want a beer or—"

"Coffee," she said, and lit a cigarette.

"Place is heating up. Pity you aren't sticking around for Carnival."

Lorraine stubbed out her cigarette. "Okay, can we get down to why we wanted to see you?"

"Sure, fire away."

Lorraine spoke quickly, detailing the events that led up to Nick Bartello's death and mentioning the fact that he had been in Fryer Jones's bar the previous night, and might possibly have returned.

"Look, I know he was your pal, right? But he was crazy to go to ward nine late at night and to get involved with anyone there. Now, I know we investigated this, we asked around, because he was found close to the bar, you know, about a block away down an alley, but nobody there saw him. Nobody saw him down the alley either."

Lorraine leaned forward. "Okay, so you're sayin' with Mardi Gras comin' some poor fucker is gonna walk off the main drag by accident, go into Fryer Jones's bar, have a few beers, walk out and get his throat cut? And all the cops are gonna say is that he shouldn't have been in that district? You got notices up there saying, 'Beware, you could end up fucking dead'?"

Harper wrinkled his pig-nose, annoyed at being spoken to by a woman in that tone.

Lorraine ticked off on her fingers. "We know he went

there, we know he pissed off some kids because they were shooting a pistol and shoving it up Fryer Jones's nose. We know he made them look dumb, we know all of that. We know that Fryer Jones gave Nick a necklace, a gris-gris, which wasn't on his body when he was found, nor were his wallet or his driver's license. He used to keep them in separate back pockets.''

''Uh-huh.'' The fat face wobbled.

''Fryer Jones admitted to me that he had met Nick, and I want to know who was in the bar that night. I want to know who was in the bar the following night—in other words I want to know if Nick Bartello went back to Fryer Jones's bar and somebody there cut his throat. So if it means getting a search warrant, if it means—''

Harper shook his head. ''You are an impatient lady, that's for sure.''

''Well, we only got the room booked for one more night,'' she said with a tight-lipped smile.

''Okeydokey. This area that your friend went into is well known as the wrong neighborhood for whites to go drinking in the early hours, unless they are known or trying to score dope. Your friend use dope, did he?''

''No, he didn't,'' snapped Rooney.

''Okay, so he was acting dumb. But we don't like going into bars like Fryer Jones's without real good evidence. We don't like doing that, because Fryer is an informant.''

Lorraine leaned back. ''Is he? That's why you arrested him on the night Anna Louise Caley was missing?''

''Yes, ma'am, we did arrest him and we hadda knock him around a bit. We needed to ask old Fryer if he had heard anythin', you know, if he knew where she might have disappeared to, because there is nothing down in that section of town that Fryer Jones don't know about. But we have to always make it look real good, because if it was known, then it'd be old Fryer with his throat cut like your friend.'' Harper rested back in his chair and belched; he thumped his chest with a curled fist. ''Better out than in.''

Lorraine lit another cigarette and looked up and down the street, inhaling the smoke. ''Okay, let's try this another way. You're telling me you couldn't get a warrant to search that bar, maybe haul a couple of guys into the station? That is what you are saying, isn't it?''

"I guess so. We don't like to rock the boat."

"Right, so what would it cost to rock it?"

"I'm sorry?"

"Come on, you heard me. I am asking you what it would cost to get maybe four or five of you to back me up, get yourselves armed with more than your wooden bars. They can be cops, or they can be cops not acting as cops, if you follow me?"

Rosie could feel the nonalcoholic beer churning in her stomach. Rooney turned to stare down the street, but the sweat was trickling off his face.

"How much?" Harper asked.

"You tell me," she said softly.

Rooney flicked a glance at Rosie. Her face glistened with perspiration, and she was twisting a bit of the tablecloth round and round one of her fingers.

Harper caught a drop of water running down the neck of his cold beer bottle. He licked his finger. "Are you gonna be around until this evening?"

"Back at the hotel, sure—we can wait for you to contact us."

Harper pushed back his chair. "Be in touch. Been nice talkin' to you, Mrs. Page, Bill, and nice to meet you, Rosie."

He waddled off, seeming to make a wave through the people in the street, his girth not something to push around but to bounce off.

"How much do you think he'd want?" Rosie asked.

Lorraine stood up. "Why, you worried about parting with your hard-earned money, Rosie?"

"No, just being cautious. And you should put that check in the bank before you lose it."

Lorraine laughed, and swung her purse around her shoulder. "Sure, and I guess you both want a check for your cut, but you mind if I wait until it's actually in my account?"

She walked off, and Rosie reached over for Rooney's hand. "I didn't like him and I'm getting to not like her."

They both looked toward Lorraine. She was standing on the pavement, slowly turning to face them as she saw a red convertible Mustang on the opposite side of the road cruise past. It was driven by Raoul Corbello, one hand trailing down over the door, the other lazily holding the white steering wheel. Rap music blared out, and his eyes, hidden behind mirrored shades, were checking out a young black chick selling postcards. He drove on, he could do a lot better for himself than a street vendor, and he needed to get to his uncle's bar, Fryer Jones's place. Raoul was hyped up on crack and needed to get easy, chill out for a while so he could face his family and see his precious Ruby crowned. That's what he'd come home for: Mardi Gras.

CHAPTER
19

Raoul Corbello sneaked into his uncle's bar, and stayed near the doors, just where the old wooden counter ended. He leaned back against the windowless wall as the barman sauntered down toward him.

"Mexican, and a shot of bourbon on the rocks," he said, collar turned up, his shades still on.

"Sure, Raoul, but let's see your money."

"Fuck you, Zachary Blubber." But he slapped twenty bucks down.

Zak opened a beer, banged it on the counter and sauntered back for the bourbon. "So how's LA, man? You get all that fancy gear there?"

Raoul shrugged. His nose was running, and he sniffed as Zak leaned against the bar, sliding the bourbon glass forward.

"Cool, it's cool."

"You look like you need to chill out."

Raoul knocked back the bourbon and reached for the beer.

"Your brothers are workin' out back."

"Uncle Fryer around?"

"Sleepin', like always at this time. Place was jumpin' last night, he played so much he got his big old lips swollen up, but he sure as hell can play that beat-up bugle o' his."

Raoul sniffed again, wiping his nose with his shirt cuff. He took out a thick roll of notes and peeled off another twenty. "Same again, have one yourself."

Zak eyed the wad, and slowly moved back along the bar. "Don't mind if I do, brother, don't mind if I do."

Raoul had to wait awhile, as a couple of customers needed refills. He was beginning to get the shakes and wondered why the hell he'd come back. He'd get more than the shakes when he showed his face back home. What had seemed like a good idea was now beginning to pale.

Zak passed another beer and bourbon along, holding up a glass to indicate he'd taken his drink, and started to chin-wag with two old guys huddled at the far end of the bar.

"Zak, eh, Zak man, come on down here a second, will ya?" Raoul said loudly, gulping down his beer.

"What you want?" said Zak, handing out beers and toss-ing the empties into a crate beneath the bar. He kind of knew, so he opened a drawer under the till and took out a packet. "This what you want, bro?"

Raoul put his hand over the plastic bag. Zak leaned for-ward, whispering that it was good homegrown stuff, he could vouch for it.

"You got any rolling papers?" Raoul asked, peeling off fifty dollars.

"Shit, man, what you want me to do, smoke it for you?" He reached into the back pocket of his pants and tossed down a squashed pack of rolling papers.

The two Corbello boys were filthy from stacking all the crates, ready to load up the truck, when Raoul appeared in the back doorway of the bar. They yelled and flung their arms around him, and then sat in the outside john as he rolled up three big joints, one for each of them.

"How come you workin' out back here?" Raoul asked. They were hesitant at first, but after a few drags they told him that Fryer was getting heavy. They giggled as they said that when their Aunt Juda got hold of Raoul he'd get some heavy-handed activity. Raoul laughed, saying he was cool, and started telling them about his Mustang, his dealin' and his thievin' of their aunt's hoard of cash from under her bed. She could try beating it out of him, but he wouldn't tell her where he'd stashed what he hadn't spent. They were both in awe of their older brother, and the more stoned they became, the more they got to bragging about carvin' up a whitey. Raoul listened, his eyes drooping, not really believing their stories, not really caring. They rolled up some more joints, and started messing around as Raoul took a leak, having to prop himself up against the shack wall to piss straight.

"Eh! How's Ruby?"

"Oh man, she's gettin' so in with Mama and Juda she don't have time for us."

"She getting into all that voodoo shit, huh?"

The two boys, now hurling empty bottles against a wall, didn't really pay any attention. Fryer Jones looked down from his dirty window, pulling the sacking curtain aside. He could see his three nephews who might even be his own sons, but he sure as hell didn't like what he was seeing. They were whooping and hollering and smashing up bottles. He drew on his dirty old jeans and had a good scratch before he made his way down the stairs. He was well hungover. It had been a good night, too good, and he was still buzzing.

"Eh, Zak, gimme a pickup, will ya?" he shouted down, and Zak was waiting for him with his usual glass of snake's eye.

"That Raoul's turned up," he said.

Fryer knocked back his pick-me-up in one gulp, and kissed his swollen lips. "Yeah, I see him, and I had enough o' my fucking relatives to last me a lifetime. Give us another, I need something to waken me up before I get my belt off to those little no-good shits."

Lorraine was washing her hair: she'd had a good few hours' sleep and was feeling, if not a hundred percent, at least a lot better. She had stopped drinking, and hadn't had a drop since she left Caley's hotel, but she wasn't congratulating herself, just hoping she'd be able to keep it up. All around her in the room was Rooney's and Rosie's baggage, but where the two were she had no idea. A second later, though, Rosie banged on the door.

"It's us, Lorraine," she shouted.

"It's open," replied Lorraine, still rubbing her hair dry.

Her partners came in and Rooney sat heavily on the bed—unlike Lorraine, he hadn't caught up on sleep from the night before, and he yawned, resting back on the pillows.

"I deposited the check—I got them to call her bank to clear it, got us a slice of it in cash. Where have you two been?" Lorraine combed her hair and began to dry it with the hair dryer.

"With Harper," Rosie answered, raising her voice above the noise.

"He's got five guys, plus him makes six, and you and me. He doesn't want you to go in, Lorraine." Rooney also had to shout over the roar of the dryer.

"I want to be there. Did he get a search warrant?"

"What?" Rooney shook his head. "He didn't say, but I doubt it. They're all ex-cops, two grand each."

"What?" Rosie said, astonished.

"For twelve thousand dollars, it's worth it," Rooney yelled. "Turn that goddamned thing off!"

Lorraine switched off the hair dryer. "And Nick Bartello's dead. If he was alive, Bill, he'd get a hell of a lot more from his share of the one million bonus, so quit beefin'. And you, Rosie."

"I never said anything!"

"Right, but you were thinking about it," Lorraine said, checking her hair. The ends were still damp, so she turned on the dryer again and began to curl them over a brush. She watched Rosie and Rooney in the mirror: both looked exhausted, Rosie yawning and Rooney's eyes drooping as he leaned back on the pillow.

Nobody spoke, and Rooney nodded off and began to snore. Eventually Lorraine switched off the dryer and went back into the bathroom to dress. When she came out, Rosie was also fast asleep. Lorraine smiled sometimes the pair of them were like two kids, and she felt worried about involving them in the scene at Fryer's bar. She didn't want anything to happen to them, not now that they'd found each other at last.

She stared at them, and then sat down and wrote a note. She left it on Rooney's big heaving chest, packed her bags and carried them out, closing the door quietly behind her. Neither woke. The note said: "Don't stay for Mardi Gras, see you back at *my* new place. Good luck. L."

Lorraine left her cases at the desk and walked out to pay François. He was still hovering, even after she settled his bill, asking if she needed him to take her to the airport, astonished she wasn't going to stay on for the Carnival.

"Thanks, but no thanks, François. You take care now."

She walked off, and he counted out the dollars. She'd given him a bonus, fifty dollars more than he'd asked for. He grinned, a happy man.

Lorraine walked out into the French Quarter. It was a muggy evening, and the street was crowded as more and more tourists flooded in. Purple, green and gold were everywhere and there was already a carnival feeling in the air, but she didn't feel in a festive mood.

The six men were waiting in two patrol cars down a side street. They were smoking, wearing dark glasses, all the car windows open. Lorraine got in beside the obese Officer Harper, and smiled as he introduced her to the men squashed in the backseat.

"Cash up front, Mrs. Page."

She opened her purse and took out an envelope. "Twelve grand, right? Half now, half when we're through."

Harper turned to look at the officers behind him—they shrugged. He got out of his car and waddled to the car behind him, leaned in the window, had a brief conversation and then returned.

"Okay, but you'd better not try to put anything over on us."

Lorraine smiled. "You think I would really try to pull a fast one on you guys? Come on, I know you're taking a big risk."

It seemed to do the trick. He nodded, his jowls wobbling.

"So how do we work it?" she asked quietly.

Rooney grunted, and his body jerked. He lifted his head. "Shit, what time is it?"

Rosie murmured as he eased himself off the bed. The note fluttered to the floor and he picked it up. The room was in darkness, so he turned on the bedside lamp.

"Rosie, wake up, girl. Rosie!"

She blinked and swallowed, and then sat up with a start. "She's gone. Read this."

Rosie took a moment to adjust to the light, and then read the note. "What should we do?"

Rooney hesitated, then crossed to the bathroom. "Check if there's a flight out of here. If there isn't, we'll stay."

"We're going to leave her?"

"Just see if there's a flight, sweetheart."

Rooney splashed cold water over his face and patted it dry with one of the damp towels Lorraine had used. It smelled of shampoo, and he lowered it from his face, staring at himself in the mirror. He felt old and tired, wondering what the hell he was thinking of doing, getting himself engaged at his age. Had he really suggested she move in with him? He sat on the edge of the bath, wishing he'd taken his shoes off before he fell asleep; his feet felt swollen.

Rosie called out that there was a flight in an hour and a half.

"Gimme a second," he shouted back. He didn't know what to do. Not knowing what the hell Lorraine had arranged with Harper or when they were going to do it, or for that matter why. What did she expect to gain? He sighed.

Rosie was brushing her hair when he walked out. "I gave them your credit card number; that okay?" She watched him plod across the room, and she turned. "Bill? You want to leave or not?"

"I'm thinking about it, Rosie."

She'd been thinking about it too, and asked him virtually the same questions he had just asked himself.

"I mean, what does she expect to find at the end of it?"

"I dunno, Rosie—maybe someone scared enough to say they saw Nick, who knows? I think she's throwing away good money, but that's just my opinion."

"It's mine too. I liked Nick, of course I did, but it's a long shot, isn't it? We don't even know if he was in Fryer's bar the night he got killed. Even if she was to find the gris-gris, even if whoever did kill Nick was dumb enough to hang on to it, they wouldn't have it in the bar, would they?"

"I don't know, Rosie." He hadn't meant to snap at her. It just came out that way.

"Listen, if you feel guilty about going, we'll stay."

"I don't feel guilty."

"Fine, then we'll leave, yes?"

He sat down, said he needed a drink, and Rosie flung the brush on the dressing table.

"We can't hang around, Bill, the flight goes in an hour and a half."

"I heard you the first time, Rosie."

"So, I'm repeating it."

Rooney stood in the lobby as Rosie checked out, looking at Lorraine's suitcase waiting behind the desk.

"Bill, if you want to wait, you'd better say so—they got people wanting her room. Which means if we do check out and stay on we'll have nowhere to stay for tonight. It's Mardi Gras, Bill, the hotels are all filling up."

He suddenly made up his mind. "You stay with the bags, I'll go over to Fryer's bar."

"But what about the plane?"

He turned on her angrily. "We fucking miss it. Hell, if we have to we'll hire a private plane, okay? Just wait here."

Rooney walked out. Rosie felt near to tears; he'd never been angry at her before, never snapped at her the way he just had. But then she understood why—he was worried about Lorraine. For all his complaints about her, he really cared about her, and if Rosie thought about it, so did she.

"Excuse me, is Mrs. Page checking out or not?"

Rosie glared at the receptionist, who was getting more frazzled by the day. It was always the same at Mardi Gras; she hated it.

"Yeah, I'm checking Mrs. Page out, but we need to leave the bags here, is that all right?"

The receptionist sighed; she was knee-deep in people's luggage, as it was. "I guess so, but the hotel can't take any responsibility for them."

"Fine, I'll take the goddamned things out with me."

Rooney tried in vain to flag a cab down. The pavement was crowded; there were people walking arm in arm down the streets. More jugglers and clowns had appeared on the scene, passing out leaflets for all the forthcoming events; people were already getting into the spirit. Fireworks were going off in all directions, they whizzed and banged overhead, and lit up the dark sky. A Dixieland band was playing, or rehearsing, stop-starting. It was as if he had stepped onto a fairground Ferris wheel and couldn't get off. He pushed and jostled his way along the street, eyes peeled for a vacant cab, and he couldn't stop his rising panic. He didn't know what he was getting so het up about—his personal life or Lorraine. Or maybe it was just the memory of Nick Bartello, but he had a hideous feeling of something coming down, and his frustration at not being in control of it made it worse. She was somewhere with a bunch of guys, and probably bad ones. She was alone, and he shouldn't have let her go without backup. He was her backup man, her partner now, and he'd never be able to live with himself if something happened to her, because for all her faults and her headstrong ways, he cared about her, more than he ever dared admit. And one thing he knew, she was one hell of a cop, in the force or out. Lorraine was in a class all her own.

"Taxi!" he yelled.

Rosie sat outside the hotel in the small terraced area. She was not the only person sitting by a sea of luggage. There were a lot of backpackers and families, some licking ice cream cones, some becoming irate with their tired-out kids, and the persistent noise of the fireworks was giving her a thudding headache.

François tooted his horn and waved over. Rosie jumped up and waved back frantically. He grinned, then realized she was gesturing for him to join her.

"Can you get all these bags on board?"

"Sure, you want to go to the airport?"

"Yeah, eventually, but first can you get me over to Fryer Jones's bar in ward nine? Lorraine's there."

He jumped out, opened the trunk, and began hurling the bags inside.

Rooney was sweating. He had got into a near fistfight with a drag queen who had flagged down the same taxi, but as he or she was a good foot taller than Rooney, he'd walked away. Now he turned as he heard his name shouted out, and he looked this way and that. Then he heard Rosie's voice and he pushed his way through a crowd of people before he saw her waving to him from across the street in François's car. His panic rose as he nearly got knocked down by a kid on a bicycle with three other people somehow balanced on it as well.

"What's happened? You heard from Lorraine?"

"No, get in and shut up," she said.

Rooney sat beside her, and she nudged François to get a move on.

"We going to the airport?"

"No," she snapped. "Fryer Jones's bar, all right?"

He grabbed her hand and pulled her closer. "She's my partner, Rosie."

"She's mine too, in case you've forgotten."

Boom went another firework, and a rocket exploded over their heads. "Carnival getting started!" shouted François gleefully. "Man, this place heats up, don't you just feel it all coming down all around you? This place is crazy, man, it goes wild, real wild."

Ruby placed the steaming bowls of crawfish stew on the newspaper that served as a tablecloth. Juda, Edith, and Sugar May dug in. They had chilled beers and big chunks of bread, and they ate hungrily, as they had been working all day on the float. Baskets and baskets of fresh flower heads had been delivered, and each one was to be placed around the throne to make a sea of color for the queen to step over as she was led to her throne.

Ruby was barefoot, wearing just an old slip. Her hair was pinned up off her face, as she'd worked up a sweat. They were tired, but they would all be up and working the following morning. It took a lot of time and loving care to get the floats ready, and all the hard work only built up the excitement until it was like being drunk with it all.

Juda dunked her bread and sucked on it; it was good to be back home, good to be free. She had decided not to go back to LA, even if Elizabeth Caley offered her a fortune. She was not leaving home again. She broke off a piece of bread and was just about to dip it into her bowl when she saw the newspaper article: MISSING MOVIE STAR'S DAUGHTER—BODY FOUND!

"Move your plate aside, Sugar May."

Juda inched the newspaper around to read it. "They found her, they just found Anna Louise Caley." She pulled the paper from the table and wiped off the crumbs. "Oh, my Lord, she was buried in . . . Oh my, oh my."

Edith looked at her sister. "What's that, Juda?"

Juda folded the paper into a roll, staring at Ruby.

"They found poor little Anna Louise Caley buried in a garden, under suspicious circumstances, it says."

Ruby continued to eat, sucking her bread loudly.

"Where, Juda?"

Juda kept on looking at Ruby. "In Miss Tilda Brown's backyard. You know who she is, don't you, Ruby?"

Ruby looked up and her eyes were glittering, her voice soft, almost purring. "I know who she is, Aunty Juda, she tied a dressing-gown cord around her neck and hanged her little self."

Sugar May put her hand over her mouth and giggled, and received a slap across her head with the newspaper. Edith now looked in confusion at Juda, who slowly pushed her chair from the table and stood up. She wasn't wearing makeup or her wig; her cropped gray hair looked thin at the crown.

Ruby tried to be nonchalant, still dipping her bread into her bowl, but she would not look up, did not want to face her aunt. She was afraid of her, even more so when her big body loomed over the table.

"Ruby, remember what I told you, play with the devil and he'll come for your soul."

"No he won't. And whatever I done, Fryer's taking care of, like he's taking care of my brothers. Nobody is ever going to know nothing."

Edith was still confused, looking from her sister to her daughter. "What you two talking about?"

Juda walked to the door. "She knows, Edith, Ruby knows, and Fryer never took care of nobody but himself. That is the way he lives. He sold to the devil a long, long time ago."

Edith was really worried now, and she pushed her half-finished supper away, following Juda out.

"What you done?" Sugar May asked in a whisper.

Ruby had just taken a mouthful of water, and she turned on Sugar May, hissing, and the water sprayed from her mouth like a jet.

"I just used my powers, Sugar May, I just used my powers."

Sugar May scuttled out after her mama, and Ruby sat alone. Then after a moment she reached for her mama's bowl, and tipped it into her own. She continued eating, delicately dipping her bread into the bowl and sucking it. She felt no guilt, no remorse for what she had done, or what she had begun. After all, she had only given them what they had wanted.

Elizabeth Caley sat at Lloyd Dulay's side, looking composed and as beautiful as ever. She wore black, out of respect for her daughter, and everyone there had whispered their condolences. The Dulays were old money, and the whole of New Orleans society had accepted the invitation out of curiosity, wanting to see Anna Louise's grieving mother with their own eyes. Elizabeth did not let them down. She was composed and distant, as if frozen with grief and shock. She was starring in another movie, and she acted the part to perfection. She knew Robert would ask for a massive settlement, but she didn't care. She had more money than she knew what to do with. Money had never been a priority for Elizabeth; she had grown up with it, always had it and never considered being without it. She was going to be invited to every Mardi Gras ball and top-level function in New Orleans, as she had been since she was a child. She was famous, now even more so because of her tragic daughter. She was sitting next to Lloyd Dulay, the man she had always loved. She was his prize guest of honor, but tonight she didn't relish it—tonight she no longer cared. She had determined there would be no more secrets; all she was waiting for was the right moment. It came when Lloyd rose to ask his guests to lift their glasses to Elizabeth Seal.

There was a polite murmur, none expecting her to speak, but she stood up like a queen. She held her glass in her right hand, lifting it a fraction.

"A long time ago I was given the leading role in a film called *The Swamp*. I was sixteen years of age and excited at the prospect of becoming a star. I paid no heed to the fact that I was to portray the great voodoo queen Marie

Laveau. I did not consider the culture that Marie Laveau brought to her people; it was just a movie, and I was going to be a star.''

Elizabeth gave the performance of her life, but it wasn't scripted; it came from her years of torment, from the nightmare during filming when she had been taken and raped, curses written in blood on her body. She told them all about the doll she found in her trailer, a doll bearing her face, cursing her and any offspring that she might conceive to live in the hell of the living dead, and condemning Elizabeth Seal to spend the rest of her days feeling the weight of the great queen's coffin lid pressing on her heart. And as those gathered became frightened by her driven, emotional declaration, they knelt before her as she at last admitted, ''I am black and I have hidden behind a white skin. I have been punished and cursed for abusing the great voodoo goddess Queen Marie Laveau. Every child my womb conceived was also doomed to live under her shadow.''

It was all so clear to Elizabeth what she should do, exactly what she should say, and the impact her words would have made her feel stronger than she had ever felt in her wretched life. She was going to free herself, she would be free. No need for Juda anymore, no more nightmares, it was all over.

Elizabeth still held the photograph of her daughter Anna Louise; as the drugs distorted her mind she truly believed she was there, dining alongside Lloyd Dulay, and that it was all taking place. He was in fact waiting impatiently downstairs when Missy came running from the bedroom, unable to wake Mrs. Caley. She had screamed to him that something bad had happened.

Lloyd Dulay felt for Elizabeth's pulse; it was very weak. She opened her eyes only once, and smiled at him, saying that everything was all right now, it was all over. Her black gown was laid out in readiness for the dinner, with matching shoes and sequined purse. By the time the doctor arrived she was dead. She looked peaceful and calm, a sweet innocent smile on her lips. Dulay sat down in a chair close to the bed.

''Oh, Elizabeth, my little queen.''

Harper looked at his men. He was sweating as he listened to the radio and then rehooked it back on the dashboard.

''They're standing out back ready. We go in via the front, let's keep this as tight as we can, no shooting unless . . . Well, we done it before, so here we go.''

He looked at Lorraine. ''Stay back. Once we got the place quiet you can come in, but not until I give you the word. Let's go!''

Fryer Jones was sitting with Raoul at the far end of the bar, trying to get him straightened out enough to take him home and face his Aunt Juda. His two brothers were out in the yard lying stoned among the beer crates they were supposed to have been stacking. There were only the usual regulars dotted around the bar—it never became lively until after midnight. Sugar May had crept in, and was hiding out down the back, talking to one of the hookers, thinking she was someone to emulate, when it happened.

Fryer looked in astonishment as the big motherfuckers charged in from the backyard and through the front door. Even Zak gaped. Nobody had busted them for years—they paid a high price for it not to happen—so nobody was sure what the hell was going down. Glasses were shattered, mirrors cascaded into jagged pieces as the thugs came in, screaming and shouting for everyone to back up against the wall. It was a raid. Some customers raised their hands in terror as they were thrown up against the wall; others ran for cover under the old bar tables.

Fryer turned on his barstool and yelled in fury, ''What you motherfuckers doing, for Chrissakes?''

Batons clipped heads, boots kicked groins, as everyone inside the bar tried to disappear into the walls. The more the cops yelled and hit out, the more Fryer Jones screamed abuse. The cops were laying into the customers, asking between fists and batons what their names were. One of the thickset cops had thrown the Corbello kids on the floor and they lay curled up as the boots went in, screaming and shouting they hadn't done anything.

Raoul was hauled by his hair from his barstool next to Fryer, but not one cop touched Fryer himself.

''You better have a fucking good reason for this, you motherfuckers,'' Fryer screamed.

Lorraine couldn't wait any longer and walked into the bar.

It was mayhem, screaming and shouting, people huddled in corners, crying and hunched up as the boots and batons still went in.

Lorraine shouted, "This is for Nick Bartello, *Nick Bartello!*"

Fryer squinted in the darkness down to the end of the bar. "His throat was cut down an alley, one block from here."

Fryer shook his head and pointed. "You are a crazy bitch, you know that?"

As they spoke cops were hurling the drugs taken from the drawer beneath the till onto the bar. Two more moved up the narrow back staircase to Fryer's private quarters.

Rooney walked in as Fryer Jones spat a spray of his beer over Lorraine. "You gonna pay for this, you fucking whore. Nobody comes in here and takes over my bar. Nobody!"

"You want to bet, Mr. Jones? I wouldn't bother, we already took it over."

Rooney edged closer and said to one of the cops kicking the shit out of a guy caught between the tables, "I'm with her, I'm with Mrs. Page."

Lorraine turned, and seeing Rooney she gave a quick grin before turning back to Fryer.

"We will all walk out, Fryer, when you give us the names of whoever cut Nick Bartello's throat. That's all we want, all I want, no charges, you all hear me? No charges, but we want who cut my friend's throat."

One of the cops searching upstairs appeared in the doorway behind the bar. "Mrs. Page?"

Lorraine turned to the cop, who gestured for her to come closer, and chucked Nick Bartello's wallet onto the bar. Fryer looked, and then pursed his lips, swearing. He had fucked up, he had meant to destroy it. But he kept smiling. "This is gonna cost, you motherfuckers, this is gonna cost."

Lorraine moved closer to him, and then reached out. He had on the necklace or a necklace similar to the one Nick had been wearing.

"This is yours, Mr. Jones, is it?"

Fryer looked at her, and laughed. "Sure is, honey, we make 'em for the museum, how many you want, huh? You fuckers are not even here on a warrant, are you?"

The second cop walked in from the back stairs. He held

up Nick Bartello's license in a small plastic bag and tossed it down.

Harper looked over the wallet and the license, then at Lorraine. "These your friend's?"

Lorraine fingered the empty wallet, looked at the license, and said, "Yes, these belonged to Nick Bartello."

Harper held his hand up. "Okay, back off everyone, come on, quiet down in here. Quiet!"

He turned to face Fryer Jones and took out his handcuffs. "Okay, Fryer, you overstepped yourself, this is one you won't wriggle out of."

"I never saw them before in my life!" Fryer said calmly.

Harper clipped on the handcuffs, roughly pulling Fryer's hands behind his back.

"Well, they was under your pillow, Fryer, and they may very well have your prints all over them. So let's walk out nice and quiet, shall we?"

Fryer Jones bowed his head. He could see Raoul shaking in one corner, his brothers huddled under a table, and Sugar May crying with the hookers. Fryer eased off his stool, his hands cuffed behind him. He was pushed past Lorraine, and he stared at her.

"You got the devil in you, lady."

Fryer Jones leaned back in the patrol car and closed his eyes. He could never name his own kin—maybe one of them even his own blood—so he sighed, and asked if they could bring him his trombone. It made Harper turn and stare, because he had reckoned in all honesty that Fryer had nothing to do with this Nick Bartello. He leaned out of the window and shouted to one of his pals, "Get this old buzzard his fucking trombone."

Lorraine sat in the back of François's car and wept, Rooney on one side and Rosie on the other. They just held her tightly between them; she didn't need to say anything. In fact, they all felt tearful as François asked if they still wanted to make it to the airport.

They got there with five minutes to spare, bags and baggage intact.

Fryer Jones played his trombone in his cell until other prisoners asked him to shut up because they couldn't sleep. He sat there in silence, staring up at the small window of his cell. He wouldn't name the Corbello boys or Ruby or any of them. He guessed it was time he took responsibility, time he paid his dues, so he admitted to killing Nick Bartello. He didn't ask to talk to a lawyer; the only call he made was to Juda Salina. She came, as he knew she would, all done up in her turban and false eyelashes.

"Elizabeth Caley's dead."

"Uh-huh."

"Anna Louise Caley's body was found."

"Uh-huh."

She sighed, not meeting his eyes. "Ruby is ready to be crowned, no guilt, no remorse. That girl worries me—she'd better straighten out."

"Uh-huh."

"Raoul's back, with only half my savings."

"And I'm goin' away for a murder I did not commit." He gripped the bars with his gnarled hand. "I'm doing it for you, Juda. You take over my bar, you keep those two young ones in line."

She gently stroked his hand. "Why are you doing this, Fryer?"

He gave her that gappy gold-toothed smile. "Because once you were young and beautiful like Ruby. Nothing stays young or beautiful, Juda, only memories. Take care now."

Juda wanted to cry, but she just walked away. She could hear him playing his trombone a long time after she left. She could still hear it in her small bedroom at Edith's. Life played tricks on you like that, hearing things that weren't there, seeing things that were about to happen. Life was full of strange things, especially in New Orleans and always just before Mardi Gras.

Rosie stood with her bags all packed, and two big boxed crates. Her apartment seemed suddenly bare.

"Well, I got everything," she said sadly. She looked around again—stripped of her things, the place looked bigger. "If you're staying on, Lorraine, you should get a better kitchen put in."

Lorraine smiled. "I intend to, Rosie, I'll get the place

done up. It's a waste of money moving somewhere else, this will do me fine."

Rosie chewed her lip. "You can always call me if you need someone in the office, you know, part-time. I'll always be willing."

"And able. Yeah, I know, you told me four, no, five times. Now, the checks, you got the two checks?"

"I certainly have," Rosie said, patting her purse.

Lorraine smiled. "You know, I never thought I'd be writing out checks for that amount, and from my own bank account. We're rich, Rosie, we all got over three hundred thousand, so, you feeling happy?"

Rosie nodded. "Well, not quite up to the brim, but I guess we'll make it work. I'm gonna give it a try, and you try to keep up the meetings, won't you? Keep on going, because I'd hate to see you blow this chance, Lorraine."

"Rosie, I know I almost lost it, but I promise you I'm off the stuff now, and if it makes you feel any better, I give you my word that I'll keep going to the meetings. I'll contact Jake to be my sponsor, how's that?"

Rosie kissed her, and then hugged her tightly. "Oh, hell, I'm gonna miss you."

Before Rosie could become tearful, Rooney arrived and honked from the street. Rosie began to take her bags and boxes and cases down, and he appeared, moaning as he helped her carry all her bits and pieces: "I don't know if this is gonna work, Lorraine, but at least . . ."

She laughed. "You'll give it a try? And you know there will be always be a job open for you at Page Investigations, I've told Rosie that too. Office will be open Monday morning—you got the number?"

"Right, thanks."

Eventually it came to the real good-byes; it was a bit awkward. They didn't really know what to say to one another because for all the offers of work in the future Lorraine knew it was the end of their partnership. Neither Rosie nor Rooney had actually said it, but she just knew. They all knew.

"We might sort of go on an extended honeymoon," he muttered.

"Great, you do that, but I will be invited to the wedding, won't I?"

"Hell, don't be stupid."

There was nothing left to say, but it was the last moment and they hung on to it. They seemed not quite to know how to walk out the door, so Lorraine pushed them through it, saying that when they were settled they would all have a big celebration dinner, but until then they should just piss off and leave her alone.

Rosie started to cry, so Rooney told her to go on ahead, then turned back to Lorraine, half closing the door.

"You know, if you need me for anything I'll always be there for you, anytime you feel, you know . . . if this drinking problem rears its head. You call me, call us, and we'll be right with you."

Lorraine reached out and held him close. "Bill, I'm okay, but I appreciate what you just said."

He stood holding her for a few moments more, then turned abruptly and walked out, the screen door banging shut behind him.

Lorraine slumped down on the sofa bed, which she would no longer have to sleep on. She would have Rosie's room all to herself, and she suddenly felt good, looking around the room. Her room. Her apartment. She would start to redecorate the next day, and lay on the old sofa thinking about color schemes, and drapes, and then she sat up abruptly, swearing. She'd forgotten him; in all the excitement of returning home and banking the million dollars, she'd forgotten him, forgotten her promise.

The kennels were just closing when she arrived. She'd made the promise, and she wouldn't go back on it, but she began to doubt it when the kennel worker started saying that the dog been a handful of trouble from the day he'd been left. He had attacked every one of the helpers and every canine they had in residence, and was now kept in solitary confinement.

Tiger didn't greet her; he sat at the far end of his wire meshing, his blue eyes beady and angry.

"Hi, kiddo, it's just me, I'm afraid. Nick's not gonna be able to take you home."

He still sat, and then he bared his teeth.

"Listen, man, it's up to you, but I am the best bet you got. I walk away and it's the lethal injection, know what I mean?"

The beady blue eyes froze, and she bent down.

"Come on, Tiger, they want to close up, and I'm tired."

Tiger slowly got to his feet, his head hung low as he padded toward her. Then his big bushy tail started to wag slowly.

"Okay, man, we're out of here."

ABOUT THE AUTHOR

Lynda La Plante started her career as a television actress before turning to scriptwriting. She made her writing breakthrough with the phenomenally successful British television series *Widows*, and her four subsequent novels, *The Legacy*, *Bella Mafia, Entwined*, and *Cold Shoulder*, were all international bestsellers. In the United States she is best known for her television miniseries, *Prime Suspect*, and is the winner of two Emmys and the 1993 Edgar Allan Poe writers award, as well as top British awards. La Plante has recently been made a fellow of the British Film Institute. She divides her time between writing novels and screenplays, and lives in East Hampton, New York, and London.

"*The Magician's Tale* is truly original—atmospheric, seductively written, and compellingly suspenseful."
—Richard North Patterson

DAVID HUNT

THE MAGICIAN'S TALE

"David Hunt introduces us to the bleak world of a San Francisco photographer named Kay Farrow and what she sees when she looks out from eyes that are completely color-blind. [Her] nocturnal prowls through the Tenderloin district take on a terrible purpose after the bizarre murder of a handsome street hustler who was her favorite model and only friend. The voice of the storyteller grows more intimate, more mesmerizing, once the narrative begins to explore the shadowy secrets in the victim's past. But it is Kay's extraordinary vision that arrests us; with the starkness of a reverse negative, it shows us light and dark, truth and deception, reality and illusion, even good and evil, in ways we never imagined."
—*The New York Times Book Review*

__0-425-16482-9/$7.50

Prices slightly higher in Canada

Payable in U.S. funds only. No cash/COD accepted. Postage & handling: U.S./CAN. $2.75 for one book, $1.00 for each additional, not to exceed $6.75; Int'l $5.00 for one book, $1.00 each additional. We accept Visa, Amex, MC ($10.00 min.), checks ($15.00 fee for returned checks) and money orders. Call 800-788-6262 or 201-933-9292, fax 201-896-8569; refer to ad # 799

Penguin Putnam Inc.
P.O. Box 12289, Dept. B
Newark, NJ 07101-5289
Please allow 4-6 weeks for delivery.
Foreign and Canadian delivery 6-8 weeks.

Bill my: ☐Visa ☐MasterCard ☐Amex _____ (expires)

Card#_____

Signature_____

Bill to:

Name_____

Address_____ City_____

State/ZIP_____

Daytime Phone #_____

Ship to:

Name_____ Book Total $_____

Address_____ Applicable Sales Tax $_____

City_____ Postage & Handling $_____

State/ZIP_____ Total Amount Due $_____

This offer subject to change without notice.

#1 *New York Times* bestselling author of
Airport* and *Hotel

ARTHUR HAILEY

DETECTIVE

Serial killer Elroy "Animal" Doil is hours away from the electric chair. In his last hours of life, he wants to make a confession—to Detective Malcolm Ainslie, the man who put him away. And as much as he'd like to, Ainslie can't ignore the criminal's request. Because although Doil is guilty of a gruesome double murder, his confession could close ten other unsolved slayings.

What Ainslie learns, however, will thrust him into an investigation that leads directly to elite levels of city government—and some of his trusted colleagues...

___ 0-425-16386-5/$7.99

Prices slightly higher in Canada

Payable in U.S. funds only. No cash/COD accepted. Postage & handling: U.S./CAN. $2.75 for one book, $1.00 for each additional, not to exceed $6.75; Int'l $5.00 for one book, $1.00 each additional. We accept Visa, Amex, MC ($10.00 min.), checks ($15.00 fee for returned checks) and money orders. Call 800-788-6262 or 201-933-9292, fax 201-896-8569; refer to ad # 798

Penguin Putnam Inc.   Bill my: ☐Visa ☐MasterCard ☐Amex _____ (expires)
P.O. Box 12289, Dept. B   Card#_____
Newark, NJ 07101-5289
Please allow 4-6 weeks for delivery.   Signature_____
Foreign and Canadian delivery 6-8 weeks.

Bill to:

Name_____
Address_____City_____
State/ZIP_____
Daytime Phone #_____

Ship to:

Name_____ Book Total $_____
Address_____ Applicable Sales Tax $_____
City_____ Postage & Handling $_____
State/ZIP_____ Total Amount Due $_____

This offer subject to change without notice.

MINETTE WALTERS

THE DARK ROOM

"Hitchcockian"—*USA Today*
"Engaging Mystery"—*People*

Jinx Kingsley, a prominent photographer and millionaire's daughter, wakes up in a private hospital. She does not remember the car accident. Or her fiancé leaving her for her best friend. Or the grisly murders of her fiancé and her best friend. She must piece together memories that will save her—or convict her...

___0-515-12045-6/$6.50

THE ECHO

"Cunning"—*New York Times*
"Twisting"—*USA Today*

A destitute man is found dead on the property of a wealthy socialite. But the reporter investigating the dead man's identity—and the woman whose home became his deathbed—are swiftly ensnared in a web of deception as tangled and complex as the hearts and minds that spun it...

___0-515-12256-4/$6.99

Prices slightly higher in Canada

Payable in U.S. funds only. No cash/COD accepted. Postage & handling: U.S./CAN. $2.75 for one book, $1.00 for each additional, not to exceed $6.75; Int'l $5.00 for one book, $1.00 each additional. We accept Visa, Amex, MC ($10.00 min.), checks ($15.00 fee for returned checks) and money orders. Call 800-788-6262 or 201-933-9292, fax 201-896-8569; refer to ad # 777

Penguin Putnam Inc.	Bill my: □Visa □MasterCard □Amex _____ (expires)
P.O. Box 12289, Dept. B	Card#
Newark, NJ 07101-5289	
Please allow 4-6 weeks for delivery.	Signature
Foreign and Canadian delivery 6-8 weeks.	

Bill to:

Name_____

Address_____City_____

State/ZIP_____

Daytime Phone #_____

Ship to:

Name_____ Book Total $_____

Address_____ Applicable Sales Tax $_____

City_____ Postage & Handling $_____

State/ZIP_____ Total Amount Due $_____

This offer subject to change without notice.

LEE CHILD

"Terrific."—*New York Times*

"Combines high suspense with almost nonstop action... Reacher is a wonderfully epic hero: tough, taciturn, yet vulnerable. From its jolting opening scene to its fiery final confrontation, *Killing Floor* is irresistible."
—*People*

KILLING FLOOR

Ex-military policeman Jack Reacher is in Margrave, Georgia, for less than a half-hour when the cops come, shotguns in hand, to arrest him for murder.

All Jack knows is he didn't kill anybody.

Not for a long time...

__0-515-12344-7/$6.99

Now available in hardcover from G. P. Putnam's Sons:

DIE TRYING

Prices slightly higher in Canada

Payable in U.S. funds only. No cash/COD accepted. Postage & handling: U.S./CAN. $2.75 for one book, $1.00 for each additional, not to exceed $6.75; Int'l $5.00 for one book, $1.00 each additional. We accept Visa, Amex, MC ($10.00 min.), checks ($15.00 fee for returned checks) and money orders. Call 800-788-6262 or 201-933-9292, fax 201-896-8569; refer to ad # 781

Penguin Putnam Inc.   Bill my: ☐Visa ☐MasterCard ☐Amex_____(expires)
P.O. Box 12289, Dept. B   Card#_____
Newark, NJ 07101-5289
Please allow 4-6 weeks for delivery.   Signature_____
Foreign and Canadian delivery 6-8 weeks.

Bill to:
Name_____
Address_____City_____
State/ZIP_____
Daytime Phone #_____

Ship to:
Name_____   Book Total $_____
Address_____   Applicable Sales Tax $_____
City_____   Postage & Handling $_____
State/ZIP_____   Total Amount Due $_____

This offer subject to change without notice.